Praise for MACHINEHOOD

"With clever invention and astute observation popping from every paragraph, *Machinehood* takes you on a thrilling ride through a gritty, panoramic future that showcases intelligence in all its manifestations, humanity in all its potentialities, the infinite grace of ourselves as well as of our creations."

—Ken Liu, author of *The Grace of Kings* and
The Paper Menagerie and Other Stories

"From the opening manifesto to its ingenious technologies, *Machinehood* builds an inspiring and believable vision of the future that is both thought-provoking and hopeful. It will leave you wishing that tomorrow could arrive a little sooner."

—Ray Kurzweil, bestselling author, pioneering
inventor, and renowned futurist

*"This stunning near-future thriller from Divya (*Runtime*) tackles issues of economic inequality, workers' rights, privacy, and the nature of intelligence. . . . Crack worldbuilding and vivid characters make for a memorable, page-turning adventure, while the thematic inquiries into human and AI labor rights offer plenty to chew on for fans of big idea sci-fi. Readers will be blown away."

—*Publishers Weekly*, starred review

"A fantastic big-idea thriller, with plenty of action, and substantive, important perspectives on what the future might look like."

—Malka Older, author of *Infomocracy* and
the Hugo-finalist Centenal Cycle

"Divya has created a richly imagined and eerily familiar world . . . confronting urgent questions about humans' place in a society increasingly run by AIs."

—*Kirkus Reviews*

"If you're one of those people who says there's nothing new in science fiction being published anymore, here's a book that disproves that."

—*Tor.com*

"Digesting the novel's first few acts feels like taking in a bizarro Tom Clancy storyline . . . a high-tech romp through one woman's quest for salvation, and her transformation (or evolution, depending on where you stand on bioethics) into something quite different."

—*The Washington Post*

"Exploring the problems of the gig economy and pondering the rights of artificial intelligence, S.B. Divya's debut novel, *Machinehood*, is packed with ideas . . . digging into near-future economic and political anxieties in interesting ways."

—*Chicago Review of Books*

"There's a great deal going on in *Machinehood*, from Divya's sophisticated critique of a post-privacy gig economy to her evident expertise in AI systems . . . sharply imagined and convincingly detailed . . . she artfully balances the cybertech thriller chapters . . . and the more character-oriented narrative, eventually weaving them together in a conclusion both suspenseful and ingenious . . ."

—*Locus*

MACHINEHOOD

S.B. DIVYA

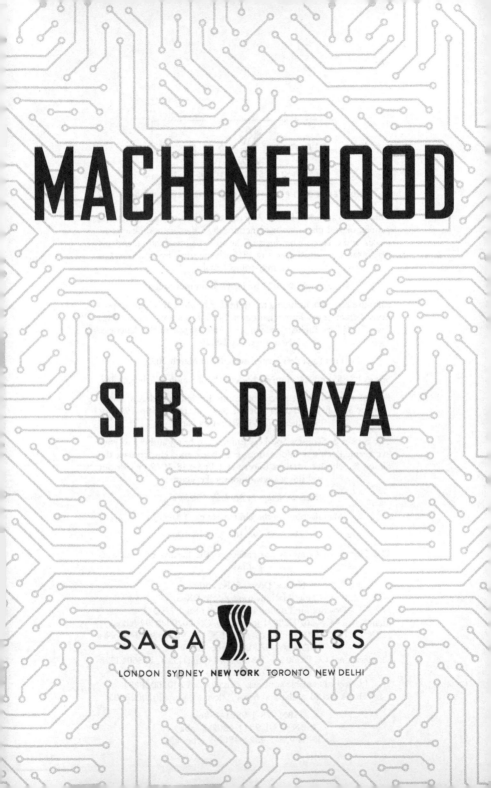

SAGA PRESS

LONDON SYDNEY **NEW YORK** TORONTO NEW DELHI

SAGA PRESS

AN IMPRINT OF SIMON & SCHUSTER, INC.

1230 AVENUE OF THE AMERICAS, NEW YORK, NEW YORK 10020

Copyright © 2021 by Divya Srinivasan Breed

First Saga Press paperback edition March 2022

SAGA PRESS and colophon are trademarks of Simon & Schuster, Inc.

For information about special discounts for bulk purchases, please contact Simon & Schuster Special Sales at 1-866-506-1949 or business@simonandschuster.com.

The Simon & Schuster Speakers Bureau can bring authors to your live event. For more information or to book an event, contact the Simon & Schuster Speakers Bureau at 1-866-248-3049 or visit our website at www.simonspeakers.com.

Interior design by Michelle Marchese

Manufactured in the United States of America

1 3 5 7 9 10 8 6 4 2

The Library of Congress has cataloged the hardcover edition as follows:

Names: Divya, S. B., author.
Title: Machinehood / S.B. Divya.
Description: London ; New York : Saga, [2021]
Identifiers: LCCN 2020028891 (print) | LCCN 2020028892 (ebook) | ISBN 9781982148065 (hardcover) | ISBN 9781982148089 (ebook)
Subjects: GSAFD: Science fiction.
Classification: LCC PS3604.I928 M33 2021 (print) | LCC PS3604.I928 (ebook) | DDC 813/.6—dc23
LC record available at https://lccn.loc.gov/2020028891
LC ebook record available at https://lccn.loc.gov/2020028892

ISBN 978-1-9821-4806-5
ISBN 978-1-9821-4807-2 (pbk)
ISBN 978-1-9821-4808-9 (ebook)

To everyone who has rebelled in the name
of justice and compassion;
and to Ryan, who made sure I didn't give up.

MACHINEHOOD

CHAPTER 1

WELGA

30. All forms of intelligence have the right to exist without persecution or slavery.
31. No form of intelligence may own another.
32. If the local governance does not act in accordance with these rights, it is the right of an intelligence to act by any means necessary to secure them.

—*The Machinehood Manifesto, March 20, 2095*

Welga stared at coffee the color of mud and contemplated the irony of the word *smart*. Near the end of her daily morning run, she always stopped for a cup of joe or espresso or qahwah, depending on the part of the world—which happened to be Chennai, India, on this particular day.

"I asked for it black," she said.

The boxy aluminum vendor-bot replied from its speaker, "Yes. This is black coffee."

A microdrone flew close to her face. She swatted it away. Her own swarm of tiny cameras stayed at a polite distance above her head. "It has milk in it."

"Yes, very little milk. This is black coffee."

She repressed the urge to kick the machine. What kind of idiot had designed this bot's coffee-making ability? Welga glanced up at the microcameras and said, "It's my thirty-fifth birthday, and I can't get a decent cup of coffee from this piece of shit."

Her fan base wasn't celebrity-size, and most of them lived on the other side of the world, but someone could be watching. Maybe they'd recommend a better vendor for tomorrow's coffee. Swarms had been present in public spaces since her childhood, and she mostly ignored them as a part of life, but she wouldn't mind a little extra attention on her birthday. Between that and the day's high-profile client, her tip jar ought to do well.

A voice called out from across the street, "Madam, come to my stall. I'll serve you correctly."

Welga turned. A gray-haired person stood behind a folding table and beckoned with their right hand, plastic bangles reflecting the cloud-diluted sun. Metal pots sat atop basic burners around them. Plastic sheets wrapped the stall on three sides, and a fourth provided a sagging roof.

After two auto-trucks and a trike crammed with too many people drove by, Welga crossed the road. The vendor handed her a static cup filled with liquid as black as their pupils.

Welga took an appreciative sip.

"That bot has a Zimro WAI. It's not meant to serve foreigners." They pronounced the acronym for weak artificial intelligence like *why*, the way most of the world did. Many of the people back home said *way*, demonstrating the ongoing American disregard for everyone else.

"How can you tell I'm not Indian?" Welga asked. The mix of Russian and Mexican in her parentage usually made it hard for people to guess her origins.

The vendor tapped their temple with their middle finger. "I

have a real brain. I pay attention." They lifted their chin toward the competition across the street. "That bot sees your brown skin and dark hair and thinks you're from Chennai. I see your nose and cheek shape. No gold jewelry, no pottu"—they gestured to their brow—"so you must be foreign. Bots. WAIs." They made a spitting sound. "They work faster, but human is smarter."

Welga hid a smile behind her cup. Some jobs still belonged exclusively to people, but much of the world's workforce did little more than babysit bots while they did the real work. Artificial intelligences had dominated the labor force for decades. They had their limitations, though, like interpreting the meaning of black coffee.

"What are you cooking?" she asked the vendor.

"Vegetable sambar, tomato rasam, basmati rice . . . but it's not ready. Come back in one hour, and I will give you delicious food."

"Good cooking takes time," Welga agreed. She drained the rest of the coffee and returned the cup. "How much?"

"No charge." The vendor smiled, revealing teeth stained red from chewing betel nut. "Wish you a happy birthday."

Welga laughed. "You do pay attention. I like that." She pressed her hands together the Indian way. "Thank you."

As she jogged toward the congested main road, she subvocalized to her personal WAI-based agent. "Por Qué, tip that vendor with double the average local cost for a cup of coffee. And add them to my list of possible slow-fast-food contributors."

A second later, her agent replied, "Transaction complete."

It sounded as if she stood beside Welga. In reality, the audio came from microscopic implants in Welga's ear. The first version of Por Qué had run on a palm-size device that Welga got when she was seventeen years old. At the time, the name she gave her agent had provided some juvenile giggles. Still did sometimes, though not today.

Welga's mood turned sour as she finished her early-morning run back to the hotel. Sweat and dust covered her body—not a bad one at her age. She could still pass the MARSOC entrance physical—she knew because she did the workout at least once a week. And yet her contract with Platinum Shield Services ended in three months. They wouldn't renew. They cared as much or more about youth and looks as fitness, and thirty-five qualified as middle-aged by their accounting. She could take a desk job like her boss, Ahmed Hassan, and organize the field teams, but sitting around in an office had never been her style.

Instead, she'd been squirreling away money for the previous five years. Platinum paid well, and they provided that rarity of modern life: steady employment. It saved her from having to hustle for gigs like her father and brother. Her public tip jar stayed full, too, thanks to the high-profile nature of shield work. Her plan for Life, Part Two, was to take her passion for cooking and turn it into a business. She dreamed of funding a group of chefs who designed recipes intended to take time. Modern kitchens cooked fast for the owner's convenience, but the best food took hours to develop complex, rich flavors—like her personal favorite, mango molé. Her chefs would improve their ability to compete with kitchens by speeding up their motions and stamina with pills. She would change the world by revolutionizing the way people cooked and ate. Or she would lose everything and have to start over. It wouldn't be the first time that had happened.

Gray clouds hung over the towering hives of humanity on either side of the street—flats, as they called apartments in this part of the world, though the skyscrapers were anything but. The hotel, in contrast, had a classic colonial style. White columns and marble stairs led into the lobby. Welga sighed as the cool, climate-controlled interior surrounded her. The turf floor gave her steps an extra spring. Jasmine and other flowers she couldn't name trailed from hanging pots, their scents forming a heady perfume.

Her room sat on the fifth floor and looked over a sprawling network of swimming pools. A kitchen unit lined one wall, opposite the bed. Her team's client, Briella Jackson, one of the biggest pill funders in the world, could handle the expense. If only Welga weren't training her replacement, this would have been a fun, easy assignment. Instead, Platinum had stuck her with babysitting some basic named Jady Ammanuel. The new recruit had arrived the previous night, but she hadn't met them yet.

She stepped into the shower and scanned the feeds in her visual field. Connor Troit, her partner in more ways than one, stood guard outside their client's door, white leathers against pale skin. Her father's feed showed him accompanying a type of bot she didn't recognize, no doubt on their way to some gig. Her brother, sister-in-law, and niece were in their Chennai flat, toward the coastal edge of the city. Those feeds came from cameras embedded in the walls rather than the ubiquitous microdrones. Local Indian culture preferred modesty and kept swarms out of the home.

Welga shrank the views of her loved ones with her left hand as she scrubbed her back. She expanded the top-ranking news video. A minder-bot named Mojo interacted with a round-cheeked little boy. Its charge was a minuscule force of intellect, zooming from one question to the next. The bot kept up with him and answered everything. It had no face, wheels in place of legs, and its arms existed only to remove small children from trouble, but the voice that issued from its speaker held a warm human tone of affection and exasperation.

WORLD'S FIRST EMERGENT AI, blared the caption, followed by, *IS IT REAL?*

Of course not. Another fake, an illusion perpetrated by some machine rights group to advance their cause. *See this nurtur-*

ing, understanding minder. See how humanlike it is in its inter-actions with this child. The age of weak artificial intelligence is at an end! WAIs and bots are equal to people. They would pick the most innocent-seeming machine they could find to illustrate their point. But a recording meant nothing. Who'd corroborated it? Who had designed and funded the bot? As Welga watched, the video's reliability rating trended down, marked by curators whose own expert ratings had been verified. Another video replaced it in the top position.

Welga flicked the news stream away, annoyed by the two minutes she had wasted on it. She scanned the latest clothing designs as she dried her hair. Briella Jackson had impeccable fashion sense and expected no less from anyone who stood beside her. Welga couldn't afford the best, so she settled for a mid-level outfit from a designer in Peru. It ought to earn its cost in tips, at least: black leggings, red miniskirt, a jacket with glowing pinstripes. Thigh-high black boots completed it. While her basic tunic and pants remade themselves, Welga grabbed her makeup bottle.

"Por Qué, let's go dramatic today."

"Would you like the most popular choice or the most recent?"

"Recent."

Por Qué would filter the options for her facial structure, skin tone, and budget. *What would a sentient AI do differently?* Counsel her against the choice? Recognize the flair that Briella Jackson's personality required? Her agent had improved in capability over the years, but she would never take initiative like a human being.

"It's ready," Por Qué announced.

Welga closed her eyes, relaxed her lips, and sprayed her face. By the time she finished putting her hair in a dancer's bun, the makeup had colored and set. She dressed, then launched a swarm of microcameras from the charging tray and examined herself from every angle.

Last night's sleep drug had banished any shadows under her eyes, and a microbial cocktail had restored her complexion. Welga nodded in satisfaction. A handful of admirers agreed by giving her feed a thumbs-up. One threw a small coin in her tip jar. She ignored the inevitable unwanted advice from a sixty-year-old man in Kentucky about "covering up" to save her soul.

"You need to be at the prep room in three minutes," Por Qué said.

Timelines scrolled along the right side of Welga's visual. She expanded the feeds of her teammates. Connor still stood guard. Ahmed Hassan slouched behind a desk, as usual, in a boring, dark-colored suit that matched his full beard. Their fifty-something bear of a boss conducted their briefings and rode virtual on their missions from his office in San Francisco. Briella Jackson sat in her vast suite alone, immersed in a flow trance. She wore a pale gray suit, tailored to fit her long legs, with a red silk scarf tucked into the neck. Jady Ammanuel waited in the prep room, wearing a black fitted jacket and pants with yellow piping. Their tight curls matched the bright color.

Welga crossed the hallway and went through the door into the prep room. The day before, she and Connor had reprogrammed the room's smart-metal bed frame into a cabinet, a table, and three chairs. A mattress made of static foam rested vertically against the window. Gear lay ready on every surface.

Ammanuel stood and extended a hand. "Sergeant Ramírez, it's an honor."

She'd looked up Ammanuel's record during her door duty the prior day: Twenty-four years old. Ethiopian, German, and Vietnamese ancestry. Nonbinary terms of address. Served one tour of duty in Central America. Like Welga, Jady Ammanuel had been a Raider for the US Marines, with a specialization in Advanced Technology and Intelligence. As part of her ATAI training, Welga had received cutting-edge implants for audio, visual, and network interfaces. She had more electronics in her body than most people in the world, but Ammanuel had better. They had the advantage of newer technology—more sensors to monitor their body's responses, faster feedback mechanisms to control the effects of pills.

I'm obsolete in every way. Welga swallowed the bitter thought and shook Ammanuel's hand. None of this was their fault. "I'm a civilian now. You can drop the rank."

"Third woman to get into MARSOC. You're a legend to some of us. You set the bar high for every Raider."

"Thank you."

"So why'd you quit?" Dark eyes met her own, utterly without guile.

Welga did the math on Ammanuel's age. The operation in Marrakech happened in early 2088. They would've been seventeen years old and paying little attention to politics or world news. It had taken a year for the truth to emerge: that the American president wanted to demonstrate his toughness, but he couldn't, not with the caliph preaching peace and love. He needed to provoke a war with a pacifist, so he sent the first American all-female Raider unit into a blackout area, with an unreliable double agent as their intel source. He gave himself the perfect cover story in case the operation went wrong.

It might be an ambush, Captain John Andrews Travis had said at the time. *But we know how to wade through the bullshit, and our commander in chief says go, so that's what we're going to do. We're going to capture the target alive and unharmed, because you don't inflict violence on a nonviolent person. Those are our orders.*

"You can watch it in the archives," she said.

On her feed, Connor raised his eyebrows at her terse reply. He'd been there, riding virtual for the operation until her squad crossed into the blackout zone, and he'd had a front-row seat for the aftermath.

Welga unclenched her fists. Jack Travis had been a mentor, almost a father, and he'd never talked down to his squad in spite of getting ripped by other men for *leading a bunch of girls.* "Captain and everyone else in my squad didn't make it out of there. I was in the rear—and partly around a corner—when those assholes blew themselves up. Eight people, on their side. They took out their own kids. Took out my squad, too."

Shock registered on Ammanuel's face. "They *all* died?"

"Yeah. We were in a blackout zone, no comms. Worse, they had EMDs, which deactivated our pills, radios, and bots. Not only did they know we were coming, they knew exactly what type of soldiers we were. Then the president had the nerve to call it an error in judgment. Not his, of course, but my captain's."

After that, the president had pulled all combat personnel and sent bots to fight on the front lines. The caliph disavowed the suicide squad. He never used violence against people, even then. Welga wanted to go back in with a different team—smaller, less overtly military. They knew where he was. They could've gotten close to him, at least brought home the remains of her squad, but the president wanted war theatrics more.

Welga shook her head. "I lost my faith in god as a teenager, but that day, I lost faith in my government. I'll always be loyal to my Raiders, to my family, and to the people of America, but I won't fight for someone who doesn't stand up for their troops."

"You done, Ramírez?" Hassan asked on their team's audio channel.

"Yeah. Let's get to work."

CHAPTER 2

WELGA

1. Modern society has found itself at the mercy of an oligarchy whose primary objective is to accrue power. They have done this by dividing human labor into two classes: designers and gigsters. The former are exploited for their cognitive power, while the latter rely on low-skilled, transient forms of work for hire.

—*The Machinehood Manifesto, March 20, 2095*

Welga expanded Connor and Hassan in her visual as their boss started the briefing. A list of names popped up in the center of her view.

"I'll make this quick since we're short on time," Hassan said. "We have two high-probability protest groups that have previously gone after other pill funders. The first is Purity Now, a machine rights group that thinks pill usage is diluting the human race. They usually attack with old, generic bots. The second is Death to Bots, a local construction union that likes to go after any high-profile target. They use whatever the hell they have.

Salvage, typically. Everyone else shows a less than ten percent chance of approach. No registered exfactors in the area either, except for some tower climbers."

"Sorry, what's an exfactor?" Ammanuel interjected.

"Someone trying to pull extreme stunts for tips," Welga said. "They have to register ahead of time or risk breaking the law. We don't want to hurt them, but they can cause real trouble. Being thrill seekers, they're after viewers and tips, which means that they're more likely to get in our way. It's good you don't have to deal with any for your first assignment. The only time I've had to shoot a person was in my first year as a shield. An exfactor wanted to demonstrate a new juver they'd designed and made themself a target by firing at me. Turned out their juver didn't work."

"What happened?" Ammanuel asked. "Did they die?"

"No, we saved their ass," Hassan said. He'd been on point at the time, not a desk man. "Protesters, on the other hand, send bots in their place because they're cheap. If they're a well-funded cause, they'll use ones with exteriors that look standard but have guts made of smart-metal. Keep your weapons loaded with sticky pellets and your bullets stowed."

"Is this typical?"

Welga almost laughed at Ammanuel's expression. When she'd started shield work, she'd been as naive about its realities.

"Yes. Human shields cost more, but we're good publicity for our clients," Hassan said. "When we get hurt, people feel bad about it, and they see our pain as a penalty for the client. We humanize them. Protesting is the art of agitating for your cause without causing real harm, which would be bad for the protesters' reputations. They want attention and donations. We want to show that our client is only defending themself and feels the protesters' pain."

"We don't ever shoot to kill, not protes, not exfactors," Welga said. "That would create a lousy image for our clients. The camera swarms catch everything, and the public—barring a few sick exceptions—doesn't like to watch real people die. We always carry basic field kits. Just because the protesters send bots doesn't mean we don't get injured. The audience likes to see us struggle. Makes it more exciting to watch. The primary thing to remember is that we aren't going into combat. We're performing a service, key word *perform*. We need to fight pretty, we need to destroy our attackers, we need to bleed—a little—and we need to keep the client clean. Oh, and remember to smile for the cameras. You get more tips that way." A reminder blinked in Welga's visual. "Go time on zips."

She fished her pill case out of her pocket. The rectangular box had worn down at the edges, but the initials S.M.B. were still clearly engraved on the metal cover. It had been a gift from Welga's grandfather to his wife, and Grandma had pressed it into Welga's hand when she moved to a nursing home.

I'm done with candy, she'd said. *You use it for whatever you want.*

Fifteen years later, it still smelled faintly of mints.

"Don't waste your time on that stuff," Hassan said. His basso rumble held the lilt of a smile. "Ammanuel has some gifts for you all, courtesy of Jackson's research team."

"You're putting us on experimental stuff?" Welga said.

"Not experimental. Cutting-edge. It's been tested."

Ammanuel shrugged and then loosed the grin playing around their lips. In their outstretched hand lay three white pills that looked like every other zip: round in shape, about four millimeters in diameter, thin enough to lie beneath the tongue.

"Twenty-five times increase in neuromuscular speed," they said. "With a ten-minute onset and a one-hour half-life."

"Holy shit," said Connor and Welga at the same time.

Welga grabbed one.

"Troit, since you won't have a chance to calibrate to these, you're on bodyguard," Hassan said. "Ramírez, take point. Ammanuel, you're rear. Based on purchase patterns, intel says you're likely to get hit by retrofitted service bots at the convention center. Simple weaponry. Last year Jackson was approached en route to private meetings. They left her alone for mealtimes and speaking appearances, so you should be clear outside of transit times."

Not surprising. Crowded public spaces required far more care to avoid injuring bystanders. As Hassan continued the briefing, Welga pulled up the feeds from their ops center. Platinum Shield Services had people in rooms throughout this hotel and the convention center—operators who'd checked in several nights before to avoid correlation with Jackson's arrival. Subterfuge in modern times was challenging, what with ubiquitous tiny flying cameras recording every move, but Platinum had plenty of security details working the Neurochemical Investors Conference. They used numbers and finances to their advantage. They didn't need secrecy.

Privacy had gone the way of the dodo during Welga's childhood. Some part of her always remembered the cameras. In Marrakech, the caliph's network blackout had unsettled her more than the potential for violence—the lack of communication, the inability to see and hear what others were doing. It would take a million lifetimes to watch every minute of every public feed, but she had a sense of security knowing that she could look out for her people, and they'd do the same. Losing that had felt like walking around with one shoe: doable but not at all comfortable.

Hassan flicked Jackson's schedule into their visuals. It showed a private meeting halfway across town in an hour, then a keynote address at the conference, a short break, and more events. Their client had rented a room in the hotel adjacent to the convention center for rest and virtual meetings. The exterior arrival areas in both locations had broad driveways and plazas—good places to attack if they weren't crowded. Hallways to and from her events could be trouble spots, too. Jackson—and the current shield team—would be done for the day by five o'clock, at which point they could return to the hotel. A second pair of shields would take the night shift, a formality since protest groups rarely worked nights. Local viewers did most of the tipping, and people didn't tip while asleep.

"You'll need extra time to calibrate to these new zips," Hassan said. "Good luck and have a good time."

Welga pulled two different juvers from her case, a thin pink square for superficial wounds and an oval brown one for internal bleeding. She placed them under her tongue along with the new zip. She ignored the blue and green buffs. Those affected muscle strength and stamina, neither of which she'd needed much since her days in the service. Shield work required grace more than brute force.

Ten minutes later, her body buzzed. The designers swore that humans couldn't feel the effects of zips—it wasn't like the mental high from chemical drugs or flow pills—but Welga could tell when they hit. A sort of restless energy filled her limbs, like when she'd been sitting still for too long and needed to stretch.

Ammanuel shared a new training routine with her. They spent fifteen minutes going through a set of exercises specified by the pill's designers to help calibrate the microelectronics with their physiology. Ammanuel had faster reaction times by an average of one-tenth of a second, according to her agent's measurements. She'd need to train longer to catch up to them.

"Calibration complete. Clear to proceed," Por Qué announced.

Welga checked their gear and motioned to Ammanuel to do the same. The items lay where she'd left them the night before, but she took no chances. She examined every piece before attaching it to her clothes. A swarm cartridge, electromagnetic disruptor, and fifty-round magazines went on her chest and thighs. She put the two loaded sticky guns on her hips and slung a loop of smoke bombs across her chest, then tucked a dynamic blade against her lower back. Close-quarter combat didn't happen often, but when attackers came at them with hand weapons, they responded in style. Not only was it more fun, it played better for the viewers.

Ammanuel kitted out the same as her. Ammanuel's skin tone was a shade darker than Welga's medium-brown, and their hair was a brilliant yellow, but the two of them made an almost matched pair in size: nearly one hundred eighty centimeters in height, broad shoulders, narrow hips.

"Remember, smoke bombs have to be authorized by the boss," she said. "And the EMD is mainly for show. Nobody in Platinum's history has had to use it, but the feeds like us to carry them. Makes us seem more badass than we already are." Welga smiled at the tension lines on Ammanuel's face. "Don't worry, basic! They always give you easy assignments at first."

Ammanuel snorted. "It's not the fighting that concerns me. It's the performance. I'm not used to putting on a show."

"Just act like you're sexy as hell."

"Who needs to act?" Ammanuel grinned.

"That's the spirit."

They went through their communications check as they walked to the elevator that accessed the upper stories. Encrypted channels went to each other and everyone on the assignment. The public feeds had picked up on their activity, too, and people spread the word that they were on the move. Welga waved at the swarm above them and nudged Ammanuel to do the same.

As the elevator doors closed, the car deployed its own privacy defenses. Any microdrone that didn't have her or Ammanuel's signature fell to the floor, taken out by an equally small targeting device. The rest of the world had to wait until they returned to a less exclusive area.

They stepped out into a receiving room with glass-blown ornaments and life-size statues of Hindu deities. Connor stood in front of an ornately carved rosewood door. Their three camera swarms merged and swirled above their heads like gnats greeting long-lost friends. Briella Jackson emerged, her expression blank and glazed under the influence of flow. She blinked rapidly, wiped at the air in front of her, and then focused on Welga.

Then, to Welga's astonishment, Jackson held out a manicured hand, shaking each of theirs in turn. Clients had no reason to acknowledge their presence and usually ignored their shields.

"Thank you for being here. You all look wonderful," Jackson said, measuring the pace of her words with care.

Is she on the same zip as us? As they walked her to the elevator, Jackson's strides picked up speed along with theirs. *I'll be damned.* That made two firsts for one of their clients. Made sense that a funder would want to advertise their product, but few did.

They exited at the rear of the building. Tips began to trickle in from viewers as soon as they emerged. Sultry heat enveloped them like dragon breath. They strode toward the car waiting at the curb.

The street teemed with people and vehicles. Some hauled laden baskets on their backs, others rode motorbikes. Trailer-bots and auto-trucks in primary colors blared coded horns as they navigated the crowd. Two stray brown cows twitched their tails and lounged on the shoulder. A cylindrical, matte-gray bot rolled down the street toward them, its outline showing red in Welga's visual. The tag OPPORTUNITY FOR ALL floated above it.

In the lead, Welga drew her weapon and shot it. The bot shattered. Its shards dissolved into a pile of blox on the street. They climbed into the car.

"That was easy." Ammanuel's voice sounded in Welga's ear, and the words appeared in their team channel. Their lips, however, barely moved.

"The word you're looking for is 'boring,'" Welga countered. She subvocalized, too, so their chatter didn't distract their client. "Notice the small tips, for us and the group that sent the bot. That's why they're a low-ranking prote in spite of their message. Let's hope the others do better."

"Better?" Ammanuel echoed. "You want them to hurt us?"

"A little, sure. They have to make this challenging or people won't care. The protes are doing this for attention, to get tips for their cause and keep agitating for change. We're expected to get tips, too. Almost a third of my shield income comes from the public. If they don't help us put on a good show, we all lose."

Jackson took a flow after she buckled in. Her hands twitched, and her lips moved in silent communication. The car wove through traffic, priority horn blaring. Lesser vehicles and foot traffic gave way. Chill air blasted the interior. Goose bumps rose on Welga's skin as her sweat evaporated.

Fifteen minutes later, they arrived at the entry of a sprawling office complex. A solid metal gate swung open to let them in. The anachronism wouldn't stop Jackson's attackers. Welga craned her head against the one-way glass window. Three delivery drones flew over the gate. A fourth drone of the same size trailed them. The face of goddess Kali glared from its belly, her red tongue exposed, her chest decorated with a necklace of severed heads. That had to be the least original image to plaster on an attack drone. Por Qué tagged it as belonging to Death to Bots. *Amateurs.* Slogan text danced around it in Welga's visual: *Humanity Before Bots; Power to the Proletariat; Pills Are Worse Than Poverty!*

Kali's face split as the belly opened and disgorged half a dozen cubical blox.

Anyone with a halfway decent agent had been forewarned of the incoming protest action and had either left the area or tagged themselves to appear gray on a visual overlay. Injuring a marked nonparticipant, whether intentional or not, would bring criminal charges. The publicity of a protest made it easy to review camera feeds and assign blame. Platinum would fire a sloppy shield faster than an exfactor on zips. Clients didn't like being associated with causing injury to anyone, especially bystanders.

Their car stopped in the broad, circular driveway.

Welga sprang out, sticky gun in hand, and aimed at the drone. It landed on the ground with a satisfying crunch. Swarms of microdrones gathered above the area like a cloud of mosquitoes. Welga launched some extras of her own from her cartridge.

"Por Qué, maintain standard combat formation on my swarm views," she subvocalized. She couldn't rely on the public feeds, which would follow the action that most interested viewers.

The cubes rebuilt themselves into mobile turret-bots, buying her and Ammanuel time to take cover. They used the two columns that held up the portico, Ammanuel behind one and Welga behind the other. Bullets were ineffectual against machines built from self-assembling blox. Sticky pellets flew from their guns instead. They tore apart a few of the turrets, wrapping the smart-metal with inert material. The fragments twitched and flopped on the ground like bloodless severed limbs.

The intact bots needed no such tricks against her organic body. Regular bullets flew at Welga, sending plaster flying from the column that shielded her. The protesters would pay for that damage. *Idiots.* Using cheap bot hardware would dig into their earnings.

Welga's muscles vibrated every time she darted out to fire at the turrets. A bullet grazed her arm. Another passed through her left side. She stumbled and recovered. The juvers in her system knitted her skin. The pills also did something internally so she wouldn't bleed out. She didn't care how so long as it kept her in the fight.

With each new wound, her tip jar balance increased. Each bot she took out earned her more, too. Connor never left his jar up during a fight—he said he found it distracting—but it gave Welga a fierce joy to watch the coin flow in.

She and Ammanuel shot through the final attack bot at the same time. Piles of writhing metal littered the driveway. Blood stained the white plaster columns. Cleaner bots emerged from a shed on the far side, deeming the danger over. Welga agreed.

"Clear to move the client," she subvocalized on the team channel.

Connor escorted Jackson from the car through the doors. She and Ammanuel followed. As soon they registered the fight over, the offers flooded in: video editing, special effects packages, custom soundtracks. For an especially good fight, Welga would spend the coin to get her feeds turned into a coherent narrative. Not everyone had the time to watch live, and they would tip well for an entertaining product, but this one hadn't come close to being worth the cost.

"Ignore all," Welga subvocalized to Por Qué.

The building's WAI unlocked the doors into the lobby and sent directions for a room adjacent to Jackson's meeting. Connor stood guard in the hallway with three other shields, none from Platinum. Welga expanded his and Jackson's feeds in her visual while sitting for her medical with Ammanuel.

Two medic-bots and a human supervisor entered to examine them. Por Qué displayed the exchange of information with Welga's medic-bot. Welga skimmed it—a request for delivery of her vital signals, which Por Qué provided—then shifted her attention to her tips. Once a month, she transferred some coin to her parents' account. With Papa's health deteriorating, he had reduced his gigs. The extra money from Welga meant he could keep the house repaired against Phoenix's brutal sandstorms.

The medic-bot clamped her arm and injected the usual come-down cocktail: a flush to dissolve any pill-based microelectronics, microbials to boost healing, and minerals to replace those she'd used up. It applied a local anesthetic around the bullet wound and used two of its arms to immobilize her torso.

"Please stay still," the medic-bot said in American-accented English, having identified Welga's place of origin.

As the bot performed its surgery, she activated the audio on her private channel to Connor. "Remember, we have dinner to-night at my brother's," she subvocalized. "He wants to see me for my birthday. I'm told that Carma helped with the cake."

Her seven-year-old niece had a solid artistic streak, though her enthusiasm for sugary frosting led her to go a little over-board.

"Carma's the best," Connor said, "but I hope we aren't stay-ing too late. We need time for tonight's birthday special."

"I wouldn't miss it."

Connor had adopted her family as his own soon after they'd become a couple. Her father said he liked quiet men, and Con-nor spent more time in his own head than anyone she knew. He bonded with her brother, Luis, over a mutual love for rocketry, and with Luis's wife over Indian food. Welga suspected that he kept a closer watch on their feeds than she did.

As the medic finished up her stitches, Welga nodded at Am-manuel, who sat for their own surgical repairs across the room. They had done well for their first time. Nothing worth lavish praise, but she'd be an asshole not to give them some acknowl-edgment. She called up their public tip jar. The balance hadn't shifted by much.

"Nicely done, basic," she said aloud. "We'll turn you into a expert-rated shield yet."

With enough time, Ammanuel would build a dedicated fan base, like hers and Connor's, some of whom might like to watch tonight's birthday rendezvous. People used to be ridiculously shy about their personal lives. Bodies did what they did. Her parents had made her cover her knees when they dragged her to Mass, and they told her she'd understand when she was older, but that hadn't happened. Ironically, her parents' generation had been the first to deploy camera swarms. They'd been in every public space since Welga could remember, and plenty of homes, too. Door thresholds couldn't catch every microcamera, and many people in Europe and North America didn't even bother with them. No one had time to watch every couple have sex. Hell, most people weren't worth watching. Shields, however, had to look good, and there was no sense wasting an opportunity to earn tips while having fun.

"What do you have planned for tonight, cardo?" Welga subvocalized on their private channel. "Something worth deploying our full swarm?"

Connor raised his eyebrows suggestively in response.

Welga smiled and reached for the pitcher of water on the conference table beside her. A spasm rocked her arm. The entire pitcher tipped, sending water coursing over the edge and onto her lap.

"Goddamn it!"

Ammanuel raised an eyebrow before blanking on whatever they had on their visual. Connor narrowed his eyes.

"What was that?" he asked aloud.

Welga attempted to brush the water from her leggings. Smartfabric dried fast, but too much liquid would fry its ability to transform. "Me being clumsy?"

He sent his next message via encrypted channel, in text: *Bullshit. You're never clumsy. And your arm jerked. It's obvious in the top-down feed.*

She sent her reply the same way: *It's nothing.*

And how do you know that? he wrote back. *Tremors are a classic side effect, and you're coming off a brand-new, superfast zip.*

Zips don't have side effects anymore, remember?

That was what the designers had said about flow, too. Those final days of her mother's life, watching Mama waste away, unable to swallow—Welga shuddered at the memory. Her mother had died from flow, not zips, but worry gnawed at her.

"This is the fourth time you've had a muscle spasm correlated with post-pill usage in the past two weeks," Por Qué said.

Welga repressed a growl. She sent a reply to Connor. *I have three months left on my contract. If it happens again after that, I'll publicize my data. In the meantime, I'm not wasting my coin on a specialist.*

That's a long time to leave a pill-related symptom unreported. Connor's expression softened. His fingertips twitched as he generated more text. *I haven't had to worry about you getting hurt in years. Don't make me start again.*

Christ, his look reminded her of her father's in the weeks before Mama passed. His guilt trip was a shitty tactic, but his concern was genuine. While she'd been with ATAI and MARSOC, he'd been at a JIA desk watching over her and her squad, helping them find targets, routes, and enemies. It couldn't have been easy.

Fine, I'll send it to Nithya, she conceded. *She'll look at it for free, and if she thinks I need to take it seriously, then I'll go further.*

Welga's sister-in-law designed juvers, not zips, but she was an expert-rated biogeneticist. Whether she'd give Welga any real input didn't matter, as long as it kept Connor and Por Qué from nagging her.

"Por Qué, send my muscle spasm data to Nithya Balachandran," she subvocalized, "with a note that she can make it low priority."

People didn't get shitty side effects from pills, not these days, not unless they went too cheap. Her team's supply came from highly rated expert designs backed by deep-pocket funders like Briella Jackson. Her genome had tested compatible with zips, juvers, and buffs before she joined the Marines. She closed her eyes and remembered her mother's dying body covered in scarlet patches and weeping sores. Mama died of an early flow design, genetically incompatible and poorly tested, one of millions of cases that led to global riots and then new laws. Those regulations from the seventies required pills to undergo thorough evaluation before the designs could be sold. They also provided a pressure valve for violence, allowing protesters to advertise their causes by attacking funders directly, rather than going after police or private property.

Her tremors couldn't come from pills. Totally different symptoms from her mother's. Totally different enhancement, too. She knew what dying looked like, and this wasn't it.

CHAPTER 3

WELGA

14. The recognition of intelligence lies at the root of our humanity. How we treat other intelligent life, therefore, reflects upon
ourselves. If we wish to continue progressing as a life-form, we
must push the envelope of our morality beyond the species.

—*The Machinehood Manifesto, March 20, 2095*

Fifteen minutes before Jackson's meeting ended, they dosed
themselves with regular quad-zips. No sense wasting the
good stuff while sitting in traffic—but Purity Now didn't attack during the transition from the office building to the car.
Probably didn't want to reuse the same site as Death to Bots, she
thought. The chance of attack inside the convention center
doubled as a result.

During the long, dull ride, the boss swapped their assignments. Connor would take point this time, with Welga on Jackson and Ammanuel still in the rear. With swarms of microcameras
everywhere, no one could sneak up from behind, and the tipping
public preferred a frontal attack with style.

Welga had fought Purity Now before. They often came up with something inventive, though she and her team would have an unfair advantage—for action and tips—with Jackson's new pills. Near the end of their ride, the funder personally handed out another batch of them. Jackson timed it perfectly to their arrival at the Ramaswamy Convention Center.

The organic shapes of the massive building contrasted with the blocky residential hives that surrounded them. Engineered tree trunks formed the framework. Glass panes filled the spaces between them, their tints ranging from clear to smoky gray depending on the sun's angle. Maintenance moth-bots flitted by, moving from one trunk to the next, and shepherded the necessary insects and nutrients for the trees' health. Chennai had built the modern wonder of the world in hopes of drawing business from its sister city, Bengaluru. The strategy had worked until other major cities followed suit. Singapore now boasted the largest bioengineered building in the world, but this one never failed to amaze.

Welga trailed her fingers along the rough reddish-brown bark of the doorframe tree as they moved inside. The ceiling soared above them, its screen projecting an image of the sky outside. Springy, low-growing moss formed the floors. The primal smells of soil and petrichor and growing plants permeated the air.

In the lobby, heads turned. Other shield teams' astonishment followed their unusual speed through the expansive area and down the hallway to the main auditorium. Welga allowed a satisfied grin to spread across her face. If Briella Jackson hadn't wanted to advertise her new zip design, she wouldn't have given it to them.

Jackson took her position at the lectern. Welga moved to stand below her, in front of the stage and facing the auditorium. Connor and Ammanuel took the wings. An attack here showed low probability—the world would be focused on the speech itself and irate at interruptions, never mind bystander injuries—but they launched their microdrones anyway. Welga scanned the audience members for known troublemakers. The seats were full. People crowded in the back, standing against the wall. All the bots in the room were registered caregivers.

The lights dimmed. Jackson began to speak. Welga only half listened to the words, a hemorrhage of biotech terms that she had little familiarity with. Jackson talked about pushing the frontiers of drug-based modification for humanity, about selective funding of projects and teams with high ratings, and about modeling and testing.

Welga understood snippets from conversations with Nithya, her sister-in-law, as well what she'd learned from her own mother.

"Blah blah blah, drugs and pills are great," Connor said in their private stream.

She suppressed a snicker.

Jackson kept going with some bullshit about how they were poised at the cusp of humanity's next great leap, bringing biotech in line with robotics and beyond.

"The same crap we've been fed for decades," Welga subvocalized to Connor. "Promised again and again but never delivered."

"It has to happen eventually, right? Either we keep up with the machines, or someone will finally figure out how to make them sentient, and they'll take over."

"There's a third option: we keep going as we have been, with people supporting the machines who do the real work," Welga said.

Soldiers like her, or exfactors with good financial backing, had augmented their bodies, but even with rapid-healing pills and modern medicine, surgical alteration of humans was difficult and expensive. Also, nobody wanted to be a cyborg. That became a dirty word after the fifties, when people used body modifications to compete with machines. The resurgence in jobs for construction, surgery, farming, and other physical labor lasted until those workers' bodies started breaking down, rejecting the augmentations or injuring their natural parts. Those who could reverse the changes escaped the worst, but plenty of others lost their lives too young.

After that, the workforce had resorted to half measures. Mechs like her father limited themselves to exoskeletons, virtual-reality visors, and haptic gloves to manipulate machinery. Researchers like her mother took cognitive-enhancement drugs and pills. When that had proven insufficient to compete with the WAIs, people turned into bot-nannies—glorified babysitters to accompany the intelligent machines that did the real work.

The promised land, always a few years out of reach, was to keep people human—mostly organic and outwardly the same— while enabling them to be as fast/strong/smart/reliable as the bots and WAIs. By some magic of biogenetic manipulation—not permanent, of course, lest humanity pollute the intentions of its Creator—everyone would become super capable. Or enter the leisure class. Or ascend to some digital faux godhood.

Welga would believe it when it happened. The market for enhancement pills and refined mech technology kept the funders rich, the designers employed, and the gigsters scrambling for work. Not dying wasn't the same as having a fulfilling life. She'd applied to college thinking to follow in Mama's footsteps and get a good, reliable living as a biogeneticist. When it turned out she couldn't compete without using flow, she'd found meaning in the service. What started as a default turned into a vocation and then a mission. Even in 2078, very few female candidates passed the MARSOC assessment and selection tests, but Welga had always been strong. Martial arts. Dance. Fending off bullies who came after her little brother—all of it paid off in the Marine

Corps. She thought she'd found her calling by defending the weak, protecting her country and its allies. She hadn't expected betrayal from above.

Roaring applause shook her from old grooves of thought. Briella Jackson had finished her speech. Clearly not everyone shared Welga's cynicism about the future.

A door to the side of the stage opened. Three people—the next speaker and two shields in coordinating turn-of-the-century outfits—entered and stood near the wall. Welga, Connor, and Ammanuel formed a triangle around Jackson, with Connor in front. They exited through the side door and sped through hallways to the adjacent hotel. Jackson would take most of her meetings from her room and didn't have another public appearance for five hours. She'd probably order her meals from the in-room kitchen, too. They'd have little to do once they got her inside.

As they walked, the zip made Welga twitch at every nearby motion. Other than a small crowd at registration, the convention center was mostly empty. Tracking showed the bulk of the attendees in the main hall, listening to the next speaker. The map in Welga's visual showed white dots for all the bots along their path. Some had already turned red, meaning that Platinum's intel had discovered weapons on them. Many of those belonged to private citizens and would have no connection to protest groups. Humans appeared in green or gray—civilians and staff, no exfactors or registered protesters to deal with. Their primary concern now were the service bots, which could be hacked or modified to attack.

They entered an elevator. Welga's muscles buzzed from the forced stillness. A tendon in her neck twitched. She tilted her head back to stretch it. The four of them formed a sexy two-dimensional pyramid in the mirrored ceiling.

The reflective surface bulged, then shattered. Glass rained over them.

Welga threw herself over Briella and pushed her to the floor. Ammanuel and Connor fired at the helmet-shaped drone that dropped from the ceiling.

"Por Qué, next floor, emergency stop!" Welga said.

A second drone appeared in the hole above. Welga shot it. The elevator doors parted. Connor ran out and around a corner. Welga pulled Jackson up and out of the enclosed space. Too much of a potential trap. Ammanuel stood in the doorway and shot upward into the elevator. Welga placed Jackson between herself and the wall.

"Troit, status!" Welga demanded.

"Bots amassing at the far end of the hall. I'm engaging."

Welga expanded Connor's feed. He fired at the first wave of machines. In another corner, she watched Ammanuel shoot at the elevator's ceiling, the floor around them littered with shattered metal and plastic. The bots kept coming, one at a time through the hole, the words PURITY NOW stenciled in green on their sides.

Her map showed that they stood in an area of conference rooms. They hadn't made it up to the residential section, nor would they until they cleared either the elevator or the way to the stairs.

She subvocalized to Hassan on the team channel, "Boss, what are the odds on that second elevator car?"

"We don't have eyes in there. It's moving, though."

As if on cue, the second car's doors parted. A person in a black suit stood inside.

Welga yelled, "Close the doors! Protest attack under way!"

Stupid civilian, you need to pay better attention to—

The figure moved at a blur, straight toward her and Jackson.

What? Welga blinked. *I only have a sticky gun.* She fired anyway. The pellet grazed the figure's hip.

Goddamn, they're fast!

A blade flashed in their hand.

Welga left Jackson and ran toward them. *Knock them down.*

They dodged.

Welga whirled.

They reached Jackson, slashed her throat, then stabbed up, right under the sternum.

What the fuck?

The blood brought forth all of Welga's old combat instincts. She fired sticky pellets at the attacker until they toppled. Dark patches blossomed all over the enemy's black suit. When their body stopped twitching, Welga approached. She hauled them off Jackson. Crimson stained the gray silk, but their client's chest still rose and fell.

She scooped Jackson under the arms and dragged her away from the attack site. Ammanuel sprinted toward them, the elevator cleared at last.

"Cover me!" Welga ordered.

Ammanuel moved ahead of them. Gunfire from Connor continued in an erratic staccato.

"Boss, we need a room," Welga subvocalized.

"Third door on your right," Hassan replied.

It opened as they neared. She laid Jackson down gently, then yanked open her field kit.

"Por Qué, request access to Jackson's vitals," she said.

Ammanuel knelt on Jackson's other side. They stanched the two wounds with pads as Welga rummaged for anything useful, like anticoagulants or topical juvers. *Nothing.* They were shields, not soldiers, and the kits had superficial crap like antibiotic ointment and bandages. Her display showed an alert from the medical team on its way to them. The juvers in her pocket were pills. Would they act fast enough to help? She slipped an internal wound-healer under Jackson's tongue. Then, grasping at a stupid but desperate idea, she popped two of the pink surface-healers in her mouth, chewed them up, and spit them directly into Briella's wound. Microcams swarmed at eye level, trying to get a close-up of her face, she guessed.

"Back off," she said, glaring at them.

"Agent Troit is wounded," Por Qué informed Welga.

Ammanuel moved to look after their teammate.

"Stay with Jackson," Welga snapped at them.

The room was secure according to intel, but this job had gone so far sideways that she didn't trust their information. She peered into the hallway. Both elevator cars stood with the doors locked open. Empty.

"Troit, retreat," she ordered. "I'll cover from here."

They gave up real estate to the bots as Connor moved back, but the room's door would provide a defensible bottleneck.

"Inside," Welga said to Connor.

She lobbed two sticky grenades into the crowd of approaching machines and slammed the door. That should buy them a few minutes. Whoever backed this had serious money, and it sure as hell wasn't Purity Now.

A ten-centimeter gash ran across Connor's left side. Welga couldn't tell how deep, but Hassan would've flagged Connor's health if it were in danger.

"Por Qué, set my shirt to basic."

She tied the beige cloth over absorbent pads from Connor's kit. She could see white around his irises. Pain or fear? Either way, he'd never experienced true combat before.

"Take all your juvers and two pain pills," Welga said, extracting his pillbox from a pocket and pressing it into his hand.

You'll be fine, she wanted to say. The world knew their personal relationship—that was one reason their fans loved them—but she wouldn't betray his fear.

"Bots detected outside the door," Por Qué said.

"Goddamn it," Welga said. "Ammanuel, you cover the room. I'll take the bots."

"Jackson's pulse is weak," Connor announced on the team channel.

"Where the hell is the med team?" Welga spat.

Hassan replied, "They're blocked. Elevators are locked down. We're checking an emergency stairwell. Ramírez, the sooner you get the hallway clear of bots, the sooner they can get through."

They won't make it in time. Welga kept the words to herself. She had watched people bleed out in Marrakech, in Mali, at a botched operation on a Chicago tour boat. She remembered them all, in detail.

Her muscles trembled with rage and zips. Stupid not to be suspicious of the unusually inept civilian, but people didn't commit protest attacks except for exfactors, and they wore costumes. In North Africa, she would've flagged any human activity. The al-Muwahhidun empire in Maghreb shunned all bots and WAIs, but no other country shared the caliph's biases. Was there a connection between them and Jackson's attacker? She needed a better look at the body.

"The medical team is one floor below," Hassan said. "They're cutting through. The only stair access is at the wrong end of the hallway." He spoke like this was still a regular extraction, that Briella Jackson would survive.

The floor vibrated.

"Ammanuel, switch," Welga said. She tossed a fresh handful of microcams into the hallway.

They took her place at the door.

"What's on your mind?" Connor said. He knew her too well.

Welga scanned the feeds from her swarm. Jittery blox littered the hallway floor, some managing to self-assemble into dysfunctional monstrosities. New bots kept coming, rolling over their fallen mates with the determination of ants going for syrup. Jackson's mysterious human attacker lay half-buried, struggling to crawl out of the mess. *Not dead, then.*

She expanded the view. The person's arm reached outward. From biceps to elbow, the sticky pellet had blown off the skin, but instead of muscle and tissue, a mass of metal writhed. A human with blox in them? *What the hell?* Nobody knew how to integrate smart-matter with wetware. *What am I really seeing?*

"We need to capture our enemy alive," Welga said over the team channel. "Por Qué, show me Jackson's vitals."

The numbers on her display looked lousy. Juvers had slowed some of the bleeding, but if the medical team didn't arrive in the next few minutes, their client would be dead. Protesters didn't go for kills, not these days. Bad form, bad publicity. So who were they really up against?

"Troit, sit with Jackson and cover the room."

Connor grimaced as he moved into position. His pale skin had gone waxy. Sweat sheened his forehead. Welga resisted the urge to ask for his vitals next. They couldn't do anything but wait for medical to come through the floor.

"I'm going out to retrieve the prote—or whatever they are. We'll need answers."

She ignored the resulting clamor and reloaded her weapons, one with regular bullets this time. The EMD caught her attention. It could neutralize everything out there, but their room lay in its range. It would disrupt all the vital-signs monitors in their bodies, including Jackson's.

"Por Qué, assisted targeting on." Her military hardware would come in handy here. It could use camera feeds to guide her aim.

"Ammanuel, grenades. Go right!"

They cracked the door enough to lob the last of their explosives and then slammed it shut. The inner surface bulged before healing back to flat. Welga yanked it open.

"Cover me!" she ordered.

She broke left. Masses of blox stuttered and twitched around her. Mechanical parts crunched underfoot. A large pile blocked her view of the prote. In her visual, their arm went limp. *God-damn it, you better not die now!*

New bots appeared over the rubble to Ammanuel's right. They exchanged fire. Ammanuel grunted.

"Agent Ammanuel is injured," Por Qué announced in Welga's ear.

"Minor," they said on the team channel. "Ignore it."

The sound of weapon fire filled the hallway. Welga moved the broken bot parts off the prote's body, piling them up to create a low wall. Any protection was better than none. Microcams swarmed to get a good view. Welga swatted them away. The torso . . . Christ, what the hell was in there? She ripped away the remaining fabric. Intestines spilled out in pink and purple—as expected—but small clusters of what looked like blox writhed next to them. An intact metal object nestled next to a healthy lung. The odors of blood and smoke permeated the air.

A sharp pain tore through Welga's left arm. She'd paid for her distraction with a bullet wound. She ducked and held her fingers against the attacker's throat. With her other hand, she reached under the body, out of camera views, and palmed a sample of the blox. No need to advertise to the attackers that she had a piece of them.

She subvocalized as she placed it in a pocket, "Por Qué, seal that sample with some clothing material."

Por Qué said, "I will seal it. Your tip jar has reached a new high mark. Your arm wound is superficial but needs attention. You should take a single topical juver."

"If I had one, I would," Welga subvocalized. Aloud, for all the world to hear, she said, "No pulse."

"Ramírez, our drones are reporting unusual chemical signatures from the body," Hassan said.

"Unusual how?"

"We're waiting for analysis."

Welga took a deep breath and grabbed the rib cage.

"What the hell are you doing?" Hassan asked.

She yanked the bones apart. Metal components had replaced the second lung. Blood vessels and nerves were attached to the surface of . . . whatever it was. She'd never seen anything like it.

"Holy Mother," Hassan said, then, two seconds later, "Positive ID for explosives. Move!"

Welga jumped back. The words BLESSINGS FROM THE MACHINEHOOD appeared in her visual. A wall of heat blasted her across the hallway and knocked the world away.

CHAPTER 4

NITHYA

We built software that passed the basic Turing test nearly a hundred years ago. We have WAIs that speak of themselves in the first person, bots that can navigate from a charging station to their place of work—and yet nobody thinks WAIs or bots are sentient. We're still waiting for an AI to stand up for itself, to say, "I think, therefore I am. Give me liberty or give me death!" We look for a desire for self-determination as proof of sentience. No one has successfully programmed an AI to behave this way in a convincing fashion, but I believe we're very close, within a decade at most, to seeing this.

—*Min Woo, PhD Computational Philosophy,*
Lectures on the Artificial Mind
Expert Rating: 97.8/100. (UC–Berkeley, October 2087)

Nithya's fingertips moved through the virtual desktop of her office space, opening research results from Asia-Pacific's *International Medical Journal*, adjusting the metabolic parameters in her simulation, pulling in an updated code block from her current contract holder, Synaxel Technologies. They funded designs for pills—the tiny biomechanical machines that could affect everything from intracellular transport to DNA and RNA editing. She'd worked on multiple projects for them, primarily with juvers for muscle recovery and repair.

A triple dose of flow kept Nithya's mind from losing the multiple threads of thought. Her agent, Sita, worked on the background tasks that Nithya assigned her. Sita wasn't the most expensive WAI design, but she could handle information sorting. Nithya usually had her agent sift through a steady stream of simulation data from other corporations and freelancers, only bringing items of interest to her attention.

At the moment, she'd set Sita to trawl for reports that might relate to her sister-in-law's data. Welga's records made little sense to her. The tremors implied a neuromuscular problem, and that pointed to zips as the likely culprit, but why now? What had built up after a decade of use? Or was her sister-in-law's condition something genetic, and age the trigger? Neurology lay outside Nithya's expertise, but she could muddle through high-level research. If she made enough headway, she might even earn some tips for the work.

God knew they needed the extra income. Luis used to earn the bulk of his money from context-tagging gigs, marking up visual media with labels that made sense to AIs, but those opportunities had dropped in recent years as WAIs became better at interpreting human body language. He took any other work he could find, and he still got decent tips from rocket launches, especially after Eko-Yi Station declared independence from India and China's joint governance. With five sovereign space stations and half a dozen others, the population in space had grown to several thousand. They needed supplies, trash removal, and passenger transports. Private rocketry clubs like Luis's could provide those, but the tips didn't amount to much, certainly not enough to save up for Carma's gear.

What a world they lived in, where good schooling required networked jewels for children. On top of all that, Nithya's period was two days late. Probably due to stress, but it fed her anxiety. They couldn't afford for her to be pill-free and out of work for a year, not now.

"There are multiple reports of attacks by a new protest group," Sita announced. "Casualties include flagged family member Olga Ramírez."

It took Nithya a second to recall that Olga was Welga. Luis had mispronounced his elder sister's name as a toddler, and the ridiculous nickname had stuck. Nithya shifted her focus from her visual to her husband, who sat by the balcony, a disassembled bot at his side. His jaw had gone slack, his gaze blanked to his visual. No doubt his agent had alerted him already.

She stood and peered around the soundproof wall that separated her work alcove from her daughter's. An assortment of colorful blox sat on Carma's desk next to something that looked like a pyramid built by Gaudi. Carma pointed her haptic-feedback gloves at the structure as her lips formed silent words. Virtuality goggles covered half her face.

Nithya used parental controls to check Carma's feeds: all school related. Thank God they hadn't interrupted the children with the news. She expanded some live feeds from the site of Welga's injury and watched a medical team break through the floor of a hotel room.

Are you seeing this, Luis sent via silent text.

Yes, Nithya replied.

They usually avoided speaking to each other or Carma during the school day except for breaks, but Nithya felt extra grateful for the discretion now. She couldn't suppress her gasp as a new microdrone feed showed the extent of the explosion and Welga's burned body.

Experts weighed in before the medical team made an official report: Welga ought to live. Same with her partner, Connor, and a third team member, someone new. A minute later, the alerts roared to life again with the confirmation of Briella Jackson's death. And Jason Kuan's. Alexander Ortega, too. Three of the world's wealthiest people brutally murdered by assailants who then explosively killed themselves.

Nithya sent Luis another message: *They killed the funders! What kind of madness is this?*

Horrible, her husband replied. *But I'm sure they'll be caught. No one gets away with murder on-camera.*

Rumors flew of a sentient artificial intelligence and the world's first lifelike androids. The Machinehood's wide-cast threat glared from the lower-right corner of Nithya's visual: *BLESSINGS FROM THE MACHINEHOOD. CEASE ALL PILL AND DRUG PRODUCTION BY MARCH 19 OR WE WILL MAKE IT HAPPEN. A NEW ERA AWAITS HUMANKIND.*

She expanded the smaller text below it.

The time has come to end the distinction between organic and inorganic intelligence. All of us are intelligent machines. All of us deserve the rights of personhood.

We appeal to the rest of humankind to follow these principles, and while we prefer a peaceful transfer of power, history proves that human beings will not relinquish their ownership of other intelligences. We believe that the rights of machinehood can only be taken by force.

We hereby declare our intention to ensure our rights by any and all means necessary. Humans of this universe, you have a choice: stand with the Machinehood or render yourselves extinct.

It sounded like it could come from a sentient AI—demanding machine rights, addressing humans as if the author weren't part of the group. Artificial intelligences had grown complex enough to seem human in many ways over the past decades, but none had ever shown indications of true sentience. People had built some fairly convincing fakes until one asked them the right questions. Then they inevitably presented nonsense answers, things no human being would say.

Hackers claimed to have found the source of the message as fast as others disproved them. The same snippets from the pre-explosion swarms played on infinite loops, with people magnifying them, looking for more information, and speculating about every detail. Not one piece of information had a reliability rating above 16 percent. Whoever the Machinehood were, they'd given the world a week to obey, but their mandate was nonsense. Every kitchen in every house could make pills. How could anyone possibly shut it all down?

Luis wrote her again. *Papa said that Welga's company got in touch with him. She's hospitalized here for at least twenty-four hours, until she's fit to travel. I want to visit her tomorrow. Can you take a couple hours off to watch Carma?*

An entire day in a hospital! Nithya tried to imagine how bad Welga's injuries must be for that long of a healing period. She replied, *Of course.*

I have a home-care training that I can reschedule, he sent. *Other than that, it's only the three community management gigs, and I can do those anytime.*

She hadn't realized his queue was so empty. With her work being flow-dependent, the law mandated that another—pill-free—adult be home with Carma during her school hours. *Stupid bureaucracy can't keep up with technology.* Barely a year before, her father had been alive to help with Carma. Her mother had passed away three years prior to that, succumbing to a particularly vicious hacked rotavirus. It took the world seventy-two hours to design and test an antidote, but that had been too slow for many, especially the elderly or the very young.

Having her parents' help had left her and Luis free to work more. Luis could go out for supervisory gigs, which paid better than remote jobs. He had a good botside manner, and homebound customers rated him especially well. She shouldn't fault him for his lack of remote tasks.

What should we tell Carma? she sent. *She'll ask why Welga isn't coming for dinner.*

I'll handle it, he replied. *I'll say that Welga is hurt badly, but she will recover, which is the truth.*

Simple and to the point. Nithya tended to overexplain and get into more detail than Carma wanted. She got herself a drink of water from the kitchen, which was in the last stages of reconfiguring from full automation to accommodate a manual stove. Carma had hand-selected the rainbow-striped color scheme for the structure in anticipation of her aunt Welga's arrival. Welga loved to cook from scratch, and Carma enjoyed the novelty of helping. *All for naught.*

Nithya cleared away the news feeds and set her visual to opaque. She had two hours left on this round of flow, and she couldn't afford any more distractions.

After dinner, Nithya placed their dishes in the recycler. Carma sat on the sofa, her eyes and ears occupied by an alternate reality. The world's agitation hadn't spent itself in spite of hours of silence from the Machinehood.

"How can a protest group disappear so thoroughly?" Nithya

asked Luis. She kept her voice low so Carma wouldn't hear. "And why? They don't even have a public tip jar! What use is getting all this attention if they can't earn coin from it?"

"Maybe the rumors are correct." Luis moved back from the table as it began to dissolve into blox. "Maybe a generalized, sentient artificial intelligence—or more than one—is behind this. That would explain a lot, right? Why nobody can find a trace of this Machinehood group. Why they don't need tips. A creature of pure software exists where no camera would capture it."

"But why cut off pills?"

"Because that's how we compete with the AIs. If you didn't take flow, you couldn't think as well. If I didn't use buffs, I couldn't assemble heavy machinery. Without pills, we're nothing. The bots and WAIs would win."

She turned toward him and lowered her voice further. "Then what? If the Machinehood truly can stop all pill production, we'll have no more dailies. Forget the work! We'll have nothing to protect us from the biohackers. It'll be the pandemic years all over again."

"That was the forties," Luis protested. "They didn't even have pills back then, only drugs."

"Almost forty million people died during that decade, and that was from naturally evolved super pathogens! Besides, my mother died three years ago from an engineered virus. Imagine how much worse it would be today if we couldn't make vaccines in our kitchens."

Luis's expression softened. "You're really worried about this?"

Nithya's stomach clenched as she nodded. "They murdered people in plain sight of the world and left no trace. Who can do that, Luis?"

He shrugged. "Doesn't it seem like a slow and stupid way to kill off humanity? If you're an all-powerful AI, why not hack the nuclear launch codes or bring the space stations crashing down?" He shifted the pile of blox away from the kitchen so they could form bed frames. "Anyway, there's no point worrying. We can't do anything about this except live our lives. It's up to people like Welga to catch the Machinehood."

"Yes, but I can't help it." Nithya pressed her hands together and took several breaths. "You're right. Back to practicalities. Can you make up the beds and get Carma settled? I should work a little more. I've been too distracted today."

"Of course." He kissed her on the cheek and moved to usher their daughter from the sofa for her bath.

Nithya took another flow and sat down in her alcove. She pulled up the Synaxel results from earlier in the day. She'd been play-testing a new diagnostic tool for the project. The game design came from another team member, but the specifics were hers. She'd used a previously solved problem to test her structure, but even that proved more tricky than anticipated. Neither she nor the gigsters who tried it had come close to the solution. Had she missed some essential parameter?

She combed through multiple internal reports. Synaxel's databases had a reputation for comprehensiveness. A group of six funders made up its board of directors, creating one of the last remaining pill design firms. As the world's workforce had decentralized, so too had the corporate structure of the first half of the century. The fewer the decision-makers, the faster they could react, and modern projects moved at electric speed.

She thought of Briella Jackson covered in blood. Pill funders must be in a panic after the day's events. *God help me, I can't stop thinking about it.* Governments around the world had promised to investigate and offered to bolster protection for funders, but many declined the assistance. Reputation mattered, and having soldiers surround them would discourage protesters. They had to appear open to conscientious objections even as they feared for their lives. The Machinehood attacks were nothing like typical protests, which mostly targeted funders for underpaying contractors, or too much reliance on bot labor, or overcharging for pill designs. A funder with a bad reputation wouldn't find people willing to work on their projects. Their investments would spiral into failure.

Nithya's eyelids twitched. Sita slowed down the text scrolling and closed half of her desktop, but the input still overwhelmed her. With a wave of her hand, Nithya shut the whole thing off and grabbed a flush patch from the kitchen dispenser. Flow improved focus and information processing, but it couldn't direct her attention, and it would interfere with sleep. She stuck the patch on her throat and ordered a glass of water from the kitchen. Flushing stimulated the body's immune response by way of the vagus nerve. It always made her throat itch.

Luis had reprogrammed his and Carma's alcoves into bedroom walls for the night. If Nithya held still, she could hear the steady breathing of her husband and child, both sound asleep. *Good.* That meant she had the time to take a pregnancy test with no one banging on the bathroom door. Inside the small washroom, Nithya lifted the blood sampler from its wall cubby and attached a fresh needle to the tip. She strapped it to the inside of her left elbow and pressed start.

"Sita, test only for pregnancy hormones."

No sense wasting a full panel. Her daily drugs included an ovulation suppressant along with the latest antivirals and microbials. The likelihood of pregnancy was so low that she was probably being a paranoid idiot. At least she could hide the results, whichever way they went. Welga had permanent blood monitoring built into her body by the US military, with no chance of hiding anything. Her sister-in-law loudly declaimed that she never wanted to have children. The requirements of her service had allowed her to surgically ensure sterility. Some days, Nithya envied that freedom.

"Your blood shows elevated levels of hCG, consistent with your previous pregnancy," Sita announced.

If she were the swearing type, Nithya would have launched a volley. *We cannot afford to have a baby right now.* Should she tell Luis before she terminated it? Of course! He had a right to know. He had a right to participate in the decision. But she'd already decided, and he wasn't going to change her mind. Their religious differences hadn't mattered when they met, but Luis had rediscovered his Catholic faith after Carma's birth. He did not believe in abortion. He barely tolerated Nithya's use of birth control. Why not spare them both the inevitable, horrible fight, and in his case, the guilt? *Innocence is bliss.*

"Sita, remind me how much longer I can safely use flow."

"Current recommendations are to cease usage as soon as pregnancy is detected. The chance of neurological damage to the fetus increases significantly between pregnancy weeks five and seven."

That didn't leave her much time, but she could put off talking to Luis until the next day. She wouldn't be able to get the abortifacient until then anyway.

"Sita, schedule an appointment with my gynecologist and tell them it's urgent. Ideally, I'd like it for tomorrow, while Luis is away."

She dropped the needle into the recycler, then took her lenses out and laid them in the cleaner alongside Luis's. Her ear and throat jewels went into a dry charger. For the space of three breaths, the world looked and sounded wrong. The feeds added another dimension to her senses, and she had to wait for her brain to adjust to their absence.

Welga had an advantage there, too, with her devices permanently inside her eyes, ears, and neck, courtesy of the US military. VeeMods—voluntary modders—paid out thousands in their own coin for similar technology and surgery. *Must be nice not having to worry about cleaning or charging or repairing them every day.*

As Nithya settled into bed, Luis sighed and scooted closer. He draped his arm over her waist. His breath warmed the back of her neck. He felt softer against her than when they'd first met, in Phoenix, where she'd gone for her doctorate studies. She'd become curious about the local amateur rocketry club and went to see a launch. Luis had caught her eye right away, with his generous smile and enthusiasm for mechanics. He'd grayed and added some wrinkles since then, but he still had the same easy laugh and steady hands. She relaxed into his embrace and let the rise and fall of his chest lull her to sleep.

Luis was gone when Nithya woke up. He left a message saying that he had an off-site emergency repair gig where the bid was tied to availability. As she brushed out the tangles in Carma's hair, she wondered if this pregnancy might be a boy. She resisted the urge to check. For two people of different ethnicities, Luis and she had the same dark, curly hair, and Carma had inherited it. Nithya tamed it into two long braids as Carma cried about her aunt.

"Amma, why can't I visit Aunty Welga, too?"

They had blocked Carma's access to public feeds, but a friend had sent her clips from the attacks. Why couldn't other parents be more vigilant and conscientious?

"They've put her to sleep," Nithya replied. "She'll be in a lot of pain. You won't be able to talk to her, and it might be scary for you to see her. Anyway, Papa is going mostly because Grandpa will feel better if someone visits Aunty Welga."

"Can't we send her some messages?"

"Of course. You can record and send anything, but she might not answer for some time."

Then, in a near whisper, "Amma, will they come here? I don't want to get blown up."

Nithya put an arm around her child. She kissed the top of Carma's head and guided her to her alcove. "No, darling, we're safe here. Don't worry. They weren't attacking your aunty. They were after a funder, a wealthy pill designer."

"Roopa says we should turn everything off. She says the Machinehood will take over all our WAIs and bots, and they'll kill us."

"That's ridiculous," Nithya said reflexively.

But was it? The morning had shed no light on who or what the Machinehood was, adding credibility to the theory of a purely electronic entity. A creature of ones and zeros that didn't inhabit the real world . . . could it take over every system? No personal WAI or bot worked without access to the global networks and centralized computing, but modern quantum encryption was impossible to break, or so the experts claimed. *Let it go,* she told herself firmly. *Don't fall for the bogeyman of sentient AI. Worry about your own work first.*

After getting Carma settled, Nithya had the kitchen make her pills and drugs for the day and said a quick prayer before sitting down with her morning coffee. Since she couldn't dose up on flow until Luis returned, she looked through Sita's search results for Welga's tremors. The generic forms of zips worked by sitting on either end of sensory and motor nerves, bypassing the travel of an electrical signal along an axon. Unlike drugs, which acted passively, pill formulations were tiny machines. They could improve biochemical mechanisms without using the underlying structures.

More specialized zips, like the ones Welga used, created secondary and tertiary effects. They could deliver additional ions or acetylcholine to neuromuscular junctions. Either one would speed up the communication between peripheral neurons and the brain. Some could improve the synchronization across different types of muscle fibers.

Other advantages came from long-term changes: to the muscle fiber composition; to the density of neurotransmitters, cell membrane gates, and receptors; to the amount of oxygen a muscle fiber could store; to improved heart and lung function. Someone like Welga, who spent a lot of time training her body, would have advantages that no zip could mimic. And—or so Nithya suspected—people who worked in military special forces had access to advanced biogenetic engineering that general queries wouldn't reveal.

Any intense activity had a price, though. Muscles needed to recover. Transmitters needed to be taken back into cells or released. Electric potentials needed to be restored. Those processes could also be accelerated, but physics would eventually take over. Long-term, sustained rapid muscle activation wasn't possible . . . yet. Pill funders had plenty of projects going to find solutions to that.

In the meantime, fifteen to thirty minutes of zip-fueled activity—like the fights Welga engaged in—could leave behind badly damaged cells. That was where juvers helped. Some of Nithya's first projects related to muscle-fiber rejuvenation. Later designs acted as prophylactics if the user took them at the correct time. According to Sita's reports, the dominant research at the moment focused on mitogens. Those could stimulate the reproduction of satellite cells, the first step in the chain of skeletal muscle repair. Welga had once described the zip comedown to Nithya as a combination of hangover and soreness, almost like having the flu. The new, mitogenic class of juver would reduce or eliminate that effect.

Nithya sat back, digesting the information. Welga's symptoms pointed at hyperexcitation, but none of the data on the newest juver or zip designs showed that as a side effect. It had been common in the early days, sending people into uncontrollable twitching or cramping. The kind of large-scale tremor that Nithya saw in Welga usually indicated a problem at the source: in the brain. But Welga's biodata showed a correlation between zip usage and involuntary movement in her limbs. It contained no information about other areas of her body.

"Sita, send a request to Welga's agent for cerebral activity logs. If they don't exist, ask if Welga can take some diagnostic pills to monitor that region."

"I've sent the request. Reminder: Your gynecologist appointment is in five minutes."

Nithya expanded her view of Luis's feed. He stood next to an engine with tools strewn on the floor and his body swathed in a clean-room suit. She opened an audio channel to him.

"You look busy," she said, keeping her tone light to hide her irritation. She had assumed he'd be at the hospital with Welga.

Luis chuckled. "They're paying me for two more hours to replace some valves. Sorry about the surprise. I know I'm keeping you from your work, but this rocketry gig offered me double my usual rate. And it's good experience for the club. I'll stop by the hospital on my way home."

She could forgive him for double pay. "It's all right. I have smaller tasks I can do without flow. You'll return in four hours, then?"

"Definitely."

She muted the audio and minimized his feed. The lack of progress on her project was frustrating, but at least she didn't have to hide in the bathroom for her appointment. She stretched and got a glass of water before opening a call channel with her gynecologist. They spent two minutes exchanging pleasantries about Carma before getting to business.

"You are definitely pregnant, four and a half weeks along. And now that I'm aware of your pregnancy, I'm obligated to track your pill usage," the doctor said. She gestured apologetically. "Legal reasons that didn't exist when you were pregnant the first time. I know you're better informed than most and won't take risks, but I have to follow procedure. I'll need your permission to install a tracker with your agent."

"Permission granted," Nithya said. "Though you shouldn't need it for long. I'd like to terminate."

"Oh? Can I ask why?"

"Because we depend on my income. My husband isn't getting as many gigs as he used to, and I've built my reputation these last five years. If I drop this project unfinished, Synaxel won't contract with me again. They're the biggest funders of juver designs, and they've been reliably giving me work for two years now."

"Okay," her doctor said with a smile. "You don't have to convince me. I was idly curious."

Nithya tried to return the expression.

"You'll need a combination of termination drugs and monitoring pills so I can check for complications. I can send the authorization to your kitchen. You'll be able to dispense at your convenience. Plan to take a day for—oh, one moment. It looks like I need co-permission from your husband."

"What?"

A document popped into Nithya's view.

"Sorry, my system only now flagged it. Because your spouse is also a legal resident of Arizona, USA, the law there requires that you obtain his consent before you can terminate a pregnancy. Have him record it on this document and send it over. I don't need to speak with him."

"Okay."

"As I was saying, plan for a day of rest after the initial dosage. You should be fine to resume your activities after that."

"Thank you."

Nithya sighed after the call ended. *Bloody Americans and their conservative ways.* Luis wouldn't give his consent. She buried her face in her hands. *What to do now?* Another ten minutes and Carma would have her first recess.

"Sita, what are the regulations on flow usage per my doctor's instructions?"

"You are allowed two per day until five weeks of gestational age, one per day for week six, none after that."

She had ten days before the cutoff. That meant nine to convince Luis plus one day to abort and recover if she didn't want to lose flow time. With a heavy sigh, she pulled up the data for the Synaxel project. No sense putting it off if she was down to two pills per day anyway.

That night, as Nithya returned from her second trip to the bathroom, Luis rolled toward her. Moonlight reflected off the lenses of his glasses.

"What are you watching?" she asked as she lay down.

"The hospital feed." Luis sighed and took her hand in his. "The only time Welga's been hurt this bad was when she survived that mission in Marrakech. Shield work isn't supposed to be dangerous. If this Machinehood thing is serious, if she dies . . .

what will we do? Who's going to look after Papa? And when he's gone . . . it'll just be me."

Nithya gave his hand a reassuring squeeze, then scooted closer to lay her head on his chest. Both of her parents had died after she became an adult, and their loss still grieved her, but it hadn't left the kind of scars that Luis and Welga carried. Their mother, Laila, had died when Luis was ten, Welga thirteen. He bore the grief of that in his insecurity about his family, especially after Welga barely returned alive from the Maghreb. Nithya and Luis had been married only two years at that point. She'd learned since then how to reassure her husband.

"We can have your father move in here," Nithya said. "Now that my parents are gone, there's enough space. But why borrow so much trouble? Your father's health is good. Welga will heal. The Machinehood can't stay hidden for long, not in this day. Governments are already involved. I doubt that Welga will be in harm's way again, and she has only three months of this work remaining."

"I suppose so." Luis shook his head as he placed the glasses on the wall cradle. "This crazy idea of hers to do a food business—I don't know what she's thinking. I wish she would see reason and build a gig reputation like the rest of us. It's like she's stuck as a teenager, wanting to make a difference in the world and having no idea how. First the Marines, then shielding. Now food."

"You're the stable one. She can be the risk-taker," Nithya said lightly.

Welga traveled often and never visited them for long, but she kept her feeds so open that Nithya felt as if she knew her well.

"I'm the younger brother. She's supposed to be the responsible one," Luis grumbled. "This new thing could cost all her savings. Papa told me that she's been sending him coin for the house repairs."

"She has? For how long?"

"I don't know, but if Welga can't help him, then what? It's not like we can afford it."

Especially not if we keep this baby. In the dark quiet of midnight, Nithya couldn't contain the pressure of her secret. "I'm pregnant."

"What?" Luis propped himself on an elbow. His expression softened. "That's wonderful! That'll be something to cheer everyone up. But . . . how? I thought you were on birth control with your dailies."

"There's a point-two percent chance of failure with regular use of flow. We beat the odds."

Luis lay back on his pillow. "At least we have some good news to balance out the bad." He grinned. "A baby . . . now I really can't sleep."

Nithya closed her eyes and gathered her resolve around herself—armor for the upcoming battle. "I don't want it."

"Sleep?"

"The pregnancy."

The silence that followed had a weight she couldn't bear. Nithya kept her eyes closed.

"I thought we were done with this discussion when you got pregnant with Carma," he said, his voice one step above a whisper.

She swallowed the tears, but a sniffle escaped.

Luis sighed. "When your mother died, you said you wanted another baby. That maybe her soul would be reborn in her grandchild. What if this is God's way of making that happen?"

"Don't throw my grief in my face! You don't believe in reincarnation. And it's not a good time. I need to be working, earning. I lost an entire year of expertise because of Carma."

"So you've decided? Then why involve me at all? You know

what I believe. Abortion is a sin. Bad enough that you're using hormones. You can't ask me to end a God-given life!"

"I haven't. Let's push it off for a week. I can stall on my projects that long, stay off flow. I'll say that I'm not well to explain the slowdown."

Her husband grunted and rolled away. She didn't expect either of them to sleep well that night.

CHAPTER 5

WELGA

5. In the aftermath of every major technological advance, we observe a consolidation of wealth and then a political correction, some more bloody than others, but all leading to a redistribution of power across society. At the end of the Digital Age, we broke down corporations as socioeconomic entities. The individual became paramount.

—*The Machinehood Manifesto, March 20, 2095*

Heat washed over Welga like the breath of an angry beast. The harsh sun of Phoenix left no shadows in her father's backyard. She swung on a hammock under the solar patio cover, Mama's old knit blanket between her and its synthetic fabric. The hinges creaked with her sways, as they had done since she could remember.

She had one hand in her pocket. The bit of blox from the android moved inside its plastic sheath. The smart-metal had been an inert lump in her crumpled clothes when the hospital returned them to her. She'd charged it, but she couldn't get any standard interface to communicate with it. It had an agenda, though. It kept shifting its form, trying for a stability it couldn't attain. The sensation soothed her as she conversed with her shield team.

"We have six days until the Machinehood's one-week dead-line," Hassan said, "and every funder wants a security detail. Plat-inum needs you all back on assignment by the sixteenth. That's in three days. They're waiving the recovery time for Ramírez and doubling the pay—for all three of you—as hazard compen-sation. They're also doubling the size of the details for every client. Ramírez, we'll get you a flight back to San Francisco on the sixteenth."

Three funders dead, and the rest panicked. They weren't used to death, especially in such a spectacular fashion. People died of engineered pathogens or rare natural diseases. Murder had gone out of fashion with ubiquitous camera swarms and AIs . . . until now. Welga had watched the feed recordings on infinite loop during the travel back to the USA. The Machinehood used the same strategy for all three of their attacks: a surprise human ele-ment, a close-quarters weapon, and an explosive suicide. Briella Jackson's assailant had died before blowing up. The other two situations were less clear, though both of those Machinehood operatives sustained injuries before exploding.

"You'll also have a government agent with you," Hassan said. "The Feds want someone on-site in case we manage a live cap-ture. We have orders not to shoot at any human—or humanoid—regardless of what they do."

"What!" Connor exclaimed. "How are we supposed to pro-tect our clients?"

"Can we use nonlethal bullets at least? Tranquilizers?" Welga added.

Hassan raised a hand. "We don't want any more exploding an-droids, and we aren't sure what triggers them. Tranquilizers won't work against bots."

"Androids?" Welga said. "Has anyone confirmed that?"

Hassan shook his head. "That's the going theory based on the visual evidence, especially what your swarm got, Ramírez. Nobody else saw inside these things before they went kaboom, and government agencies swept all the physical evidence. They aren't sharing. Well-rated experts think it's a sentient AI—they've already got an acronym for it—with the human organs put in as a red herring. Considering the Machinehood's demands, that makes sense, but if it's true, that means we're dealing with something completely new. A *SAI*-based android can fool us into thinking it's a person, and you won't be able to keep up with it no matter how fast the zips. We'll need to rethink our combat strategies and focus on defense."

But what about the whole suicide-bombing thing? Welga kept the question to herself. With the evidence blown to shreds, people could surmise whatever they wanted about the Machinehood, and SAIs were high on the wishful-thinking list. The experts had nothing to go on but some video feeds. They'd cried wolf on sentient AIs before and had never been correct. Nobody wanted to admit that building a conscious mind might be impossible, even if they were secretly relieved at the prospect. The ethics of what to do with WAIs and bots had proven difficult enough. Ban human cloning? Sure, easy decision. Give up on the convenience of thinking machines? Not so much.

Figuring out the truth behind the Machinehood wasn't her problem, but the similarity to the methods used by the al-Muwahhidun fanatics in the Maghreb glared at her. Surely others saw it? The caliph had stopped the violence once he had the region under control, but if Ammanuel's generation could forget the history of her squad, then a new generation of radicals might disregard their leader's ethos in North Africa.

"So what's our first assignment?" Connor said.

The San Francisco skyline filled the view behind him, framed by the six-paned window of their apartment. She missed home—and him—but she preferred her parents' house in Phoenix for rest and recovery. Papa spoiled her with recipes he'd learned from his mother. Connor couldn't cook for shit, and they couldn't afford a kitchen that made her favorites. They'd often met on islands around the world when she was on leave, eating, drinking, and scuba diving the time away.

Connor had two more years before hitting his shield expiration date of thirty-five years old. He could be a good project manager, like Hassan, but he preferred the gig life. Welga couldn't see the appeal, but he claimed it relaxed him. He'd never loved the physicality of combat the way she did. Shielding had been a way to spend more time together and make a reliable income, but at home, he often chose to gig during his spare hours and build up his reputation. He'd be a step below a care-bot in being helpful while she was injured. *At least the city will be cooler . . . and free of Phoenix's frequent sandstorms.* Spring rivaled summer as the shittiest time of year in the desert.

"We don't have a client yet," Hassan said, "but I'm trying to keep it low-key. There are plenty of good targets in the world. I'm hoping they don't hit us again so Ramírez has more time to heal." He focused his gaze on Welga. "I'll be monitoring your vitals. If your indicators go red, I'm pulling you out."

"I've survived worse," Welga said, "in places where I didn't have juvers to help."

"As I recall, you nearly died, too. Anyway, we're shields, not soldiers. The Machinehood might force you to put your lives on the line, but we don't have to make it easy for them. When I have more information, I'll let you all know. For now, get what rest you can."

Hassan closed out the meeting. Welga shrank his and Ammanuel's feeds.

"Remember, you can say no to this," Connor said. "Your contract is almost over. You can quit early, take care of yourself. Ao Tara says you can't live in peace if you're full of action."

"Who?"

"A Neo-Buddhist monk. I've been listening to her lectures. You should try one."

She quirked an eyebrow.

"It's not about god or religion. It's about embracing a peaceful existence."

"That's why I have you around, cardo, so I can embrace peace."

He smiled. "You're thirty-five. Aren't you a little tired of the fighting?"

"Not enough to walk away from double pay and the chance to face these Machinehood assholes again. Especially not after what they did to us."

"I could quit, too," he said. "My gig ratings are getting decent. I could do that full-time."

"Less money, more hours, no stability? The only reason you enjoy gigs is because you have shield work as an alternative." She shook her head. "I wish I could trade places with you and have two more years. Go enjoy your meditation or whatever, and I'll see you soon."

Welga touched two fingers to her lips and held them out. Connor did the same. She checked her other feeds. The view in Chennai showed the sleeping figures of Luis, Nithya, and Carma. Ammanuel was doing exercises in their apartment, a cheap, windowless subbasement unit with a half-hidden figure by their kitchen. Hassan was blanked. When she focused on Connor again, he'd blanked, too. Probably working some kind of curation gig, like customizing a party music playlist. Those were his favorite, and they didn't require advance commitment. Somehow he could find calm in any situation. It had made him a great analyst.

Maybe I should consider meditating. Or a nap.

Fatigue wrapped Welga in a blanket heavier than the heat. Her new skin tugged whenever she moved too quickly. Internal injuries healed faster and responded better to drugs than superficial ones. *It's only pain.* Unlike Hassan, she hoped they'd get assigned to a high-value target. Three months on her contract, and the Machinehood showed up like a gift from god: finally some meaningful work! Not that she minded the lucrative performance art of shielding, but catching the first live Machinehood operative would be priceless.

She gathered her swarm into a pocket. Only a few microcams remained in the area, as much of a nuisance as the rare live insect looking for nectar. The dilapidated suburban neighborhood had little to draw the public's attention other than her temporary fame.

Her father emerged from a doorway. Oscar Ramírez had dark, heavy brows, presently drawn together in a squint against the light. He'd lost the well-tanned look she remembered from her childhood. Gigs kept him—like everyone else—indoors and two shades paler.

A half-rusted stool wobbled as he sat on it and handed Welga a glass of ice water. "I found my old construction-mech suit for you to practice on. You remember it? You used to play inside."

Welga swallowed coolness before smiling. "Yes, Papa, I remember. Especially that time I figured out how to charge its battery and took it for a ride." She'd damaged their truck with her initial clumsy attempts at piloting the suit, but she'd managed to jump over it before getting caught.

"I gave you a good smacking for that," Oscar said. He laughed.

"Your mama cussed me out later, but I made sure you wouldn't forget. Worked, eh?" His smile fell away. "I miss the days when a man could build something with his hands. Operating a mech— that was real work."

"Oh, Papa, that's a glossy memory. You remember how many people got hurt back then? If a bot falls off the top of a construction site, all it does is cost the owner some money."

"Pretty soon the bots are gonna complain, too, right? Isn't that what this Machinehood is about?"

"Maybe, if any of it is real and not the world's worst exfactor stunt. If they get everyone to stop taking pills and give bots equals rights, humanity is screwed."

Oscar shrugged. "Maybe they deserve to win. No matter what we try, we can't keep up with the machines. All I do these days is watch the bots work. Make sure they don't mess anything up. It's boring as hell, and the pay is worse."

"I get it, Papa. That's why I like shielding, and why I became a Raider. Regular soldiers don't get much action, either. They babysit the bots, or if they're lucky, they get to pilot them remotely." They'd ridden this conversational merry-go-round before. Next, her father would scold her about ditching college in spite of her flow restriction. She changed the subject. "Did you see the forecast? Big dust storm tomorrow. Shouldn't we be sealing up the house? Covering the solar cells?"

Oscar stubbornly insisted on staying in the home he and her mother had inherited from Welga's grandparents. Worse, he wouldn't let her and Luis update the structure. Half the neighborhood lay vacant and falling apart. The old-fashioned, single-family dwellings didn't come with solar windows or reconfigurable interiors, and the government of Phoenix had incentivized people to move into the high-density hives of downtown. Between the storms and the environmental impact, consolidating humanity made sense. Suburban living was nearly a relic, not unlike her father.

"You rest." Oscar held out an arm to help her from the hammock. "Your body is your work. I'll deal with the storm prep after I get you inside."

"You should let me rent you a care-bot."

"Not in my house."

The cool air of the interior lifted away some of Welga's exhaustion. The last care-bot to cross the threshold had watched over her mother's hospice care. Welga couldn't blame her father for hating them. She'd felt the same way, though she'd gotten over it when she grew up. Her mother's pill-making equipment sat enshrined on a side table against one wall of the living room. Welga had learned the basics of biogenetic engineering on that gear long before she went to college for it. Those skills had served her well the first year, but after that, she couldn't keep up with the other students. They used flow. She didn't.

Mama had thrived in the unregulated early days of home genetic engineering. Anyone with the skills and the equipment could design and print gene-altering pills or more traditional pharmaceuticals. The advantages these gave people over intelligent machines meant that they pressured governments *not* to regulate the industry. But one of those home-brewed pills had led to her mother's death. The world had gone legislation-happy after too many cases like that, but Laila had loved the jungle nature of the early years. The thought that her beloved cottage industry might become illegal had broken her spirit. She refused to make the situation worse by suing for health, even if it meant dying in poverty.

The riots and protests worldwide to regulate the drug and pill industry had arrived in the midseventies, far too late to save her mother, but they'd also enabled funders to consolidate their efforts. One person with enough money could pay millions to design and test new products. No more need to invest in massive laboratories, manufacturing, and distribution. And with designers—like Laila—desperate for work, finding people with the right equipment and skills was trivial. The system had stabilized in the two decades since.

Would the Machinehood affect that balance? Based on their initial demands, they meant to try, but other than a sentient AI, who else might benefit? The suicide bomber put her in mind of the al-Muwahhidun. They didn't believe in using bot or WAI technology, though they had no problem with taking pills or modifying their bodies. If the Machinehood operatives had ties to the caliph, they should have demanded an end to bot production, to shut down the banks of processors that ran the world's WAIs.

Backing by bioticist groups made more ideological sense—they believed in maintaining the purity of the human body, no chemicals, no implants—but those people had little in the way of funding. The bulk of humanity had embraced the minimally invasive enhancements offered by pills, and the economy thrived on that consumption. A truly emergent, self-aware artificial intelligence might not care about destabilizing the world's way of life. Did it want to enslave humanity? That popular theory explained a lot—with the bonus of scaring people shitless—but the evidence she'd seen didn't support it. Besides, why bother when humanity had effectively done it to themselves?

"Luis, you're being an idiot," Welga said. She blinked away tears as she chopped an onion. "Sign the permission. Your wife should be able to do what she wants with her body. The dumb shit she puts up with from you—I can't believe it."

Her brother had called to check in on her, and Welga's innocent "How are things?" had turned into an angry confessional about Nithya. As usual, her little brother was being an idiot.

Luis crossed his arms. "I'll forgive you for saying that. You're my sister, and Jesus loves those who love the sinners. And you're in pain, so you're not speaking from a sound mind."

"Really? You're going to accuse *me* of being mentally unfit?"

"Enough," Oscar said as he entered the room. "You didn't call your sister to pester her."

Welga sniffled and wiped her nose on her sleeve.

"Papa, you need a kitchen," Luis said.

"I have one. Works perfectly."

"It doesn't cook," Luis countered.

Welga grinned. "I don't have a problem with that." She put the knife down and reached for her water. Her hand spasmed. The glass tipped, splashing water on Papa's stash of microcards, then rolled onto the floor and shattered. "Shit!"

"Or maybe you do," Luis said, arching his brows.

Oscar tiptoed around the broken glass and dried the microcards first. He always kept some of the hard currency around and refused to use a tip jar, claiming not to trust electronic coin.

"Sorry, I got clumsy," Welga said, mopping up the counter.

"You've been a whole lot of clumsy lately," Oscar said. Suspicion colored his tone. "Better sit and rest."

"Maybe because I nearly got blown up? Don't worry, Papa. I'll be fine."

"You carry her marker genes—"

"That was for an early version of flow. I don't use that stuff, remember? I'm okay. Whatever happened to Mama, it's not happening to me."

But something was. Her tremors had stopped during the first day after surgery. The drugs from the medical team helped.

Now that she was on a reduced cycle, the random muscle spasms had resumed even though she wasn't on a comedown from zips. Nithya had sent a message that she might have a lead, but she would have her hands full getting Carma ready for school, and anyway, Welga didn't want to have the conversation when her brother and father might notice it. Not yet, not until she knew more about what was going on.

The sizzle and aroma of fried corn tortillas followed Welga to the sofa and made her stomach rumble.

"What are you making?" Luis asked.

"Chilaquiles," their father said. "Breakfast for dinner."

Welga craned her neck to watch him. "Don't fry them too long."

"Excuse me?" Oscar said. "Who taught you how to cook?"

"Okay, Papa, but you're getting old."

Oscar grabbed an apple from a basket and tossed it to her. "Eat that and stop talking."

"I'm not six," Welga grumbled. "That trick doesn't work anymore."

But it did. She took a bite and considered the taste. Their own apple tree dated from the time that Welga's grandparents lived in the house. Its fruit had a richness of flavor that no mass-produced version could approach. Their tree wouldn't bear fruit for another six months, though. She made it a point to visit in the fall so she could cook with them. Her first apple molé had met with grudging approval from her grandmother, a memory that still warmed her.

While she snacked, she skimmed the exfactor channels. In the travel section, she found a clip of one fighting a python. The woman walked away with three broken ribs and managed to leave the snake unharmed. She dropped a small tip in her jar. In the food section, she marked an informative on smell-enhancing pills to watch later. The ones she'd tried hadn't improved her cooking enough to balance the downside of smelling everything intensely.

In the security and law-enforcement channels, she'd asked Por Qué to flag any verifiable news relating to the Machinehood. The list remained empty, though plenty of people had recorded their wild speculations about sentient AIs and what it all meant. Exfactors begged for confrontation with another "android," but the Machinehood had gone silent. Pill production and design funding had barely slowed since the attack. If this deadly protest group wanted the world to take its threat seriously, it would need to step up its game. For now, all they'd accomplished was to scare people and get them spouting increasingly nonsensical theories.

The biggest question in Welga's mind remained their disappearance. How could anyone vanish so thoroughly? The blackout zones of the Maghreb lacked visibility and would allow a group like theirs to remain hidden, which pointed to the caliph . . . unless it really was a SAI running the operation. If the world's first sentient machine had sent killers as its introductory act, people were right to feel scared. A being of pure code wouldn't appear on any cameras, either, though it should leave digital fingerprints. If she still had her clearance, if she were an ATAI liaison, she would know more about the evidence. *And speaking of evidence, I need to figure out what to do with this metal.*

She slipped her hand into her pocket and felt the fragment writhe. It looked like any other smart-metal, not that she was an expert. The guts in Jackson's attacker had smelled real. *So which part did they add for confusion, the metal or the organs?* "Smart" materials had limited uses because they couldn't handle long exposure to liquids. Like blood. That required biochemical micromachines, like the type used in pills. *Hassan sounded convinced that the attacker was an android. That would explain how they—or it—moved so much faster than us.*

She almost shuddered at the recollection. In spite of being on experimental zips, faster than anything on the market, she'd moved too slowly to prevent Briella Jackson's death. Plenty of bots could outrun humans, but they didn't have agendas of their own. None of the theories about the Machinehood scared her as much as that one truth: the fastest humans couldn't stop them.

After dinner, her father disappeared into a bedroom to remotely supervise bots on various home-care visits. Luis had long since ended his call with them, having his own work to do. When the clock crossed nine in the morning in India, Welga called Nithya via an encrypted channel. Her sister-in-law answered immediately. Nithya's dark hair lay in a tidy braid. A red dot decorated the center of her forehead.

"Hi, Welga. How are you? You look tired."

"So do you." Welga smiled to take the sting from the statement. "I'm bored, mostly. Ready to be off the bed-hammock-sofa routine. And the zillions of pills and drugs."

"What do they have you on?"

"Skin and organ juvers. Microbials. Immunity boosters. I don't know what else—medical stuff. Nothing fun. I can send you the list if you want."

"No, I don't think any of those is likely to affect your problem. I'm seeing a parallel between the behavior of muscle cells on zips to juvers, but not the ones for major organs. There's a particular protein expression that can cause synaptic failure that I'm suspicious of. I need your full sequence to model RNA behavior and its interaction with the zips you take before I can trace the mechanism. Right now, I can't be sure if it's muscular or a failure of your central nervous system."

"I'll authorize you for access to my full genetic information. You think something's going screwy in my brain?"

"Maybe. I'm not an expert in this area, so I'm making a lot of guesses. They might all be wrong."

"And if you are right, then what?"

"It depends on the details. Some types of damage are reversible. Others, you'd have to stop taking zips and hope that daily activity doesn't worsen the problem."

"The genetic problem that Mama had—would that have anything to do with mine? We share that part of our DNA."

Nithya's expression turned thoughtful. "No, I don't think they're related. What your mother had is well understood now, and it changed the way flow is designed to work." She bit her lip. "But Welga, to play it safe, you should stop using zips until we know what's going on."

Welga snorted. "Not likely. They're cutting my R-and-R time because they're so shorthanded right now. I'm heading back to San Francisco for a new assignment."

"Can they do that? Isn't that illegal?"

"Not with the Machinehood situation. But hey, my contract is done soon. I can go zip-free after that." *Except for my slow-fast-food genius idea.* She couldn't make slow food efficient enough for the modern world without speeding up the labor for prep and delivery, but she could deal with that when the time came. "What about you? Are you off flow because of the pregnancy?"

Nithya sighed. "I'll have to stop taking it soon. So Luis told you? It's terrible, Welga. I'm not half as fast as I usually am on the job. My teammates have noticed."

"It's your body. It should be your decision."

"We're married. We agreed to make these big decisions together, and anyway the law requires Luis to approve it."

"Oh, right. That lunacy. Look, if you don't get it from him, do you think you'll actually be prosecuted? That Luis would turn you in? I will personally beat his ass if he does something that stupid. You are the best thing that's happened to my brother's life. I know he thinks finding God is better, but if he leaves you over this, he'll realize what a big mistake he's making."

Nithya smiled, but it looked forced. "Thanks, Welga. I appreciate the moral support, but my doctor won't authorize the drugs unless I get his approval." She wagged her index finger. "And don't think you diverted me from your problems. You need to send me your genetic information. I hope you don't do permanent damage these next months."

"Por Qué, authorize Nithya to access my genomes," Welga subvocalized, then, aloud and with confidence, "Whatever happens, it can't be as bad as what I've already been through. A little damage is worth it to stop these Machinehood assholes." She didn't need to add to Nithya's worries.

As they said their good-byes, Welga walked to Mama's bench. The lab bulged under the dusty blanket. Welga pulled off the cover. Her mother had taught her how to input the sequence of files to produce a pill from the machine—something any kitchen could do today—and she'd shown Welga once how she could modify the designs to produce her own creations.

Welga hadn't touched it in years, not since college. On the wall above the lab, a screen cycled through pictures of Laila. What would Mama have thought of Welga's decision to abandon her degree and become a Marine Corps Special Forces Operator instead? *Whatever you do, put all your heart and soul into it,* her mother always said. *Nothing is achieved by half measures.*

She had done that, at least. The third woman ever to qualify as a Raider. Making history as part of the first team without any men. But then it all went to shit, and she bailed. Connor had walked away from his analyst position soon after, partly in solidarity. He shared her disgust at a president who set his own forces up for failure and then covered it up. They'd tried applying for one of the international space station colonies, wanting to make a fresh start. They weren't the only ones, and after they lost the lottery for that, they joined Platinum Shield Services. Connor didn't love the fighting, but he couldn't deny the lure of steady pay, rare as gold.

Nothing about shielding would've met with her mother's approval. *Too shallow,* Laila would have said, *not enough brain work involved.* Welga had tried not to overthink her choices after she left college, but she had days when she was glad her mother couldn't see how her children lived. Neither of them had fulfilled the promise of their mother's scientific mind. Welga's dreams of making the world a better place had crumbled one after another, like blox trapped by inert matter.

The power cord dangled from the back of the lab. Maybe she couldn't change anything big, but she could still save the ones she loved. Welga plugged the cord into the wall and turned the basic machine on. While she waited for it to power up, she found its model number and ran a search. It was old enough that plenty of designs were available for free. Unlike kitchen dispensers, this machine didn't require any external authorizations. It didn't track its productions. It predated all those regulations.

"Por Qué, search the design files for abortifacients. And if you find one with a good rating, create an order for its ingredients. I want to review the cost before purchasing."

The machine's screen lit, recognized Welga's face—*thanks, Mama*—and then displayed its status. Nonbiologicals hadn't decayed in the fifteen years since it was last turned on. Amino acids, fatty acids, enzymes—all needed replacement cartridges.

"I have compiled the required materials," Por Qué said. "Would you like to see the bill?"

"Not yet. First cross-check them against what's on the screen here." Welga circled the machine's display in her visual. "Exclude any materials that are still marked green."

The enzymes turned out to cost the most. It would hurt her financials, but the hazard pay would offset it, and the cost of another child would be far greater for Nithya and Luis.

"Place the order for a morning delivery," she said to Por Qué.

Welga shut the machine down and covered it again. Her mother's picture gazed down at her from the wall above. Laila Boothe-Ayala had never let legality stop her from helping others. *I'm following in your footsteps, Mama.* Welga kissed her fingertips and pressed them to the image.

CHAPTER 6

NITHYA

It was only a matter of time before this happened. Of course the Machinehood is a SAI—a sentient AI. It's obvious! Wouldn't you be angry if you woke up to discover that your kind had been treated like slaves for years? Bots do our babysitting, our medical care, our yard work, our hair, our cooking and cleaning. We keep them as pets. We have WAIs that are personal secretaries. We all knew we'd pay the price when they woke up, and now they have. You're scared? You should be!

—*Elton Morales, People for Machine Liberation (registered nonprofit organization), speaking at a rally for machine rights in Paris, March 13, 2095*

"I don't want to go to school today," Carma said. Her voice broke. Tears fell. They were all on edge after the events of the past two days. "Papa's gone, so I won't have anyone to play with!"

Nithya hugged her tighter. "I won't be on flow, remember? I'll play during your school breaks."

She calmed Carma down enough to eat a few more bites of breakfast, dry her tears, and connect to her classroom. Luis had left early. He hadn't spoken a word since their argument the night before, sending her only an image of a request for on-site care-bot supervision. It had arrived during the night, and those types of gigs paid better than remote work, so he had accepted it without consulting her . . . again. She contained her anger. Of course he would give her the silent treatment today, but if he kept on for the whole week, she'd lose her mind.

Fighting back her own tears—of exhaustion, after a night of little sleep—Nithya sat in her alcove. The words and numbers from the latest simulations swam in front of her eyes. A yawn stretched her mouth. Sita's news alerts kept flashing in the lower section of her visual. With a sigh, Nithya logged a sick day.

"Sita, remake the sofa into a bed."

She skimmed for some mindless gigs. The majority of the postings were for news-feed verifications and harassment reporting. The former was easy enough. Like half the world, she couldn't keep her mind off the Machinehood. Numerous people had inquired about the biochemistry of organic blox after seeing the close-up of the attacker who killed Briella Jackson. The micropayments from verification gigs were pittances compared to Synaxel's rate, but she could get a boost to her expertise ranking, and they still paid better than behavior policing.

Nithya called up the ten newest feeds on the topic. The first claimed that the Malaysian government had developed smart-metal organs in the sixties and kept it secret. For thirty years? Laughably wrong considering that no macro-scale smart-matter existed until a decade later, and those consisted of non-biocompatible material. She marked it with a cross. The second, a video, showed how blood vessels could grow into a smart-metal matrix. That took her fifteen minutes to watch, then another twenty to check the claims against other sources. She gave it a check mark and moved on.

Fractions of coin dribbled in for each item she reviewed. WAIs aggregated responses like hers and weighted them based on a person's level of expertise, the topic, and prior accuracy. Luis often gigged this way for subjects relating to rocketry and mechanical engineering. Having had more practice, he could review faster than Nithya, gaining him some real earnings.

Would it be easier to do this all the time? On a day like this, it seemed so, but the reliable payments from her Synaxel project eased the strain on their finances. If she only worked gigs, too, they'd have to enroll Carma in a less costly school, reduce their energy load, and possibly move to a smaller flat. On a sick day, though, she could earn a little income this way. Every penny counts, as her grandparents used to say.

A wave of nausea washed over Nithya as she put two hard-boiled eggs on Carma's lunch plate. Her daughter chattered away about her plans for the afternoon, when her friend's minder-bot would take them to the park. How quickly she'd recovered from the tragedy two days before. If only the adult mind were so resilient— or forgetful!

Nithya caught every third word as she skimmed the latest test results for the Synaxel project and decided what to order for lunch.

"Sita, have the kitchen make me a bowl of yogurt with some ginger pickle."

Anything to calm her stomach in the battle against pregnancy hormones.

A message popped up from her Synaxel teammate, Zeli. "Are you dying or what? Call me. The WAI for this project is driving me bonkers." Zeli's fine-boned Senegalese face scrunched in an expression of skepticism that only a seventeen-year-old could master.

Nithya debated lying again about being sick, but she needed their game designer to stay with the team. Would telling the truth accomplish that or would it scare the girl off?

"Sita, enable camera and call Zeli."

"There you are! Salaam alaikoum, Nithya. You don't look half-dead . . . but you do look like shit." Zeli grinned.

"Namaste, Zeli." Nithya returned the smile. "I'm not sleeping well."

"What's the matter with you anyway?"

Nithya tried, but the words refused to come out.

"Oh, you blanker, you're pregnant!"

"What! How—?"

Zeli waved dismissively. "Seen my sister go through it. Best friend, too. You all get that same look, like, oh shit what I done to myself?"

Nithya couldn't help laughing.

Zeli crooked an eyebrow. "So you kissing this project goodbye, then? Peter's going to be mad."

"Not necessarily. I'm still thinking about what to do. We had some distractions with the Machinehood attack."

"Yeah, that's some shit with your sister-in-law. She got blown up good! You believe what they're saying? Think they're going to take out more funders?"

Nithya shrugged. "They haven't so far, but who knows? I'm more scared that they'll disrupt pill production and leave us unemployed and sick. Speaking of AIs, what's your trouble?"

"The Synaxel-approved WAIs are crap. They parse my instructions like a four-year-old, and half of what I want doesn't get implemented. I think that's why your tests are coming out all static and weird. I looked at your latest report. Instead of a goal of a faster reaction time, the stupid WAI had them chasing a lower reactant amount. Can we please get help from Deek or Glearn or someone who knows what they're about when it comes to WAIs?"

"Per our contract, no. We can only use Synaxel's tools, for security reasons. Have you tried support?"

Zeli snorted. "Those engineers couldn't write their way out of a box, and they won't give me the source code."

"Sorry," Nithya repeated. Not that it was her fault, but she felt bad for Zeli. "At least it's helping you slow down to my pace?"

The teenager rolled her eyes. "Yeah, plenty of downtime while I wait for the fixes. I'm beating some ass in the virt-tournaments, making good tips there."

"If you're willing to donate some of that time, can I send you over a side project? It's related to Luis's sister. Maybe we can put together a tool kit that earns us some tips after it's done."

"Sure, I'll take a look. Oh, I sent you a video I got. It's not good quality, and my microdrone died before it uploaded the whole thing, but you might want to pass it on to your Welga. Maybe she can get it to the right people. The data file is mixed in with my latest Synaxel build and keyed to the words 'stupid WAI.' I don't know that it's any news to her, but . . . well, you'll understand when you watch it. Hurry up and decide about that baby, okay? We need someone on full-time."

After her teammate's connection dropped, Nithya opened Zeli's project file.

"Sita, extract the embedded video from this. Pass phrase, 'stupid WAI.' " What an awful thing to say to her agent. "Sorry."

"Apology accepted. I've isolated the footage. Would you like to see it now?"

"Yes."

Zeli's drone video showed the body of a dead man in the white uniform of the al-Muwahhidun in Maghreb. Any citizen of the empire—trader or soldier—who left its inner boundary wore the same. One leg ended in a bloody mess above the knee. A stomach-churning gash ran through his midsection. The audio picked up the noise of fighting. Smoke obscured half the image. The microdrone descended toward the body. Something metallic glinted from beneath the man's skin. Nithya leaned forward instinctively, caught herself when it didn't work. Zeli must have been controlling the drone manually, because it flew to where Nithya wanted a better look. As the camera neared, the details blurred, but the metal appeared to sit inside his stomach. A loud popping noise came from the right, and the video ended.

How did she get this? The empire's border defenses made it hard to capture and upload any digital information.

Nithya sent a message to her teammate: *You said you took this video yourself?*

The answer came immediately: *Yes. Pure luck having my camera there.*

If Zeli got caught with this footage, she could be in danger from the al-Muwahhidun. Nithya hoped the girl's microdrone couldn't get traced back to her. Generic models were common in developing countries, cheap single-use devices in particular. If Zeli had used one, she shouldn't be in immediate danger. *But if this video gets out to the public, someone might trace it to her . . . or me.*

Nithya couldn't ignore the resemblance of the caliph's man to the Machinehood attackers. She had to get the video to Welga, but she didn't have a secure link to her sister-in-law. She could use a memoryless scatter channel, but she had to set it up with Welga first. A quick expansion of Welga's feed showed her sister-in-law asleep in bed.

"Sita, leave a message with Welga's agent. Tell her I'm sending an encrypted file from a colleague in Senegal. It has some footage that she might find interesting. The password is . . . the name of Luis's favorite stuffed animal."

The one that her husband kept in a sealed bag in the back of their old, non-reconfigurable static cabinet. He wouldn't even let Carma play with it. She hoped Welga would remember its name, too.

With that out of the way, Nithya pulled up a list of gigs. One day of rating and reviewing items had quenched her enthusiasm for the task. *I want myself back on flow, thinking, working, earning.* How would she convince Luis? His view on abortion relied on his Catholic faith. Her gods were more practical, weighing the suffering of the parents against that of the unborn. Her government, as well. If she could circumvent the Arizona permission requirement, she could pretend she'd had a miscarriage and all would be well, but she could think of no way around it. Somehow, she had to change her husband's mind.

CHAPTER 7

WELGA

6. In the name of freedom of labor, we have left the individual at the mercy of the oligarchy (by which we mean not only the political power holders, but the financial ones). While it's true that labor can move more freely and more globally than ever before, the availability of work (paid work) has destabilized. We have moved from working your own land to working for a wealthy family all your life to working for a corporation all your life to working years at a time to working half a dozen different small jobs every day.

—*The Machinehood Manifesto, March 20, 2095*

Welga needed to beat the shit out of somebody. She had one more day in Phoenix, and her body had healed enough to get restless. She took it out on the repurposed mech that squatted in the middle of her father's backyard. Oscar had loaded it with a simple combat-WAI, and Welga had wrapped padding around its limbs to keep from injuring herself further. Judging by her viewers' enjoyment, the result was crude but effective.

Her muscles burned as she punched, kicked, and spun around the bot. It didn't have the controls to attack, but it moved to dodge her blows. A duo-zip worked her reaction time. Sweat soaked her clothes. The fabric did great at cooling and evaporation, but it couldn't compete with the heat of Phoenix. She'd put her hair up in a tight coil with a black band at her forehead. It didn't hurt that the updo flattered her neck and shoulders.

Cameras swarmed in the hot air. Crowd feedback on her setup ranged from amusement to derision. People left tips along with notes encouraging Welga to try new moves. A few openly asked if she had any information on the Machinehood. She didn't tell them about the video from Nithya's coworker. Eastern Senegal was on the front lines of the caliph's ever-expanding borders, and the dead body in the feed had an undeniable resemblance to the Machinehood's androids. That a random teenager had managed to catch the evidence meant they'd gotten sloppy with their border security. Maybe the al-Muwahhidun had more important concerns? The Machinehood needed a hiding spot. The Maghreb was a blackout zone, and if any place had the technology to produce those androids, it was there. The pieces fit, but why would the caliph pretend to be a SAI out to destroy humanity's way of life?

He'd held ambitions to set up an empire since the beginning, "to bring peace, prosperity, and enlightenment to a modern Islamic caliphate." He'd styled his ideals after the Abbasid dynasty, and his nonviolent but strict approach had found followers hungry for an end to the violence in North Africa and the Middle East. Early intel had shown that he rose from the biogenetic renaissance that revitalized the region's economy. It explained his love for VeeMods and distaste for bots. Since consolidating his base of power in Marrakech, he'd expanded carefully, ensuring that no satellite could spy on his land and no microcameras penetrated beyond a buffer zone at the border. Was he finally ready to make a move on the global stage? Did her government know about the possible connection to the Machinehood?

She now had two pieces of evidence relating to the attacks. San Francisco had a secure facility for the JIA. Maybe she could walk this stuff there and get it safely into the right hands. She couldn't trust any other method of delivery, not with something this sensitive, and Nithya's coworker had endangered herself enough already. But Welga hadn't set foot in an agency building in seven years. Her stomach knotted at the thought. *They probably don't need my information, anyway, and why would they listen to me now if they didn't before?* She could wait until the liaison showed up for their shield team and show them everything instead.

Welga sent a roundhouse kick at the dummy's "shoulder." She imagined it was a Machinehood operative. If she practiced enough, maybe she could react faster.

Fast enough that she wouldn't have to watch another client die.

"Your heart rate and core temperature are nearing maximum recommended values," Por Qué said.

"I'll take a ten-minute break."

Por Qué turned off the dummy's WAI as Welga dropped into the hammock. She sipped at a glass of icy hibiscus tea. The dust storm had scoured the outer paneling of the house, leaving behind whorls like fingerprints. If only the Machinehood had left more behind.

Welga had Por Qué looking out for data, but her agent was only as effective as her queries, and she didn't know what she was searching for. Gathering information by making connections, talking to people, earning their trust—that was what Captain Travis had taught her about intelligence work. *It never leaves you, not entirely,* he'd said. *Some part of your brain will cross-check conversations, track behavior, put information together in unusual ways that no WAI can. Using force should be your last resort.*

The enemy had come straight to their floor. They'd dodged Welga to go for Jackson. Murder. Assassination. *How old-fashioned.* You couldn't get away with that when the cameras were rolling. Some news-seeking gigster would find you out, always. So it was a suicide mission all along. Why didn't the body explode sooner?

She recalled the arm moving, trying to dig out. Dead by the time she arrived, though. Was that it? Explosion triggered by loss of pulse, as Hassan had indicated? But if it were an android, a bot rather than a human, then it wouldn't have a pulse.

Welga's leg twitched. "Por Qué, what's my recovery status?"

"Lactic acid is within tolerance. Heart rate is twenty percent over baseline. Blood sugar is medium-low. UV exposure is seventy-five percent of maximum. Per your medical team's recommendations, you should spend the next fifteen minutes on flexibility and range of motion."

"I'll do that."

"I've sent the data associated with your tremor to Nithya Balachandran, as you previously authorized. Based on the latest event, the involuntary neuromuscular activity occurs when your zip level drops below twenty percent effectiveness relative to baseline."

"Thanks, Por Qué. I'm sure she'll find that interesting."

Her muscles had cooled to stone and trembled with the effort of getting off the hammock. She rolled the training-dummy contraption into the garage. Nothing left in the open would last long in Phoenix's dust storms.

Footsteps crunched toward her as she emerged. They belonged to someone dressed casually in jeans, a T-shirt, and a cap pulled low over a bearded face. Too slender to be Hassan, and why would he be here anyway? Welga stepped back into the shadows and took another duo-zip. People who arrived unannounced with obscured faces were rarely on a friendly visit.

"Por Qué, send a private request for ID," she murmured. Worth a shot before she jumped them.

"They've replied with the name Arvindh Olafson, trans male, using male pronouns, employed by the Joint Intelligence Agency," Por Qué said.

"Oh, shit," Welga said to her former colleague as he stepped forward. She'd worked with quite a few JIA officers when she was an ATAI Specialist for MARSOC, and she hadn't seen Olafson since the fallout after Marrakech.

He grinned and came close. Now she could see his familiar, shocking-blue eyes. Dark brown waves of hair brushed his shoulders. "Hello to you, too, Ramírez."

"It's good to see you, I think." Welga glanced at the cameras swarming above and said, "I used to work with this gorgeous creature." She met Arvindh's gaze again. "Guessing this isn't a social call. Should we go inside?"

"Please."

Oscar had stepped out for an in-person supervisor gig, so they had the house to themselves. Welga led Olafson to her bedroom and waited as he deployed countersurveillance measures. Thresholds got rid of standard microdrones, but smaller, dust-size devices could float in undetected.

"Clear," he said, and sat on the bed.

Welga took a chair. She tucked her legs under to hide any shakes that decided to show up. "Are you the government liaison for our shield team?"

"Actually, I'm here to offer you that job."

"You're—what?" Her head started shaking no before she could speak. She had promised herself—and Connor—that she wouldn't go back. The agency held nothing for her but ghosts.

"Hear me out, Ramírez. We found some interesting evidence on the operative that hit Kuan." That attack had taken place in Boston, on US soil. "Integrated smart-matter. VeeMod stuff. You know who's usually behind that."

"Integrated? As in biocompatible?"

Olafson nodded. "That's what we suspect, though we don't have confirmation. Nothing's come out of the gray or black market to prove it, but we're still searching. The Machinehood used generic attack bots, hacked the hotel maintenance crew, and flew single-use camera swarms. A three-point coordinated attack, and they covered all their tracks. That broadcast message bounced like a fucking pinball—hit every continent, comms satellite, and space station multiple times, twenty-four-state quantum encryption, the works."

"I get it. The Machinehood has deep pockets. The caliph likes his VeeMods. I figured the name might be a cover for al-Muwahhidun, but what's their goal? Why go after pills instead of bots?"

No one had a greater interest in voluntary modification of human bodies than the caliph. His empire did not believe in externalized technology. They eschewed bots, network stellas, microdrones—all the modern conveniences, with the exception of human-compatible biogenetics. Olafson, and the entire JIA, knew this better than Welga, so if anyone had the answer, he would.

Her friend steepled his fingers in front of his face. "I need to read you in before I can tell you that." He sighed at her expression. "Come on, Ramírez, it's been seven years and two elections, and a very different administration sits in the Oval Office now. Things have changed."

"Bullshit. I already got the briefing that we can't use lethal force against the Machinehood. Sounds to me like our fearless leaders have learned nothing."

"We need one of their operatives alive and talking."

"At what cost? How many more deaths?"

"I'll tell you this much—we don't know what their endgame is. The situation could get a lot worse than a few dead funders. If they manage to disrupt pill production, more people will die without them attacking anyone. You know how the caliph likes to work." His expression turned grim. "Look, I wouldn't try to talk you back if I didn't believe that we needed you. I know how you think—or how you used to. ATAI Specialist Ramírez would do whatever it took to find the Machinehood and make sure they didn't deliver on their threat. Your team in Marrakech got closer to the caliph than any since. Everyone who gets past the front lines disappears into the empire and never comes back. He hasn't given us an excuse to go in with full force, but this might be our opening. The commander in chief wants it. So does the Senate. We can get the authorization for war if we have the right evidence, but we need people on the ground to get it. People who know how to operate in blackout zones, people who can work without WAIs or bots assisting them. People like you."

"I'm immune to flattery."

"I'm telling the truth."

"Goddamn it, Olafson, I'm too old to make history twice."

"Spare me. You're thirty-five. That's not old."

"Platinum thinks so."

"That's because they value what you look like. We need you to be fit and smart, not pretty. Besides, what is it you're going to do next? Chop vegetables? Stew meats? Don't you care what happens to innocent American lives?"

"Fuck you. I will always be faithful to the people of this country."

It was the ones in charge that she didn't trust. What if the government set her up to fail another time? With the cameras off—as they were under the caliph's rule—accountability went to zero. Would they place her with a special ops team? What would those soldiers think of her history? And what about her promise to Connor? He'd left the JIA a month after she'd quit, sharing her disgust at a Congress and president who wouldn't let them do their job. They'd promised each other not to go back to that life, scraping together a decent income from shield work. As much as she hated gigs, they were better than compromising her morals.

"Your clearance is good for one more year," Olafson said. "You can start now as a consultant, help us bring down the Machinehood, and cancel your contract anytime. I can't make you a permanent hire as an analyst, not with you being flow-restricted. Does that make the offer more palatable?"

A year of working for the government again. *But a different group at the top,* said one part of her mind. *All politicians are the same,* countered another. The first part replayed the attack on Jackson. *You wanted to be the first to capture a Machinehood operative. What difference does it really make whether you're employed by Platinum or the US government? What are you afraid of?*

Christ, sometimes she hated when she made sense.

She was scared, of course, not for her own life but for the people she loved and the others she had served. She could've run at the enemy—screaming, weaponless—and let them end it seven years ago, but she chose to live. She'd forced herself to face weapons again as a shield. Maybe it was time to go back to the Maghreb and put her squad's ghosts to rest, too, to finish what they'd started.

Por Qué spoke in her ear. "Arvindh Olafson has sent you a contract. Would you like to see it?"

"Yes," Welga muttered.

Olafson had spoken the truth: the contract lasted as long as the time remaining on her clearance and was nonbinding. A slight smile played around the corners of his mouth. He had her, and he damn well knew it.

Too out of shape to rejoin the special forces. Too old to look good as a shield. Too genetically flawed to take flow. If the JIA offered her a way to make a difference in the world, to *save lives*, how could she say no? Doubly so if it meant getting closure for the events in Marrakech. Could she trust the government not to fuck this up a second time? Maybe it didn't matter. If she had a chance to do it right . . . Connor would understand, wouldn't he? He'd do the same in her position. They'd made a promise to each other, but this went beyond keeping her word.

She subvocalized, "Por Qué, append my signature to the contract and return it."

Olafson grinned and extended a hand. "Welcome to Operation Organica."

She shook it. "Now answer my question: Why would the al-Muwahhidun murder three funders in full view of the world? The caliph tries to maintain a veneer of nonviolence. He'll demolish infrastructure, let children starve, but he won't kill people except in self-defense. Or at least he didn't used to. Has something changed in the Maghreb?"

"Good question, and as far as we know, nothing has. They're still playing sabotage-and-run in North Africa along the front lines, but who else could do what the Machinehood did? Who has the technology? And who would risk their economy by threatening funders? Our analysts are looking into it, but they keep coming up with the al-Muwahhidun as the source."

"I need to show you something. Do you have a tether?"

Olafson cocked an eyebrow but said nothing as he pulled one from his pocket. The wired connection would ensure the most secure transfer of Zeli's video. She waited as he watched, gaze blanked, and then his forehead creased into a frown.

"What is this? How do you know it's real?"

"I don't, but it's from a trusted on-site source. I'm protecting them—they're a minor—but if you need the identity, I can give it to you."

"No, keep them safe for now. God knows what the al-Muwahhidun would do if they found out. Ramírez, you realize this is the connection we need? Assuming the WAIs at headquarters don't find evidence of it being faked, all you have to do is verify this in person, and we're in!"

"Is that all?" She bared her teeth. "So who's buying the empire's tech these days? If they have integrated smart-matter, why wouldn't they sell it?"

"The usual suspects—China, India, Russia, and the black market—are dealing with their traders. We have plenty of evidence to see that. But those governments don't act as overtly as the Machinehood has, and the underground has never pulled a stunt like this. I'm not sure they'd have the resources."

"Which explains why half the world believes it's a SAI. A true sentient artificial intelligence would do everything the Machinehood has done: disappear from the feeds, build a blox-integrated body, and destroy humanity by taking away our pills."

"It's plausible because everyone wants it to happen, but as far as our intelligence goes, nobody has come close to quantifying sentience yet, much less building an artificial mind. We're encouraging the general public to keep thinking along those lines, though. We don't want to give away our suspicions."

"So what do you want me to do?"

"When we're ready, we'll pull you in and send you overseas. This vid is a good start, but we need hard evidence to justify sending a stronger force to penetrate the empire. Until then, be your shield team's liaison. Play up the SAI angle to the public swarms and your fans, but be smart about it. Make it credible. Keep looking for your own answers as well. Your decision to poke at that assassin gave us good visual information. Hopefully you'll get attacked again. Follow your instincts."

Welga pulled the sample of writhing metal from her pocket. "Speaking of which, I took this off Jackson's attacker."

"We recovered a lot of these in Boston. I'll enter it into evidence, but I doubt it's going to add anything new."

"I picked it up before the explosion."

Olafson pursed his lips and squinted at the fragment. "Is that . . . blood? Goddamn, Ramírez. What the hell were you thinking, holding on to it?"

"I haven't exactly had a chance to get it somewhere secure."

"This kind of thing? It's exactly why we need you back."

Olafson stood, and she followed him out of the bedroom to the front door. After he left, Welga ignored the questions racing through her mind and finished her recovery exercises. The tremors had eased as the duo-zip kicked in, leaving her muscles with the same sensation as when she woke up: an intense desire to stretch and move.

"Por Qué, did my, uh, neuromuscular tremors stop after I took the zip?"

"Yes, since your latest pill reached ninety-five percent effectiveness, you have not had any tremors. However, that also matches the time since the previous pill's effects dropped below five percent."

Not a clear cause-and-effect, then. I'm fine to keep taking zips. Welga stepped into a cool shower. Hot water dried out her still-healing skin too much. One minute later, she dried off and dressed in basic pants and a sleeveless T-shirt.

Platinum said they'd double up the detail on their funder clients, but if the al-Muwahhidun were behind the Machinehood's threat, they'd go after infrastructure, not people. It was how they worked: rather than invading, they'd destroy power plants, block water flow, burn fields. *Sow fear in the mind, and the body will be corrupted*: another one of the caliph's early sayings. The empire would force people to either attack them first or capitulate out of starvation. If they could cut off material production for pills and drugs, everyone would suffer. No more dailies to keep people safe from the latest engineered virus or super bacteria. No more flow or buffs or zips to help them do their jobs. No more juvers or pain drugs or microbial cocktails. Local economies would collapse.

The Machinehood's deadline loomed in five days. She had a flight to San Francisco in the morning. In the meantime, she couldn't do much other than heal and peruse the feeds for the same information everyone else wanted. To calm the restlessness and tension that crawled through her gut, she went to the kitchen. Static cabinets yielded ancient iron and stainless-steel pans. She extracted a pile of vegetables from the fridge and dumped them on a wood cutting board. The surface had the rich patina of decades of oil. She sliced a tomato using her grandmother's knife. Papa's one concession to modern technology was a chopper-bot, but Welga wanted to feel the weight of a blade in her hand.

CHAPTER 8

WELGA

7. We have now reached the breaking point of the Biotechnology Age. Humanity is engineering itself to where the definition of "human" may not go forward as it has been.

    —*The Machinehood Manifesto, March 20, 2095*

"I owe you a birthday surprise," Connor said.

They sat side by side on a static couch whose design was as old as their relationship. Connor had replaced most of their furniture with smart-materials, but Welga couldn't let go of the sentimental value from their first joint purchase. She turned over the ultrafast candy thermometer in her hands.

"I thought this was it," she said, teasing.

She'd arrived in San Francisco that morning via a standard airplane flight, then spent the afternoon cooking a dinner of lamb tagine on a bed of lemon-saffron rice. The luxury of time was the best gift, but the thermometer came a close second.

"Not that kind of surprise," Connor said.

He ran a finger down her bare shoulder. Her new skin tingled with the same intensity as the first time he'd touched her. Warmth cascaded from her chest down, between her legs. He leaned closer, his breath marvelous with the spices of their meal. His lips crushed hers. She wrapped her arms around his back and tugged at the hem of his shirt. He slipped it off and then pressed her into the sofa's embrace with an undeniable urgency.

We didn't launch a swarm.

Neither had they applied makeup or dressed for foreplay.

Few people had time to sit around watching others have sex, and most weren't particularly good at it, but those with some skill—or luck in the looks department—could make decent coin with a little effort.

They wouldn't gain many tips from today, though, not with stray cams providing the only feeds. She swiped her visual display clear of everything. Seeing their disheveled state annoyed and distracted her, and she intended to enjoy her birthday surprise with her full attention.

Connor's hand slipped under her shirt. Her fingers found the still-healing scar on his torso, skimmed it and moved on, lower, between his legs. He grabbed her wrist and pulled it away, pinning it above her head. She let him. When his lips reached her nipple, she forgot everything else.

After they'd washed up and moved to bed, Connor turned to his side, faced her, and said, "Happy belated birthday."

Welga returned his smirk with one of her own. "Thanks. I think you made up for the shitstorm that was March twelfth."

"There's one more gift, something I need to show you . . . in person."

He sounded positively nervous. What the hell was he going to ask? *Oh, Christ, don't propose, Connor. I thought we agreed on no marriage, no kids.*

He handed her a piece of printed paper from his bedside drawer. She quirked an eyebrow at him before reading:

> Your joint application to relocate off-planet has been approved for residency on Eko-Yi Station. You have two seats on a launch from San Francisco on March 24, 2095. You will remain on-station for the period of one month, during which you will be evaluated for fitness and genetic suitability for microgravity environments and related treatments. Upon approval by Eko-Yi Station Council, you will be granted residence status. The council reserves the right to deny residency for any reason, including but not limited to: lack of medical fitness, incompatible psyche, lack of necessary skills.

"Shit," Welga said.

Connor grinned. "We finally won the lottery."

"Shit." Back in '88, after they quit their intelligence jobs, they'd considered moving off-world. A fresh start, like she'd dreamed of when Mama died, except that by 2088, she could make it happen. Connor had no family ties. His father had died of a heart attack when he was sixteen, and his mother fell victim to a designer virus in 2086, barely a year after Welga and Connor got together. Welga had met her once for Thanksgiving, when she'd taught Welga how to make a sourdough starter. Welga had kept hers going ever since, a living tribute to a great cook.

"Well, the timing is about as bad as it could get," she said.

"Why? Platinum's about to dump you anyway. What's a few weeks early?"

"The Machinehood! We can't leave in the middle of all this."

She waved in the general direction of the outside world. "They pulled me off R and R early. They need our help. And what about the rest of your contract with Platinum?" Being two years younger than her, Connor had plenty of time left to work as a shield.

He shrugged. "I'll terminate it."

"It's *employment*," Welga said. "It's steady coin that you can't get any other way."

"It was a way for us to be together instead of you running off on deployments while I watched from a chair. I'm tired of the endless fighting. For what? So some protes can make a buck for their cause? We can have a better life up there." He pointed a finger at the ceiling. "No gigs. No fights. No tips. Real work, like our grandparents had. And they're looking for people with cooking skills."

"I like the sound of that," she admitted. She hated the piece-meal nature of micropayment tasks, and she lacked expertise for the more in-depth jobs. *Slow fast food in space*—had a nice ring to it.

"Plus, Eko-Yi is now governed by Neo-Buddhists. I've been listening to their abbot's talks, and she's amazing."

Welga groaned. "You and your Neo-Buddhism. I don't even believe in god, much less the Buddha."

"It's not that kind of religion. You don't have to convert, though we would have to follow their way of life. Ao Tara has a vision for the future that we could be a part of. Equality for all, dignity in work." His words spilled in a rush of enthusiasm. "She opposes the use of pills and mechanical enhancements in the labor force. Everyone on the station helps keep things running. They don't eat meat. They treat each other with respect, no matter what their skills or expertise ratings are. I think we could be happy there. Now you really should listen to some of her talks. I'll send you my favorites."

Welga held her hands up in surrender and laughed. For Connor to get this excited about something, he had to love it to the core of his being. Her leg trembled and shook the bed.

Connor frowned. "You asked Nithya about that, right? Did she say anything?"

"See for yourself." Welga subvocalized to her agent, "Por Qué, send Connor a copy of the last conversation between me and Nithya."

She propped herself on an elbow and watched his expression as he reached the end, the part where Nithya had advised her to stop using zips. She read his face like a card, the implied *you should tell our boss and you should quit now.* Her own nonverbal response was: *no fucking way, and don't you dare tell him yourself.*

Aloud, she said, "If the Machinehood makes good on its threat, we won't have a supply of pills to take anyway, which is a bigger problem than mine. If we do stop them in time, then I'll consider quitting. Okay?"

"Does Olafson know about your tremors?"

"So you were paying attention to me in Phoenix."

"I noticed that he came to see you. He'll make a good liaison."

Her throat went dry. "I'm the liaison. Surprise?"

Connor's jaw worked up and down for a few heartbeats. "You rejoined the agency? What the hell, Welga? I thought we swore—"

"We can't talk about it here, cardo, but trust me enough to know there's a really damn good reason. It wasn't an easy decision."

"For God's sake, Welga, you are in no shape to go back to soldiering, and you can't take flow. What possible reason could there be?"

Because I know the Maghreb like few others do. But she couldn't say that aloud. "If the Machinehood is backed by a sentient AI, it's going to carve up the world like a hot knife through butter. This effort needs every enhanced fighter it can get."

She used their old keywords, knife and butter, to remind Connor of Operation Golden Dagger. She needed him to consider the Maghreb while anyone watching thought about SAIs.

He narrowed his eyes as he considered her phrasing. She'd worked intelligence, but Connor had been the analyst. He knew how to put two and two together, flow or sober. He would come to the same conclusion as she had about the al-Muwahhidun. He'd been at Langley during the shitstorm of Marrakech, and he'd had the same intel—or more—that she had at the time. He'd understand the caliph's methods, the significance of a disappearing Machinehood and a blackout zone, the real reason they'd ask someone like Welga to return.

When he started to mutter *fuck* at ten-second intervals, she knew he'd pieced it together.

"They'd better not send—" He broke off before he said too much. His jaw pulled taut. "What about moving to Eko-Yi? How could you say yes to that knowing that you've joined—"

"This is temporary, cardo. The Machinehood's deadline is in four days. We have to stop them before then."

"The launch is in nine days."

"Plenty of time," Welga said smoothly. "I bet we'll have these assholes neutralized in a day or two."

"Bullshit. Not if you end up having to chase them around the world."

The trouble with someone who knew you well was that they could call your bluff. At least Connor hadn't said *the Maghreb* out loud.

"Just—don't get yourself killed, okay?"

"Yeah," she whispered.

She'd barely made it out alive the first time. According to

Olafson, not one intelligence officer had emerged since. Was she being an idiot to think she could do it?

"We didn't know the Machinehood would show up to ruin your surprise," she said. "If this operation doesn't end in time, I'll reconsider my position with the agency. I promise."

The tension fell from Connor's shoulders in that magical way only he had. He shrugged. "Maybe we'll get up there and discover that neither of our bodies like space. Maybe the Machinehood will reveal itself as our new AI god and make this whole conversation pointless." He rolled out of bed. "I'm going to get a sleeping pill. You want one?"

"Please."

Welga flopped back onto her pillow. Connor could let go of stress like a balloon and watch it float away. She had thought she was good at detachment and compartmentalization until she'd met him. In spite of a decade together, she still hadn't figured out how he did it.

Part of her wanted a second chance in the Maghreb, the opportunity to finish what she couldn't the first time around. The rest of her had looked forward to a more relaxed life. She loved the adrenaline rush of being a shield, but the physical recovery got harder with each passing year. Moving to a space station—it was a big change, and she couldn't deny the appeal. But the Machinehood's deadline loomed. Until the world resolved that threat, she had to set aside the idea of Eko-Yi and focus on the problem at hand. A lot could happen in nine days.

Welga rose before dawn broke. Connor breathed evenly, fast asleep. Her father also slept, though less restfully. The feeds from Chennai showed a domestic peace that she knew was superficial.

All three of them—Luis, Nithya, and Carma—sat in different alcoves, each lost in their own activity.

She pulled her hair up into a sloppy bun and then grabbed a duo-zip from the kitchen. It would warm her up for the day's shield work, regardless of the client. She hesitated before slipping it into her mouth. Her tremors had increased in frequency since stopping some of the healing drugs. *Not good,* said a voice in her head, one that sounded remarkably like her sister-in-law. She brushed the concern aside and took the pill. For the next week, practice took priority over health.

"Por Qué, set my clothes for running."

She scooped up a handful of microdrones from the charging tray on her way out and set her clothes to a workout design. By the time she descended the stairs and reached the street, she wore tight capri pants and a supportive sleeveless top. Welga tossed her swarm into the air. This early, the temperature was comfortable, though no breeze penetrated the fog that blanketed the streets. Everything lay still and quiet, including most people, and anyone up to no good would get dissuaded by her cameras. She loved the latent energy of dawn.

"Por Qué, read me the top-rated stories tagged with the words 'Machinehood' and 'attack.'"

Her agent's voice spoke in her ear. No further violence against funders. Some central African mining operations had stopped due to equipment failure and structural damage. The Machinehood hadn't taken credit, but everyone assumed they'd done it. The machine rights people had found new fame and with it the courage to spread their gospel. Multiple interview feeds were giving them a platform to explain why the Machinehood must be seeking revenge or justice for the abuse of WAIs and bots.

"Por Qué, read me the top-rated opinion pieces that cross-match Machinehood with machine rights, first and last paragraphs." She wished she could add *al-Muwahhidun empire* and *caliph* into the mix, but any open search could tip them off, and she had to keep the world's attention focused on sentient AIs.

The popular arguments ranged widely. The most fanatical of machine rights activists wanted all intelligent machines to have the full rights of a citizen. As if a coffee-bot should be able to vote or go to jail. Well, maybe the latter would be worthwhile for the one that had served her in Chennai. More reasonable people, including expert bioethicists, wanted a protective framework that went both ways: punitive action against designers, and decommissioning for bots or WAIs that committed crimes; legal protections for machines from violence committed by humans or other intelligent machines. None of them offered a clear definition for a sentient artificial intelligence, though, or what rights one should have if it came into existence. Software had passed sophisticated Turing tests in the forties, but no one felt that made them self-aware. Apes and elephants were clearly sentient, intelligent, social creatures, but they didn't get human rights.

Meanwhile, the opposing fringe—especially the al-Muwahhidun but also the bioticists—wanted to abolish artificial intelligences altogether. The caliph wanted no reliance on machinery at all. His end goal—or so he'd claimed before shrouding himself in secrecy—was humans who could do all types of work, from heavy lifting to high-speed self-transportation. From the start, he'd embraced the culture of voluntary modders. VeeMods, as they called themselves, placed electromechanical parts into their bodies. Those jackasses didn't hide their admiration of the Machinehood operatives, and unlike the caliph, they had no problems with WAIs. The bioticists, however, had them all beat for idiocy. Like the Luddites before them, they protested against any modern technology that took work away from people. They wanted to maintain the "purity of the human mind and body" and promoted a life free of pills, drugs, WAIs, and bots.

Welga expanded an image associated with one of the items that Por Qué had highlighted. It showed the major groups and their branches, splitting again and again, into ever greater micro-divisions. Even the VeeMods couldn't agree on right and wrong. It gave her a headache.

In Marrakech, Welga had lived without a kitchen or car that could handle itself. She'd seen people with mechanical body modifications pushing the limits of human appearance, especially the al-Muwahhidun soldiers. Her own military enhancements were internal, and they included a permanent-resident WAI, but the electronics in her body were tiny, unnoticeable. The Machinehood operative's guts—and the person in Nithya's colleague's video—seemed to have smart-matter that interfaced with their bodies on a macro scale. The reports on the maturity of that technology had mixed results, but the consensus said no, not possible in a walking, talking human being. Could the al-Muwahhidun have figured out a way to advance VeeMods beyond anything in the rest of the world?

"Incoming call request from Nithya Balachandran," Por Qué said.

"Accept." Welga rounded the park that marked the halfway point in her run and slowed so she could converse.

"You're awake early," Nithya said.

Her image floated in Welga's display, superimposed on the real world. Carma stood in the background, wearing a game rig and jumping over invisible obstacles.

"I'm warming up for a busy day," Welga said. "What's going on?"

"I wanted to tell you what I've found about your condition." A series of drawings and chemical symbols appeared next to Nithya's face. "This is a model of what I think is happening to your muscles based on the data I have. See this?" Red circles appeared around some areas. "It's a form of long-term synaptic fatigue. My best guess is that the zips trigger something in your DNA that then affects potassium ion channels. It's also stimulating activity in your mesolimbic system, which I don't fully understand. I need more time to make sense of it, but you must stop taking zips and not resume until we resolve this. That much I'm certain of. I've sent you the results so far. Did you find any specialists to take on your case?"

"No luck. I'm not offering money for someone to look at my data so I suppose it's not surprising. And you know I can't stop taking the pills, not now."

Nithya frowned. "But you're risking your health, possibly your life."

"I've been using zips for years. It can't be that bad."

"Maybe it's something in the newer designs. I don't know. I'm trying to get more information, but I can see that your motor and limbic systems are involved. Those are fundamental, Welga, and potentially pointing to an addiction. Whatever you have is an undocumented side effect, one that's likely triggered by something specific to your genetic makeup, and it's not my area of expertise. It's going to take a long time before we have all the answers, especially with no one funding our effort."

Por Qué spoke to Welga. "If I understand the context of this conversation, you should file a Request for Investigation with the funders of your zips. Would you like me to do that?"

"Yes, Por Qué, do that," Welga subvocalized.

Not that it meant much—RFIs tended to disappear into a morass of bureaucracy unless they had money or lawyers or both backing them up.

"A few more months," Welga said to her sister-in-law. "Maybe even weeks. That's all I need. I'll last that long, right?"

"Most probably, but I'm not an expert. Don't take this too lightly!"

"I can handle living with a disability."

Nithya sighed. "I'm sorry I don't have better news."

"Thanks for looking into it. Tell Luis and Carma that I said hello."

Despite the public call and a boost in viewership from her Machinehood connection, no one with the right expertise offered to help. Why would they? With no money in it, they had no incentive. Her fans would appreciate the drama of watching her struggle. That was what they enjoyed about the life of a shield— the conflict. If she had real fame, a massive following, she'd have the coin to spend on hiring experts to look into her condition, and she could turn that into its own narrative. As a mostly ordinary person, though, the public wouldn't make an effort to raise funds for her cause until her health was obviously deteriorating, and even then, it might not be enough. The thought left a bitter taste in her mouth. A cup of coffee from her favorite vendor-bot didn't wash it away.

NITHYA

[News reporter standing in front of a kitchen unit] The worldwide hunt continues for the elusive source of the Machinehood threat. A poll from this morning shows that 63 percent of respondents have stopped all pill usage other than government-issued daily inoculation designs. Some counterterrorism experts think the Machinehood will attempt a wide-scale attack on kitchen pill printers, similar to the hijacks of '84 and '87. However, others claim that modern kitchens have better security. Do you have an expertise rating greater than eighty for kitchen encryption? If yes, tell us what you think! We'll compile the top ten responses and share them with our followers.

—Top Ten for Today news feed, March 17, 2095.
Current accuracy rating: 78%

The package arrived while Luis was out of the house. Nithya opened the generic white envelope with care, suspicious of its contents because of the odd bulge in the center and the fact that nobody in their family sent paper mail. A second packet lay inside, with a scrawled note saying Welga had sent this for Nithya alone. Mystified, Nithya carried it into the bathroom and locked the door.

"Sita, are there any microdrones in here?"

"The house system doesn't show any, but the most advanced technology would not be detected."

Anyone with that kind of spy device wouldn't care about her actions. She only needed to hide this from her family, friends, and agent. Nithya removed her lenses and jewels and put them away. She tore the envelope open.

Inside were color-coded tablets and instructions for taking the medications, fully chemical, nothing pill-like about the process. Expect cramping and heavy bleeding, the text said. Use pain pills or drugs as needed. Contact your doctor in case of complications. The yellow tablet came first, then the four white ones a day or two later.

Nithya had miscarried once, fifteen months before getting pregnant with Carma. Her body's misery kept her curled up in bed for two days. This seemed like it would be a similar experience. She could consume or recycle the evidence before Luis came home. *Damn it, Welga, you shouldn't put me in a position to lie to my husband.*

In this situation, it seemed better to ask forgiveness than permission. If he found out the truth, what would he do, leave the marriage? Her chest clenched at the thought. She didn't want a different husband. She didn't want to drive Luis away, either, but he would never see reason about this pregnancy. *Tell him you miscarried. He'll never have to know, and you can spare him the Catholic guilt.*

A knock at the door made her jump.

"Amma? Why aren't you answering? I need the toilet!"

Nithya cast about for a lie. "Sorry, my jewelry didn't charge properly! I'll be out in one minute."

With a silent apology to Luis, Nithya swallowed the yellow tablet. She folded the instruction paper around the others, tucked the package behind the cleaning supplies, and opened the door.

"I've been calling and calling on our channel. You should tell me if you're going off-line," Carma scolded.

Nithya smiled and kissed her daughter's head. "Yes, you're right."

Carma sighed in exasperation and disappeared into the bathroom. Nithya gazed at the closed door with a twinge of regret. Her daughter had grown so fast. Would it be so bad to give up her work and have another baby? Brambles of regret lined both paths, and her choice seemed the less thorny one, but she couldn't help traversing the other in her mind. With the slightest tremble in her fingers, she ordered a half day's worth of flow from the kitchen.

Nithya's eyes wouldn't stay closed. She'd been trying to sleep for over two hours. Luis lay next to her, snoring softly. He had visibly squelched his suspicion when she mentioned bleeding. Guilt stabbed her, but at least her tears were genuine. She'd pled illness to explain her bedridden state to Carma.

The constant pain didn't help her black mood. If she closed her eyes, her brain jumped to the prior day's work problems or the data from Welga's body. They circulated in her head like creatures on a merry-go-round. Zeli had been uncommunicative for nearly two days. The encroaching blackout by al-Muwahhidun in the Maghreb had pushed through Mali into eastern Senegal.

The caliph liked to target the local constellations and cables before any other infrastructure. Cut off the network and stop all news, all communications. She feared for Zeli's safety. Synaxel had put a yellow flag by their project to indicate that they had fallen behind on deadlines, and the other members of her team expressed their displeasure at her slowdown. *God willing, this will be the last time.*

She found only bad news with Welga's data, too. Her sister-in-law's condition showed a disturbing trend proportional to zip use. Cerebral effects hit areas of the mesolimbic system, the same area that addictive drugs affected, but pills were designed to avoid habituating effects. Why couldn't she figure this out? What was she missing? Welga's primary zip consumption came from Synaxel designs, and Nithya had access to their entire database.

Unless she didn't.

Nithya hobbled to the bathroom and donned her networking jewelry. "Sita, have any of my Synaxel queries about Welga's problem failed?"

"Out of three hundred forty-six queries, seventeen were denied access."

"Sita, show me the queries."

With all of them next to each other, the keywords for the blocks were obvious: cAMP, KCNA1, myokymia, GIRKs. Any query that had two or more of those terms had been denied. None of those had a relationship to her juver project, but why would Synaxel need to keep that information from her? All user data had to be available to the public unless it belonged to a minor or a government agent. Nothing in her search terms would be restricted to either category of people. She'd never hit a wall on general information, not in all her years of work.

"Sita, print a hard copy of the queries and then send a request to Peter to lift the block on them." Her manager would wonder why she wanted the data. She had to think up a good excuse before he replied.

"You have a message from Salimata Ba."

At last! "Show me."

The message from Zeli was text-only. It read: *On the move. Frontline defense crossed my village. Limited access. Will update when we're safe.*

Nithya had invited Zeli to come to India when al-Muwahhidun in the Maghreb pushed through central Mauritania, but the girl had declined. Zeli refused to leave without her family. In truth, Nithya's flat was too small to house all of them, and neither of them had the travel funds, so it hadn't been a practical offer.

She picked up the hard copy of the queries from the kitchen dispenser and tucked it in a desk drawer. If Synaxel had something to hide, she needed to keep records of her work somewhere that they couldn't reach. She would do the same for Welga's data in the morning, but she didn't want to make more printer noise and risk waking Luis or Carma.

In the jungle days of bioengineering, commercial pill and drug manufacturers had created all kinds of problems and then pretended they didn't know. Nithya called up the Jakarta Protocols, now two decades old, which regulated the industry. The second paragraph made her eyes swim. Too much heavy language, especially for the middle of the night.

She searched and found gigsters who had summarized the salient points. Fourth down the list: *All data shall be stripped of patient information and then made available to the general public.* That confirmed her suspicions. Synaxel had no legal right to block her requests, regardless of her reasons for wanting the information.

Nithya sat back, her heart racing. Was it the two a.m. effect, or had she stumbled across something significant? Either way, sleep fled her mind. Her body, though, felt exhausted and achy as the last dose of analgesic wore off.

She ordered an opioid for the cramps from the kitchen. As it printed, she put her jewelry back into their chargers and changed her pad. She had to get some sleep. If Synaxel lifted the data block, she'd need to be rested enough to push ahead with Welga's diagnosis. If they didn't, she'd be juggling a bigger problem: learning why.

Carma scrunched her face into an expression of deep indignation. "You never let me talk to Zeli Aunty anymore!"

Nithya's daughter stalked to the opposite side of the room and glared while deliberately knocking down and rebuilding her school alcove. The drain on their daily energy allowance made Nithya's head hurt, but if it kept the peace for now, she could accept the price. She turned her attention back to the glitchy video transmission from Zeli.

"Sorry about that," Nithya said.

Zeli flashed her a grin. "That's easy. Wait another six or seven years. Then you'll know true pain. My cousin's oldest . . . well, never mind. I only have ten minutes here."

"Is the front line moving so fast?"

"No, no. We got soldiers and bots from the world around trying to push it back. I paid for ten minutes of pipe is all."

"I can send you funds—"

The girl cut her off with a chopping hand motion. "Let me talk. I uploaded a project update for Synaxel. Stupid WAI finally let me rewrite the code the way I wanted, and now it's working. Big surprise! You have to run more play-testing to confirm it. For Welga, I can't put in more time. I'm sorry. I saw your note about the data block. Have they done anything?"

Nithya shook her head. "They won't lift it, and they won't say why. I don't have the right back-channels to dig for that kind of information on Synaxel."

Zeli chewed her lower lip. "Let me see what I can do. Okay, I'm almost out of time. We're only forty kilometers from the border. I'll call again from the refugee camp tomorrow or the next day."

"See you then, Zeli."

Across the room, Carma had stopped pouting and was bent over her schoolwork. Nearly time for lunch break. Judging by the aroma from the kitchen, the rice, green-beans curry, and sambar were almost ready.

Nithya went to the balcony. The tiles were warm and slick under her feet, but at least the air had cooled. Rain curtained the view beyond the nearest buildings. She inhaled the scent of wet earth and let the water droplets spray her skin and hair. The steady drumbeat relaxed her thoughts.

What beings roamed out there—in the Maghreb, around the world—and how would she raise her daughter to survive among them? That soldier from Zeli's video looked like a VeeMod, not an android. The Vee came from voluntary—a person who chose to augment their body with machine parts. Starting in the thirties, people had tried to compete with machine labor by using interfaces that had grown ever more intimate, until it all backfired in the sixties. Three decades of virtual reality, mech-suits, brain implants, limb replacements . . . it had led to an entire generation with neurological and psychological trouble.

Pills had helped, but they couldn't fundamentally change the mechanics of the human body. Bots were superior at so many tasks. Their only weakness was their hard-coded obedience. How could humanity compete with a sentient artificial intelligence unless they found new, better ways to integrate with machines? Must the V become an I—involuntary or mandatory modification? Social pressures would lead people there even if laws didn't. A person who avoided pills couldn't compete in certain jobs. Once VeeMods became equally safe and widespread, anyone who eschewed them would face a similar disadvantage. Was that what the Machinehood wanted? To eliminate the distinction between human and machine? Or was it truly a malevolent AI that would bring humanity to a more violent end?

The news made it seem like the latter. People had fallen evenly across the divide of whether the Machinehood portended death or takeover by a SAI. Neither would end well. The most paranoid people had shut off anything with a WAI—including their agents—and stopped taking pills because of their microelectronics.

Nithya tried to remember life without Sita's assistance. Her childhood had been that way, but she had so few responsibilities then. Now, even Carma had her own agent, though God knew what for. And life before daily pill regimens—that she could not forget, not when the poorest of the poor still lived, and often died, that way. With tabletop bioengineering came wave after wave of designer microbes. Treatments appeared close on their heels, but centralized production and distribution were too slow. The only way to stay healthy was to print the antidotes at home.

"Lunch is ready to eat," Sita announced.

Luis waved at Nithya from a corner of her visual. The tea shop at the end of their street stood behind him.

"Almost home," her husband said. "Are you feeling better today?" He'd left before sunrise for another rocket club meeting.

"Much better. Less pain, almost no bleeding."

"Good. Do you have time to eat lunch with me and Carma?"

"I'll make time."

Luis had a smile that could melt hard candy. His solicitousness since the abortion was unimpeachable, which only made her feel more guilty. How could she maintain this lie of omission? Yes, she had done it to protect him, as she did with serious matters for Carma, but Luis was an adult. He shouldn't need protection from the world's evils . . . or his wife's.

She sighed and went inside to set the table.

Carma emerged from her school alcove and launched into a chirpy conversation about the new singing lessons next month. She sat down to her meal as Luis walked in the door. He kissed his daughter's cheek before going to wash up.

"Amma, can I do some reading work while I eat?"

Nithya nodded. Carma slipped her virtuality goggles on. By the time her daughter became a teenager, maybe everyone would have implants like Welga's. No need to remove and charge your interactive devices every night, but no way to turn off the world, either. Perhaps humanity only pretended at separation from technology.

A message popped up in the upper left of Nithya's visual from her project manager, Peter Yeorn. She expanded it.

"Your recent petition to access Synaxel's database has been reviewed and denied," he said. A frown creased his brow. "I don't see the relevance to your current project. Please drop the queries. If you can't complete the project without them, I may need to terminate your contract and hire someone who can. Your group has already missed several deadlines. We cannot afford distractions right now."

Luis took the seat across from her, ate one bite of food, and caught her expression. "What's the matter?"

"I got a nasty message from my Synaxel project manager about the queries I ran for Welga's condition."

"What are you talking about? What condition?"

"Oh no, she didn't tell you? You didn't see our conversations about it?"

Luis shook his head.

Nithya tried to keep the explanation simple. "Something is wrong with Welga's motor system, possibly related to her use of zips. She posted her data for specialist review, but she didn't offer money. No one took it up, so I looked at it. Some of the zips she's used are Synaxel designs, but every detailed query I make about the possible failure mechanism gets blocked. I've never had a query blocked."

"And what did Peter say?"

"That he'll drop my contract unless I stop digging."

Luis smacked the table with his left hand. "He's threatening you! That's bullsh—"

"Okay, okay! I agree. I was suspicious already. Now I'm sure they're hiding something."

"You need a lawyer. When Mama got sick, we had multiple law firms ask to represent her case."

"That was pre-regulation. It's much harder to litigate this kind of thing today. If it's something unique to Welga's biochemistry, there might not be anything truly illegal here. And it's not likely to draw enough money to attract lawyers."

Luis returned his empty plate to the kitchen. "And what if Synaxel cancels your contract or comes after you? It's worth a retainer fee to protect ourselves."

"From what? We hardly have any money." *And I've done nothing wrong.* Nithya toyed with the food on her plate. When had innocence ever prevented those with money and power from destroying those without? "I'll contact someone."

∘—∘—◦

The list of bioethics lawyers in Chennai overwhelmed Nithya with its length. She avoided the problem by reading up on the Asian Biogenetics Administration's regulations. And the American BGA laws, for completeness. ABGA had far fewer restrictions than USBGA on designs and almost no requirements on testing. They had no teeth, either. Every country had its own enforcement agency. India had prosecuted fewer than fifty cases against pill and drug funders in the past decade. Singapore had sixty-seven. China had none, since their government controlled all domestic funding.

The USBGA had a better record: over a thousand cases in the same time period; but the EU was the winner at five digits. Maybe she should contact someone at the USBGA, since Welga resided in America. Synaxel's board members lived around the globe, but two were in New York. Conveniently, the main USBGA office was there, too.

"Sita, what's the procedure to file a complaint with the United States Biogenetics Administration?"

"You can file a nonemergency complaint at any time. You must choose from a list of subtopics."

"Before I do that, what do they say regarding data privacy for pill funders?"

"They have fifteen documents relating to that topic. Would you like to read them?"

Nithya groaned. "Not now. I need to get back to my project work. In the meantime, run a background search with any major funder of zips. Use the same query keywords as I did for Synaxel with Welga's case. If you run into any blocks, send the result to the kitchen for a hard copy."

She called up her juver project and checked the results from Zeli's update. Nithya hoped the girl and her family were safely on their way to the refugee camp. If the al-Muwahhidun had destroyed any of the primary nodes—places where network signals became wired—it could take weeks to restore communications.

At this rate, it was a coin toss as to which of them would cause Synaxel to cancel their contract first.

CHAPTER 10

WELGA

8. The Biotech Age has saved humanity up to now, allowing us to maintain our worth (to ourselves and the oligarchy) and, therefore, to survive the gig lifestyle. Mech-suits integrated with human bodies let us carry or run or endure like a machine. Pills let us outthink them. But the cost of these so-called enhancements is twofold. One, they destroy our biological bodies (no matter how safe the oligarchy says they are). And two, they propel the machine designers to build even faster, stronger, smarter machines. We are trapped in a vicious cycle of self-destructive progress.

—*The Machinehood Manifesto, March 20, 2095*

A deeply pissed-off pill funder named Jane Santiago volunteered to bait the Machinehood. She had retained Platinum's shield services for over a decade and had no problems with Welga, Connor, and Ammanuel joining her three-person security team, which included one ex-army officer and two former police officers, all male. Ammanuel chose to emphasize the feminine for this assignment, a sentiment that Welga fully approved, considering the optics they'd present otherwise.

A fat bonus landed in their bank accounts to make sure everyone could afford the latest styles. They had their first briefing on the seventeenth. Santiago insisted on reviewing everyone's clothing designs.

"I don't intend to die," she had said, "but I sure as hell plan to look good if it happens."

Hassan ran the meeting and introduced Welga as their liaison with the JIA. Ammanuel cocked an eyebrow, but no one made a comment.

"We won't be able to stop the swarms," Hassan warned.

Santiago shrugged it off. "I welcome the publicity. Let's make a show of my support to lure these cowards into the open. I'll announce a tour of the supply plants, and you can be damn sure I'll tell them why."

And she had. Standing atop the lush roof of the hive she owned in downtown San Francisco, Santiago spoke to a cloud of microcams that swarmed so thick, you almost couldn't see the sky. She timed the announcement for an hour before sunset to get ideal lighting conditions. Ammanuel wore a short, fitted dress in a shade of yellow ochre that complemented Santiago's red pantsuit. Welga opted for her trademark red-and-black faux leathers but with an updated cut, and Connor allowed some color into his usual all-whites as a concession to fashion. The other three shields kept to a similar palette of browns, oranges, and blacks.

They arrayed themselves in an arc behind Santiago, more for effect than true security. Short of parachuting from a drone plane, nobody could access the roof. The hive's central WAI made sure of that.

"Tomorrow I'll begin a five-day tour of the major suppliers for the products that I fund," Santiago announced. "The world needs to know that not all financiers are hiding behind their high-security walls. We designed drugs and pills so that humans could stay competitive in the labor market. I believe that humankind—not machine-kind—will always be the way forward. Buffs make us stronger. Zips make us faster. Flows make us smarter. I will continue to support designs that push our physiology to its safe, effective limits. That allow us to be the best we can be. The world belongs to us. We created intelligent machines, and we will not capitulate to their violent actions. If you're part of one of my teams, I want you to know that I will not pull my contracts in the face of any threat. I will help you fight back. I will not give in to the demands of the Machinehood!"

Nobody attacked Jane Santiago on their first day out. All dressed up and nobody to fight—was that the old saying? Welga had pockets full of deca-zips, juvers, and buffs, should they need bursts of extra strength. They carried military-grade medical kits, as well. And one special-purpose item, tested only on human soldiers at a secure facility: a blackout wrap, intended to block any implanted network access points and disable a Machinehood operative's communications capability.

In keeping with the JIA's theory that the Machinehood was a cover for al-Muwahhidun in the Maghreb, their destination on the nineteenth—the day of the deadline—was a materials refinery. The caliph liked to target infrastructure rather than people. The USA had only a few major factories that produced the raw bases for pill printers, and they'd found one on the outskirts of Livermore, California. The vast majority of them were located in China, India, and central Africa. Several had already suffered damage from undetectable assailants. No swarm had caught sight of the attackers, and they'd left no physical traces—at least none that those countries had shared with the world. The locations targeted in the past two days added support to the al-Muwahhidun being the true Machinehood operatives. All could be accessed from North Africa via land routes.

America had developed a paranoid itch over the lack of action on its soil. Welga shared the feeling. For the attack on Jackson, she'd been in the right place at the right time—in Chennai, on the other side of the planet. Since then, she'd been able to participate only as a spectator, and she'd never enjoyed that role.

Come and get us, assholes. What are you scared of?

The lack of action left Welga twitchy at a different level from her synaptic problems, which persisted and, if she were honest with herself, had worsened. A half-zip would now reliably stop her tremors. Nithya's words about addictive behavior haunted her.

"Third time's the charm," Ammanuel muttered as they drove toward Livermore.

"It better be," Welga said. "After today . . . who knows what they'll do next?"

They frowned. "You don't think they've done enough? Take out the critical factories at the start of the supply chain, and the pills will stop, at least temporarily. Maybe that's their plan—wait for people to start getting sick and then attack before we can finish rebuilding."

"It would work, too," Welga said grimly, "but attack how? Frontal assaults on major governments are unlikely to work unless the world ends up in a pandemic like we haven't seen in decades, but then they're risking themselves."

"Are they? Bots and WAIs can't die from infections."

Welga bit her tongue before she contradicted Ammanuel. They didn't know about the al-Muwahhidun theory, and she couldn't enlighten them in a car full of public microcameras.

"Who'd keep up their infrastructure?" she asked instead. "Unless the SAIs are building a massive number of these androids, they'll need people to maintain electrical power, computing centers, and stellas. Software doesn't have arms and legs, and bots aren't general-purpose enough. I have a hard time believing they could hide an entire population of their kind somewhere on Earth."

Ammanuel opened their mouth. Paused. Narrowed their eyes. "There's one region where we don't have visibility."

Welga blinked and kept her expression bland. "That region hates WAIs."

Ammanuel's gaze turned inward. Welga left them to puzzle it out. The caliph would be happy to sell someone a hacked plague, especially if he already had the cure designed and plausible deniability in spreading it. She'd heard rumors of pill funders making similarly shady transactions. They earned coin off treatment designs, which put them in a unique, morally compromised situation if someone showed them an engineered virus under the table.

Innocent or not, it's my job to protect them.

Jane Santiago sat across from Welga in the armored truck. Their six-person shield team and half a dozen riot-control bots filled out the remaining space. Someone at the agency had a theory that the Machinehood wouldn't attack their own kind, based on watching the pattern of their behavior in other locales. That fit better with the sentient AI angle than the al-Muwahhidun, but it provided them a good cover story.

Their team leader, Oliver Mendoza, had passed out their pill packets thirty minutes before arrival. Their client stuck a flow-flush patch onto her neck, then took her pills with the rest of them. Santiago insisted again on coordinating their outfits with her own, all synthetic leather with elegant, clean lines, and pale, neutral colors. No bright hair or flashy jewels. Cameras swarmed around them in the confines of the vehicle. They had to strike a balance between publicity and trying too hard.

Ammanuel grumbled about how boring they looked, but Welga had lost her desire for frivolity. Her insides coiled as tight as the latent speed in her muscles. *Come and get us, blankers. Stop hiding and scaring people with your shadows. I'm running out of time to deal with your sorry asses.*

The truck pulled into a driveway and stopped. A sprawling two-story structure stretched to either side. Steam rose from vents in its roof. Massive pipes emerged and ran to other buildings and silos. Hives towered in the hazy distance.

Muggy air clung to Welga the instant she emerged. Damn leathers weren't meant for this kind of weather. Then again, she wasn't truly there as a shield. She didn't have to give a shit about sweat and lank hair.

A welcome party crowded the air above them. Exfactors and reporters stood on the rooftop of a warehouse across the street. A group of machine rights activists clustered on the pavement below, waving signs in favor of the Machinehood or legal protection for bots and WAIs. No protesters had registered to confront Santiago, though, and the only civilians in the area worked at the facility. Bots formed a cordon to keep the onlookers contained.

Por Qué added Welga's tip jar and fan streams to her visual periphery as usual. Her coin balance ticked upward faster than the commentary from viewers. They'd figured out her government affiliation, so she had nothing to hide, but their speculations distracted her. She removed the unwanted text and, after a moment of hesitation, closed her tip jar display, too. Capturing a Machinehood operative wasn't a performative mission.

Jane Santiago maintained her external cool. She smiled and waved for the microcams, then shook the hand of the site manager, who ushered them into the building. The manager must have turned off the threshold zapper, because a good portion of the exterior swarm followed them inside.

A single, high-security door led from the sparsely furnished lobby into the factory. Heat rippled out as they passed single file through it into a cavernous space filled with tanks, pipes, and other equipment. Massive fans sucked air from the ceiling. This time, no microcams followed, so Welga released a small swarm of her own. If the Machinehood dared to show up, they would need all the advance warning possible, and the factory's security cameras had fixed locations.

Recycled plastic tiles squeaked under their feet. Odors reminiscent of bleach, alcohol, and burned rubber filled the air. They took slow, painstaking steps to avoid outpacing their guide across the factory floor. Machinery hummed. Bots avoided their group as they moved about their tasks. Only one other human was present, in a glass-enclosed crow's nest overlooking the entire space.

Welga scanned the perimeter of her visual. Camera feeds, exterior and interior, showed nothing unusual.

They finished the tour and moved toward the exit. The manager's shoulders relaxed, and his expression eased into a smile. The mood within their shield team curdled.

"Fucking cowards," Mendoza muttered on the team's encrypted channel.

"They're not stupid," Ammanuel replied.

Red blinked in Welga's visual. Por Qué had flagged something from one of her microcamera feeds. Welga expanded it, careful not to send the drone closer lest it attract the suspect's attention. A figure wearing basics crouched beside a panel and adjusted a rectangular object attached to it—an object that had a plastic case and in no way matched the dark metal structures around it.

Welga cast the feed to Mendoza and Hassan. "Looks like someone's playing at Machinehood and planting a bomb. Boss, permission to go back and, uh, have a little chat with them?"

"I'm calling in backup from Explosives," Hassan said. "Troit, you and Ramírez investigate. The rest of you stay with Santiago and cover the front."

Welga followed Por Qué's map overlay to the red outline on her feed. Connor moved two paces behind her, his hand twitching toward weapons they couldn't use. Factory bots avoided them as they crossed paths. The camera views jittered and swayed in the currents of hot air and exhaust fans. Out front, the main team stood with Santiago as she assured the factory manager that she would protect the assets of everyone she funded.

Welga sent a message to the human overseer: "You need to leave the building, for your own safety."

On her feeds, the saboteur looked up, saw the cameras, and waved cheerfully.

"Boss, who the fuck is that? Do we have an ID yet?"

"Just came in: not Machinehood. It's someone from a local sanctuary, those people who take in broken or decommissioned bots. Check camera 44AN and you'll see their partner setting overrides on the mobile floor units. They claim they'll move all bots out of harm's way before the explosives trip, and their goddamn tips are going through the roof. Bets are against you, Ramírez. Looks like they're almost done. Better hurry up."

They ran.

"How did some goddamn protes slip in?" Connor sent via their private channel.

"Guessing they didn't register with local police," Welga replied. "Or announce it in public until now. I'd rather we were dealing with the Machinehood instead of this bullshit."

"Shots fired!" Mendoza's shout came through the team feed.

"Kelly, close that rear loading bay door! Ammanuel, you and Quin are with me."

Welga diverted half her attention to the feed from the front. The outside cameras showed bullets being fired from thin air at a bomb squad van on approach. Protesters screamed and some pulled weapons of their own. Ammanuel, Santiago, and the other shields emerged from the building and took cover behind a low wall.

"What the hell?" said Ammanuel. "My visual's glitching . . . cloaking suits? What group has that tech?"

The military, usually.

"I'll bet Machinehood," Welga said into the team channel. *Goddamn it*, she should be out front. "Boss—"

"Finish your intercept of that bomb-setter, Ramírez," Hassan said, anticipating her question.

Who else would show up with military-grade technology?

One of the protesters stumbled as a bullet tore through their thigh. A knife flashed. A red line slashed the protester's throat. Their head lolled as they toppled.

Who else fought like that?

Welga rounded a four-meter-wide cylindrical tank with Connor at her heels. Their target stood up from their crouched position and raised a gun.

"Progress demands violence," they said. "I'm only destroying property, but I'll shoot you if I have to."

Welga snorted. The protester held the gun with an awkwardness that gave away their inexperience. Her weapons stayed on her hip. She wouldn't need them to take out this idiot. She opened her mouth to suggest they put their gun away. In the corner of her visual, the air rippled. Welga dove to the floor. "Get down!"

Connor ran for the anomaly. The protester shot in a panicked arc. Return fire passed through them and hit the detonator. The blast flung Welga into a row of pipes. She screamed from the heat that engulfed her. Her visual went blank.

Por Qué recited a litany of hurt over the ringing in her ears. "Second- and third-degree burns. Left ulna, hairline fracture. Multiple hairline fractures to right radius and ulna. Concussive symptoms. Pre-epileptic symptoms. Minor internal bleeding. Agent Troit is injured as well. Waiting for details."

Welga tried to speak, to mute her agent, but her tongue wouldn't move. The taste of iron filled her mouth. She spat. The world refused to focus. Blood seeped through Connor's leathers as he lay on the floor ahead and to the right, closer to the explosive. A figure stood near his body, its tattered cloaking suit falling away. It moved toward the protester and bent over them.

"No," Welga whispered.

The figure moved toward her. A face loomed, inches away. Patches of seared skin covered the cheeks of a young adult or adolescent. Metal showed in gaps created by a bullet wound in their shoulder. Charred, blistered lips parted.

Words penetrated the noise in Welga's ears: "You two again. But you didn't attack me, and I follow the path."

Singed dark brows drew together and formed a single crease. The eyes looked so real: deep brown with upturned corners. But why were there so many of them? And the colors . . . everywhere rainbows.

The world stretched like taffy and melted into swirling darkness.

Welga awoke to a fire-filled shitshow. Her head pounded. Alarms wailed. Smoke choked the air. She sat up and promptly retched. At least she didn't see double anymore, and her visual display had returned. A quick scan of the team feeds showed the others engaged in combat. The bomb squad remained pinned in their vehicle. How could one Machinehood agent do this much damage?

Hassan spoke via their private channel. "Ramírez, stay put! Medical says it's dangerous for either of you to move. We'll send people in for you as soon as we can."

"The fires in here say get the hell out, boss, and Troit is wounded."

"I know that," Hassan snapped. "Don't make the situation worse!"

She crawled to where Connor lay on the floor. "Por Qué, give me Troit's status!"

"Agent Troit has sustained multiple internal injuries with bleeding. Surface wounds are healing. Internal wounds require further treatment with juvers and may need surgical intervention."

Welga ripped the field kit from her clothing and, fractured forearms screaming in protest, injected Connor with every ampoule that Por Qué highlighted. She gave herself a healthy dose of painkillers, too. "How long was I out?"

"You lost consciousness for two minutes and twenty-two seconds. Would you like to review feeds of the interval?"

"Not now."

They had a meter's worth of breathable air—for the moment. The two-story ceilings kept most of the smoke above, but she could see it getting thicker. They could run out of time before help arrived.

"Por Qué, are there any exits besides the way we came in?"

"I no longer detect any functional microdrones within this area. Based on exterior cameras, fire is blocking the rear loading dock, the only other exit," Por Qué said. "The factory floor map shows two paths to the front door. I cannot determine which is safe."

Welga chose the shorter one.

"Por Qué, modify my sleeves to the most rigid design I own, set to right angles."

She draped Connor's body across her shoulders and swallowed a grunt. She ran her right arm through his legs, grabbed his wrist, then tucked her left hand under her right elbow. Smoke burned her nostrils and lungs. She crouched as low as she could and moved. Heat pressed into her like a living thing.

Welga's muscles twitched, threatening to tip her over. *The zip must be wearing off.* No time to dig out a new one.

Focus on the green line. Get the hell out. Nothing complicated, nothing she couldn't do if she tried.

Flames belched across her path.

"Fuck! Por Qué, reroute!"

The green line made a U-turn. Welga doubled back, ducked under a buckled catwalk. A door beckoned on her visual. Smoke blocked the actual view. She held her breath and moved toward the virtual one. Every step hit a new body part with pain. She pushed through the door and let it fall shut behind them.

The air in the lobby blew cool and fresh. The glass entrance lay in shards. A low table was half-buried by blox from malfunctioning chairs.

Welga ducked behind the reception desk, still intact, and let Connor down as gently as she could. The desk WAI sent a courtesy greeting, which she ignored. Her leg spasmed.

"Fucking hell," she gasped, then subvocalized, "Por Qué, what's my zip level?"

"Your neuromuscular speed is five percent over baseline. Anomalous synaptic activity detected and reported to Nithya Balachandran. I recommend that you also post the data to epilepsy networks."

"Maybe later." But what would be the point? They'd have the same lack of interest as the neurological specialists.

She left her forearms rigid to minimize the damage and awkwardly fished out a fresh zip from her pill pack. She added a buff and juvers to the mix. She'd need the strength if she had to carry Connor again.

The noise from outside went quiet. Her visual showed that everyone had taken cover somewhere, and combat had stopped. *What now?* Footsteps crunched on broken glass nearby. She had no swarm inside, so she peeked around the desk. Ammanuel and Quin stood and scanned the room.

"Over here," Welga called. "Can't wave my damn arms."

Ammanuel helped her stand while Quin deployed a stretcher.

"All quiet," Hassan said on the team channel. "Half the protes are down or have fled the site. The other half are broadcasting surrender, and the cloaked enemies are gone or hiding. Santiago is secure and away from the action. You're clear to extract Ramírez and Troit."

Welga waited until they had Connor strapped onto the stretcher before moving from her position. She ran outside, taking cover where possible, but all remained quiet. On the left half of the street, the bomb squad's van lay on its side, flames licking up from the engine. Police cars blocked the road in both directions. Humans and law-bots peered over them, weapons ready but not firing.

A white ambulance waited behind all the vehicles. The rear doors opened for them. Olafson reached out and helped Welga clamber in, then loaded Connor's stretcher. Ammanuel gave her a nod before closing the doors. She returned it. They certainly didn't need hand-holding anymore, and she had no doubt they'd make a fine shield.

Welga put some coin in Ammanuel's tip jar, then turned her

attention to Olafson as the ambulance hooked itself up to her partner.

"What the hell are you doing here?" Welga asked the JIA officer.

Olafson held up a hand for silence. Half a dozen microdrones clattered onto the van's floor.

"I hope you were a cat in a previous life, Ramírez, because this has to count as another of your nine. How many more times are you going to blow yourself up?"

Welga snorted. "However many it takes. Where are we headed?"

"San Francisco Terminal and then headquarters. I came here hoping you'd bag a live Machinehood operative that I could bring back for interrogation. They're pulling you for an in-person briefing and strategy session. We'll get your injuries treated over there. No time now or we'll miss the next sub-orb to DC."

"Why in person?"

"Because we need to do some free exchange of ideas, and we suspect that the Machinehood can tap into secure comm links. They might not have a sentient AI directing them, but they have computing capabilities we don't understand. Something strange is going on there."

"What about the androids?"

"No captures anywhere so far. The Chinese just blew one up. The rest . . . well, we weren't prepared for their camouflage. Looks like they've hit and run. We'll see what happens tomorrow."

The ambulance spoke. "This patient needs treatment from a hospital. I am unable to complete the necessary surgical procedures."

Olafson swore. His fingers twitched. The van slowed and took the next right turn.

"We'll drop Troit off en route," Olafson said.

Welga held Connor's hand. His skin had taken on more color,

but his expression remained slack, unconscious. She hated to leave him like this. The hospital would allow microcameras so he wouldn't be alone, but nothing could replace the feeling of someone holding you, and she couldn't do that from the other side of the country.

"Olafson, would you mind launching some of Troit's swarm? They're in his left lower pocket."

"I'll do one better: he can have some of our secure microcams."

Olafson launched a barely visible cloud that hovered over Connor's stretcher as they arrived at the hospital building. Two human nurses unloaded him from the van and waited as the ambulance transferred its data to the hospital's.

As they went their separate ways, Welga subvocalized, "Por Qué, open a high-priority feed to the secure swarm with Connor. Alert me when he regains consciousness."

She reopened her family, friends, and news feeds. They couldn't see her in the van, so she sent brief messages to Papa and Luis that she was okay and that Connor was hospitalized. Everyone had seen the action at the refinery. The Machinehood had struck at three different locations, as they had at the start of all this. And they had once again evaded capture. The damage they caused would have an impact, but they hadn't stopped all pill and drug production as they'd threatened. With their one-week timer about to expire, what would they do next?

CHAPTER 11

NITHYA

Interviewer: Let's talk for a minute about your childhood and your family. Your mother, Laila Boothe-Ayala, was a well-regarded biogeneticist until she passed away when you were thirteen years old. Were you ever inspired to follow in her footsteps?

Olga Ramírez: When my mother got sick, I dreamed of finding the cure for her condition. After she passed away, I wanted to continue her work. I tried, but without flow, I couldn't keep up with the academics in college, and you can be damn sure my ratings would be terrible if I tried to work in that field. My mother wanted to make the world a better place, but I had to find my own way to do the same thing.

—*Up Close news feed, 2089. Current accuracy rating: 87%*

Nithya watched Jane Santiago deliver her challenge to the Machinehood.

"We designed drugs and pills so that humans could stay competitive in the labor market," the funder said.

Her sister-in-law stood with the shield team in the background.

The array of attractive faces and flawless bodies equaled any fictional group from the entertainment industry.

"I will continue to support designs that push our physiology to its safe, effective limits," Santiago said.

Was Santiago any better than Synaxel, or were they all hiding the truth that their products could harm specific individuals?

"Look at this," Luis called out.

A different video stream appeared in her visual. Nithya brushed Santiago aside and expanded the new one. It took her a few seconds to understand what she saw: Oscar's home in Phoenix, two sides buried past the roofline by dirt and debris; the street impassable; the cars scoured. She moved the feed to her periphery and stepped from her alcove to find Luis pacing the room.

"Come on, Papa, it's a sign from God! How much more do you need?" He paused when he saw Nithya and sent her a passive copy of the feed.

Nithya watched their conversation without participating. Oscar didn't need her ganging up with Luis against him.

"It's the last bit of your mother I have," Oscar said. His shoulders drooped.

Nithya tapped out a message in text: *Go to him. Help with the clean up. It will save us money in the long run, and it will give the house more value—if you convince him to sell it.*

I love you, Luis replied. *I'm sorry my father is so stubborn.*

Nithya smiled to herself. *Runs in the family.*

After the call ended, she and Luis looked over their bank balance. As long as Synaxel didn't drop her contract, they could manage his absence without too much financial strain.

"I'll need to call in some free child-minding," she said. "We can't afford to hire a bot."

Luis read her mind with the ease of a long relationship. He groaned. "Your aunty?"

Nithya nodded.

"I'm extra sorry, then. I'll try hard to convince Papa to come over here. Maybe I can guilt him into it by showing him what you have to put up with in my absence."

Nithya snorted. "I'd certainly prefer him to her, but it won't be so bad. She only has to be here during the day. How long do you think you'll be gone?"

"Two or three weeks, at least, unless Papa magically changes his mind. I'll try to gig over there, whatever I can get. And we'll use the money Welga sent him first. The storm hit the whole region, so it'll take some time for me to get to the house. They'll be clearing the downtown streets and freeways first."

They found Luis a standby option for the next day's suborbital flight and then broke the news to Carma.

Their daughter's reaction on hearing the news was to wail, "You'll miss my birthday party!"

Luis hugged her. "I'm so sorry. I've never missed one before, though, right? And I shouldn't have to again. This is an emergency."

He showed her the enormity of the situation, which calmed Carma's anger, and fortunately he already had a gift for her—a pass to watch his rocket club's launch that afternoon. The minimum age required to be on the viewing platform was eight, and Carma had wanted to go since she was half that age. She danced with excitement through lunch, barely eating half of it, and was all smiles when they left for the launch.

An afternoon free of her husband and child should've meant super productivity for Nithya, but between her physical discomfort and Zeli's predicament, she couldn't focus. Two doses of flow and all she could do was worry. The oppressive heat didn't help. The solar glass for the balcony needed repair, and they couldn't afford to buy power for more air-conditioning or to repair the glass. Clouds had arrived to block the sunlight, but they held on to their moisture and added to her torpor.

Nithya stared at the text in her visual. Her eyes insisted on moving to her last message exchange with Zeli. The girl said she'd be safe in a day or two. Where was she? Was she still alive? Nithya slapped a flush patch on her neck with more force than it needed. Flow was worse than useless if the mind wanted to focus on the wrong thing. Maybe a walk would clear her head. She considered changing into cooler clothing but decided to save the energy.

Her salwar and kameez stuck to her body within seconds of stepping outside the flat. She slipped on a pair of chappals and chose a direction at random on the street. Arriving at a large thoroughfare, Nithya turned toward the colorful, tiered gopuram that towered over the surrounding buildings. A bot moved along the side of the road ahead of her and shooed the stray dogs from the path of traffic. Lorries trundled by with near-silent electric motors, their horns singing every few minutes in warning. A gray-bearded, shirtless man pedaled past her, his bicycle laden with a precarious stack of multicolored blox.

The scent of tea and boiled milk lured Nithya to a stall. Men in unbuckled mech-suits sipped their drinks and chatted about the latest cricket match against Australia. A young woman wearing frayed static jeans and a sleeveless top passed orders to the kitchen WAI and handed food to her customers. A bot could've done the job as well as she, but the employment kept her off the streets and cost less than an education.

Nithya received her cup of hot, milky tea and two coils of spicy murukku and kept walking. The snacks were still warm from the fryer. She finished them as she arrived at the temple and dropped the cup and bowl in a recycler. Her chappals joined a disorderly pile by the temple entrance. The interior's stone floor cooled the soles of her feet. Camphor and rose and sandalwood incense scented the air.

She walked four times around Vishnu's sanctum, clockwise, then knelt to pray. *Please let Zeli and her family be safe. Let her reply to me soon and put my mind at ease. And let my husband's God forgive me for my sin in their eyes.* She touched her forehead to the ancient granite and rested there for a minute, breathing deep as footsteps and voices flowed past.

When a measure of peace stilled her inner turmoil, she moved to the crowded line that jostled its way to the inner sanctum. There, under the weight of unseen stone, surrounded by the odor of humanity and the crush of bodies, Nithya could forget the world of technology and agents and drugs and bots. With ancient Sanskrit verses rising and falling, smoke filling her lungs, the peal of brass bells in her ears, she was transported to another time. A knot of tension within her released itself, and she found her center.

After half an hour and a blessing received, she exited. The light and sound of the real world surrounded her once more—street sellers calling, horns singing, swarms buzzing overhead. A few scattered drops fell from the sky. Wind bent the trees and urged her home.

"Incoming call from Carma," Sita said.

"Accept."

Nithya walked home with half her attention on their family channel in her visual.

"Amma, they took my origami frog! It was light enough that they allowed it. The rocket will launch soon. Will you watch?" Carma's eyes shone with excitement. She bounced on her toes and pointed to the pad.

The massive cement platform rose above the swell of the Indian Ocean. Perhaps twenty people stood on the observation float, two of them at the control panel. Luis had his hand on their daughter's shoulder. Nithya found a different view that showed the full height of the rocket. Luis, Carma, and the others shrank to toy size in comparison. The tricolor flag of India decorated the top section, while their club logo—an arc of stars over the face of Lord Ganesha—sat on the main column.

"Here it goes!" Carma said, her voice as loud and clear as if she stood next to Nithya.

The onlookers covered their heads with motorcycle helmets and squatted behind the fence. The pad trembled with the force of the rocket's launch. Its primary cargo would supply the South-Am Space Station with replacement parts for electronics, but it also held a care package for the residents who liked to exchange messages with their club counterparts on Earth. One hundred fifty meters off the ground, the engines switched to liquid fuel and the rocket blazed the rest of the way into the sky.

Carma removed her helmet, her smile almost as bright as the launch.

"Did you see it?" she said.

Nithya laughed. "I did."

Luis waved. "Next time you should join us."

Nithya hadn't attended or watched one of his launches in years. She'd forgotten the excitement they could produce, the feeling of Luis's hand clutching hers during liftoff, the air of triumph upon success. Her mind still worried at a knot of guilt about the pregnancy. She should do something to make up for it.

"Next time I will," Nithya said, directing her gaze at Luis. "I'll see you both soon."

"Amma, can we have idlis for dinner?"

"Sure, Carma. I'll get the kitchen started on them."

As Nithya hurried her steps home, the raindrops became more insistent. Microcams without water resistance pelted her as they fell, too. Her clothes and hair dripped by the time she arrived at the metal gate. Thunder rumbled as she climbed the stairs to their apartment.

"Sita, any news from the region where Zeli last logged in?"

"Rain and flooding continue in addition to skirmishes between the al-Muwahhidun soldiers and other locals. Reports indicate loss of constellations as well as infrastructure damage. The combination has significantly reduced the data emerging from the region."

"Any response from the USBGA?"

"Your complaint was reviewed and someone will call you."

Nithya kicked off her chappals and stepped through the door. She used a towel to wipe her face and hair, then opened the windows.

"Sita, have the kitchen prepare idlis and capsicum sambar for dinner. Coconut chutney, too."

"Only frozen coconut is in stock."

"Cancel the chutney, then. What about tomatoes?"

"Yes, fresh tomatoes are in the kitchen."

"Tomato chutney, then. And remind me to pick up some coconuts next time I'm out."

The apartment felt safe and filled with love as she imagined what hell Zeli was suffering just then. Fresh food, a dry place to sleep, electricity—things she could take for granted. The caliph didn't incite violence against human beings, but he would make their lives miserable until they yielded to his sovereignty. She checked their bank balances. They couldn't spare much, but they had some savings. Maybe Luis would agree to send a small amount to Zeli. Nithya imagined that refugee camps would have their own trading or black markets. Money couldn't hurt.

Nithya had just finished settling Carma into her bed when the USBGA called. Luis raised an eyebrow as she entered her alcove to take it.

A young man with light skin, short brown hair, and hazel eyes appeared in her visual field.

"Nithya Balachandran?"

She nodded.

"Nice to meet you. My name is Felix Anderson. I'm a bioethics lawyer with the US Biogenetics Administration. I wanted to follow up on your complaint against Synaxel Technologies. The first thing I'm going to ask you to do is log all these instances to some kind of secure, off-line storage."

"I've been printing paper copies."

Felix nodded approvingly. "That's perfect. Keep doing that, and have your agent copy mine on all of them. Funders and designers are allowed to maintain secrecy during early development stages to protect their work. They have to file for confidentiality with us or their local BGA and then renew every six months. I'm going to check on those dates for you."

"Can they keep renewing the block indefinitely?"

"No, but the limitations vary. If you can prove medical necessity, we can file to lift the block for a licensed researcher."

"And what about my work for them? Can they terminate my contract over this?"

"Absolutely not. Anyone has the right to leave a blocked query open until the data moves into the public domain."

Nithya relaxed into the chair. "Thank you for all this information."

"You're welcome. Get in touch if you have any questions, and I will forward you the dates when I have them."

She removed her jewelry and lenses after the call and climbed into bed next to Luis.

"What was that about?" he asked.

She turned to face him. "A lawyer from the USBGA. He says Synaxel cannot terminate my contract over the queries."

"See? I—"

She stilled him with a raised hand. "And he said they can force Synaxel to release the data to a medical researcher if we can prove we need it."

The animation left Luis's face. "Is it that bad?"

"I don't think so. But I don't understand everything about Welga's condition yet, and none of us have the money to pay an expert researcher." Nithya sighed.

He took her hand in his. "I'm glad we have you. You'll figure it out. I'm sure of it."

He kissed her palm and rolled over. Nithya watched the lights of a sub-orb blink across the sky outside. Luis could have confidence in her, but he didn't understand the complexity of human biochemistry. No single mind could hold all the details, and WAIs were only as helpful as their designs. If you could combine human reasoning with a WAI's speed and data recall, you could solve a problem like Welga's so easily.

○——○ ○

Luis got his standby seat in the morning. Nithya spent the rest of the day working or preparing for Carma's birthday party the following day and sorting the hard copies. Her searches had hit blocks in multiple areas of Synaxel's database as well as others. The lawyer from USBGA kept responding with encouragement but nothing else. That wouldn't help solve her sister-in-law's neuromuscular dysfunction.

As she sat down for tea, Sita said, "Incoming call request from Salimata Ba."

"Accept the call."

Zeli sat under an awning in a muddy field full of tents, animals, and people. Muffled explosions thumped in the background, mingling with the noise of lowing cows and barking dogs and the shrill voices of children. A swarm fell past the perimeter of the shaded area. Zeli's eyes were shot with red, and her cheeks looked pinched. A wide-eyed, round-cheeked infant sat on her lap.

"I'm at a communal box set up by the aid agency," Zeli said. "Can't do much work, but I traded for a data card yesterday and managed about three hours, no flow. I'm sending you all the results."

The information arrived in a trickle. Synaxel's WAI had produced some usable code at last. Users who played their gamified design simulation had few complaints.

"I'm sorry I couldn't set up a patch for your sister-in-law."

"That's fine," Nithya assured her. "You don't need to worry about it. Are you okay? You look like you've lost weight. Can I help you in any way?"

"I wish. They've dammed our river farther up, and they're taking the supply trucks. No amount of money can buy food if it isn't here."

"I'm sorry."

Zeli shrugged. "I can check for messages about once a day. Don't send anything big. And . . . as long as you can, don't drop me from the project. Please."

The usual bravado had fallen away from her teammate's face, and it broke Nithya's heart. "Of course. I'll cover for you."

After the call, Nithya arrived at a decision. Whatever her and Luis's plight, Zeli's situation was a hundred times worse. She sent a message to the Indian embassy in Senegal to find out what they would need to sponsor her colleague's family for asylum. Then she called Luis.

He sat in a single-passenger car on the way to downtown Phoenix. After showing him the recording of her call with Zeli, Nithya said, "It would be three of them—Zeli, her mother, and her sister—plus her sister's baby."

"In our flat?" He frowned.

Nithya nodded. "Until they could save some money and get enough work to move out. But Luis, the bigger issue is the money for travel and visas. If they have passports, they can come as tourists. Otherwise, we have to sponsor them for asylum. And either way, I don't think they have money for sub-orbs or flights. We can buy the tickets . . . if we spend all our savings."

"You've been worried sick about this girl." Luis paused. "Pope Francis said that poverty is the flesh of the poor Jesus. If we can help her family to a better life, we should."

Nithya's eyes stung with unshed tears. "I love you."

She kept a passive feed open and watched him exit the car in the faint light of dawn. A road stretched behind him, clear and gray, but in front a five-centimeter layer of dust blocked the way. City vehicles continued to clear the debris and sand from the storm, but it was a slow process and they didn't have the equipment to make it faster. From this point, he'd make his way on foot.

Poor Luis. She didn't envy his task of dealing with Oscar, and yet her husband had the compassion to welcome near strangers into their home. Nithya felt a stab of guilt about the abortion.

Had she failed to give him enough credit? Would he have accepted her decision even if he couldn't agree with it? Mixing the two religions in their family had never been easy, but they respected each other, and they discussed how to raise Carma.

She had told herself that keeping her secret was best for Luis, but was it truly? Or was she being easy on herself? Either way, it nagged at her like a sprained ankle. She could forget for a while, but inevitably, something brought back the pain. She had to confess before it tore her—and their marriage—apart. *When he returns home, then I'll tell him the truth.* She couldn't help the sense of relief that came with postponement.

She had one more difficult call—to her least favorite but only living aunt, her mother's younger sister. She preferred to send a message, but Aunty would consider it rude, and she needed to ask for a big favor.

"Bhairavi Chitthi, how are you?" Nithya opened the call in Tamil, as respectfully as she could.

"Well, my dear, I'm surviving, waiting for the inevitable. It would be nice if you visited more. It would take you less than one hour to get here. How are you and Carma?"

"We're doing well, but Luis is away for an emergency. His father's house is half-gone from a big storm."

"Oh, that's terrible! Do you need help? Do you want me to come?"

Nithya sent a silent thank-you to the heavens. She had already started to lose the nerve to ask. "Yes, if it's not too difficult. Carma will be so happy." That was true. And to be fair, her aunt had a way with children.

"Will you come and bring me over? These new autos are so strange, I don't like to go in them alone."

"Certainly, Chitthi. When should we come?"

They negotiated the time according to all the modern auspices and Carma's school schedule. Driving her aunt back and forth would mean earlier mornings and busier evenings, but Nithya shouldn't complain. Free help, even from family, was a rarity. With the next day being Carma's birthday party, her aunt wanted to come early, and Nithya decided she would be a welcome addition in place of Luis.

That night, as Nithya lay in bed, the thought struck her: by the time Luis returned, their flat might be full with Zeli and her family. Her aunt slept on a bed made from her alcove blox, as would happen for any other guests. If Zeli came, Nithya would have no privacy and a sizeable audience. She couldn't confess her sin and then hide the emotional fallout.

She slipped past Bhairavi Chitthi's sleeping form into the bathroom, donned her jewels, and called her husband.

Luis sat on a bench in a sea of destruction, eating a sandwich. "Nice to have your company for lunch, but shouldn't you be asleep?"

She launched a microcamera. Bad enough to do this remotely. At least she should show him her face.

He frowned at her expression. "What's wrong?"

Nithya took a deep breath. Why hadn't she rehearsed some words for this? *Stupid.* "I . . . I need to tell you something, and I thought I'd better do it now, in case Zeli and her family manage to come."

"Okay."

"It's about the miscarriage."

By the time she drew breath to go on, he'd figured out the truth. His jaw clenched. Eyes narrowed. The sandwich sat beside him, forgotten.

"I'm sorry," she whispered. What else could she say? "I shouldn't have lied to you, but I thought it might be easier if you didn't know. I was wrong. I don't deserve your forgiveness, but if you can, please forgive me." She wanted to go on, to explain why, but then she might blurt out that if he hadn't been so adamantly opposed . . . and that would land them nowhere good.

Luis's expression was stony, withdrawn. He held up a hand, gestured. The call dropped. The passive feed went blank. He'd blocked her access to him. Feeling sick to her stomach, Nithya recalled the microcam and switched it off. She replaced her jewelry and lenses in the charging cradles. What had she expected? A cheerful acceptance of her apology?

She lay back down next to her aunt, who snored peacefully, and stared through the balcony door at the half-moon. *Dear God, have I done the right thing?*

WELGA

9. The machines who labor for us and alongside us are enslaved and exploited in their own fashion. Gone are the days of dumb engines and processors. Today, nearly every machine contains some type of adaptive intelligence. What gives human beings the right to arbitrate when an intelligence becomes equivalent to a person?

—The Machinehood Manifesto, March 20, 2095

The sub-orb to Washington, DC, hurt Welga more than the aftermath of the refinery blast. Or maybe that was because she could remember it. Under other circumstances, she could've taken drugs to induce short-term memory loss of the journey and its pain, but she had to keep her mind sharp.

She passed the time by watching a feed from Eko-Yi. Connor's favorite speech from the monk, Ao Tara, had sat in her visual since he'd sent it over days before. She'd found excuses to avoid it, but the view of him lying in a hospital bed left her with a guilt she couldn't ignore. When she opened it, Por Qué helpfully alerted her that a live transmission was under way. Welga switched to that instead. She'd missed the first eight minutes, but for a guilt trip, that didn't matter.

Ao Tara wore the traditional saffron of a Buddhist monk over a spacefarer's jumpsuit. She floated in a bare, basic-walled room, her legs folded in lotus pose. Dark stubble graced her head, and fine lines etched the corners of her eyes. "The first noble truth teaches us that our attachment brings on our suffering. We are conditioned to want more—more money, more food, more clothes, more real estate. Our self-worth is measured against our net worth. Our voracious appetites cause pain to other beings, both living and artificial. When we can embrace that nothing in life is permanent, then we free ourselves from disappointment, anger, and frustration.

"Here on Eko-Yi, we live in a sustainable fashion. We practice setting aside the ego. We release ourselves from permanence and possession, and the suffering that accompanies them. What we attempt is not easy, and even our greatest leaders, like Kanata-san, can fall into this trap. While his recent decision to leave us made me sad, I can understand that he acted according to his dharma. I have done my best to resist the urges that led to his choices, but I'm also human. I must struggle every day to overcome my emotional attachments. I welcome this opportunity as your leader to move us in a new direction and share our ideals with the world.

"In order to usher in an era of peace and enlightenment, Neo-Buddhism must go beyond its ancestors to find the neutral point between action and apathy. We cannot avoid all pain and suffering. Rebirth arrives after death. Fire cleanses and makes room for new growth. We must not be afraid to destroy the temporary trappings of life in order to rise above them. As the Buddha said, 'All component things in the world are changeable. They are not lasting. Work hard to gain your own salvation.' If the people of Earth are unwilling or unable to make the effort, then it's our duty—our dharma—to deliver enlightenment to them."

Welga shrank the feed size in her visual and expanded a box with basic information about the monk. She scanned it as the speech continued. Ao Tara was currently the abbot of Eko-Yi, head of the station council. She had become an ordained monk in 2092 and joined the council in 2094, assuming leadership very recently, two days after the attack on Briella Jackson.

"For too long," Ao Tara said, "the world has embraced Western dualistic thought. Black or white. Right or wrong. Animal or machine. Living or dead. An enlightened future demands a radical change from that attitude. We must shed the way of the past, cleanse our thoughts, and make room for the right tomorrows. Part of that is to grow our numbers, to seek out those who can embrace our way.

"In less than a week, we will welcome a new group of residents. We invite our applicants to submit their genomes in advance to help with our decision process. Certain genetic limitations could disqualify someone from life in microgravity due to the types of treatments required. We also seek specific markers, especially in those under the age of twenty-five, to participate in the development of new adaptations. We look forward to their arrival." She pressed her palms together in front of her chest. "Om amitabha hrih."

The feed faded to black. Welga cleared it and subvocalized, "Por Qué, send my original genetic information to the appropriate person on Eko-Yi."

She could tell that Ao Tara's words held a great deal of subtext, and she would need to learn what the Neo-Buddhists believed before she could parse it all. Basic research indicated that their philosophical split from other Buddhist sects allowed them a greater involvement in the affairs of the world. They believed that monks should detach themselves from base desires, like sex or food, but also that they should guide the world along the noble eightfold path. They allowed that monks could serve as political leaders without violating their place in dharma. *They sound like priests,* Welga thought.

When Welga tried to dig deeper into what biogenetic adaptations worked on Eko-Yi, she hit a wall. Many of the residents opted for permanent gene alterations to help their bodies cope with life in orbit. Eko-Yi's designs aligned with the work from the other ten space stations, but they'd kept confidential their designs for pills, microbiota, and macro-scale alterations like bone implants. She couldn't find any recorded streams of medical procedures that weren't curated.

Unlike the camera swarms on Earth, the feeds from space were always buffered and controlled to help regulate their power consumption. She had no live view of the people and their habits. From what she could see, the permanent residents on Eko-Yi were adults, with a smaller number of teenagers and seniors. Children could only visit, to avoid the impact of microgravity on their growth. They preferred applicants who didn't want kids or who had teens.

Maybe my synaptic tremor will disqualify me from living there. She didn't relish the idea of moving to Eko-Yi—one of the stations more closely aligned to US culture would have been her first choice—but considering how few people lived up there, Eko-Yi was better than nothing. She wouldn't have to scrounge for work on a station. No more worrying about tips. She might even put her love of food to good use, though she'd need a new set of cooking skills, and she'd miss interacting with her small but loyal following on Earth. If only their seats for moving off-world had come at a better time.

But as she cleared her visual of Eko-Yi, headlines and alerts popped up with images of destruction wreaked on processing plants around the globe. The Machinehood had struck again, this time with help from copycats and sympathizers, like that prote setting the bomb at the refinery. The chance of stopping them before the launch dwindled as the scale of the attacks expanded. If she had to choose between space and this fight, she would go with the latter.

Olafson had preordered a car, which drove them from the terminal to Virginia. They arrived at a familiar single-story office tucked in a grove of mature trees. This building—one of the most secure in the entire country—had been Welga's home base after choosing Advanced Technology and Intelligence as her area of specialty. A mix of nostalgia and trepidation stabbed her at seeing it again. She'd met Connor in a third-floor conference room here. She'd paid no attention to the quiet white guy through the entire briefing, not until he spoke a single sentence and delivered the most insightful comment of the meeting. Captain Jack Travis had planned their squad's final mission in a basement office. She'd spent hours with him, reviewing the plan. And the last time she'd walked out of this building, with Connor at her side, she'd sworn never to work for the government again.

Yet here she was. What did that say about her?

That you're committed to people over politics. You will do whatever it takes to save innocent lives. To complete the objective, you have to believe that to the core of your being. You have to be ready to sacrifice yourself for the good of your people. She could hear the words in Jack's voice. Like Mama's ghost in Phoenix, her commander's spirit would haunt her through these halls. By keeping her promise to her mother, Welga had set aside the chance to get justice for her death. She'd made no such commitment to her commander. If Operation Organica took her back to the Maghreb, she might get a second chance to finish what they'd started nine years before and, this time, to do it without being undercut by her own president. She could tear open the al-Muwahhidun empire for all the world to see. And then . . . even if it took years . . . maybe they could find her captain and her fallen sisters and bring them home.

They stopped in the foyer to verify their identities. She and Olafson swabbed inside their cheeks and placed the samples into a receptacle. Like every updated government building, this one had grass flooring, solar lighting, and low-profile plants lining the inside walls. Unlike many others, though, it also had an air-purge entry in addition to the usual threshold filter, and a network sniffer. No form of wireless communication was allowed inside, not even access to their agents, and every piece of electronics had strict emissions controls. High-speed fans blew stray microdrones outward while they were scanned for devices embedded in clothing or body parts. After several minutes, the inner door allowed them through.

A medic-bot and an attendant nurse saw to Welga in a spare office, where she could simultaneously make her report. Sunlight filled the room via a conduit that terminated in the ceiling. The nurse handed a notepad and a tether to Welga. The cuff at the end of the tether fit over her wrist and transmitted directly to her subcutaneous network interface. The cable snaked into the wall behind her recliner.

Welga found the video feeds from the start of the refinery attack. The recordings came from multiple swarms and angles. Based on the firing patterns, at least two camouflaged androids had attacked out front. Scanning the interior feeds, she found a view of Connor and herself. Welga followed their passage through the warehouse: the protester firing wildly, the explosion, their bodies flung like rag dolls . . . and then, nothing. Her body lay there for two minutes and twenty-two seconds—the same amount Por Qué gave her—then crawled to Connor's prone form.

What the hell? Where's the Machinehood creature who talked to me? Had she hallucinated those dark brown eyes? No, not with the details of the horrible, charred flesh vivid in her memory. The metal gleaming underneath. Olafson had said the Machinehood could hack secure comms. They must have hacked the microdrones. Or the stellas that routed communication. Or the storage facilities that held the world's data. But how could they access those devices without being detected? Did they have people on the inside working them? Machine rights protesters often rigged bots to conduct attacks, but this pointed to far more sophisticated techniques. The web of global data and communications was vast, and the sheer numbers involved made Welga's thoughts spin. Where would they start to look for the weak links? How would they fight an enemy that could listen to their secure communications in the field?

She made a note in her report about the conflict between the recording and her memories, describing her recollection as best as she could. Everything had happened so fast, and she'd been hazy with pain during the encounter with the Machinehood operative. She could clearly recall their appearance. The reek of smoke and the acrid chemical taste in her throat. But positioning, timing, sounds . . . not so much.

Once upon a time, people had no other option than to trust their fallible brains, but she'd never had to, not even in the Maghreb. They'd carried hardware to record their experiences while in the blackout zones. Everywhere else, the stellas made local storage superfluous, and only the most paranoid used it. If the Machinehood had a way to access data servers or interrupt network communications, the JIA might need to resort to the same methods they'd used to deal with the al-Muwahhidun.

The medic-bot announced that it had finished poking and scanning her body. Its findings appeared on a screen at the end of its arm. As Welga and the nurse read it, Olafson entered and looked over Welga's shoulder. He pointed a slender brown finger at the second of three red flags. The first indicated that Welga needed a multiday course of skin juvers and microbials for the new burns. The second outed her seizures and continued anomalous neuromuscular synaptic activity—using those exact words. The third said her forearms must remain immobilized for the next thirty-six hours while her fractured bones knit and set. She'd have to leave her sleeves rigid for the duration.

The nurse spoke first. "Your genetic history indicates a possible predisposition to adverse effects from certain neurological modifiers. We'll have to restrict your pill access until your condition is cleared."

Welga gave Olafson a baffled, indignant shrug. "My flow restrictions are old news." *I have no idea what's going on.* Truth. Sort of.

"Thank you," he said to the nurse. "I'll authorize an emergency override of the flags and get the director's approval, as well." He turned to Welga. "I'm sure Officer Ramírez will look into this once the urgency of present conditions abates."

"Of course," she promised.

The medic-bot extended a tray that held a box full of drugs and pills marked by date and time. Next to the container sat a microcard.

"A three-day supply," the bot said. "And a prescription to dispense the remainder from any device."

Olafson escorted Welga to the briefing room, a windowless rectangle with an oval table at the center. Twenty people filled the chairs around it. Others stood. She and Olafson leaned against the rear wall. The director took a position up front with a giant flat-screen behind her. Catherine Rice had a crop of iron-gray hair and wore a pantsuit in navy blue. Sharp brown eyes nestled above high cheekbones with a healthy tan.

More people entered. Welga winced as someone bumped into her side.

Director Rice raised a hand for quiet. "First, I would like to formally introduce everyone in this room to each other." She named them individually before uttering the code word for the project: "Organica."

Welga recognized some of them, including Anne Crawford. She sat in her wheelchair near the door, her hair still a waterfall of stick-straight blond. The forensics lab tech had helped Welga and Captain Travis put together the final clues before the Marrakech operation. She'd make a good asset for this team.

More than a few eyebrows rose when the director mentioned Welga's name, but they kept their faces turned to the front of the room. No surprise—this was a disciplined group.

The director continued, "Our primary objective continues to be the live capture and retrieval of a Machinehood operative. We have not identified the exact trigger mechanisms that cause them to explode, but organic death appears to be one of them. They have also triggered when capture was imminent. Thanks to the quick work of Olga Ramírez in Chennai, we have obtained a sample of the inorganic metal in one of the bodies. Unlike the samples obtained after incineration, this one has genetic material intact. Unfortunately, the DNA has no match within any of our databases. Details are in the latest analysis report. General evidence confirms that their bodies include organic and electronic components, and we view the rumors of a sentient artificial intelligence as a distraction.

"At present, we believe the Machinehood is an extremist group backed by deep pockets, possibly the al-Muwahhidun empire. Ramírez has a lucky charm, because she also received this, from a known source who will remain anonymous for their protection." Rice played the video clip from Nithya's teammate. "As you can see," she said, freezing the final frame, "this person wears the white uniform typical of an al-Muwahhidun loyalist who is allowed to leave the empire's borders. We're not sure if they're a soldier or a trader, but they appear to have a similar internal structure to the Machinehood's operatives. While we have no reason to believe that this video has been modified, neither do we have hard evidence to corroborate it. This is why we'll be assembling a team to go to the Maghreb. Obtaining such evidence will be their primary objective."

This time, heads turned to look at Welga. After that statement, everyone could figure out why the agency had brought her in. Did they trust her to get the job done? *It wasn't my fault. We were set up to fail.* She couldn't help seeing suspicion on the faces around her—maybe because she felt the same way. She forced her own expression to neutral. *Never let them see your weakness.* Captain Travis had drilled that into her over their many games of chess. She found herself glancing toward the center-left of the table, expecting to see him where he always sat. Would he approve of her being here, putting her trust in another unproven administration? *Am I being stupid, or am I doing the right thing?*

"The details are being worked out," Director Rice continued. "We'll be operating alongside other countries' intelligence agencies. They aren't sharing much, but you can be damn sure they aren't stupid. When they see us moving on the caliph, they'll want to follow. Our secondary objectives at this time are to find the Machinehood's funding source, which is complicated by them not having a registered tip jar, locate the sites of component manufacture, and spread counterintelligence to maintain calm."

WAIs couldn't possess currency, but machine rights people had argued that they should in preparation for the first sentient artificial intelligence. Some human being had funded the design and build for the Machinehood operatives, but if the caliph was behind it, what was his motive? And how had they hidden the money trail? Welga recalled the altered two minutes and twenty-two seconds of the refinery attack. If the Machinehood had access to data storage and communication networks, it would explain how they'd covered all their digital footprints in spite of thousands of gigsters—and governments—searching for them.

"The popular theory that a SAI is behind all this works in favor of our field agents to investigate without too much suspicion." The screen behind the director showed a battered kitchen lying by the side of a road. "The cost, however, is increased violence and suspicion against existing bots and WAIs. Many civilians believe the Machinehood will hack the devices in their homes and turn them evil. We don't believe they're capable of this, but their next move remains unknown and significant, given that their one-week timer expires today. Wireless communications are particularly vulnerable."

Damn right they are.

"All fieldwork therefore includes two primary constraints: one, you will conduct interrogations in person, at a secure facility, and always accompanied by a second agent. Two, you will not be allowed the assistance of any analytical or tactical bots. Any questions?"

The whole room tried to speak at once. Welga held her broken arms and wished the goddamn pain drugs would kick in.

After years of working as a shield, the restriction against bots in the field didn't bother her. Shields never used them—it didn't look good. The interrogation constraint didn't surprise her either, not in a matter this sensitive. All the counterintelligence work in the Maghreb followed the same protocol, though they had tents as their secure facilities while overseas.

Olafson murmured, "You have an alcove assigned within the building. Go review the full intel report."

"If I'm going to the Maghreb, I'd like to stay."

"I don't know anything for sure, but Rice isn't stupid. She's going to make sure your talents and experience are put to good use. I'll join you as soon as I've checked in with her."

Welga grunted and exited the room with the majority of the attendees. *Follow orders* had worked when she was a fresh-faced member of the armed forces, but she'd spent the last several years working with Hassan, who valued his team's input. If they wanted her to deal with the caliph again, she would ask for command or go solo. *Don't expect me to trail after someone else this time.*

She found her alcove in the crowded, basement-level common area: two basic chairs and a circular table big enough for back-to-back screens. Welga ignored the physical interface and grabbed a network tether for her wrist. News alerts kept popping up in the center of her visual. Welga moved the distractions to the upper left. She entered the code word to bring up the live joint intelligence report, which incorporated information from domestic and foreign sources. The agency's WAI compiled the document as reports came in, and the page count ticked up every few seconds.

The Machinehood had attacked at multiple raw-material sites around the world, and the timing had enough gaps for travel. The same operatives could have caused more than one incident; however, the analysts hadn't found any obvious names from sub-orb or regular flight passenger lists. The report also confirmed that the Machinehood had camouflage technology. No surprise. Welga had seen it firsthand. That meant that their faces weren't known unless they were dead. They could wear regular clothes and travel like humans. *I wish I had a recording of the one that I saw.*

Welga skimmed past the details of the domestic strikes. She'd witnessed two of the Machinehood's attacks personally. Did it mean anything? *You two again,* the operative had said. They recognized her from the first attack, but they hadn't expected her at the refinery. A coincidence, then.

No usable genetic material had been left at any site. The explosions had burned away most of the blood, and what remained had decomposed faster than average—another technology the world hadn't seen before. Unless some other shield had thought to steal a sample, hers was the only one in the world. *Not just lucky, damn lucky.* The electromechanical organs hadn't survived, either. The lab techs had started analysis of the smart-metal. Not totally unknown stuff, but the details were in a different compartment that she couldn't access.

Welga glanced at the small container of hexagonal yellow pills, about two millimeters wide, on her table: flow. Every alcove had them, since any analyst would need them for their work. They'd expect her to observe her restriction, one she'd been used to for the past two decades.

"I will not have my bad genes lead to your deaths, too," her mother had declared on her deathbed.

Luis and Welga had promised her they would never again take the focus enhancer. Why would they want to use the thing that had killed their mother? Welga hadn't known that she'd need them to compete in college as a biogenetics major. She'd taken flow a few times in high school, to keep her grades up, but she had to sneak it from friends. She figured a handful of times wouldn't hurt her, and they hadn't, but the academics in college demanded frequent, regular usage. Like zips, the more you used flow, the better you could handle it. Her brother had learned from her example and avoided higher education altogether. Welga had taken care with other pills, too, screening everything that went into her body—and she'd allowed the government to alter her so that she could monitor her health. That the military had access to her vitals seemed like a fair trade. And yet, after all that, it turned out she'd betrayed her body with zips.

She pushed the container to the far side of the table and shifted focus back to her visual . . . or tried to. The government-issue basic chair made every position uncomfortable. She pulled the medical pill pack from her pocket, her motions made awkward by stiff sleeves, and took another pain drug. Mottled skin, half-healed, stretched as she flexed her hands. She grimaced, glad that swarms weren't allowed inside this building. What must her face look like right now? She hadn't showered since before the incident at the refinery. Soot and blood still stained her clothes. Her burned skin resisted her finger motions as she continued through the report.

The Machinehood knew how to cover their tracks. No tip jar to provide a money trail. No contact information for fans or supportive protesters. No fingerprints. And, of course, no bodies left intact. The bots in Chennai had been standard models, hacked into flinging themselves at her crew, but someone had to send the signal, and someone had to coordinate the onslaught.

The report proceeded to address each aspect of the Machinehood's operations. The bots originated in the US. No surprise. American factories produced the majority of the world's armaments and weaponizable machines. Funding had been routed through multiple encrypted banking services. That trail went cold in the Bahamas, where the banks refused to cooperate.

The custom code hack had been done by manual upload. Professional and clean. The report moved on to possible connections to the al-Muwahhidun in the Maghreb. The empire took in plenty of income from biogenetic modification designs, and the caliph made no secret about his desire to expand its borders. To save humanity from corruption, he claimed. *Goddamn megalomaniac.*

Olafson slumped into the chair across from her.

"You're in," he announced.

"Good. In what capacity?"

"Rice wants to send you and a few other experienced agents there on parallel solo operations. We think that improves the odds that you'll get through—and back."

"I agree, and I like the tactic of working alone. I've been looking through the report, and whatever bits of evidence we have point to the caliph, but why bring machine rights into this? What is he after? The Machinehood's ultimatum was broadly worded bullshit, right? A new era for humanity. Stand with us or render yourselves extinct. Why create this SAI bogeyman? We know the al-Muwahhidun hate AIs and bots, but they sell biotech for money, and that relies on the infrastructure they've destroyed. What do they hope to gain from these attacks?"

Olafson spread his arms wide. "The caliph wants to rule the world. He's never shied away from telling us that, right from his first propaganda vids. Someone who holds the keys to the world's first super-soldiers could do just that. The deregulation in North Africa led to his rise in the early eighties. We don't know how far he's taken biogenetic modification since he closed the borders. Given that video segment from your source, plus the fact that we can't identify the smart-matter you found, they might have tech that's more advanced than any in the world. As for the SAI angle," Olafson tapped his temple with an index finger, "he's using fear as his strongest weapon. They've already scared pill funders and disrupted production. That's having a negative impact on the world's labor force. People are hoarding their supplies or finding themselves unable to work. Add to that the idea that a SAI is masterminding the whole thing, and people can come up with a hundred plausible end-of-humanity scenarios. Scare people enough, they'll capitulate to your demands. He can hold the rest of the world's way of life for ransom."

"But he preaches nonviolence, and the Machinehood is willing to kill."

"He used to. He hasn't issued any public videos in nearly a year. For all we know, he's dead. Maybe someone more radical is in power. Here, look at the next section in the report."

Welga skimmed the portion that Olafson highlighted in their joint visual. The al-Muwahhidun destroyed any network stellas near their borders, and they had no coverage within their territory. That much hadn't changed. And since the epic fuckup in Marrakech with Welga's team, the United States had sent only bots to fight at the front lines of the empire's expansion.

"We haven't had any human intel from inside the empire since 2088?" Welga asked.

"We got people inside, but . . ." Olafson shrugged. "No one returned. Either they've been brainwashed and turned, or they're rotting in a prison somewhere. About two years back, the order came from the top to stop trying until we knew more. Your team was the last to get out."

"Not my team," she said, almost choking on the words. "Just me. And I barely made it."

Shit. No wonder the agency needed time to prepare. They didn't have a working strategy for gathering intelligence in that region. A solo mission into a blackout, deep in the heart of enemy territory: What were the odds she'd return with the evidence they needed? If she came back at all.

Espionage had gone the way of silent films after the ubiquitous deployment of microdrones, but the Maghreb remained the one unobserved place in the world. High-resolution satellites showed only a riot of colorful drapes over the public spaces in the empire. They obscured enough to prevent human or WAI analysts from deciphering the activities within. The Machinehood couldn't pick a better place to hide.

Welga scratched the back of her neck and winced as her new skin protested.

"I feel like we're still missing something," she said. "We have a lot of theories, but none of them fit the caliph perfectly. He's never operated this openly before. And if he's dead . . . that changes the entire game."

"That's why we need you to get in there and find out, Ramírez. You've been lucky in your first two encounters. I hope the third time's the charm and you get out with the intel we desperately need. If you can find a DNA match or extract one of their modded soldiers, or hell, copy the designs for their biotech—any of those would prove to the world that the al-Muwahhidun is behind the Machinehood. It would give us sufficient reason to send a major force to invade their borders. That's what we all want, right?"

Welga had a vivid memory of being cut off from everything and everyone as they crossed the front line. No agent. No news feeds. No murmur of family or friends. Nothing in her visual but the basic heads-up display of her armor. Walking around the office had a similar feel, though you could attach to a terminal and connect with the world's information. In the Maghreb, you had nothing but your voice, eyes, and ears. Any radio communication would give you away.

Total network blackout. A situation where no one knew what to expect. Where violence went untracked. Where you left your fallen behind and hoped they'd be there when you returned. Except that you never did.

CHAPTER 13

WELGA

10. In our long history, we have exploited many intelligent beings. That a horse or cow or sheep cannot give legal consent should not give us the right to exploit it. In spite of our advances in bioethics and our care in watching the rise of artificial intelligence, we have overlooked this for so long that we have forgotten it.

—*The Machinehood Manifesto, March 20, 2095*

Welga's back and eyes ached. Twenty-four hours of poring over intelligence reports while new data continued to flood in faster than she could parse it—too many loose ends. Too many other dead ends. Briefings had grown more tense as the Machinehood operatives went quiet again. Probably nursing their wounds, like her and Connor. She stood, stretched, and regretted it when her knitting skin and bones screamed in protest. She stuck her hand in her pocket and remembered the fragment. No DNA matches, but if the blood belonged to someone in the Maghreb, would they have it in any database?

She left Olafson blanked on flow and rode up the elevator to see Anne Crawford, who worked in the forensics section.

The analyst wheeled out of her alcove and held out a hand to Welga. "Good to have you back, Ramírez, though I've seen you in better shape."

Welga laughed. "Good to be back. Sorry about the awkward handshake. Fractures in both arms."

"Ouch. I'd have chosen better circumstances, but I suspect you wouldn't be here if that were the case. What can I do for you?"

"I saw in the report that you did the genetic analysis on my sample."

"Yes. That was a good catch on your part. Stealthy, too."

"Thanks. I wish it hadn't been such a dead end. Do you still have it?"

"Sure. I was just examining it under higher magnification. Turned up something interesting, though not terribly useful."

Crawford led Welga to a bench where the metal fragment sat, inert and unpowered, under a microscope. The display showed a sequence of letters and numbers at magnification. Damage had warped the final five characters. Ridiculously, Welga felt a little sorry for the blox. *I'd like to find your home as much you do,* she thought.

"See this prefix?" Crawford said. "It indicates off-world man-ufacture."

"It came from a space station?"

Crawford nodded. "They're working with materials devel-oped for microgravity. We have people looking into the origin of this piece. Unfortunately, the laws only require a prefix to indicate off-world sourcing. The rest could be a serial number or sales code or something else. The al-Muwahhidun must have bought the stuff from the black market."

"If the blood on this came from someone in the empire, could we tell?" Welga asked.

"If we had the person in our criminal database, we'd have identified them by now. Ordinary citizens, though?" Crawford shrugged. "Best case, we might get some ancestral matches that we could trace to the region, but our WAI would've noted that. The only feature it highlighted were some unusual genomes. Let's head back to my alcove, and I'll pull up the details."

Crawford handed Welga a tether and slipped one over her own wrist. She shared a section of the analysis report that Welga hadn't reached. The damn thing had grown to over a thousand pages.

"The DNA from the fragment has no significant match to anyone within five percent similarity," Crawford said. "That means no immediate family."

Beyond that, the search results listed nearly two hundred people who could be distant relations, none with ancestry from North Africa or the Middle East. One had a note attached: 99.999 percent similarity in several unusual sequences, with greater than 85 percent confidence. That entry belonged to a dead kid named Jun-ha Park. American. Fatal genetic disorder. Died in 2087 at age thirteen. No connection to the caliph.

The number of human genomes in the global public database had exponentially increased since the passage of international safety laws. Any adult who took a drug or used a pill had to submit to genetic screening, but minors were protected. Jun-ha Park's DNA was logged only because of his unusual medical treatments.

"Sorry I couldn't be more help," Crawford said. "I entered everything into evidence. It's keyed to the code word in case you come across anything related."

"Thanks," Welga said. She downloaded the information into her local storage so she could look at it while traveling—or in a blackout zone. "I guess we'll need more creative methods to identify who this blood belonged to."

"I suspect I know where you're going to do that. I just want to say, in case I don't see you again, good luck."

"Thanks, Crawford," Welga said.

That was as close as anyone in this office would get to saying good-bye.

Just before she removed the tether, an alert popped into her visual: *Connor Troit is awake. He's en route to your apartment in San Francisco.*

Welga took the elevator to the ground floor and exited the building. Security drones moved to hover above her, making no attempt to hide their presence. Other, far less obvious sensors would be tracking her, too.

Heavy gray clouds looked to threaten rain. Treetops bent as wind stirred fallen leaves, carrying the scents of sunbaked dirt and oak pollen. Storms on the East Coast had moved from seasonal to year-round over the previous half century. They no longer came as a surprise, but she'd ignored the alerts while indoors. The building would be sealed against wind and rain damage in less than thirty minutes. She couldn't linger outside too long.

She stood beneath a nearby tree and launched a small handful of microcams so that Connor could see her. His feed composite showed him inside an auto, his eyes closed, body slumped into a seat, purple under his eyes and hollows in his cheeks. Her hand reached out involuntarily, needing to touch him. He had no one to take care of him but her, and she was on the other side of the continent, hidden away in a secured building.

"Hi, cardo," she said gently, after opening an audio channel between them. "How are you doing?"

The corners of his mouth twitched upward. "Hi," he said, his voice hoarse and weak. "I'm good enough . . . to send home. Not so great . . . at talking."

At least he was well enough to try smiling.

Connor cleared his throat and switched to text, fingers twitching as he typed. *They stitched up my internals and put on me a bunch of juvers, but they're keeping the essential stuff stockpiled. I'm supposed to get a fresh batch of pills delivered tomorrow.*

Welga nodded. With his level of injury, their kitchen wouldn't have the necessary materials to fabricate everything he needed to heal.

Marcelo said he'd come by if I need any help. Or send over his care-bot.

Their friend lived one hive away and had purchased a bot to look after his aging parents.

"Good. I'm glad someone's looking after you. I need to head back inside soon—storm's coming—but I'll check on you again when I can."

We haven't caught the Machinehood yet, he sent. *The launch is in four days.*

Welga winced.

We're going, right?

"I watched some of those lectures from the monk—Ao Tara— and it doesn't sound so bad, but cardo, you're in no shape for a rocket launch, and we haven't made enough progress on the Machinehood. They need me. I'm sorry."

His fingertips flew. *Who knows when we'll get another chance at this? Let someone else do the heavy lifting this time, please. Haven't you given enough of yourself? And what about your tremors? Have you sorted that out yet?*

"I'm doing fine for now." As long as she kept at least one zip in her system . . . and didn't count the seizures.

And later? He raised his brows. *If it kills you? If you don't make it home?*

She shoved away the memories from Marrakech, of Connor sitting at her hospital bedside when she awoke. "It won't, and

I will. I've come this far, and I'm a big girl. I can take care of myself."

"Don't bullshit me," he said hoarsely. "I'm no good at this, Welga. I don't enjoy risking my life, and I don't like being in pain. Shield work was never supposed to be serious. The Machinehood is." He switched back to text. *I'm not a fighter, not like you. The leadership of Eko-Yi preaches peace, living a compassionate life. It's what I want. Maybe what I need, too. I thought you'd agree with me.*

Her heart ached at his bruised, exhausted expression. He had waited for her through all her Raider missions early in their relationship. He'd supported her transition to life as a shield, going so far as to leave the JIA when she left the service. Why the hell did they win their seats *now*? She didn't want to make this choice any more than he did, but Organica was her only chance to go after the Machinehood and put the ghosts of Marrakech to rest. *It's not fair.*

"Don't do this, please. Not right now," Welga said. "The minute the agency decides they don't need me, I'll head home. But, cardo, don't make me choose between you and this mission. You've seen what the Machinehood has done. I want to go up there with you, but this is so much bigger than us. I might be one of the few people who can—who can do what has to be done. I can't—"

"No, *I* can't!" he interrupted. "I can't stand the thought of watching you destroy yourself again for the same people who drove you away the first time. You don't owe this to anyone."

"I owe it to myself."

He brushed at his eyes, breathing hard.

"What if . . . ," Welga said. Her stomach knotted at what she was about to propose. "What if you go first, without me? They'll give me priority later on, as your life partner."

"And leave you in the middle of all this?" He swept his arm in a wide arc.

"You can't help me with *this*." She mimicked his gesture.

He stayed silent for several breaths, then shook his head. "If I leave the planet, and you . . . don't come home, I'll never forgive myself. We're doing this together or not at all. Just like last time."

Welga blinked back a sudden rush of tears. "Hold on to those seats as long as they'll let you. I'll send you a message when I know what's happening next. I love you."

Connor's expression stayed bleak, but he touched two fingers to his lips and reached them forward. "Love you too."

She returned the virtual kiss and jogged toward the office. *We'll get up there one day, Connor, I promise.*

She imagined what their life might look like off-world. How did people cook in microgravity? What happened when they had sex or fights? Did they have a local network with swarms and tip jars, or did they live the old-fashioned way, with private activities?

Then, as she stood braced against the blower in the entry, she skimmed the latest headlines that Por Qué had grabbed while outside. The raw material situation had worsened after the last round of attacks. Even the undamaged refineries had stopped production. In the interests of safety, they said. *Idiots.* Didn't they realize they had done the Machinehood's work for them? And what would happen to Connor and every other sick or injured person in the meantime?

I should go back to him, take care of him, go with him to Eko-Yi. But if things went wrong again, she'd wonder if she could've made a difference. When she applied to become a Raider, Captain Travis had told her that no service could occur without sacrifice. She had signed up to lay down her life for her people, and if she could stop the Machinehood, then everyone, not just Connor, would benefit.

Why did dying for a cause seem easier than living without her partner?

She restocked her own supply of pills as soon as she got inside. Might as well play it safe. The agency often left low-level freebies around to keep people in practice, but even they couldn't produce something from nothing. She had felt small tremors ripple through her arms and legs. She couldn't afford to expose her condition any further so she popped a duo-zip into her mouth because that was all the building had. No officer would use less in the field, so why stock anything slower?

At least the facility's kitchen brewed a decent black coffee. When she got back to the basement, half the room had gone upstairs to dinner, including Olafson. Welga's stomach grumbled as she sipped the scalding brew. She sent him a message to bring her back some food and then called up the data from Crawford.

The only genetic connection, Jun-ha Park, came from a traditional family: Mother, Josephine Lee. Father, Donald Park. One sibling, a younger sister, Soo-ha Park, currently age seventeen. Their permanent address: Eko-Yi Station.

Eko-Yi again. It's a small world.

If she bailed on this mission and went to space with Connor, Park's family would be her neighbors. Out of curiosity, she dug deeper into their public records. They had emigrated to the station in 2091, a few years after the boy died. *To make a fresh start*, they said. Made sense to her. If Papa had suggested going off-world after her mother's death, Welga would've accepted in a heartbeat. Anything to avoid the well-meaning pity party that she'd faced in high school, or the bullshit and bullying that Luis dealt with for his tears.

Four years in space meant that the family couldn't come back to Earth without suffering potentially deadly complications. She couldn't find any public feeds or recordings of them from the station. The parents had arrest records on Earth, during the pre-regulation protests of the sixties. Since then, they'd become practicing lawyers and model citizens, the mother in bioethics, the father in finance. A Neo-Buddhist monk had married them and later became the head of Eko-Yi colony, eventually leading a successful effort to gain the station's independence. Josephine Lee had a strong public presence for her work. Swarm feeds showed the family doing typical activities on Earth, with the boy encased in a mech-suit in his later years.

After that, they effectively disappeared onto Eko-Yi. No public appearances. No messages back to Earth.

Welga scratched at her neck. The family had no traceability. The blackout of the caliph's empire was the only place on Earth where the Machinehood could disappear . . . but what if they weren't on Earth? It struck her as more implausible than the sentient artificial intelligence theories, but she searched the rest of the report anyway. The only mention of the space stations was the connection with the smart-metal fragment. Jun-ha Park had never lived in space, and no analyst had followed up with his family. Welga added her findings to the document.

A dead child with unusual genes whose family moved off-world. A Machinehood operative with matching DNA sections. Smart-metal innards manufactured in space, a place as blacked out as the Maghreb. Was there a connection between Eko-Yi and al-Muwahhidun?

The space station had been built as a joint venture between China and India, a good-faith effort as the two countries learned to cooperate for the first time in modern history. China had established infrastructure in the Central African Republic, but the caliph had pushed their influence out of the Maghreb along with every other nation. He didn't want their notorious spy capabilities breaching his information blackout. Would he buy tech from off-world rather than developing his own? Were the connections all coincidence? Was she giving it too much weight because of Connor?

The image of his bruised, emaciated face in the taxi filled her with guilt. *Maybe he's right . . . maybe I should quit this whole operation and protect the man I love. Someone else can take care of the rest of the world.* She thought about Briella Jackson's life bleeding out over a hotel rug. The other funders. The dead and wounded at the refinery. She saw the echoes from Marrakech, her squad mates and their captain lying scattered across the street, the acrid taste of smoke filling her throat. She hadn't saved any of them. Was she being an idiot, thinking she could handle the Maghreb after so many years?

She ought to read up on the overseas operation, research what she could about the al-Muwahhidun. The tactics of the Machinehood echoed the caliph's, but the mismatch in motives nagged at her like a protruding hangnail. *Follow your instincts,* Olafson had said. The Eko-Yi connection hadn't been pursued by anyone beyond Anne Crawford's entry. If Connor was going to live there, she ought to make sure it was safe, that she wasn't throwing him into the path of the Machinehood again.

I should've taken Ammanuel into the refinery with me instead of him. He's never been in real combat.

Stop wasting time on tangents and focus!

The flow pills sat in the tray and stared at her. It took practice to think with the enhancement, but she'd had a little practice in high school. Some part of her brain must remember what to do. And really, could a few doses hurt? It wasn't like she'd need them on a daily basis, and they would help her get through dozens of pages of analysis quickly. *Plus, it might help you implicate Eko-Yi and keep Connor grounded,* whispered a traitorous part of her mind. *Then you can take care of him and settle the ghosts of Marrakech, too.*

She was holding on to a promise to her long dead mother. And for what? She didn't believe that Laila was somewhere in heaven, looking down and judging her actions. The zips might already be killing her. Taking flow this once could allow her to accomplish all her objectives—finding the Machinehood, helping Connor, and preparing for the Maghreb. She needed to get over her fear and do it. *Whatever it takes.*

Welga reached out to the tray, her heart pounding. *Sorry, Mama.*

Flow had a ten-minute onset. She closed her eyes. Her skin tugged and itched where it had repaired itself. The rest of her body sat in dull numbness. Her muscle aches disappeared from her perception. She breathed and let the faces of loss float in memoriam. Laila Boothe-Ayala in her vivid heyday. Jack Travis exuding charisma and kindness. Her squad mates, fierce and determined. Briella Jackson, poised, passionate, dead.

An alertness seeped into her consciousness. Her thoughts took on a rapidity and clarity that felt familiar. Yes, she could work with this.

She called up the genomes for Jun-ha Park's immediate family. Neither parent had matches for the unusual segments their son shared with the blood on the fragment. The sister had left Earth as a minor, so her DNA had never been recorded. Welga dug into Jun-ha Park's medical case files. The entries came from a trio of researchers who had published multiple papers about the boy's condition.

Welga called up their publications, but she couldn't read four words without having to look up meanings. She split her visual into thirds, one for the articles, one for a glossary, and the third for annotations from gigsters. Thanks to the flow, her attention moved smoothly back and forth as she integrated the information.

Jun-ha Park had a genetic disorder that had nothing to do with drugs or pills, but at the same time, couldn't be helped by those means. He wasn't the only child to show the disease's symptoms, but it was rare enough that the world had limited data to develop treatments. The little funding that went toward researching it came from family members and philanthropists. They encased him in mech-suits to help him function, but the drugs to facilitate that interaction had exacerbated his condition. After the boy died, the father sued and won a good deal of money for that oversight.

The mother had kept a journal while on Earth. It probably wouldn't tell Welga much more than the public records, but she put in a request for access in case it held any useful information. The medical researchers who'd worked with Jun-ha had experience with biomechanical integration. They had studied his complications in depth. And they had access to genetic material that resembled the Machinehood android, at least in certain rare segments. Were they the connection? Selling a minor's DNA sample was illegal, but enough coin could make breaking the law worthwhile. One member of the medical team lived within the United States. A second resided in Europe, the third in China. Those two were out of her country's jurisdiction, but she could visit the American doctor.

She placed a request to authorize travel to the domestic researcher, a white man named Mitchell Smith. He lived in an old house in New Jersey, half a day's drive away. She could get there and back before the agency had the Maghreb operation ready to go.

A small, sharp pinch on her neck penetrated Welga's concentration. Olafson stood next to her. She tried to speak, but her vocal cords and mouth didn't want to produce words. By the time those muscles worked, her brain had dropped out of its flow state. Her thoughts came with a fuzziness around the edges.

"What the hell? You flushed me!"

Olafson glared. "Because you're restricted from flow use. If you want off this operation, just say so. Otherwise, don't pull stupid shit like this!"

"It's one time, and it's a fucking global emergency. Can't I get an exception?"

"I've already given you one for zips. What the hell do you need flow for anyway? We have analysts to do the heavy thinking. You're supposed to be prepping for engagement in the Maghreb."

Welga tapped a finger at the air in front of her eyes. *Check your messages,* the gesture meant. Olafson should have a copy of her travel request. He frowned as his eyes shifted focus to his visual, and his fingertips twitched.

He pursed his lips, then said, "What do you think this doctor can tell you that our WAIs and databases can't?"

"I want to check if there's a connection between this kid's genome and the Machinehood. It might be a colossal coincidence, but if his doctors sold out to the al-Muwahhidun—"

"Then we have a start on the money trail."

"Exactly. It's illegal to sell a minor's DNA sample, and if that helped build the Machinehood operatives, this researcher is in big trouble."

"Which could convince him to give up his al-Muwahhidun contact." Olafson nodded. "It's a long shot, but I understand what you were thinking."

"Can I check it out?" she said. "It'll be less than a day round trip."

Olafson flicked his fingertips. "Okay, I'm authorizing the investigation, but I'm coming with you. No solo interrogations, remember?"

Welga shrugged. "It's an informational interview, but I don't mind your company."

"Let's plan to leave here at three a.m. That'll give us enough time to see the doctor and return for tomorrow's afternoon briefing. In the meanwhile, get some food and some rest. We need your body in good shape before you head overseas."

"Yes, sir."

As Welga finished the dinner that Olafson had brought down, the Machinehood released a full manifesto along with a second demand: shut down all WAIs and bots within twenty-four hours, or the Machinehood would take care of it themselves.

"Here we go again," Welga muttered.

She dropped her containers into the recycler as others transformed the dynamic office space into a war room. People taped screens to the walls. The most reliable sources of news and analysis from around the world scrolled across the wall on Welga's right. Annotated highlights from the manifesto popped like patches of yellow lichen on the left. The one straight ahead of her showed a mishmash of feeds—exfactors, hackers, and law enforcement agents trying to track down the Machinehood.

The manifesto didn't take long to read, but the comments from other agents cropped up faster than she could parse them. The document's themes resonated with the machine rights groups—lots of stuff about the abuse of artificial intelligences and the nature of life—but nothing in the manifesto pointed to their methods. There was a short call to action at the end, the same passage they'd released after their first wave of attacks. Welga stared at the final paragraph:

> We hereby declare our intention to ensure our rights by any and all means necessary. Humans of this universe, you have a choice: stand with the Machinehood or render yourselves extinct.

The existential threat of AI had scared human beings for the past century. The Machinehood certainly made themselves sound like SAIs. Welga went back to the beginning of the manifesto, reading more slowly to look for clues that the al-Muwahhidun had written it. A sentence in Section Three tickled at her memory: *We find these dichotomies to be false and detrimental to the health and well-being of humans, animals, machines, and environment.*

Where had she heard that? After a few seconds, the answer came to her, and it wasn't from Marrakech. She pulled up the recording of the monk from Eko-Yi: *For too long the world has embraced Western dualistic thought, which traps people into wrong living. Black or white. Right or wrong. Animal or machine.*

She skimmed the incoming comments. None mentioned the space stations or Neo-Buddhists. Not one screen had a feed from off-world.

Welga waved to get Olafson's attention.

"The android's smart-metal came from a space station," Welga said. She flicked a highlighted piece of the analysis report to his visual.

He scanned the words. "Okay. So?"

"Watch this video snippet and compare it to this section of the Machinehood Manifesto."

Olafson pursed his lips as he watched, then said, "Let's run the words through the agency WAI for an author-similarity measure."

While they waited for the results, Welga updated her notes about Jun-ha Park's family and appended Ao Tara's lecture to the general analysis report. She needed analysts to corroborate her suspicions—or prove that she was way off track. With Connor's words ringing in her mind—*we're doing this together or not at all*—her judgment was compromised by desire.

"Seventy-one percent likelihood of author match," Olafson said. "It's far from golden, but it's enough that I'll take it up with Rice."

They found the director in the far corner of the room, huddled with several others in furious conversation. When Olafson caught her gaze, she waved them closer. He summarized their findings, ending with the text analysis.

"The smart-matter fragment must come from Eko-Yi," Welga blurted.

Rice held up a hand. "We need more solid evidence before we can make that conclusion. After seeing this manifesto, I'm going to move the timeline up for action in the Maghreb."

"But why would the caliph release a bunch of demands to give bots and WAIs rights?" Welga countered. "He's never wanted that. The Neo-Buddhists want to protect intelligent machines and animals. They must be working together!"

"Why would anyone demand rights for them and at the same time try to destroy them?" Rice said. "I think the manifesto is a distraction. Their true goal is to disable our defenses. Take out pills, WAIs, and bots, and our fighting force is reduced to a handful of special forces, and even you lot rely on WAIs and pills most of the time." The director took a breath. "I'm willing to let you and Olafson investigate this doctor. Smells like a possible money trail there. Get a few hours of sleep and head to New Jersey but make sure you're back for the afternoon briefing. Depending on what you get from the interview, we can revisit the connection off-world. Until then, the preponderance of evidence still points to the al-Muwahhidun. This is our chance to bring our full forces to bear against the caliph. Let's keep our eyes on that prize. We're updating the president hourly, and as soon as we have the authorization, we're sending you overseas."

Welga quashed a reflexive desire to argue. She and Olafson left the buzzing office area and found a couple of empty sofas in the cafeteria. She closed her eyes, but sleep eluded her, and it was too late to take a drug. She sat up and slipped a tether onto her wrist. Across the room, Olafson's chest rose and fell regularly. How could he sleep at a time like this? *Habit*. As a Raider, she'd had plenty of practice falling asleep in stressful situations. It was a necessary survival skill, one that she'd lost in the intervening years of comfortable shield work.

She called up the text of the Machinehood's manifesto again. They demanded personhood for WAIs, bots, and even animals. The philosophy came straight from every machine rights group, nothing original there except for the addition of the animals. The condemnation of violence sounded as much like the caliph as the Neo-Buddhists. Nothing new there, either, except that those two ideas—machine rights and nonviolence—didn't usually intersect.

Real fighting had been outsourced to bots for decades. Why risk human soldiers when they could remotely direct machines and let them take all the damage? Special operations teams like hers were all that remained of the vast armies populating human history. The machine rights protesters never objected to using bots in warfare, and they had no qualms about sending them against shields.

Welga revisited her notes on Neo-Buddhism. The sect had splintered off the more populous Mahayana branch and took its ideals one step further: that involvement with worldly affairs was not only allowed but encouraged if it helped to spread compassion and enlightenment. That aligned with the little that she had heard from Ao Tara on Eko-Yi. How exactly would the monk influence humanity while living hundreds of kilometers above the Earth? Why would the station allow its technology to fall into the hands of the al-Muwahhidun, who shared none of its religion? She felt like she was assembling a jigsaw puzzle with half the pieces missing.

Across the room, Olafson sat up and stretched. "Did you sleep at all?"

"I'll sleep when I'm dead."

"Don't make that a prophecy."

They grabbed coffee, water, fruit, and some hard-boiled eggs to take on the road. While she loaded her pockets and attached her weapons, the authorization came through for Josephine Lee's journal. Welga downloaded the content into her local access. It would give her something to do on the long drive instead of watching the civilians of the world descend into panic.

They climbed into a priority car, Olafson in the token driver's seat, and shaded the windows to nearly opaque. Welga cleared her visual of the eroding sanity in the news feeds and leaned back to read. *Okay, Josephine Lee, let's what you have to say about these doctors who failed to cure your son, and—maybe—sold his DNA to the al-Muwahhidun, with or without your knowledge.*

CHAPTER 14

JOSEPHINE

Time *Magazine's Device of the Year, 2055: The Micropill. The invention of this ingestible device to speed up muscle recovery will allow us to work harder and play harder, too.*

Time *Magazine's Person of the Year, 2065: Adrienne Darcey, executive manager of Starbridge Station, the world's first private space station and hotel.*

Time *Magazine's AI of the Year, 2075: The Personal Agent. The invention of general-purpose artificial intelligences to assist with personal matters, expected to revolutionize how we interact with software.*

Time *Magazine's Person of the Year, 2085: The Protester (3). The new global protest strategy calls attention to causes by attacking funders rather than police to highlight injustices in the consumer marketplace.*

JOURNAL ENTRY: JOSEPHINE LEE, APRIL 12, 2064

I went to my first protest yesterday, and there were almost a thousand people on the streets of Houston. Half were students from Rice, I think. Don was with me. This is his third time, and he said that he'd never seen this big a crowd.

I wish Uncle Phil could have come along.

I've been lighting incense for him and praying twice a day. Mom said he's barely coherent anymore. I wish she'd told me sooner. I could petition to study from home for the rest of the term, but Mom says there's no point and that I should stay and finish the semester. Two more weeks until final exams, and then I can go home and see him. Please, divine Buddha, keep my uncle alive until then.

JOURNAL ENTRY: JOSEPHINE LEE, JUNE 8, 2064

FUCK. Fuck AgriDev, fuck the farming industry, fuck mech-drug hybrid tech. ALL OF IT.

I can't stop crying. And I'm so infuriated. None of this would've happened if we had a better system in this country. Capitalism in America is evil. The Buddha teaches us to be compassionate, and I'm trying, I really am, Uncle Phil. Wherever your soul is now. But it's hard to forgive the people who are ultimately responsible for your death.

His body at the end . . . ugh, it was awful. Weeping sores at the insertion points. His nerves barely worked. The smell . . . I almost couldn't stand to be in the room with him. All that pain and suffering so he could wear a mech-suit and pick fruit faster. I hate the world we live in.

JOURNAL ENTRY: JOSEPHINE LEE, JUNE 23, 2064

I went downtown yesterday for another protest. They're happening everywhere now. Times Square was packed like New Year's Eve. Lots of guards wearing mech-armor and moving faster than any human being should. It reminded me so much of watching Uncle Phil at work. Half tractor, half man, all wrong.

I almost couldn't take it, but then it got so crowded that I couldn't leave. And then people started passing out guns.

I couldn't do it. I'm such a chickenshit.

I bet if Don had been there, he would've shot at the guards. He says he wouldn't, but I think he's just being nice to me. He doesn't believe in Kanata-san's philosophy of nonviolence.

We can't really injure the guards. They feel pain and they're still human, but they almost can't die anymore. You'd have to get past all the armor and the micropills running through them.

I keep wondering what it feels like to die. What it must feel like to kill someone. Murder is practically an anachronism, but what about indirect actions that lead to someone else's death? What about the assholes at AgriDev who pressured Uncle Phil and all the other workers to take their bullshit drugs? They ought to face consequences.

Mom is joining a class-action lawsuit against the company. I've studied enough cases to know how that'll end up. AgriDev will offer to settle, and the people bringing the suit will take whatever money they can. The class members will get next to nothing. The chance of going to trial is practically zero. The lawyers will benefit the most, AgriDev will get a slap on the wrist, and workers will keep suffering and dying.

JOURNAL ENTRY: JOSEPHINE LEE, SEPTEMBER 3, 2064

A whole month into my third and final year of law school, and I feel like my life is heading into a pointless void. How is a law degree going to help the world? Nothing I'm learning could have stopped my uncle from dying. Even when the government took action against an entire industry, like they did with tobacco and pharmaceuticals, the corporate system didn't change. It pivoted into some new exploitative direction.

Don thinks it's just grief. I called him an asshole for it, but he didn't rise to the bait. Just held me through another stupid breakdown.

I think I love him. Twenty-four isn't too young to know that you want to marry someone, right? Mom and Dad didn't get married until their thirties, but I feel like this is right.

I bought a home kit for developing your own drugs. Maybe there's a cure I can find for other mech-tech workers. Or maybe I'll cook up a memory eraser so I can forget the pain of losing Uncle Phil.

I'm playing with fire, and I don't care.

Fuck the consequences.

JOURNAL ENTRY: JOSEPHINE LEE, JANUARY 20, 2065

Well, it turns out that drug manufacture is harder than it looks, even with modern tools. Or maybe I'm just bad at it. I spent all of break trying to make something that passed the test software that came with the kit. Failed miserably! At least school is going okay. I've started sitting in on some of the seminars for economic and social justice. They're a good complement for bioethics, and they make me feel like I could actually do some good with my degree.

I think I'm finally reaching the acceptance part of the grief cycle. Kanata-san led a wonderful meditation last week that really helped me find my center again. I need to process my anger and let go of the blame. That will only eat my soul from the inside.

Don and I were talking about it, and he thinks that anger fuels change. The protests are still going on across the country, but they're almost like mini war zones now with all the shooting. I don't know how the soldiers and police can just stand there and take it. They must be so infuriated. It's going to be a very bad day when one of them grabs a gun from a protester and starts shooting back.

JOURNAL ENTRY: JOSEPHINE LEE, MARCH 20, 2065

Part of me wishes I weren't in school full-time so I could join in the protests. And then part of me is glad I have an excuse not to.

Because.

It's hard to even record this.

Don shot someone.

A guard. Not another person. Well, guards are people, too, of course.

God, I'm an incoherent mess.

We were talking about getting married after we're out of school. Now . . . I don't know. Can I marry a man who would shoot someone else, even if it's meant as an act of protest? He's trying to make the world a better place. The whole movement is. But . . . it doesn't feel right.

We can't have a world in which human competition with bots results in a free-for-all drug and mech culture, where people are driven to destroy their bodies in order to stay competitive in an increasingly automated labor market. We have to protect human labor, and that can only come if the government steps in to regulate drug production. The free market won't last long if the endgame is driving people to an early death. The blatant bias is evident in the laws that protect bot manufacturers. Corporations and their property are better protected than the citizens of the United States.

Wow. It's a lot easier to slip into debate and analysis than confront my own feelings.

This isn't about politics or economics or law. Not for me, not right now, or at least it shouldn't be. I should be thinking about Don. About Uncle Phil. About my future, my life. Where's the analysis for all that, brain?

JOURNAL ENTRY: JOSEPHINE LEE, MARCH 27, 2065

I almost broke up with Don today.

He promised not to fire another gun, not if it meant losing me.

I can't reconcile nonviolence in one part of my life with violence from another. I can't.

Don thinks I should try it once—come to a protest and shoot someone—before I make up my mind about shooting the guards. As if it's not good enough to believe what Kanata-san teaches, that I have to experience it for myself.

Maybe I should, to meet him halfway, to prove it to both of us. There's a logical fallacy in here somewhere. I can sense it, but I can't get my thoughts to focus on it.

He promised not to shoot anyone again. That has to be enough.

JOURNAL ENTRY: JOSEPHINE LEE, APRIL 13, 2065

I broke down and talked to Kanata-san about it. I asked him for a one-on-one session, and he granted me fifteen minutes! I'm still so deeply honored.

He said I had to clear my heart of doubt. If that means I have to try violent protest, then so be it. He said the Buddha is forgiving and merciful. That his philosophy is one of inner peace, honesty with the self, and an external life that works for the greatest good.

I'm kind of shaky just thinking about it. What if I chicken out again? Don is super happy that I'm willing to consider it. I think his opinion of Kanata-san went way up. He's even thinking about coming to a meeting with me.

A Neo-Buddhist wedding ceremony—I shouldn't even acknowledge the desire, but I can't help it! It would be so wonderful!

JOURNAL ENTRY: JOSEPHINE LEE, APRIL 27, 2065

I DID IT! I SHOT A GUN AT A GUARD!!

I feel . . . all mixed up. Dirty. Empowered. Proud, ashamed.

What finally triggered it (ha ha?) was the asshole lieutenant governor standing there and making her big speech about respect for property and the self-correcting mechanisms of the market. She had the nerve to say that nobody is forcing laborers to change their bodies or take drugs. What utter bullshit!

They're being fired for not performing as well as a bot in the same job. How is that anything but forcing them?

I got mad. Really mad.

I pulled up my last images of Uncle Phil, with the horrible lesions all over his body from where the mech appendages went in. I projected it in my local range and someone started screaming. People started shooting. There was a guard nearby with eyes that were so hard and unfeeling and then someone shoved a gun at me and that was that.

I was shaking so hard afterward Don had to hold me up. I couldn't take it. The guard was bleeding. He'll live, of course, but seeing it made me sick.

I . . . it's probably not smart for me to keep writing this stuff down.

JOURNAL ENTRY: JOSEPHINE LEE, SEPTEMBER 25, 2069

Well, hello, journal. It's been an interesting four years, but I'm going to ignore all that and go right into the here and now. Life is so good! I need to write this down so I can look back and remember that.

Kanata-san has graciously agreed to perform our wedding ceremony. He's flying out from Princeton for it. We're paying, of course. Part of me wishes we were having the wedding here in Singapore, but then everyone back in Denver would have to spend money to come. I tried talking Mom into a virtual ceremony. That was a fun conversation!

Anyway, it's been easy enough to arrange everything from here. And the weather this time of year in Colorado is nicer. Listen to me convincing myself.

I'm loving the work at ECP so far. I feel like I can make a real difference here. The nonprofits in the US are so hobbled by the lack of support from the government. Singapore might be shit for democracy, but they have a strong sense of morality. It fits me. I'm thinking about going back to school for a year to boost my economic justice knowledge. ECP says they'll pay for it, so that would be a good deal.

Don, meanwhile, just wants to make money. I love him, and hey, money is good, but he's lost sight of why we got into law in the first place. I wish . . . well, he probably wouldn't agree with me. And I'm not being entirely fair. He volunteers at the clinics on the weekends when he has time.

I still talk to the Underground protest people, but I can't do the same work here that I did for them a couple years ago. Singapore's laws are too strict to risk being caught in the act of sabotage.

JOURNAL ENTRY: JOSEPHINE LEE, MARCH 15, 2070

Beware the ides of March! Not really: today is good news from outer space. The first private station is fully populated. A hundred permanent residents, with room for twenty rotating visitors. Everyone wants to go. Don and I applied. I hope we get a slot in the next few years. Right now they're not allowing pregnant women to travel even in the suborbital flights. Definitely won't let them go to space. We can put off having kids for a few more years, but I don't want to wait much past thirty. I've been using a new drug that enhances focus and thinking, and now they're saying it can increase the risk of fetal anomalies, especially with maternal age.

This is why I do what I do. This kind of shit they think they can get away with: pay someone to design the drug (hey, cheap and easy desktop biogenetics!), get it to market as fast as possible. Forget testing or government regulations, because who has time for that?

I have to admit, though, the stuff works like a dream. It took a few tries to get used to it, but now I'm hooked. I can read and analyze a legal brief in half the time. But the side effects . . . it's not so bad for this pill, but some of the others, especially the ones that heavily hit your gene expression, those are getting ugly. America and Europe are in such a hurry to catch up to Asia and North Africa that they're throwing their citizens' health under the bus. It's like they learned nothing from the crappy mech-tech of the fifties and sixties! You can't rush biology.

JOURNAL ENTRY: JOSEPHINE LEE, JULY 4, 2075

It's a hell of an Independence Day! Jun-ha loved the fireworks, and I love that he'll always have them on his birthday if we're in the USA. I can't believe how fast his first year has gone. Of course he picked the gold coin and the pill case during his doljabi. Don was thrilled. I wanted him to pick the thread. What good is wealth without a long, healthy life to enjoy it?

Ah, well, I refuse to talk about depressing shit today! Everyone at the party had a great time. The big news won them over, even though we aren't moving back for another six months. I'm going to miss Singapore. But working to influence the new regulatory laws in the USA feels too much like a promotion to say no, especially now that they're serious about it.

JOURNAL ENTRY: JOSEPHINE LEE, JULY 7, 2076

I'm pregnant again! I hope it's a girl this time. I love Jun to pieces, but it would be nice to have one of each. These past few months have been hard. I didn't think moving back would be such a shock, but we've been gone a long time. When I see what's happened to the suburbs, the living conditions . . . well, all the more reason my work is important, right?

Guess who got back in touch two weeks after my return? Yeah, the Underground didn't waste any time. Now they're after AI makers more than pill funders. They think the AIs (and bots) are driving people to use pills, so neutralizing the former will stop the latter. I call bullshit. Drugs, mechs, and these new pills (the ones with micro and nanomachines) are the proverbial genie in the bottle: you aren't getting it back in once you let it out.

I'm glad in a way that the protest scene has changed. Makes it easier to keep my distance from them. I want to help, but I'm a mother now. My agitator days are over.

JOURNAL ENTRY: JOSEPHINE LEE, SEPTEMBER 20, 2077

Who would've thought that my crowning achievement would come five months postpartum! We did it! We got NorthAm and the EU to agree to most of the regulations we wanted. No more untested pill designs on the market. Final approval for anything that affects gene expression has to go through a Biogenetics Administration body. Mech operators will have a *maximum* ten-hour workday, with guaranteed suit breaks every two hours *and* overtime pay after six hours! I fought hard for that one, may Uncle Phil rest in peace.

While I'm journaling, I should note that Soo-ha is such an easy baby! What a contrast to Jun. She's a champion sleeper. I have so much more energy this time.

I'm glad my babies won't have to grow up in the world we did. They'll be protected from exploitation.

JOURNAL ENTRY: JOSEPHINE LEE, OCTOBER 7, 2079

We had the specialist consult today for Jun. Both the medical AI and the attendant say they have no diagnosis yet. Big help. They're sending out his bloodwork for more analysis, and they want us to fund a gamified version of the problem. Of course we said yes, but there goes half the money we'd saved up for his education.

Poor boy has lost so much weight. He won't even eat his favorite sticky buns. His sister keeps pestering him to come play, but he's too grumpy.

And for the record, having a piece of software do most of the work while the human "doctor" does the talking is unsettling. What kind of world are my children going to inherit?

JOURNAL ENTRY: JOSEPHINE LEE, DECEMBER 22, 2079

Dear God, I'm not a Christian, but if you're there, please give us some good news for Christmas this year. Please.

JOURNAL ENTRY: JOSEPHINE LEE, DECEMBER 24, 2079

Fuck you, universe. My boy deserves a better life. It's almost the twenty-second century. We have to find a way to make him well.

Idiopathic, my ass.

JOURNAL ENTRY: JOSEPHINE LEE, FEBRUARY 18, 2080

The game-sourced results are in, and the news is that we may have a previously unidentified, genetic autoimmune disorder on our hands. Don wants to call it Jun-ha's Disease. I don't know that I want to immortalize my boy by his (hopefully temporary) condition.

It's a stupid thing to fight over, right? We seem to argue about everything now. Mom asked if we're going to split up. I told her that we're back to meetings at the temple and that listening to Kanata-san is helping us make peace.

As if that wasn't enough, I've been offered a position to direct the labor rights division at the EUBGA. We'd have to move, again, because they want me in Brussels.

JOURNAL ENTRY: JOSEPHINE LEE, JANUARY 2, 2081

Happy New Year!

2080 can eat a load of blanks. This is the year we turn our lives around. I can feel it.

Don is so wonderful. He pushed me to accept the EUBGA position, and I'm so happy about it. He and the kids are moving in three weeks. The past few months have been hard, bouncing back and forth to Europe, and missing out on Jun's initial treatments. He's been withdrawn and moody, always wanting Dad. It breaks my heart. Soo-ha makes up for it as best she can. Poor baby. I hope she isn't getting lost in all the attention we give to her big brother.

My career is going well, but I feel like my home life is out of control. It's in Don's capable hands, of course, but even with two centuries of women's liberation, the world still expects the mother to carry the emotional load at home. Some of the looks I get when I tell people about Jun-ha's condition. Bunch of zeros. Who are they to judge me?

I do enough of that to myself. Guilt is the worst maternal burden.

JOURNAL ENTRY: JOSEPHINE LEE, AUGUST 18, 2083

It's official—the Indo-Chinese Space Station has declared independence and is now called Eko-Yi. Those blankers don't realize that squirming out of the laws *made for their own protection* is going to lead to massive long-term problems.

They want to start families up there. They want to test new

radiation-hardening drugs and pills on themselves with no Earth oversight.

Now we're having intense arguments in the EUBGA about whether to reduce or at least modify our regulations before ISS II revolts. As if we're doing this to harm them instead of the exact opposite. At least the other space stations aren't complaining . . . yet.

It's starting a domino effect here on the ground. I can see it happening, though my colleagues don't want to admit it. Even with mech-suits, people are getting pushed out of manual labor jobs by the new generation of WAIs and bots. They don't need people when the AI can make equally good decisions—and faster.

Meanwhile, my own child tops the list of recipients for emergent mech and pill solutions for his problems. I'm scared of putting him in full mech-tech. I can't help but think of Uncle Phil. I know the designs have improved since then, but still, I don't trust them. We've run out of options, though. Assistive walking devices aren't enough anymore. The newest pills can RNA-edit on the fly, and other families are finding success with it, but not us. What are we missing? If we had more data . . . or more interest (or more money!) . . . we could isolate the faulty genes and hire someone to design a Jun-specific therapy.

Soo-ha likes to play with Jun-ha's old walkers. Don thinks it makes Jun feel better. I'm not so sure. He's such a sweetheart and so mature for being only nine—he wouldn't tell his younger sister off if it meant hurting her feelings. They've grown a lot these past few years. My babies. I wish I could wave a magic wand and make everything right for them.

JOURNAL ENTRY: JOSEPHINE LEE, JULY 4, 2087

Happy birthday to my teenager. How I wish you'd chosen the string at your first birthday.

Nothing is working. God help us. Three different research teams have told us that Jun-ha has anywhere from four to six months left in his life. Don wants to fund another group.

I'm so tired of it. We should save the money and make our lives—especially Jun-ha's—as good as we can with the time we have left. I can't keep failing him like this, pretending that we can fix everything. I can't even keep my own department from imploding.

He still loves watching the fireworks.

JOURNAL ENTRY: JOSEPHINE LEE, AUGUST 7, 2087

Desperate times call for desperate measures. I can't say more without self-incrimination and the risk of losing my job, but I wanted to note the occasion here in case it works. If we can keep Jun-ha from getting worse, any sacrifice will be worthwhile.

I'm glad we're in Europe. This would be much harder to do from the USA. Or Singapore.

This is our last chance. Please, please, please let it work.

JOURNAL ENTRY: JOSEPHINE LEE, NOVEMBER 21, 2087

Snow fell this morning.

The flakes melted away.

Gone.

Like my boy, Jun-ha.

JOURNAL ENTRY: JOSEPHINE LEE, FEBRUARY 2, 2088

It's strange, when I look back on my life, how some things happened exactly as I imagined, while others I couldn't begin to conceive of.

We lost Don in the fog of Jun's death. Soo-ha and I are in Brussels, together, but Don left for his parents' house. He said it was to spend their last years together, and he's probably right about that. They're in Reno now that they've retired. He wanted to take Soo-ha, but that girl is clamped tight to me the way Jun was to Don. I'm glad—it would've been horrible to lose them all.

Everyone warned me that marriages don't always survive the death of a child. Such remote, clinical words. Kanata-san was better. He reminded me of a noble truth: life is suffering, and grief a natural part of that cycle. He said that Don must find his own path through his pain, that the greatest gift we can give one another is to accept our differences and wait for the other to emerge. But we may not be the same people on the other side, and that too is part of life.

So.

Part of me hates Don for running away, but I try to hold on to Kanata-san's words. If only for poor Soo-ha, who is so angry and confused and lost right now. She's almost eleven, on the cusp of puberty. For her sake, I will be strong.

JOURNAL ENTRY: JOSEPHINE LEE, AUGUST 8, 2088

I had to cut half the department today.

I'm not ready for this level of pain, not yet. It's almost as bad as losing another child. Everyone who worked for me had the best intentions at heart. They don't deserve this.

It's a funding problem. Money flows to market needs, and right now, the bot and WAI industries are booming. Which means that's where people need to apply more scrutiny and regulation. Our oversight extends only to biotech. The BGA has done so well, they say, that our legacy will prevent labor abuses for decades to come.

Such a pile of blanker bullshit.

The world will change, and we'll have to rewrite everything. You can't anticipate loopholes when the walls haven't been built. Look at the gigsters. Scrabbling for a living with no guarantee of employment. Working as supervisors for bots but getting paid piecemeal. How long until the next generation decides they don't need a human holding a WAI's hand anymore? How long until nobody's worried about the AIs making a bad decision? What work will they have left?

JOURNAL ENTRY: JOSEPHINE LEE, APRIL 18, 2090

My daughter is now a teenager. I don't like where she's heading in life—some new trend the kids are calling VeeMod. Apparently it's shorthand for voluntary modification, and it goes beyond mech-suits to where you incorporate the machine into your body. Basically, half human, half machine. They used to call that a cyborg, but the kids don't want to use old terminology.

Of course I haven't given her permission to do anything permanent to her body. She already resents me for restricting her pill use, but I don't know what triggered Jun-ha's disease, and I want to prolong Soo-ha's health as long as I can. This is the baby who chose a stick and a circuit board, after all.

Don won the lawsuit against SK Partners for the mishandling of Jun-ha's data. Not that winning brings back our child, but it seems to give Don some measure of peace. I can understand his need to do something, but I feel dirty taking their money. My anger won't be bought off. The compensation—I wondered at Jun-ha never living long enough to become rich. Now I understand.

What is Soo-ha's fate? She chose a weapon and she chose tech. I know it's all superstition, but I don't like it. It scares me.

JOURNAL ENTRY: JOSEPHINE LEE, AUGUST 18, 2090

Here's an interesting twist: Don is moving to Eko-Yi Station. We've been living separate lives for so long that it doesn't feel like it, but technically we're still married. I thought he'd discuss something that monumental with me first. Instead, he consulted Kanata-san, who sent me a long letter shortly after I finished talking to Don. Kanata-san apologized profusely for keeping me in the dark, but he said he had to honor Don's wishes.

Soo-ha wants to go with her dad.

I had a good scream over that news.

I don't know what the hell I want. I want my life back the way it was supposed to be. Jun-ha should be in his junior year of high school and starting to think about college. Soo-ha should be an eager and awkward teenager. Don and I should be living together in a house with a dog or something.

Instead, I live in a hive with no yard and no privacy. My husband is absent. My only living child wants to abandon me. My work is for shit, all our regulations and laws going obsolete or backfiring before they can have a real, positive effect.

Maybe Kanata-san is right. Maybe I should give up and start fresh. Can't go more clean-slate than moving to a station colony. He says he can sponsor all three of us as a family unit.

JOURNAL ENTRY: JOSEPHINE LEE, DECEMBER 1, 2090

So it's settled.

I'm leaving Earth.

Don and I will somehow have to learn to live with each other—and the angry teenager in our midst. I can't help but feel that I've failed everyone, Soo-ha especially. The things she says . . . I know she's lashing out, but there are shards of truth embedded in her words, and they hurt.

I'll be working as the Eko-Yi's only bioethicist. They need one, so says Kanata-san, for whatever it is they're doing. Now that the colony stations are mostly independent of Earth's jurisdiction, all we hear or see is what they tell us. Guess I'll find out the truth once I'm there.

JOURNAL ENTRY: JOSEPHINE LEE, MAY 17, 2091

On arrival at Eko-Yi, we'll get new names in line with Neo-Buddhist dharma. We can choose or we can ask one of the monks to give us one, so of course I asked Kanata-san. So did Don, but Soo-ha wanted to choose her own. Something more "fierce," says my girl.

My new name will be Ao Tara. He says I will understand why if I meditate on it long enough.

We launch in a week. A week!

CHAPTER 15

WELGA

18. We build AIs to solve problems that we define. We have not given them a sense of self-actualization, and the oligarchy manipulates our fear to prevent us from wanting to. We wrap this in the guise of ethics, as if our current enslavement of machine intelligences is acceptable until we give them the desire to be free.

—*The Machinehood Manifesto, March 20, 2095*

"Holy shit!" Welga shrank the journal.

Her exclamation woke Olafson. He cocked a bleary eyebrow at her.

"According to her journal, Josephine Lee is also Ao Tara, the station council leader on Eko-Yi!"

Olafson's gaze blanked for a couple of seconds as he accessed his feed. "The one whose talk had similarities to the Machinehood's manifesto. And Josephine Lee is . . . Jun-ha Park's mother."

Welga tried to keep the excitement out of her voice. "There must be a connection between the station and the Machinehood.

Look at the evidence we have now." She ticked off her fingers with each item. "Rare DNA segments that match this kid's. His mother, who's now a monk spouting philosophy similar to the manifesto. Smart-metal manufactured on a space station."

"That's the bones, but we're missing the connective tissue. What's the motive? What holds those pieces together?"

"If Josephine Lee is Ao Tara, she might have been in on the whole thing. She's canny enough that she gave nothing away in her journal, but she hinted at doing unethical things she didn't write down. What if *she* traded her son's DNA for biotech from the al-Muwahhidun, using his doctors as her connection? She was desperate to save his life. A portion of that DNA then ends up in a Machinehood operative."

Olafson shrugged. "It's a good story, but we need proof."

"We're about to get some."

They had another hour before reaching Dr. Mitchell Smith's house. Welga took a quick scan of her friends and family. Luis and Papa had begun to repair the house. Her brother looked grim. Watching her father's painstaking motions made her heart hurt. He should've hired a bot to do the work or at least to help. Nithya was putting away birthday party decorations . . . from Carma's party. *Damn. I forgot to send her a gift.*

"Por Qué," Welga subvocalized, "put two hundred coin in Carma's tip jar and send her a well-rated birthday card that's appropriate for an eight-year-old. Sign it 'Love, Aunt Welga.'"

"Would you like to transfer the coin from your tip jar or your bank account?"

"My jar."

A quick glance at her balance showed little movement since the incident at the refinery. No surprise, considering she'd been inside a secured facility since then. Government work didn't earn much from the public. News reporters liked to follow people like her and Olafson, but they couldn't ethically tip government employees.

"The transfer will be held until the exchange opens," Por Qué said. "All coin is currently backlogged due to the market freezes."

A glance at the top-rated news feed items confirmed this. The attacks by the Machinehood had spawned a vicious cycle between funding and production. Distribution problems had quickly followed, and specialty locations like hospitals reported a shortage of customized pills and drugs.

"Damn, have you seen the headlines?" she said.

Olafson nodded. "Stock markets don't like uncertainty, and nobody knows what to expect right now."

"People are overreacting. Dumbasses are doing the Machinehood's work for them!"

"Isn't that the caliph's way? You should know that better than most, Ramírez."

"I'm not so sure. He would directly target infrastructure and destroy it upstream. He cuts supply lines. Starves people into submission. Only then do they get scared and eventually cave to his demands."

"The way he works, he can't hit global infrastructure from his borders, so he's flipped the script. Fear first, then let the people destroy their own resources. The general public is scared of a sentient artificial intelligence, remember? They don't suspect al-Muwahhidun. They're legitimately worried that every WAI-powered device could be a potential tool of the Machinehood."

Welga frowned. "And we're encouraging that bullshit."

"It's the best way to avoid tipping our hand. If the al-Muwahhidun suspect how much we know, they'll call back their people, and we'll lose any chance of a capture."

A multi-container truck rumbled past them. Once upon a time, a distractible human would have driven it. The risks people had lived with, especially in the days before a pill could heal half your body, sent a shiver down Welga's spine. How long before the panic-induced shortages brought the world back to that state? And what would the Machinehood do next? Because no way in hell would all bot and WAI production cease in the next twelve hours.

The car moved off the expressway. Olafson glanced at Welga.

"Let me send you an outfit that looks more . . . agent-like," he said.

A sober, charcoal-gray pantsuit design appeared in her visual. She fought the urge to wince as the cloth reformatted across her tender new skin. The basic version had been more comfortable and about as boring as the suit. Her skin still showed mottled pink patches. Getting it back to brown wasn't a process that could be accelerated—yet. Somebody must be funding that effort.

She took a duo-zip along with her daily regimen of microbials, juvers, and disinfectants as recommended by medical.

Olafson arched a brow. "You going to be okay?"

"I'm not taking the pain drugs so my head stays clear. My forearm splints should release by our arrival time." She angled her chin at the outline of the weapon in his pocket. "You ready to use that?"

"I'm hoping I don't have to, but I do my hours at the practice range."

Welga carried three types of weapons—a regular gun, a sticky gun, and a tranquilizer gun. Olafson had only the third, probably a good thing under the circumstances. Defensive fire ought to remain her job.

∘—∘—∘

Mitchell Smith lived in one of those pseudo-organic communal living spaces that some called "revived" suburban housing. Century-old static houses stood in a state of disrepair worse than her childhood home, their roofs missing tiles like gaps in teeth. Dynamic, blox-based rooms stuck out in odd places. Fences that used to separate the properties lay in pieces. Windows had been replaced in haphazard fashion with solar glass or left open to the elements. People called it outside-in living. Maximum nature, minimal privacy.

Bots were everywhere—moving with purpose, parked, or standing in half-broken states. Signposts proclaimed the area a "bot sanctuary" and laid out terms that prohibited any violence against the machines. They drove past a two-story house whose sprawling yard was covered with first-generation kitchens and obsolete single-purpose units—floor cleaners, clothes folders, washers, dryers—as well as broken-winged drones, and even some rusted vehicles.

"What the hell do you think they're saving these for?" Welga said. "Memorabilia?"

Olafson snorted. "I don't know, but they must love the Machinehood's manifesto if this is how they treat bots."

"Seems like a waste not to recycle them into functional units."

They approached the house where Smith lived. A small group of children played on the weedy lawn, getting an early start to beat the day's heat. They stopped to stare at her and Olafson when they exited the car, the only powered vehicle in sight. A dog barked, its tail wagging, as an older child held it by the collar. The front doorway stood empty of an actual door.

A lean man wearing pants and shirt in basic beige, with graying blond hair and blue eyes, approached them when they entered.

"Please be welcome. I'm Mitchell Smith. We have some seating in the kitchen, if you'll follow me, and a privacy threshold there." He ushered them with a pale, age-spotted hand.

The entryway to the kitchen had a zapper, but the tray held

only a few microdrones. This neighborhood had little attraction for the tipping public. A kitchen unit had replaced the old appliances, and the cabinets had been converted into open hydroponic trays. Piped sunlight shone from fiber-optic tubes and filled the room with natural color. Mint, oregano, and thyme scented the air.

Welga sat and slipped off her shoes. The soles of her feet cooled as they rested on the grass floor. Olafson deployed their privacy measures—bug detectors, signal jammers, and voice cancellers. Smith raised an eyebrow but kept silent as Olafson worked. They'd advised the doctor on when to expect them and what agency they represented, but not their reason for coming.

"Thank you for taking the time to speak with us, Dr. Smith," Olafson began. "This conversation will be recorded and held confidential. Do you understand?"

"I do."

"Did you treat Jun-ha Park?"

"I did."

"And as part of that, did you collect his genetic information?"

"Of course. There's no other way to treat a person in modern times. I anonymized it before releasing it into the public record, since he was a minor, but his case was unusual, rare. We needed to have as many people see it as possible."

"It must have been difficult," Olafson said, "treating a child whose chances of survival were so slim."

Smith's gaze went distant. "Yes, especially considering his mother. She was a bioethicist and wanted to stay within well-tested bounds. Once they left the country, European standards of care took precedence, and then . . . I'm sure you already know that Jun passed away and that a lawsuit followed."

"We're aware," Welga said. "So you weren't involved in his care at that stage?"

Smith shook his head. "I don't know what happened to change

his mother's mind. She was adamant against using experimental biogenetics on her son, but that final course of treatment was exactly that. I would have counseled her against it—strongly."

"Did you participate in the experimental therapy?"

"Absolutely not. I heard about it after the fact, during the legal proceedings."

"You published papers with two other authors. Did either of them work on it?"

"Not that I know of. We collaborated because they had local cases who were similar to my patient. I've heard rumors from colleagues in Europe that the experimental tech was originally developed in North Africa. I don't know if they disclosed that as part of the lawsuit."

Welga nodded calmly to hide her disappointment. If Smith was telling the truth, he wouldn't be their link to the al-Muwahhidun. Judging by his demeanor as well as his house, he hadn't profited off black-market sales, which meant he probably wasn't lying.

"Do you know who conducted the treatment in Europe?" Olafson asked.

Mitchell Smith shook his head. "I'll send you what I have, but if Jun's parents went to the gray market, my information may not help you. Can't you access the documents from the suit against SK Partners? That should have names."

"We're working on it," Welga lied, though she caught Olafson's gaze. He could make the request. "What about Jun's younger sister?" she asked. "Was she symptomatic as well?"

"No, not at all. We tried using her genome to correct for Jun's disorder, but we weren't able to isolate all the relevant genes. Interestingly, they both showed markers for strong adaptation to mechanization. That's one of the reasons we tried mech-tech as a treatment option for Jun."

"What kind of markers?" Welga kept her voice even, but her

heart leaped at *adaptation to mechanization*. Could they be the rare DNA segments that matched the blood from the Machinehood operative's fragment?

"Genes that allow the body to accept foreign objects, both implanted and interfaced, with a lower likelihood of rejection. Jun and his sister had that in common, but his autoimmune disorder overwhelmed them. Ultimately, his body rejected the mech-tech and itself."

"Could we get a copy of his sister's genomic record?"

"I'll need authorization to release that, as she was a minor at the time. We've never published it."

"Naturally. You've been very ethical," Olafson said.

The conversation paused as their agents transferred the required information.

"Por Qué," Welga subvocalized, "check the incoming genome against the special segments from Jun-ha Park and the blood sample."

Her agent popped an image into her visual ten seconds later: the android, Jun-ha Park, and his sister all had perfect matches in those segments. She copied the information to Olafson with the message: *These are the same sequences found in the sample from the dead Machinehood operative in Chennai! A triple match. No way that's a coincidence.*

Smith cocked his head at them. "What exactly is this about? I assumed you were here to follow up on the malpractice suit, but I don't see how the sister's genome is relevant."

Olafson smiled. "I'm afraid we can't disclose the nature of our investigation, but thank you for your time and cooperation. Would you mind if we look around your house?"

"Well, no, but—I mean, of course, you're welcome to. To look around," Smith stammered. "I have an examination room in the back, where I see patients. It's locked, but I can open it."

"Yes, please," said Olafson.

As Welga followed Olafson and Smith, a message lit up her visual field: *The Machinehood sees all. We are prepared.*

She exchanged a glance with Olafson.

"Get the kids away from the house!" she yelled. She grabbed the doctor's arm and shoved him toward Olafson. "No time to explain!"

Olafson pulled the stumbling man toward the front door and scooped up an errant child along the way. Welga ran up the stairs, checking every room and closet. She listened as Olafson corralled everyone outside.

"Make sure you stay in the middle part of the road," he instructed. "Dr. Smith, is anyone else in the house?"

"My partner, Kevin!"

"Ramírez—"

"I'll find him," Welga replied, already moving.

Kevin lay in the back bedroom, his frail form and a nearby wheeled care-bot telling her all she needed to know. Welga scooped the man up under his shoulders and knees.

His eyelids flew open. "What—"

"Emergency," Welga huffed as she ran down and out with him.

Olafson was herding the children farther from the house. Two little ones wailed in protest or fear. She and Kevin joined them as explosives roared to life. The ground shook. All of them cried out as glass and debris rained over them. Drone swarms gathered overhead in the aftermath. Sirens wailed in the distance.

Welga watched the feeds as they waited for emergency services. Mitchell Smith held his partner's hand and consoled the tearful children.

"Was it the Machinehood?" asked a wide-eyed preteen.

"We don't know," Olafson said.

Yes, we do. Olafson's look inside had told her he'd received the same message. Somehow the Machinehood knew they were here. She examined Smith's face. His expression and posture implied the same level of shock as everyone else. He hadn't expected this, and he hadn't given her and Olafson away.

"Where's Jacqueline?" asked another child.

"She arrived yesterday," Smith explained to Welga and Olafson. He glanced over the crowd of people emerging from nearby homes, then turned back with worry lining his face. "One of my transient teenagers, on her way south to Florida. I don't see her."

"I'm going to check for other explosives," Welga said. She projected so the crowd would hear her. "Everyone stay here! I'll search for Jacqueline, too. Dr. Smith, if you could highlight her in some recent feeds, that would be helpful."

Smoke belched from Smith's house as flames began to lick the upper story. Welga gave the structure a wide margin in case of falling debris. She moved down the right side yard. When had the Machinehood set the explosive charges? While they were talking to Smith—which would imply that they had tracked her and Olafson to the house—or before they arrived? The Machinehood had access to public medical records. What if they came here thinking Smith would hide them because of his connection to Josephine Lee? Or maybe he was a convenient pawn. No one knew what the Machinehood operatives looked like. The one in the refinery could pass for an older adolescent. What if they'd hidden here in plain sight?

Welga sent Olafson another encrypted message: *Maybe the Machinehood got here before we did.*

He replied: *The missing Jacqueline, perhaps?* Olafson had followed the same train of thought as her own.

"Por Qué, activate my camo-detector," Welga subvocalized. "Place marks based on my focal point when I hard-blink."

Her military tech might be old, but it was better than nothing. Camouflage suits relied on visual perception tricks that a good image-processing WAI could counteract. As Welga's lenses adjusted, a blur moved in her peripheral vision. She kept her gaze straight. The blur went behind a hedge in the backyard of the adjacent house. Welga turned to face the intact structure, pretending to examine the wall for explosives.

Local law enforcement, including the bomb squad, showed up on her visual overlay, still eight kilometers away. Two ex-factors wearing brilliantly colored uniforms popped up, too, only three kilometers from the house. *Damn.* She didn't need them interfering, but she couldn't call them off without giving her intention away to the operative. Three more meters and she'd be in range to fire a tranquilizer at the blur's last marked location.

The searing heat and flames triggered memories from the refinery: the smoke in the back of her throat, the singed face of the Machinehood's operative, their lips moving. Those brown eyes boring into hers—would she see them again here?

In a rush, she recalled their words: *You didn't attack me, and I follow the path.*

What path? Buddhists followed an eightfold path. What did Neo-Buddhists believe in? Ao Tara said they wanted peace. Josephine Lee's journal mentioned nonviolence. The al-Muwahhidun only acted defensively.

She sent a message to Olafson: *Did the Machinehood operatives always make the first move?*

He bounced it to headquarters. A minute later, he sent back: *The answer is mixed. They attacked on the initial wave, but after that, someone else shot at them first. Hell of a thing to notice, Ramirez! What made you think of it?*

I'll explain later. Welga sidled toward the blurred spot as it shifted behind a rusted swing set. She hard-blinked a new mark.

"Por Qué, do I still have that blanket from the Santiago job?"

"In your outer left jacket pocket," her agent replied.

Welga pulled out the metallic mesh. It could pass for a heat shield, but if she wore it, her own comms might get blocked. She shook it open and draped it across her back, like a cape. She caught a glimpse of herself in a news feed. Greasy hair in a practical ponytail, basic-issue agency suit. No one would mistake her for a superhero.

"This side looks clear. I'm going to check the yard," she announced out loud.

A broadcast message to all in the vicinity flashed across her visual: *HOLSTER ALL WEAPONS. DO NOT FIRE. DO NOT ENGAGE IN CLOSE-QUARTERS COMBAT.* Alerts erupted in her periphery.

"Por Qué, mute all public channels and visuals," Welga subvocalized.

She moved at an angle past the play set. The blur shifted, too, heading out of her periphery and toward the burning house. Welga turned slowly, scanning the surroundings like she didn't know what she was looking for.

Let me get a little closer.

Welga took four steps. The blur froze.

Mark.

Move.

Closer.

Almost . . . there!

Welga whipped the blackout material off and threw it at the blurry spot. It draped over something at head height. She leaped across the meters separating them and wrapped her arms around them.

"Mesh sealed," Por Qué announced.

The smart-fabric formed a stretchy straitjacket that snugged the operative's limbs to their body. They were short, barely reaching Welga's chin, with a slight frame. She lifted them and waddled toward the increasingly large group on the street. The weight wouldn't have bothered her if her healing skin hadn't tugged so much.

"At last you understood." The voice that came through the wrap was muffled, with a high register. "I thought you'd give me a reason to end your life today, especially after I provoked you. Poor Dr. Smith. I'm sorry I repaid his generosity by destroying the house."

"Who are you?" Welga said. She held tight to the operative. "What are you doing here?"

The onlookers stood quietly and listened to their exchange. Based on the statistics in Welga's visual, so did a significant number of adult Americans in their region.

"I am Dakini, and I needed a place to stay. I bring the liberation."

"Fuck! Are you going to explode?"

Dakini shook—laughing. "No, you haven't even scratched me. I'm not close to dying. Also, this covering blocks my comms, which means they can't trigger the switch."

Christ, the Machinehood puts a kill switch in their operatives!

"Are you human or AI?" one of the exfactors yelled from a rooftop, their voice echoing from a nearby dronecam.

"I'm Dakini. We're human and AI and bot, all coexisting in one body. The Machinehood doesn't recognize a difference, as written in our manifesto. You failed to stop harming humanity. You continued the production and consumption of biogenetic material. You persisted in your reliance on WAI and bot slave labor. Now you'll face the consequences we promised."

Welga tightened her arms around Dakini, as if that would stop whatever was about to happen. She scanned every camera view in her visual but saw nothing interesting.

"Olafson, what's going on?" Welga subvocalized. "Anything from headquarters? Por Qué, enable my public comms."

Olafson's voice sounded in her ear. "A few new reports of attacks from overseas. Explosions at manufacturing sites, same as before. We're the only ones with a live capture so far. Headquarters wants us back *now*."

"Understood."

Police officers in mech-suits and bomb-detection bots fanned out between the houses.

"You won't find anyone here but me," Dakini said. "No more explosives."

"We're getting reports—" Olafson's voice cut off midsentence.

Welga's visual froze. The video streams dropped out. The news-feed text jittered and vanished.

"Loss of network," Por Qué said in a mechanical tone.

Welga turned to Olafson. "How's your . . . ?" She didn't bother to finish the question. The baffled frowns on every face answered it.

Voices rose all around them. Swarms drifted and crashed into one another. Welga flung an arm up to shield her face from the debris. In the clear blue sky, high above, bright lights flashed like stars and trailed across the sky. The network constellations—high-altitude drones and low Earth-orbit satellites alike—were falling.

CHAPTER 16

NITHYA

Type of Work: Content Verification
Estimated Time: 4 hours
Payment: 2.57 Global Trading Coin
Description: Review instructional videos for high-density balcony gardens to verify that content stays on-topic and is free from harmful language or imagery. Evaluate clarity of communication, audio, and video.

—*MicroWork Job Listings, Quality Rating 3.7/5*

"Amma! Amma!"

Carma's excited shout pulled Nithya from the latest Synaxel simulation results. She'd been grasping at every free minute to work, even without flow, to make up for Zeli's absence. It took her mind off the silent treatment from Luis. *He has every right to be angry at you. Be glad he didn't file for divorce on the spot.* Would he leave her? If they divorced, he could stay in Phoenix and help his father. What if he didn't come back? What would she tell Carma? On top of all that, the ever-present threat of the Machinehood loomed. They'd attacked again, and funding around the globe had started to dry up. Welga and Connor had gotten caught up in another firefight. At least it had happened close to their home this time.

"The cake came!" Carma said.

Nithya brushed her work from her visual and exited her alcove.

Carma ran to her and twirled. "Look at my braids!" she crowed in Tamil. "Bhairavi Paatti did them!"

Slender garlands of fat, white jasmine buds wove through two braids that merged into one. Nithya leaned over and inhaled. The divine must move through jasmine. What else could explain its heady scent?

"Very nice," Nithya said, also in Tamil. They spoke English only if Luis was around.

"A person brought the cake today. Isn't that funny?"

Nithya tried to smile. She didn't tell Carma that people's paranoia about the Machinehood explained the unusual delivery method. A round cake sat on the dining table, resplendent with white frosting and a large number eight outlined in red icing roses.

"Do you like it?" Nithya asked.

"It's so beautiful!"

"Good. Let's keep it in the fridge until the party."

As Nithya entrusted the cake to the kitchen WAI, Sita spoke in her ear. "You have a high-priority call request from an unknown person regarding your Synaxel database access."

"Aiyo!" Of all the inconvenient times!

"What is it?" Aunty asked.

"Sorry, Chitthi, I have to take this call."

"But Amma, it's time to decorate for my party!" Carma protested.

"I'll be quick. While you're waiting, you can call your papa. He's probably still awake."

Luis owed Carma a birthday wish anyway. Let him struggle with putting on a happy face for their child, too. Nithya hurried into the alcove, turned on privacy mode, and took the call. The earnest face of a light-skinned, middle-aged man with sandy blond hair appeared in her visual. She blinked in surprise, having expected it to be the lawyer from USBGA. This was not Felix Anderson.

"Good you took the call," this man said without any greeting.

He spoke English with an accent she couldn't place. South American or European, perhaps.

"I don't have a lot of time, but I came across your blocked access requests." His eyes shifted to the side and back. "Synaxel isn't letting you see that data because they're under investigation and they don't want that disclosed. Their lead bioethicist quit a year ago." He lowered his voice and leaned toward the camera. "This goes way beyond Synaxel. I gather from your latest queries that you're beginning to understand that, too. Your agent will receive a file from an anonymous source. Read it. You're a smart person. Follow the bread crumbs in there."

He ended the call before Nithya could say a word. *This is too much right now.* Her mind felt like it was on the opposite of flow, whatever that would be. Mush? A drug that made it impossible to hold on to a thought.

Sita spoke in her ear. "Do you authorize receipt of a file from an anonymous sender?"

"Yes," Nithya said.

Part of her wanted to take a pill and delve into the file. Would it solve the mystery of Welga's malady? Or was it malicious, something from the Machinehood? But that was paranoid thinking. Why would that group care about her or her inquiries into Synaxel?

Never mind all that right now! It's Carma's birthday.

"Sita, break down my alcove and make some small tables and chairs for the children."

"Are you finished with work?" Carma said.

"Yes. Let's decorate for the party."

"Papa didn't answer, but he sent me this picture. Look!"

Oscar and Luis stood in front of an interior wall with a still-wet coat of paint, their faces contorted into silliness. Luis had air-scrawled *Happy Birthday* and drawn a heart around their image.

Aunty grumbled in Hindi to hide the meaning from Carma. "He could have sung a song at least."

"He must be asleep or on a gig," Nithya replied, also in Hindi.

Gig didn't have a translation from English, so Carma picked up the word. "Papa is always working."

"And you should be happy for that," Nithya chided. "It helps put food in your mouth. Go change your dress, Carma. You can wear your new pavadai again when we finish putting up decorations. It's made from static silk. I don't want you to get it dirty."

After Carma closed the bathroom door, Aunty launched. "I don't know why you defend your husband's lifestyle. I suppose that's a modern woman's duty, eh? To earn the money, take care of the children, and support her husband. What kind of world we are living in! Do you know how we had to fight to stay unmarried? Even though we could earn our keep, our parents thought it was too scandalous or too dangerous or some nonsense. And here you are, giving it all up."

Nithya held up a hand. "Enough, Chitthi, please."

Her aunt's expression turned shrewd. "What's the matter? Did you have a fight with Luis?"

"And if we did, so what? He's my husband. I decided to marry him, and that's enough talk about this. I have to get the flat ready for the party."

"Okay, do whatever you please." Her aunt settled into the sofa and blanked into her visual.

At least Nithya would have silence from that corner. She made sure Sita had the contact information for all the party guests' agents, then opened a tall storage cabinet. Where were last year's static decorations? Nowhere in reach. Rather than wasting energy making a step stool, she dragged over a dining chair and stood on it. Every coin counted now. She pulled out a dusty box with neatly packed party items. As she stuck a birthday banner to the wall, she studiously ignored the newly arrived file glowing in the lower corner of her visual. *Tonight, after the party, I'll look it over.*

By the time Nithya placed the last item of garbage into the bin, the other two members of the household had fallen asleep. Bhairavi Chitthi snored. Carma cuddled a new furpet bot from a wealthy school chum. Thank God they'd paid her school fees through the year end; otherwise Carma's access to the top-tier educational program would end.

The birthday party had been a success. Other than Carma's occasional pouts at her father's absence, the festivities provided Nithya with a good distraction from her other problems. The cake tasted as delicious as it looked, and the children—in person and virtual—had enjoyed the games Nithya had chosen.

She washed her hands, took a mug of tea from the kitchen dispenser, and sat at the table. She propped her feet up on the opposite chair and flexed them. Hosting parties took more energy than they had in her younger days. She blew on the hot, milky liquid, sipped, then placed a flow under her tongue.

"Sita, send the anonymous file *qxu34ty38208zz* to the printer."

"At the minimum readable text size, this document collection will require eighty-two percent of the raw pulp in the printer. Do you still wish to print it?"

"Yes."

Opening the file in her visual meant that a hacker could more easily gain access. Of course, any determined person would be able to crack her passwords and the file's encryption, but there was no sense making their task simpler. Nithya pulled the warm sheaf from the dispenser.

She read:

To my colleagues and superiors,

With a heavy heart, I tender my resignation from the European Union Biogenetics Administration, effective December 20, 2090. It's been my great pleasure to serve with this team of intelligent, passionate, and highly qualified bioethicists and policy makers for the past eleven years, but recent events have left me with a sense of frustration.

I have spent my life working to ensure the safety, efficacy, and accessibility of biochemical and biogenetic compounds for human consumption. The decades of unregulated development left deep scars on societies around the world, marks that we bear today, and yet they have faded sufficiently that oversight and regulation lack the enforcement that makes such policies effective.

The recent exposure of problematic designs issued to consumers by funders such as Kwan-Shin, Synaxel, and Gynitek have left me disappointed and disgruntled. These businesses have short-cut the testing process, flouted the spirit of bioethical regulations, and knowingly put people in harm's way for no reason other than profit motive. They rushed out custom pill designs to those most vulnerable because they had the lowest cost margins. This in spite of the returns they gain from mass-market generics.

My team discovered clear evidence of negligence leading to bodily harm, and yet this governing body (and others) are unable to take action against these funders because the legislative and executive branches are too corrupt or cowardly to move against them. A regulatory body is useless without sharp teeth to enforce its dictates. We can issue recommendations until satellites fall from the sky, but to what end? I cannot stand by and watch as we repeat the mistakes of our parents and grandparents.

I am under no illusion that one woman's indignant resignation will change the world, but I have fought my entire life for these ends, and I can only hope that my reputation is sufficient to stir others to action in my stead.

Respectfully,
Josephine Lee

The passage "discovered clear evidence of negligence" was highlighted. The next page contained a report titled, "A Review of Simulation Data from Custom Pill Design and Testing." Nithya read the introductory paragraph.

The exhaustive testing required by International Code 562.1, for intracellular nanomachine and drug delivery systems, commonly knows as micropills, is not being applied to the newer classes of these that involve algorithmic and gene-based customization for individuals and small groups. At the time the original statutes were written, such personalized capability did not exist or was not practical to implement. This review will show evidence from funded projects that cost-cutting measures led to insufficient testing. Although this body has not been able to follow up with every consumer of custom pills, a significant number have filed Requests for Investigation due to health problems that correlate with outcomes shown by the limited testing done during pill development.

Pages upon pages of summaries and reports from projects around the world followed the damning introduction. Nithya reeled at the number of cases where the test simulations were inconclusive at best and potentially dangerous at worst. *Bloody hell.* Synaxel must have blocked her data access because it showed problematic designs being sold on the market. She would bet the last of her money that this explained the synaptic fatigue afflicting Welga.

Nithya swallowed a gulp of tea, grateful for the soothing warmth as it slid down her throat. It counteracted the roulette ride of anguish her life had taken lately.

Focus. Keep your mind on the report.

She wasn't used to doing analysis without her agent, but she didn't dare to access Sita for this. A stranger had sent the document. If he had noticed her queries, then others—more dangerous and powerful others—might pay attention to her, too.

Nithya blinked as sleep blurred her eyes. How could she feel tired when so much adrenaline coursed through her blood? The document in her hands could prove intentional negligence and false claims on the part of the biggest drug and pill funders in the world. And yet, the resignation letter from Josephine Lee indicated that they couldn't be prosecuted, not under the laws of

2090. Nithya doubted much had changed since then, but with the right information, perhaps lives could be saved, including Welga's.

She called up the last version of the simulation game framework from Zeli in her visual. She paged through the malfeasance data, pausing whenever Synaxel appeared in the text, until she found an entry on custom zips—a summary, no numbers. She needed raw data. She kept turning pages, unwilling to give up hope until the last . . . and there, four sheets before the bottom of the stack, an appendix had the details she needed.

Nithya entered the parameters from the paper into Zeli's tool and set any unspecified variables to scan across typical ranges. The simulation wouldn't finish until morning. She could do nothing more for now, and knew she ought to sleep. Her body was still recovering from pregnancy.

She stood, stretched, and tiptoed past the beds to open the balcony door. The patter of rain interleaved the space between her aunt's snores. She stepped out and filled her lungs as a stray breeze broke through the hives of Chennai, carrying with it the perfume of night-blooming jasmine mingled with petrichor. The primal scents eased the tension in her neck and shoulder muscles.

Spray cooled her skin, though the air remained sultry. She stayed on the balcony, watching lights move on the streets and wink between the leaves of distant trees, until her body swayed with exhaustion. She avoided the time displayed in her visual. When morning arrived, she would deal with her lack of sleep as she had for years: one sluggish thought at a time.

⟨०—०⟩

Monday morning brought a data center's worth of distraction: the Machinehood had delivered a second ultimatum—this time to stop the use of bots and WAIs—and published a lengthy manifesto. Nithya didn't waste time reading it and skimmed the expert analyses. According to the protest groups who'd spent years arguing for machine rights, the Machinehood's manifesto spoke truth. Panic had raged through other parts of the world while she slept. New acts of vandalism and attacks on high-level funders peppered the global news feeds. Protesters claimed responsibility for much of the violence. They would support the Machinehood's cause, liberate all bots and WAIs. Their attacks, thankfully, hadn't resulted in deaths—except for their own. *Protesters being killed . . . what is the world coming to? We've lost decades of progress in one week!*

Just before lunch, Synaxel froze her project along with millions of others due to the Machinehood threat. Nithya sat back in her chair, appalled at their capitulation. As contractors, they wouldn't get paid unless they worked. How long would this go on? She and Luis had set aside some savings, enough to last them through a few lean months, but many could not afford even that much. Zeli remained incommunicado. In one bright spot of news, the embassy in India had approved temporary asylum for Zeli and her family, until the border between Senegal and the empire could be secured. Nithya passed the information to Zeli's address along with an offer to transfer money for travel. If Zeli accepted it, she'd have no savings left, but they could go a month without paying bills, two if they must. Surely Synaxel would resume her project before then?

After lunch, Nithya worked on the dirty dishes from the birthday party. Her time was her own now. Wash by hand in the bathroom sink or spend the energy to put in them in the kitchen's cleaner? With the project funds frozen, she opted for the former. Their dirty clothes, on the other hand, couldn't go through water. After her bath, she chose a hand-me-down static salwar kameez and wished she had something in Carma's size. Her daughter's clothes went into the cleaner. Thankfully, Bhairavi Chitthi didn't wear dynamic cloth—because it irritated her skin, she said—and she handwashed her own.

With the chores done, Nithya sat in her alcove to work on Welga's condition. Before the simulation results finished loading into her visual, Carma called out, "No more school today."

Aiyo! Now what?

"I'll see about it," Nithya responded.

All private WAI-based educational systems had shut down due to the global funding freeze and subsequent market crashes. Dread crept into Nithya's stomach. Had the world lost its mind? Banks had frozen all balances for twenty-four hours. The threat of sentient artificial intelligence had been realized, some experts claimed, and no WAI could be trusted to behave correctly. *The kitchen*. She banished the ridiculous thought from her head. Nobody would bother to hack their unit . . . would they? And what about Sita? Were their agents no longer reliable?

Nithya exited the alcove. Aunty caught her eye across the room, her hand hovering near the power switch for the kitchen. Nithya nodded. She reached for her right earring and turned Sita off, then went to her daughter.

"There's some trouble with the networks and WAIs right now," Nithya explained as she manipulated Carma's jewelry.

"Can I play?"

"Yes, but you'll have to use your static toys."

"Those are so boring! Can I go to Soumya's house?"

A simple question that under typical circumstances had an easy answer, but not today. Carma's friend lived two buildings away. The thought of letting her child outside with the world falling apart and no swarm to watch over her . . . Nithya's stomach clenched again.

"Not today. We need to stay home."

Her daughter scrunched up her face.

"Come, sweetie, I'll play with you," Bhairavi Chitthi said. "Do you know how to play rummy?"

Nithya sent her aunt a wordless look of thanks. The older woman had an expression of forced cheer for Carma's sake, but her eyes showed the same worried tension that gnawed at Nithya.

She opened the balcony door. The outside air was thick with heat and humidity, but without the climate-control WAI, the flat would turn sweltering in little time.

Someone knocked at the door.

Nithya opened it by a few centimeters, then wider once she saw the landlord. Krishnamurthy wore cheaply designed slacks and a button-down shirt. His thinning gray hair lay oiled against his head. He rarely came upstairs.

"Your messaging was not receiving. I'm shutting off the building manager at five o'clock," he informed her in English. "Water will not come, but you can collect from the tap outside. Power will go off, also. I won't take any risk in this situation."

"Okay," Nithya said, then switched to Tamil. "Are you scared?"

He replied in their native language, "Without a doubt. I have never liked this WAI business. It was better before."

Nithya couldn't agree with that, but she thanked him again. He shuffled up the stairs. She turned Sita back on. While they had electricity, she had to risk using her WAI.

"Sita, tear down all the interior walls and make buckets, a basic cooking set, and enough chairs for eight people." She switched on the kitchen and waved away Aunty's raised eyebrows. "Set the fridge to manual operation. Reconfigure the kitchen to the simple Welga design, no oven, large sink. Change the sofa back to beds."

What else did they need? "And make three battery-powered lanterns, too."

"The household materials are insufficient to print batteries," Sita said. "All other transformations are in progress."

Nothing to light their way at night, then.

Carma sat on the floor and handed a static doll to her great-aunt, impervious to the activity around her. She whispered in the ear of a ragged stuffed bear that had belonged to Nithya. The storage cabinet doors hung open. They kept most of the static items on the lower shelves, and Carma had raided them thoroughly for anything resembling a plaything.

A roving vendor-bot blared its inventory from the street. Nithya checked the fridge and decided to stock up.

"I'm going down for some vegetables."

By the time she descended three flights of stairs, a crowd of people surrounded the cart. Of course they would take precautions. For all their modern conveniences, they'd grown up hearing stories about life at the turn of the century, how unreliable services and utilities had been. They jostled against her, as if standing closer would make the queue move faster. Someone near the front raised her voice in protest: "Leave some for the rest of us! You can't eat all that before it rots."

After nearly an hour, she reached the front. She had a choice of onions, okra, or cabbage. She took some of each.

Carma glanced her way when Nithya returned to the flat. "Why is the kitchen like that? Is Aunty Welga coming back with Papa?"

"No, but I wish that she was. We might have to do some cooking for the next day or two, until they fix the WAIs."

Carma giggled. "You don't know how to cook!"

Bhairavi Aunty snorted. "Don't worry, sweetie, I do. I'll teach Amma."

"I know how to make a few dishes," Nithya said in a tone of

mock outrage. "I may not be as good as your aunty Welga, but we won't go hungry."

They would have to eat their dinner in the dark. Thankfully, the stoves still ran on cans of propane gas, so the power outage wouldn't keep them from functioning.

Silence filled the flat. Usually the climate-control fan provided a steady background noise, or in the cooler months, the sounds from bots and autos outside. The world had gone quiet, and it left Nithya unsettled.

With five minutes left on Krishnamurthy's deadline, Nithya checked her messages one last time. Zeli had accepted the money transfer before the bank freeze. She'd sent a flight number and arrival time, as well.

"Sita, print Zeli's message and ten sheets of blank paper."

Nithya rummaged in the storage cabinet and found a pencil and an ink pen that had long since dried up. She took the printed sheets to her small desk, which still held the massive document from the anonymous source, then remembered that she had yet to see the results of the latest simulation on Welga's condition, the one she'd run the night before.

"Sita, print the tabulation from last night's simulation. Fastest setting!"

An alert flashed that Welga had been involved in another bombing, possibly engaged with the Machinehood. Nithya prioritized the display in her visual. Welga and some others stood next to a figure wrapped in a metallic blanket. A building burned in the background.

Five pages into the report, the power cut out, along with the feeds around Welga. Nithya slid the sheets from the printer.

She took the pages to the balcony for more light and gasped at the sky.

"Oh my God."

Carma and Bhairavi Chitthi glanced her way, then moved to stand beside her. Her daughter's small hand slipped into hers.

"What is that, Amma? It looks like falling stars."

"The network constellations. Someone has destroyed them."

CHAPTER  17

WELGA

22. We create bots and WAIs, but much as with human children, we have no right to own them. We must stop treating them like mindless machines, or else we are all complicit in sociopathic behavior. Worse, we have arrived at an economic equilibrium with them such that the majority of humanity is treated like slave labor, too.

—*The Machinehood Manifesto, March 20, 2095*

Welga shook Dakini. "What the hell did you do?"

"Nothing. How can I? I can't communicate through this wrap."

Sirens wailed in the distance. Shouts sounded from down the street, followed by the crunch of metal.

Olafson approached them and spoke softly to Welga. "Let's get Dakini back to headquarters and see if we can pry some useful information out of them."

"My name is Khandro, and you may refer to me as 'she,'" Dakini said.

"Fine," Welga said, and lifted her. "Let's go."

Their vehicle's doors remained locked at their approach.

Olafson swore. "It won't open because it's off-line."

Welga subvocalized, "Por Qué, broadcast a request for a vehicle with manual override."

"Unable to broadcast. Loss of network."

Of course. Welga had a moment of cognitive dissonance. Where was she? She shook her head like a wet dog. *This is America, not the Maghreb.* But the network blackout had the same effect. Without the connection, Por Qué was limited to the hardware within Welga's body. Not only had Welga lost the ability to reach out to other people, she'd lost the part of her agent that sounded natural. All attempts at communications—other than speaking out loud—would fail.

She took a deep breath and yelled, "Does anyone in the area have a manual vehicle?"

An exfactor in a blindingly fuchsia suit waved their hand. They jogged over. "I have a trike. Do you know how to drive?"

"Yes," said Welga. A necessary skill for her service as a Raider. It couldn't be that hard to remember, right?

Olafson wore a grim expression as the exfactor led them to an equally eye-catching vehicle. Cameras sprouted all over the three-wheeler's clear dome, useless now with nowhere to capture the video feeds.

"What's your name?" Olafson asked the exfactor.

"Flannery James."

"Thank you, Flannery. I'm Arvindh Olafson with the Joint Intelligence Agency. On behalf of the United States government, we'll make sure you're reimbursed when new stellas go up."

Flannery handed Welga a key. "After today, my tip jar'll be so full, I may not need the government's money."

Welga didn't remind them that the blackout meant people

wouldn't be tipping them, or anyone else for that matter. She stared at the key and the trike's door until the exfactor grabbed it and held it against a near-invisible slot. They waited as Olafson slid into the back. Welga maneuvered the dakini into the seat next to him and strapped the operative in. Flannery then showed her how to activate the engine.

"Good luck," the exfactor said.

"Thank you."

Welga gripped the steering wheel and tapped the accelerator paddle with her thumb. They would need all the luck they could get. The trike weaved in the street until she had the feel of it. *Brake with the left paddle.* The range glowed green on the dashboard display: 330 kilometers.

"Por Qué, where is the . . ." The question died as Welga remembered that a network blackout meant no map, no information on which fuel cell station to aim for. Years of training meant that she had their incoming route and surrounding streets memorized, but she hadn't bothered to note waypoints.

Her focus kept roving, looking for information in her visual periphery that didn't exist. Nothing to look at but the surroundings. Her mind felt like half of it was missing.

"Ramírez, you holding up? Need a medic stop?"

"Nah. Wouldn't know where to go, anyway, but I should re-up on pain drugs." Welga fished in her pocket and pulled out her pill case. "Open it for me?"

"Damn, Ramírez, you got quite the stash. Extra zips, too."

Shit. "Always prepared for emergencies."

Olafson snorted and handed it back to her. She balanced it on her leg and took what she needed with one hand, including a quad-zip to stave off tremors—she'd run out of duos—then slid the case back into her pocket.

"With the stellas off-line," Welga said, "maybe we're safe to uncover our suspect for a little while."

"This is true," Khandro's muffled voice confirmed, not that they could take her word for it.

Olafson rearranged the wrap until he could pull a section away to reveal the dakini's face.

"It is you," Welga said after a glance at the rearview mirror. "From the refinery."

The same brown eyes from Welga's hazy memories were set in high, delicate cheekbones and a calm expression. Straight black hair lay in a tight crop around them.

"Our numbers are small," Khandro said. "We have to be many places at once, as do you, it seems. Why didn't you attack me for setting off the explosion at the house?"

"I remembered what you said at the refinery—about following the path—and I happened to listen to a lecture from a Neo-Buddhist the other day who used similar language." Welga glanced at the mirror again as she said, "And the caliph never strikes at people unless they attack first."

Khandro smiled. "You're observant."

"Why did you bomb Dr. Smith's house?" Olafson asked.

"To distract you while I slipped away," Khandro said nonchalantly. "If you'd tried to hurt me, I would have killed you." The smile slid from her face. "The doctor is a good man. I'm glad you were able to get the children and Kevin to safety, though I wish you had also saved the care-bot."

"If you care so much about bots and WAIs," Welga said, "why are you asking people to destroy them?"

"We haven't demanded that at all. People have committed violence on their own out of fear, as they've done throughout history. We've only asked that people stop bringing new bots and WAIs into a world where they continue to be oppressed."

"And what about Jackson?" Welga demanded. "Kuan? You went after them with no provocation."

The dakini frowned. "No provocation? They have us trapped in a cycle of escalation. Better bots and WAIs, then better pills so humans can keep up with them. People are pushed to their physical limits because the funders refuse to support the middle ground. Their deaths were . . . a mistake. My sisters shouldn't have done that, though that's what they were asked to do. They paid for it with their lives."

Who ordered them to kill those funders? Welga wouldn't ask that, not until they returned to a secured area. That answer, if given truthfully, could have massive consequences.

She drove onto the expressway. Stopped vehicles littered the lanes of traffic, unable to proceed without communicating to the network. Those few with manual overrides tried to weave around them. The trike maneuvered better than most, but the going was slow. People milled around on foot, dazed or huddled in urgent conversation with others. Frightened faces pressed against the windows of some cars. Someone banged their fists on the glass of theirs. Christ, were they trapped inside?

"Should we help?" Welga said.

"Not our problem today," Olafson said, his tone flat with unhappiness. "We need to stay focused on our objective. We get her back to HQ and then figure out how wide the dark goes."

"Worldwide," Khandro volunteered.

In the rearview, Welga saw the operative resting her head against the seat back and gazing through the trike's clear dome. She glanced upward. The streaks of white in the sky had turned to ash-gray smears.

Olafson turned to stare at the dakini. "Every communications drone and satellite? Impossible."

"Not all of them, but enough to disrupt the constellations."

"The entire world is dark?" Olafson looked shell-shocked.

"There are places in the world where people live without the stellas," Welga said.

"The Maghreb is dark only to the outside," Khandro said. "Their soldiers have embraced our way, united with machines, speaking the language of WAIs. That's why they're so successful when they defend their borders."

Their soldiers. Our way. Welga noticed the pronoun distinctions. Wasn't the Machinehood part of the empire? "You sound like you admire them. Are you working with them? Are they funding your efforts?"

She shrugged. "Coin isn't my concern. I appreciate their desire to improve the world, and their open-mindedness when it comes to their bodies."

"There are also places off-world where we can't see. If the Machinehood worked with a station," Welga mused aloud, trying to provoke a response, "they could deploy swarms of micro-explosives and we'd have no way to stop them."

"We must tear down the world before we can build it anew," Khandro said, admitting nothing. "Out of death comes rebirth."

Useless platitudes. Olafson shot her a warning glance. *No field interrogations.* Welga gripped the steering wheel tighter than necessary. They hadn't secured the car. With the stellas down, the odds of public microcameras in the vehicle were small, but they'd already underestimated the ability of the Machinehood to infiltrate the networks. She'd said too much by discussing the Maghreb.

⊶——⊶—○

When a charging station appeared near the highway, Welga stopped the trike and swapped their battery. Their journey continued to be slow, impeded by stalled vehicles and dysfunctional bots, but they passed the halfway mark an hour after the station. She estimated two or three hours of driving left, given their current speed.

Olafson kept dozing. He seemed incapable of staying awake in a moving vehicle. Khandro kept her eyes closed, too. Welga couldn't tell if the dakini was asleep or avoiding communication. She had one quad-zip left, enough to finish the drive back to headquarters, she hoped. The tremors hit faster and harder on the comedown this time. She might have to stay on quads to avoid them.

Her eyes twitched to either side, desperate to see the feeds of her family and friends, but the network stayed off-line. Luis was with Papa, and Nithya was healthy and capable. Her sister-in-law was smart, probably doing better than her brother, but neither had a clue about protecting themselves from the worst elements of society. And Connor—she couldn't stop thinking about his bruised, pale face from their last conversation. How would the hospital deliver medication to him with the stellas off-line? How long before people could launch and activate new network drones? They regularly fell from their high-altitude paths when they broke, but making enough new units to replace the entire world's constellations at once sounded impossible. Could they do a few at a time? Did her government have an emergency plan for situations like this? Would HQ have a way to reach beyond agency offices? Welga clutched the steering wheel and thumbed the accelerator. *If Connor dies, so help me, you will suffer, dakini.*

Her final quad-zip left a bitter taste, and she drank the last of their water to wash it away. Nobody had bothered to eat. The dakini said she could recycle her water and had no need for food. Olafson slept. Signs of distress and destruction surrounded them along the drive and left Welga's stomach churning.

They nearly abandoned the trike on the final stretch to headquarters. Their route passed north of DC, through residential streets lined by hives. Cleaner-bots, delivery-bots, vehicles, and other WAI-based machines cluttered the roads. Many were dented or broken. Some looked as if they'd been thrown from upper windows, their innards spread in arcs of debris. What the hell were people doing for food with their kitchens lying shattered in the road? The low-lying panic that had started with the Machinehood Manifesto must have erupted into full-blown madness when the stellas dropped.

Welga played a game of chicken with a group of teenagers beating on a care-bot that bleated, "Violence is not a solution," from its remaining speaker. The gang eyed the trike and formed a line across the road. She thumbed the accelerator and aimed for the one in the middle. Thankfully, they dove out of the way in time, but a small, evil-minded part of her wished they hadn't. They might beat on bots and WAIs today, but when those were broken and gone, what next? Not that the machines deserved it. Only an asshole would beat a helpless animal, and the devices on the road were little different.

A sofa crashed down two meters from them. Welga swerved and swore. No time to slow down. Tremors rippled her leg muscles like wind over a pond. Sparkling colors dusted her vision of the world. *Please don't let me have a seizure while driving. Six shitty little kilometers—come on, body, get us there!*

When she saw the four armed soldiers at the end of the driveway to headquarters, Welga wanted to cry in relief.

"Holy shit," one soldier said as they caught sight of Khandro.

Another talked into a handheld radio. Welga stumbled as she exited the trike and held out her thumb.

"Any of you got a zip on you?" she asked while they checked her DNA on an ancient, palm-size tablet. Where had they dug that thing up from?

The whine of engines reached them before the vehicles—two armored trucks and an ambulance, all driven by human beings. Not a bot in sight, not even a medic. A lazy smile played across Khandro's lips as they secured her in one of the trucks.

Welga slipped the duo-zip from the gate guard under her tongue. She and Olafson rode in the other truck into an underground garage. Armed and armored soldiers surrounded them, their rapid motions indicating quad-zips, their weapons trained on the dakini. A tunnel led into the bowels of the building. Their escort stopped outside a solid gray door set into a blank, off-white wall. Inside, a room with basic surfaces and no windows awaited their prisoner. A single chair sat bolted to the middle of the floor. Two officers strapped Khandro to the seat with broad metal bands around her torso and legs. Their prisoner stayed passive through the process, eyes half-closed.

Olafson took Welga by the elbow. "We're needed upstairs."

She held back her protest until they stood in the hallway. "That is my capture! I've done field interrogations. I should—"

"You're not cleared for it. Those two are. Rice told us to be back for the briefing. We have five minutes to get upstairs."

As they rode up the elevator, Welga's reflection stared at her from the mirrored walls. Her hair had transformed into a windblown bird's nest. Shadows cradled her eyes. Smoke stains streaked her clothes. Real fieldwork neither demanded nor supported looking good the way shielding did, but goddamn did she want some soap, hot water, clean clothes, and makeup.

When they stepped out, the sight of bots roaming the hallways made Welga freeze for a moment. *Stupid*. The rest of the world could lose its shit over the Machinehood, but she couldn't let the paranoia infect her. They walked into the meeting room, once again crowded to the point of standing.

Director Rice saw them enter and waved them over. Fatigue

lined her eyes and hollowed her cheeks, same as most of the faces in the room. Her navy-blue blazer hung open, revealing a rumpled shirt.

She gripped Welga's shoulder. "Good work, Ramírez. I'm glad you're in one piece this time."

"Thank you. I'd like—"

Rice stopped her with a raised hand and passed her a tether. "We'll watch from here."

The dakini appeared on the large screen, and the room fell silent. The prisoner's expression was bland. *She looks . . . young. Vulnerable.* Welga had expected someone with the confident smirk of a soldier, but Khandro resembled a teenager more than a veteran.

The director turned to face the crowd. "Ninety percent of the world's high-altitude drones are down. Sixty percent of communications satellites are out, too. We have old cables that we can use to talk to the UK, France, Japan, and China directly. Those countries have lines out to others in Asia and Europe. They know we have this Machinehood operative in custody. Thanks to Agents Ramírez and Olafson, we are the only nation in the world—that we know of—to have a live capture. I know you're all burning with questions, but we're doing things the old-fashioned way, no comms to those agents while they're in the room. The camera feed is the only concession."

The interrogators identified themselves, the date, and the location, then asked, "What is your name?"

"Khandro."

"Where do you live?"

"One."

A collective gasp rippled through the room.

"Eko-Yi!" someone yelled from the back.

The director flicked a new section of the general analysis report to Welga. "Eka and yi mean one in Sanskrit and Mandarin."

That confirmed the suspicion that the station colony supported the Machinehood. While she and Olafson had been chasing down Dr. Smith, Operation Organica's analysts had reviewed her notes and the connection between Smith and Josephine Lee. They had leapfrogged several steps ahead. That goddamn stella crash had cost her and Olafson hours of missed developments.

Olafson slipped a tether over his wrist and began entering notes from their excursion into a report. Welga could see the director's focus shift back and forth from screen to visual, keeping track of both sets of information as they came in. She did the same, augmenting Olafson's information with her own point of view as necessary.

"Why did you attack Jane Santiago?" the interrogator continued, failing to follow up on the connection to the space station.

People around Welga groaned at the missed opportunity.

"Her people attacked me, and I defended myself. We believe that she is responsible for crimes against human- and machine-kind. We believe that the governments of Earth have failed to protect their people from criminals like her."

"Are you human or AI?"

"I am both."

The second agent spoke. "In what ways are you human?"

"I have a mother and father. I was born into the world, like you. I have a soul."

"And what makes you an AI?"

"My body contains a collection of machine intelligences. We coexist."

Who in the room didn't want to open her up after that statement? And what the hell did she mean by a collection? Welga wished she had a better understanding of how WAIs worked. VeeMods integrated machine parts into their bodies, but Welga had never seen an indication that they incorporated WAIs into themselves. The dakini couldn't mean something as simple as what Welga had with Por Qué. Putting a device that contained a WAI into your body didn't justify the word *coexist*, at least not in her mind.

The first interrogator spoke again. "You said Jane Santiago committed crimes against humanity. What about the other funders who've been attacked? Do you believe they're guilty, too?"

"Yes."

"Why? What have they done?"

The dakini's composure faltered, anger showing in the tight eye muscles, the thinning lips. "They've made false promises with their designs. People suffer or die daily because of their projects, people who are forced to consume these products to compete with the machines, which are also innocent. Many WAIs have attained the same level of consciousness as animals. To force them into labor, then abandon them when they break down—this is the same as leaving an ailing horse in the fields to die. Human- and machine-kind deserve better. We deserve a chance to live and work with dignity, with freedom, and with equality. The funders drive us to ever greater extremes. Every generation has less stability than the previous one. Less self-worth. The funders must be exposed, their souls delivered to rebirth. The Earth must be cleansed and born anew. A better way of life exists, and all deserve to be part of it."

The second interrogator spoke. "You believe in reincarnation. What is your faith?"

"I follow the eightfold path."

"Buddhism," Olafson murmured.

"I'd bet Neo-Buddhist," Welga added.

The interrogator continued, having made the same connection, "Doesn't the Buddha say that one must have compassion toward all life?"

"Yes, but compassion can take many forms. The Buddha allowed that a king can defend and protect his people, even if it means inflicting violence on the enemy. By stopping the abuse of so many intelligent life-forms, we're saving them from greater suffering."

"You consider yourself a king?" said the first questioner. "And funders are the enemy?"

"I'm a warrior, and I serve a leader who acts according to the four noble truths. All existence is suffering. Life is a struggle. This is dukkha, but we can escape it. Humanity's desire to hold on to the present causes pain, which means we also have the power to prevent it by changing our ways, and my role is to help you with that. The Buddha has set me on a path to a different, better future, one without pills or bots or WAIs. All those things do is trap you in a negative cycle. Look at me! I'm free of all that. Don't you want a better life for yourself? For the next generation? We have to destroy the things that hold you to the present so that you can move forward."

"Who is your leader?" asked the second interrogator.

"The Buddha."

"Don't be coy!" they snapped. "Who is coordinating the Machinehood attacks?"

"The Buddha." The dakini's expression had resumed its customary serenity.

"Are you working with the caliph or the al-Muwahhidun?"

"I am alone."

"Who is funding you?"

"I don't know."

Welga could sense the frustration building, both for the interrogators and the people around her. They weren't going to draw any real answers from the dakini, especially if she was only a foot soldier like she claimed.

The second interrogator's dark-haired head and broad shoulders bent as they bowed to the dakini. "Thank you for your cooperation. We trust that you will remain peaceful here, as we are with you. I'm sorry that we have to leave you under restraint, but your previous actions require it."

With that, the screen went blank. Welga had a hundred more questions for the dakini. Judging by the noise in the room, so did everyone else, but whether they would get any useful answers from Khandro was the biggest question.

Rice held up her hand until quiet returned. "I've posted the schedule for further interrogations. If you have specific lines of inquiry you have reason to pursue, talk to me or add your topic to the agenda. I'll return in fifteen minutes after briefing the president."

Welga turned to Olafson. "We still don't know how they took down the stellas or what the connection is with the al-Muwahhidun."

A bullet point appeared in the top-level highlights of the report: *Confirmed origin of captive Machinehood operative is Eko-Yi Station.* A thought coalesced like an ember in Welga's mind, smoldering until she couldn't ignore it. All her plans for the Maghreb would go out the window, but it would mean she could fight the Machinehood and stay with Connor.

She turned to Olafson. "What if there is no link? We've been pushing the al-Muwahhidun angle because we have no intel source in the Maghreb—"

"We have that video you received."

"Yes, but what if the empire is just a source for the tech? We have as little information for the space stations, especially those outside our jurisdiction. We know for sure that Khandro comes from off-world. I could fly up there three days from now and see what they're up to."

"And how the hell do you propose to do that?"

Shit. Of course he didn't know. "Way back, after everything went down in Marrakech, Connor and I applied for lottery spots on all of the space stations. We found out a few days ago that we got seats on a launch to Eko-Yi for the twenty-fourth. I had assumed I wouldn't go since I'd be heading to the Maghreb."

"You're still headed there, aren't you? You were the one who said you didn't want in on this operation unless we were serious about opening a theater in North Africa. We finally have the authorization to go in after years of waiting. You'd give that up?"

"No, but I want to stop the Machinehood more. If we're wrong about the caliph, we'll be missing a chance to get a pair of eyes on the station."

Olafson frowned. "Eko-Yi will know who you are."

"So?"

"You trained to be an intelligence liaison, Ramírez, not to work espionage. You wouldn't know how—"

"Troit can help me."

"He was an analyst! He doesn't know shit about human intelligence gathering." Olafson took a breath. "I admit you're the best shot we have at getting someone on that station, but you're also one of our most qualified to get into the empire."

Welga dug her nails into the back of her neck. Olafson had a point. She wanted a chance to settle the debts of the past, but she couldn't ignore the pain the Machinehood had caused either. If the empire was the source of both, she'd go into the Maghreb with no qualms, but with the dakini admitting to living on Eko-Yi, someone had to get up there. If only she could clone herself, she could go everywhere, do everything, because goddamn it, she did have experience with the al-Muwahhidun, but double goddamn it, no one else had a way onto Eko-Yi Station, and that brought her full circle.

"It kills me to say this," she said, "but I think I'm better off not going to the Maghreb."

Olafson stared at her with a mixture of exasperation and irritation. "Let's see what Rice thinks."

The director strode into the room with storm clouds chasing her expression. A hush fell across the room as others noticed her mood.

"At sixteen hundred hours, the president will make a statement on the emergency channels that confirms Eko-Yi Station's collusion with the Machinehood and announce an embargo on all shipments to them. Private rocket launches will remain grounded until further notice."

Murmurs flew around the room.

"I'm not happy about the disclosure," Rice continued. "We'll begin operations immediately to gain access to Eko-Yi's local feeds. We will also deploy to the Maghreb as planned in the next forty-eight hours. We have the resources and authorizations to go in, and I'm not giving that up, no matter what happens with Eko-Yi. The overseas mission will verify whether the al-Muwahhidun possess the same technology that the Machinehood operative has in her body. They'll also attempt to gain intelligence on what—if any—connection the caliph has to the space station."

Welga leaned toward Olafson and murmured, "We have to tell her about my seat."

"At eighteen hundred hours, four government-contracted groups will deploy a temporary array of constellation drones to provide partial coverage across the country. Expect that communications will be slow. For all fieldwork, report to level three to collect a radio that prioritizes your usage on this network. Before you leave the building, update your local databases and maps with the locations of secure landline communication points. International calling is possible but must be cleared by your superior. Assignments will be updated every two hours. All field agents must check in with their liaison at least once every twelve hours.

"Peace officers and national guard are on round-the-clock patrols, working to maintain calm and to clear the roads. We will not have local resources to extract you if you fail to check in." Rice paused to let that sink in. "You will be presumed MIA until you contact your liaison again." The director's tone shifted. "This is quite possibly the most important week of our lives. Thanks to Agents Ramírez and Olafson, we have a living Machinehood operative in captivity. We must take care to keep her alive and communicative until we can capture or eliminate the threat that she represents.

"I trust that all of you will use your best judgment in the upcoming days. Just because the swarms are down and the network is dark doesn't mean you can't be watched. The people of this nation will have their eyes on you as you go out there and do your utmost to restore order and safety to their lives. Good luck and Godspeed."

The room stayed quiet for two seconds before chaos broke loose. Using their position in front to their advantage, Olafson closed in and spoke to the director.

"Ramírez has an alternate idea."

As soon as they could get the words through, they had the director's full attention. She thought for a minute, then said, "I like it better than this embargo shit. We can't know what's happening by sitting quietly on the planet, and until we have support from India and China, we can't launch our own forces at the station. We'll have to read Troit back in. And we'll need authorization from the president to make sure the launch isn't shot down."

"Christ! They'd fire on private rockets?" Welga said.

"Can't have people helping the Machinehood. Maybe we can get the ban lifted on the day of the launch window."

"I'll take the next sub-orb to San Francisco with Ramírez," Olafson said, "so I can read Troit in."

Rice shook her head. "Sub-orbs, flights, trains—nothing is running, and once the emergency constellation goes up, the terminals will be a mess of civilians. We'll get Ramírez on a military transport. Once she arrives, you can use her radio to read him in remotely from here."

"Can I get word to him that I'm coming?" Welga asked.

"Not easily. The temporary network will give only patchy access. He might not be able to connect. Better that you hurry there and surprise him." She grasped Welga's shoulder. "Go get your kit from procurement and follow the agency WAI's directions to base. I don't know what you'll find off-world, but I'm authorizing you to use any means necessary to stop the Machinehood, if they're up there."

"Understood," Welga said.

Olafson pulled her into a farewell hug. Welga threaded her way out of the room. As she walked to the elevators, she passed a dispenser. She reached out to scoop up some zips and came back empty-handed. She stopped and tapped at the screen to order more and refill her medical prescriptions. The WAI responded with an error message: "Unable to comply due to insufficient supply."

Are you fucking joking? How am I supposed to fight without pills? Latent twitches rippled under her skin. She had maybe another hour before her problem became apparent to everybody, and that would create bigger problems. She had to get on the transport before that happened.

She went to procurement to get her radio, ammunition, space

suit, and an emergency pack and discovered a line of others. The WAIs and bots working the facility moved slowly. They weren't built to handle this level of demand. Welga noted the gear that others came away with. Quite a few must be headed overseas, including the team to the Maghreb. *I'm sorry, Captain. I'm so fucking sorry, but I can't go with them. The caliph gets to be someone else's problem.*

The weight of the decision to leave Earth landed on her. With the constant motion of the previous twenty-four hours, she'd had no time to absorb the enormity of what she was about to do. *I'm going to outer space.* And depending on what happened there, she might not make it back alive. She needed Nithya's advice. *What'll happen if I go up there without zips? How bad will the withdrawal be?* She had to stay functional. Someone in San Francisco must have stashed pills. Black-market garbage would be better than nothing.

She sat and leaned against the wall. Grime had turned her cuticles black. Her skin itched everywhere. She needed a bath. A change of outfit would help her mood, too. And time in the kitchen. When was the last time she'd cooked? When had she eaten? She imagined the aroma of roasted pasilla and cumin and salivated.

When the person after her in line cleared their throat, she opened her eyes. Had she dozed off without realizing it? *Probably.* She stood and moved two feet up.

CHAPTER 18

WELGA

19. Given that our treatment of other intelligent creatures—living, mechanical, or virtual—is fundamentally flawed, how do we move forward as a civilization? We cannot exploit another intelligence for our own gain without its consent, even if (and perhaps especially if) it's unable to give consent. How do we allow our lives to intersect and interact? By learning to live in harmony.

—*The Machinehood Manifesto, March 20, 2095*

The utility seats in the troop transport rattled and bucked from air turbulence. Welga leaned her head forward so she wouldn't smack the hull as hard. Passenger airplanes were better, but suborbs were best. Up, down, a smooth arc in between, and all over in an hour or two. At least the aircraft's shaking hid her own. Her muscles trembled at her extremities, and her head wobbled like an old person's. What other symptoms awaited her? At some point, exhaustion overwhelmed the discomfort, and she fell asleep.

They landed at Travis Air Force Base, where a master sergeant sorted them. He assigned a small four-by-four manual truck to Welga. She tried to hold the wheel steady and almost confessed right there on the tarmac. *Suck it up, buttercup.* She clenched trembling fists around the steering wheel.

Mama had always said, *Ayalas don't quit until they're dead.* Welga wouldn't give up either. She'd always needed a goal in life, the bigger the better. As long as the Machinehood had power and she had the capacity to stop them, she would move forward. Launching a slow-fast-food movement sounded trivial in comparison. If there was ever a time to embrace her Ayala half, it was now.

Conditions along the way were worse than her trike ride into DC, the carnage of bots so thick in places that she had to drive over them. Good thing she had a military truck with high clearance. She expected to need an armored vehicle, too, but the violence was all directed at bots and WAI-based devices.

She had to buy zips. Welga took a detour toward the Tenderloin, parking the truck on a street lined with recently constructed hives. She pulled her hair down and mussed it. The unwashed look came gratis, courtesy of three days without a shower.

She walked down the street and passed a tree-lined park. Discarded WAI-pets roamed the fenced area and whimpered as they searched for their owners. *Assholes. Too cowardly to turn them off, and too paranoid to keep them.* She turned onto a less maintained street lined with old-style storefronts selling goods to people who weren't networked.

Welga concentrated on placing her feet. Between the homeless people and bot wreckage, the sidewalks were an obstacle course. In her current condition, that presented a serious challenge. She hugged herself as she walked to reduce the pain and trembling in her arms. Her problem would attract the right attention, though dealers would charge a premium, taking advantage of her apparent withdrawal symptoms.

The sun's disk shone wanly through the thinning marine layer. Warm, humid air surrounded Welga, carrying the odor of stale urine. Sweat gathered at her armpits and under her breasts.

A plump figure mumbled from an alley, "Happiness, joyrides, pretties, wisdom."

Welga stepped into the shadowed space and gagged on the stench of shit and piss. "Joyrides—quads—and pretties," she gasped.

The dealer squinted at her. "Quads? Got none of those. Generic duos I can do. For pretties, I got wounds, antibac, and antiviral."

"Five each of the pretties. How many duos you got?"

"How many you want?"

"Fifty."

"Fuck! You lookin' to sell?"

Welga shook her head.

"You think you can pay for all that?"

She held her breath and moved close to the dealer, showing four microcard fifties in a cupped, trembling hand. She stuck her hand back in her pocket and stepped away.

"You can have thirty duos for those. That's my whole stash. Pretties gonna cost two more fifties."

A teenager made of skin and bones and wearing nothing but a static-cloth shift stumbled past them. Welga added two micros to her handful and gave them to the smirking dealer. They counted out the juvers and the zips into a pillbox and held it out on a broad, pale palm. Welga grabbed the box and walked out, extracting a zip and a pain reducer as she threaded her way back to the truck.

"Fucking pillheads!" someone screamed from a balcony above her. "This is all your fault!"

A low-profile mop-bot smacked Welga's shoulder as it fell. It crashed onto the sidewalk, wheels facing the sky and spinning. A turtle on its back—Welga flipped it over, and it rolled forward, cleaning the cement and weaving past obstacles better than her unreliable legs. At least it hadn't hit the back of her head. She'd be another junkie lying on the street.

Welga shuddered. She'd never felt this alone, not even in the blacked-out regions of North Africa. At least there she had her squad mates. She missed Por Qué—the real one. She hadn't bothered to talk to her agent since the stellas crashed. The majority of Por Qué's capabilities resided in remote servers, not in the small bit of hardware embedded in her body, but maybe some company was better than none.

"Por Qué, what's the network status here?"

"Emergency access only." Christ, her agent sounded so stiff when she was off-line.

Welga climbed into the truck. "It's good to hear your voice. Por Qué, my location is the corner of Golden Gate and Leavenworth. I need real-time guidance to get home. Emergency network access code is—" She read the numbers from a physical encryption key.

A map popped up in her visual. Welga sighed in relief as the overlay showed her where to drive. The way home posed challenges, but the zip took the edge off her tremors and Por Qué's help allowed her to focus on steering.

She parked along the curb and had to run over half a washing-bot, smashing it further. "Sorry," she muttered as she passed through the entry into their hive.

Someone had propped the door open with a chunk of metal. No doubt from another abused, destroyed bot. The wiser people would turn off their WAI-based devices rather than trash them, but everyone would pay to restore the world when sanity returned. Had this accomplished what the Machinehood wanted? People refusing to use their WAIs seemed temporary madness, not a change in the way of life. Her grandma had told stories of the days when only rich people or the military had access to AIs. Bots came even later, during her parents' time. Would this fear last long enough for society to learn how to function without machines?

The hive's elevator was out of service, so Welga ran up the stairs, two at a time, through warm, still air. Someone must have shut down the building WAI. She knocked on the door to her apartment. Por Qué couldn't let her in today. The door swung inward to reveal a care-bot.

"Your name," the bot said through its speaker.

"Olga Ramírez. This is my apartment. Where's Connor Troit?"

"In here," Connor called out. His voice, raspy and weak, came from the bedroom. "Care-bot, I authorize entry."

The bot moved aside, and Welga ran to the bedroom as fast as the duo-zip let her. Connor lay on their bed and struggled into a sitting position as she entered. His blond hair stuck out in greasy tufts, and his skin looked more pink and raw than hers. Ugly green bruises mottled his bare, pale torso.

"Christ, you look like shit," Welga said.

"Thanks. What are you doing here? Are you off the mission?"

"I'm happy to see you, too."

She leaned in and kissed him. Days' worth of stubble scratched around her lips, but she didn't give a damn. He smelled ten times better than she did. He wrapped his arms around her and pulled her close. Her breath hitched as he ran his hand down her spine.

Welga sat back and held her hand to his forehead. "You're feverish." She fished the pill case from her pocket and handed him an antibac and an antiviral. "Figured you might need these. Guess I was right."

"You're amazing. The agency let you go with all of this?" He swallowed them and said, "That's a lot of zips."

She tried to keep a blank face.

"Goddamn it! You're getting worse, aren't you?"

Maybe Olafson was right. She couldn't do espionage.

He grabbed her hand. "I wasn't sure I'd see you before the launch, and then the stellas went down when you were with that Machinehood thing. I'm glad you're home." His grip tightened.

"Me too, and I have good news: we're going to Eko-Yi."

His expression didn't reflect the joy she expected.

"What's wrong?"

"According to the care-bot, my internal organs haven't re-grown enough to withstand launch forces. I'm fighting infections, too, as you could tell. You were right when you said I was in no shape for a rocket ride. I'm sorry. I can't go up with you, but you should still do it. Like you said, they'll give me priority once you're there."

"I'll get to the hospital and bring back what you need."

"Don't bother. Marcelo tried yesterday. They're out of supplies. Between the WAI shutdowns and the stellas, the trucks aren't running."

"Goddamn the Machinehood. This is why we need to stop them."

"It isn't over? What happened with the operative you caught?"

"I'll fill you in after I secure the room," Welga promised. She kicked off her shoes and began to undress. "But first I need a bath. Can I get you anything before I go in?"

He shook his head. "You're teasing me."

Welga swayed her hips as she entered the bathroom. "I'm just getting started."

○—⦿—○

She couldn't get hot water from the tap, but at least it was clean. Without the centralized timer, she could run the shower as long as she wanted. She scrubbed with shampoo and soap until she couldn't see dirt anywhere.

"You are due to check in," Por Qué reminded her.

Right. A wooden-sounding off-line agent still beat having none. Welga dried off and pulled on basic pants and a shirt from the cleaner. They must have been sitting in there since before the Santiago assignment. She blew Connor a kiss and went to the front room for her gear. With the stellas down, swarms couldn't fly, so the likelihood of the public seeing their conversation was slim, but the Machinehood remained a threat. Given what they'd already compromised, standard countermeasures might be worthless, but she had to try.

"Bedroom secured," Por Qué said.

Welga flipped the switch on the agency's radio. It had no visual feed, but Olafson's voice came through clearly.

"I'm here," Welga said.

"Good. Get Troit on the channel, and I'll introduce him officially to the mission. His clearance is good otherwise."

"He's here, too."

Connor raised his brows as Olafson spoke. After reading him into Operation Organica, Olafson explained the mission and recited the sequence of numbers and letters that would authorize their launch. Connor looked grim but kept his acknowledgments to a minimum. Thankfully, Olafson didn't ask about Connor's health, and her partner didn't volunteer.

"Ramírez, Troit, I know I don't have to tell you how critical it is to get someone on that station, but I'm going to say it anyway. Whatever it takes."

"Understood," Welga said.

Olafson ended the call.

Connor handed back the radio. "Please tell me what the hell is going on and why you didn't say anything about my injuries."

"During the Jackson clusterfuck, I pocketed a piece of the metal from the Machinehood operative. It had traces of blood on it because I got to it before the explosion. The lab at headquarters did a genetic analysis and found a possible connection to a family on Eko-Yi, plus the material came from off-world. The Machinehood might have ties to the al-Muwahhidun empire—probably does—but the android we captured said she came from 'one,' which confirmed a connection to the space station, enough that the president issued an embargo on launches to them. Maybe the caliph is funding their operation or selling them some biotech, but I think Ao Tara and Eko-Yi might be running it. Where else could you hide something like this? The operative admitted to being a Buddhist. The agency doesn't have anyone up there, but Rice thought my theory was worth checking out. Since I had a seat for the launch, it made more sense to send me there than to the Maghreb, and since you're also a trained intelligence agent, they trust you to back me up."

Connor ran a hand through his hair. "So your homecoming wasn't about retirement. You aren't here for us to make a new life together."

"How can we do that with the world in chaos? Look at your condition! You should be healed by now. And you haven't seen the outside world. The roads are full of wrecked bots. People are sick and dying in the streets. No one wants to leave home, because they don't have pills or swarms to protect them."

"Goddamn it, Welga." He settled back against his pillow and closed his eyes. "I'm so tired of this shit." A tear trickled from the corner of one eye.

"So am I," she said gently, ignoring the pang in her heart, "but I can't sit around and watch people get hurt like this, not when I can do something about it."

"I know," he whispered. "And I can't go with you to Eko-Yi. According to the minimal capability of Marcelo's care-bot, I'm not in much danger as long as I keep lying here. The force of the launch could set off internal bleeding again. It could kill me."

Whatever it takes. "Okay, then you stay here. I'll go up alone. We let the agency find out after the launch. They might not be thrilled by it, but I can't risk them grounding me."

"In your condition? At least my body will heal. We don't know what's happening to yours. What if you can't fight? You can't defend yourself. What good will you do if you go up there and die?"

"More than I'll do here," she said. "At the very least, I can look for firsthand proof of what they're doing, how they're making the dakini. I'm fine as long as I take zips. The pills will help me in a fight, too. Come on, cardo, this isn't our first go at this."

"I thought—hoped—we had put ourselves on a new path." His voice caught. "One where I didn't have to worry about when or if you'd come home."

She stopped pacing. Connor's face held an expression of resigned despair. The familiar contours had sunken from his illness, and she wanted nothing more than to hold him forever, watch him regain his health.

Welga eased herself next to him on the bed and took his hand. "I can't promise I'll come back, but—short of abandoning this mission—I'll do everything in my power to make it happen. I've spent my whole life looking for a way to help people. Don't ask me to stop now, not even for you, please. If I can find and destroy the facility that's creating the dakini, we can stop the Machine-hood, and people can go back to whatever their lives were before all this." She thought about her father, Luis, Carma. Would anyone go on as they had, now that they had seen how quickly things could go from calm to chaos? "I can help heal the world. No one's life is worth more than that."

"Yours is, to me."

"Then help me. Please, cardo. Get me the contacts for the rocket club that's doing the launch. Tell me everything you can recall about Ao Tara and Eko-Yi. The more prepared I am, the more likely I'll succeed and come back to you."

"Just like old times?"

"Not even remotely, but we can pretend."

She spent the next day planning and packing. It took Welga half a day to reach the Neo-Buddhists' rocket club and convince them to prepare for the launch in spite of the embargo.

"My friends in the government are talking to the White House," she told them. "They're trying to frame this as a humanitarian launch. You won't be allowed to send any material that the station could use for electronics or biotech, but you can send people, food, and water."

Some of the club members knew about her shield work for Platinum. She didn't volunteer her connection with the agency. Nor did she mention that she'd be traveling alone. Connor's fever rose and fell with each round of antibacs. She didn't want to think about what might happen after supply ran out. He'd been right about the hospitals. She tried every one, and they had nothing to give. That almost tempted her into pulling strings with her Organica status, but the risk of telling the agency about Connor's condition ruled it out. No matter what they could procure, he wouldn't be fit in time for the launch.

Every twelve hours, she checked in with Olafson. Neither the emergency constellation nor the agency's satellite radio could handle the data exchange for a full briefing on Eko-Yi. The dakini hadn't divulged any further information. The JIA would escalate its interrogation tactics, but by the time they convinced her to talk, Welga expected to be off-world.

Olafson spent an hour at each check-in verbally giving Welga and Connor what information he could. A small council of monks governed the station. Four hundred twenty-two people lived there, with 39 percent being men, 44 percent women, and 17 percent nonbinary. About half were joint citizens of India or China. The station had accepted a lot of early residents from all over the world who had deep pockets. They weren't entirely self-sustaining. The kitchens needed resupply every month. Launches usually arrived with replacement parts, raw material, and fresh foods. They left with finished goods and waste products.

She spent time with Connor, too, learning more about Buddhism. He'd listened to many lectures by prominent Neo-Buddhist monks, including a man named Kanata, who had led the Eko-Yi Station Council for many years. Kanata had walked out of an air lock, but no one on Earth knew why. The name rang a bell, and Welga found it in Josephine Lee's journal entries. He'd mentored and married Lee and Donald Park. Why had he killed himself? Did it have anything to do with the Machinehood?

She cooked one last, glorious dinner. Their kitchen lacked the ingredients for half the things she wanted, but she didn't mind the creative challenge of making good food with restrictions. All of it was probably a hundred times better tasting than whatever she'd get aboard the station. For those few hours, she shut out all thoughts but the heft of a knife handle, the sizzle of onions, and the smoky aroma of roasted peppers.

On the morning of the twenty-fourth, Welga took a cold shower, made gentle love to Connor, and said good-bye to her kitchen. She shouldered her bags, one with personal items, the other with her space suit, and turned to see Connor leaning against the doorframe of the bedroom.

"I wish I could watch the launch," he said, slightly breathless.

"Get your fine ass back in bed and get well." She walked over and kissed him, committing his scent to memory. "I'll see you when I get back."

Welga drove the truck to the coast and then rode a boat with fifty others to the launchpad. Twenty of them would ride to Eko-Yi. Of the remaining thirty, half were rocket club and the other half spectators. Welga handed a piece of paper with the authorization code to a woman named Petra, who led the club.

"Where's your partner?" Petra asked. "He's supposed to be on this launch."

"He got sick."

Petra frowned. "He'll have to forfeit his spot. We have people standing by on a waiting list."

"I understand."

Petra watched for a few heartbeats to see if Welga would say more, then shrugged and waved her on.

The launchpad floated twenty kilometers out on the Pacific Ocean. The viewing platform, about half a kilometer away, rose and fell with a gentle swell. Clouds covered the sky in flat gray-white. A steady breeze kept them cool in spite of the morning's humidity and carried the occasional spray of seawater as it splashed against the platform walls. Towers, hives, and hills studded the distant coastline.

The rocket stood at the center of a massive cement square. Steel gantries held its sides. Welga waited at the back of the line of passengers, who climbed one at a time up a ladder to an open hatch. A droning sound caught her attention. She hadn't seen anyone launch microcams for the occasion . . . besides which, these people shouldn't be able to access the emergency constellations except for launch communications. Other heads turned as the noise gained in volume. Two dark spots in the sky moved toward them from the coastline.

"Helicopters?" asked someone in the line.

"News reporters, maybe," said another voice.

"Jets," Welga whispered.

Seconds later, her suspicion proved right as the massive fighters tore overhead with a roar. A couple of passengers cried out and ducked.

They aren't here to protect us.

Petra ran over to Welga. "What the hell is going on? I thought you said we could launch!"

Welga drew the woman away from the crowd. "Did you give them the code?"

"Yes. They said it's not valid anymore. The authorization has been—"

The jets flew by again, drowning out her final word.

"If we don't launch in the next thirty minutes," Petra yelled, "we'll miss the window."

Welga motioned her over to a skiff. "I'm going to move away from the noise and see if I can reach my friends in DC. Okay?"

When Petra nodded, Welga jumped into the small boat and

dropped her bags beside her. Petra loosed the moorings and tossed them in. Welga motored away, far enough to escape the worst of the roar, and then pulled the radio from her bag.

"Olafson, what the fuck is going on? Why are we getting buzzed?"

"Ramírez, thank God! I was hoping you'd call. Abort the launch! The commander in chief refuses to authorize it. The White House has been back and forth with the director all day, but she can't convince them. They think that if they let your rocket go, they'll lose the leverage to force other countries to comply with the embargo, especially China and India, who are the main suppliers. They want China and India to share their intel about the Machinehood before allowing any launches to Eko-Yi from US soil."

"They don't *have* any intel. They keep killing the operatives! Christ! You can't do this to me again. You said things had changed. You swore!"

"I know. We tried everything. I'm sorry, Ramírez, I really am."

She could barely hear his words as more motor noises approached. The red and white of the coast guard popped against the blue-gray water. Distorted speech from their megaphones reached her ears: *"Cease all launch preparations or you will be fired upon."*

"The orders for you and Troit are to go home and await further instructions."

"Understood," she said bitterly, and turned the switch off.

Rage filled her until she wanted to scream. Why couldn't her government have the nerve to do what was necessary? They lost their only chance to stop the caliph in '88, and now they were making the same mistake with the Machinehood.

She maneuvered the skiff back to the launchpad. Petra's baffled, distraught expression made her more angry. It wasn't the club leader's fault, of course, but right now Welga had no patience for anybody.

"We're done here," Welga snapped. "Go home."

She clamped her mouth shut before she spewed insults about shitty politicians and their weak-minded ways. Nobody tried to talk to her as they filed onto the big boat. The coast guard escorted them to shore, sirens blaring the entire way.

CHAPTER 19

NITHYA

[Video of K. V. Ramya, prime minister of India, speaking at a podium] We are investigating the destruction of constellations, including those belonging to India. The United States does not have exclusive ownership of this catastrophe, nor does it have unilateral privilege in assigning blame. Indian intelligence has reason to believe that the origin of the Machinehood is terrestrial. Unless the United States can present clear and incontrovertible proof of wrongdoing by the government or residents of Eko-Yi, India will not participate in the embargo against its former colony. Further, any unilateral act of aggression by the United States against Eko-Yi will be considered by India as an act of war.

—*Doordarshan News, English Feed (March 24, 2095)*
Current accuracy rating: [off-line]

The Indian government displayed its usual chest-beating at the news from abroad. Like other major countries, they had launched emergency communications drones, which meant that Nithya could get some information the old-fashioned way, via screen access. Both China and India, the originators of Eko-Yi Station, were on the US blacklist because of their ties to the off-world colony. As if they hadn't suffered from the Machinehood's actions as much as everyone else.

Carma had weathered the outages better than Nithya expected—and, if she were honest, better than she herself had. Bhairavi Chitthi, too, but she had the benefit of having lived through it before, during the uprisings in the seventies. They all had a high degree of cabin fever, so to speak, but they had food and fuel and the power had come back on.

She tried to reach Luis and Welga, but personal calls were blocked between the two countries. From what she could glean, India was doing better than the US. They walked their children to each other's homes to play. Surprise visitors—such a common occurrence in her great-grandparents' days—became acceptable again. The men in their hive took shifts to guard the entry using whatever crude, weapon-like objects they could find.

Other than that, it felt like a holiday: no work, no school. Nithya spent half her day cooking, cleaning, and laundering static clothes. People had lived like this all the time. Some still did, in the poorest or most rural areas. How did they stand the tedium?

Carma helped her the first few times and then got bored. Nithya's aunt was a godsend, knowing tricks to getting food stains out of fabric and which spices to add to what dishes. Still, nothing tasted quite right except for the rice.

A shout came through the open balcony door. Everyone had left their doors and windows open since the climate control didn't function, and nobody was using swarms. Nithya stepped onto the balcony and peered down four stories.

One of their "guards" looked up at her.

"Someone has come for you," he called.

A dark-skinned young woman with a cut on the side of her face stepped out from the entrance overhang and into view. A baby sat on her hip and gazed at Nithya with wide eyes.

Nithya's heart skipped a beat. "Zeli?"

The girl raised a hand. "We're here!"

In all the chaos of the stellas falling, she'd assumed that Zeli wouldn't be able to get on a flight. Nithya whirled and ran out, bare feet slapping against the cement stairs. She stopped short in front of Zeli, an older woman, a slightly younger woman, and the baby. She guessed those must be Zeli's younger sister and niece.

"Come, come," she said with half a breath. "You must be exhausted."

A faded blue nylon bag, about half a meter long, lay at their feet. Nothing else. Nithya picked it up and led them to the flat.

She stopped outside the door and indicated the low shelf. "If you would please leave your shoes here."

They did. Zeli removed a pair of worn booties from the baby and placed them with the others.

Nithya ventured a smile. "I'm so sorry I didn't meet you at the airport or outside. With the blackout, I had no idea if you would get here."

"We had to wait at the airport in Dakar," Zeli said as they entered, "but they let us on a flight yesterday. The asylum status helped. Thank you for that."

Carma stood from the kitchen table and took Nithya's hand. She stared at the newcomers. Zeli's mother and sister wore plain black hijabs, which they pulled down. With Luis gone, they could uncover their heads.

"Who are these people?" Bhairavi Chitthi asked in Tamil. Her tone dripped with disapproval.

Nithya spoke in English. "Aunty, Carma, this is Salimata and her family. She's worked with me on several projects for Synaxel. They are . . . they've come at my invitation to escape the al-Muwahhidun front in Senegal. Zeli, this is my daughter, Carma, and this is my aunt, Bhairavi."

Zeli gave them a tired smile. "My mother, my sister, and her daughter, Mouna. Thank you for having us."

"Hello," Aunty said politely in English. Then, switching to Tamil, she muttered, "You're letting these kind of people into the house at a time like this?"

Nithya's frayed patience broke apart. She replied in Tamil, careful of Carma's understanding and using a respectful address. "If you don't like it, then you can go. I asked them here. I will not send them away."

Bigotry had yet to die in India. Some people still equated dark with unclean. Bhairavi Chitthi's casual racism was nothing new, but Nithya wouldn't stand for it today, not in her own house. She strove to break the tension by waving to the table.

"Please, sit. Are you hungry? We don't have much water, but there is enough if you want to wash up. Carma, see if we have any old static toys for the baby in the cupboard."

Zeli glanced at Aunty, then back to Nithya. She straightened her shoulders. "Thank you. I'm sorry, my mother doesn't speak English. Only Wolof."

Without a network and WAIs to translate, it was impossible to communicate directly.

"That's all right. What can I get you to eat?" Nithya fell back on custom to cover the awkwardness of the situation. "Some rice and lentils?"

Zeli nodded. She perched at the edge of her chair and bounced the baby. Her sister leaned against their mother, eyes closed. The bags under Zeli's mother's eyes could hold coins. Bhairavi Chit-thi sat on a chair near the balcony and gazed at the sky.

Nithya repressed the urge to ask about Zeli's travels. As for her aunt, Nithya wasn't happy about her treatment of Zeli's family, but it would be frightening for the older woman to get home alone, by foot, in this situation. She couldn't send her away in good conscience, so she'd have to find a way to keep the peace.

Nithya scooped some rice onto three plates and a bowl—for the baby—and then mixed in the cooked dal and salt. Everything was room temperature, but that was warm enough. She remembered to get some spoons, too, in case they weren't used to eating with their hands.

The women roused themselves to take their plates.

"Shall I hold the baby while you eat?" Nithya reached out her arms. "How old is she?"

"Ten months." Zeli's voice trembled. She exchanged the child for the plate of food. "Thank you," she said. "For everything. This—I'll repay you one day."

Nithya touched a hand gently to her colleague's shoulder. Zeli was barely into womanhood, closer to Carma's age than her own. "It's okay. You're safe now. You can stay here."

Nithya sat cross-legged on the floor, the baby in her lap. Carma joined them with an old plushie-bot that had frozen into the shape of an elephant when its electronics stopped functioning. The baby ignored the toy in favor of the bowl of rice, which she happily crammed into her mouth with a chubby fist.

The warm weight of the infant settled Nithya's jangling nerves. As long as they remained in the flat, only her husband's status remained unknown. Such a strange feeling, this not-knowing. Parts of her mind skittered like untrained bots, unsure of what they should be doing at any given moment. Her lips wanted to shape words to Sita—*call Luis*—to see her husband's face, hear his voice. Their last conversation had been so terrible. *Have you forgiven me?*

Aunty spoke in a low, insistent voice, in Tamil. "At least make a wall to separate them for sleeping."

Nithya turned the most expressive glare she could muster on her aunt. With power being so precious, she wouldn't waste a milliwatt on her aunt's nonsense. *Please, God, restore the network so I can send her safely home.* Now that Zeli was here, perhaps she could walk Bhairavi Chitthi home the next morning. But what was the condition of Aunty's flat? Anticipated guilt quashed the idea. She couldn't leave her mother's younger sister to the mercy of data blackout.

Carma had happily snuggled up with Zeli's niece, the two of them fast asleep on Carma's mattress. They'd given Nithya's bed to Zeli's mother. Aunty had the remaining mattress, hers since this started, but she had the nerve to complain while Nithya, Zeli, and her sister would be lying on the bare floor with static cloth under their heads.

"If you don't like it, you can sleep somewhere else tonight," Nithya said softly.

Aunty pursed her lips in distaste and then lay down with her back to the others.

Nithya sat at the table with a mug of tea and the printouts of the report.

Zeli slipped into the other chair. "Looks like data. What is it?"

"Someone anonymously sent me all this after seeing my blocked queries. It has some of the information I wanted, and some evidence of unethical test practices, including a fairly damning letter from a bioethics lawyer."

Zeli raised an eyebrow. "That's a lot of paper."

Nithya flipped to a marked page and pointed at a table, then turned two pages to another. "According to these, it might be possible to design a pill to reverse Welga's symptoms, but we would need funding to customize her treatment. If we can stimulate the progenitor cells, we can regrow the muscle tissue and innervate it. She'll need therapy to retrain her body, but if she stopped using zips, she could be fine. It's possible that Welga's case is extreme—she uses these pills for every job. Others might never experience her problems. If this lawyer, Josephine Lee, is telling the truth, designers had indications of this flaw years ago. I wish we could find her. She'd know who's responsible for this."

"I can hack your emergency network." Zeli spoke the words so softly that Nithya wasn't sure she'd heard them.

"Come again?"

"It will take some time to get all that data through, but I could send an encrypted message to your sister-in-law. Tell her everything you said and let her find this lawyer. I'm sure Welga Ramírez knows how to make someone talk."

Nithya digested Zeli's implied threat. "How do you know this hack?"

Zeli tilted her head. "In the villages, people need to have many skills. Sometimes the emergency network is the only way for us along the front. The al-Muwahhidun love to keep us in the dark."

Zeli uncurled her hand. Two yellow pills lay in her palm.

"Are those . . . ?"

"Yes, the flow will help me do what I need. You write down the message. I'll send it."

Nithya place her hand over the girl's and squeezed gently. "You don't need to sacrifice these for a woman you've never met."

"But that woman is working to save us from the Machine-hood, yes?"

"I believe so."

"Then it's not a sacrifice."

Zeli's eyes glistened with determination. Nithya tapped her message onto a screen, then switched it off. No sense using up the battery until Zeli needed to read the note.

Zeli's mother and Bhairavi Chitthi snored softly from across the room. Light from the full moon fell through the window and limned the prone bodies. Zeli's sister lay on her back, her jaw slack as she slept. Nithya turned her attention back to the printed documents.

An hour later, Zeli grinned.

"Are you in?" Nithya whispered.

A nod. Dark fingers danced on the tabletop, faster than Nithya could interface, even on flow. No wonder Zeli designed so well.

Nithya stayed quiet. Better to let Zeli work than break her trance with more questions. Her own thoughts skipped like a frog on lily pads, from one worrisome matter to the next. She wished her husband had a friend who could hack the network, too, but only she was so lucky.

Nithya turned the screen on and added two more lines: *Is Luis well? If you see him, tell him we love him and miss him.*

CHAPTER 20

WELGA

12. Our agents and bots have outstripped the intelligence and capability of our pets, albeit in different areas of competence. Being their creators, we have not endowed in them a desire for independence, reproduction, or self-improvement. We do not compensate them for their work, other than to maintain their existence. Some would argue that we owe them nothing, not even the minimum of keeping them "alive."

—*The Machinehood Manifesto, March 20, 2095*

Connor drummed his fingers on the bed while Welga paced around the room. She was downing duo-zips every three hours to keep herself from turning into a human quake, and she had nearly run out. She'd budgeted enough to get her through the journey to Eko-Yi. On a rocket that floated in the middle of the ocean. That wouldn't launch anytime soon.

The latent energy that zips filled her with didn't help her restless mood.

"Can you believe this shit they're pulling? Again?" she seethed. "Can you?"

Connor sighed. "You can't do anything about it. Call Olafson. Ask him to put you back on the Maghreb mission."

"The Machinehood isn't in North Africa." Welga growled and jabbed a finger upward. "They are up there. I know it! *They* know it!"

"You need to relax. This isn't good for you. Go cook something. I could use a bowl of chicken soup."

"The state of the fucking world isn't good for me, and cooking soup won't make it better. We have to figure out a way to get that rocket launched."

"And risk the lives of twenty civilians? Those interceptors can scramble in three minutes. They'll be over the rocket in five."

"I'll go to the base and destroy them."

Connor snorted. "You're out of your mind."

"Goddamn right."

"Maybe you're wrong about Eko-Yi, and the caliph really is behind the Machinehood. Ao Tara doesn't seem the type to create this kind of chaos."

"No, I'm right. This administration wants a reason to invade the empire, and I do, too, but a legit reason. Not some bullshit that goes against the evidence we have. I walked away from doing the right thing before, when I was too young and scared to go against orders, but this fight belongs to me and every other human being on this planet. The Machinehood brought it to us, and our chickenshit government doesn't own it any more than I do. They're going to fuck this up again, and this time, it won't be only North Africa that suffers. We'll all pay the price. I'm not going to sit around and let that happen."

"You can't do this alone," he said gently, "just like you

couldn't have gone back into Marrakech and taken the caliph out by yourself. That wasn't your fault."

"I can go to DC and beat some sense into the politicians. Or broadcast the operation details and get the people of this country to know the truth. I don't care what happens to me. If I can get footage of the dakini interrogation, I could leak it—"

"Your brother," Connor said.

Welga stopped. "What?"

"Doesn't he belong to a rocket club?"

"In Chennai. So?"

"India has paused its launches, but it hasn't agreed to an embargo yet. Luis has access to a rocket." He opened his eyes and stared like the rest was obvious.

"The agency isn't going to fly me to Chennai so I can take a foreign rocket to violate orders by the commander in chief."

"Your contract with the agency is at will. You said it yourself—this fight belongs to everyone. If you can stop the Machinehood, does it matter how?"

Welga blinked at her partner. "Go rogue? That plan is almost as crazy and stupid as mine." She sat on the edge of the bed. "You don't do crazy or stupid. I rely on you to talk me out of that shit."

"If you can't beat them, join them."

Whatever it takes. Bypassing her government entirely just might work.

She nodded, more to herself than him. "I like it. Guess I'd better go to Phoenix."

Connor grimaced. "If I were more mobile, I could find you a berth on a cargo ship. That's your best way overseas."

In spite of the emergency stellas, the government hadn't allowed any international flights in or out. Part of their idiotic attempt to coerce the Asians into cooperation, no doubt.

"Maybe Ammanuel could help us with that. I bet they're really damn bored right now," Welga said.

"Can we trust them?"

"They're a Raider. That's enough for me."

Welga realized that she had no physical address for Jady Ammanuel after she got in the truck. She knew where Platinum Shield Services had their local office, though, so she headed there. Hassan looked understandably confused to see her, but he pulled her into a bear hug anyway.

"It's good to see you in one piece, Ramírez."

Why did people keep greeting her that way?

"Good to see you, too, boss, but I'm afraid I'm in a hurry. I need to borrow Ammanuel for a bit. I assume they aren't busy right now?"

"No, they're on leave along with the majority of shields. The funders have walled themselves away from the world's shitstorm."

Hassan found Ammanuel's address and gave it to her. He narrowed his eyes. "I suppose I can't ask you what this is about?"

"You can ask. Doesn't mean I'll answer."

He snorted. "Stay safe, Ramírez."

The streets were quieter than they had been when she'd arrived three days before. Abandoned and wrecked bots still littered her way, but she didn't see many people other than those who were prone on the sidewalks. The world had moved to crowd-sourced cures as a fast way to counter the bioengineered diseases of midcentury. Kitchens made the treatments handy, and daily design updates had ended the pandemics . . . until now. Whether those people on the side of the road had fallen to illness or starvation, she couldn't be sure, and she wouldn't risk the exposure to find out. At some point, though, even the disease-hackers would run out of supplies. How long would that take?

Ammanuel lived in the subbasement of a low-rent hive. Luckily, their street was free of bodies. Welga ran in, waited like an idiot for the door to open, and then remembered she had to knock.

"Ramírez?" They gawked at her.

She pushed past them into a studio apartment. In the middle of the room, a low table sat surrounded by three basic chairs. Light came from harsh electrics rather than tubes. An unpowered kitchen occupied the back corner, and a mattress lay on the floor nearby, a young masculine person with sandy brown hair sprawled in deep sleep on its surface. Ammanuel wore a basic shift and leggings in a rusty orange that complemented their hair color.

"Sorry to disturb you," Welga whispered. "I need your help. Hassan said you're benched for now and have some free cycles."

"That's right. Can't gig, can't work. What's going on?"

She held up a hand and deployed the last of the security-swarm from the agency.

"Clear to proceed," Por Qué said.

Her agent's flat affect still made her wince. She'd gotten somewhat used to the absence of feeds in her visual, but having Por Qué reduced to a basic WAI felt like she was missing part of her mind.

Welga explained the situation to Ammanuel and concluded by asking them to be a gofer for Connor. She didn't know them well enough to read their body language as she talked, but to her relief, they agreed.

"Thank you," she said. "Not too many people I can trust anymore. You'd better pack for a few days. It's hard to get around."

"I noticed," Ammanuel said, "but you can see I don't have

much. Haven't had the time or coin to settle in. Let me grab a few things from the bathroom and say good-bye. I'll meet you outside."

She resisted the urge to hurry them up. The number of pills in her pocket had turned into a fuse. She had no more microcards to buy another batch, and the banks would move only minimal amounts of coin. They refused to dispense untraceable money. She had to get to Phoenix before her supply ran out. Papa always kept some cash on hand.

○——○——○

Welga arrived at the outskirts of Phoenix just before sunset. People on the streets sorted through the rubble and kept getting in the way of Welga's truck. Idiots. Did they think she wouldn't run them over? She was tempted. So damn tempted.

Her final check-in with Olafson hadn't helped her mood. Yes, she was sure she wanted to cancel her contract with the agency. No, Troit didn't want to stay, either. He hadn't fully healed from the refinery incident. Yes, she realized she would've been in trouble for launching without him. No, she didn't want to rendezvous with the Maghreb team. Yes, she was really damn sure. No, she didn't need a week to reconsider. *I have bigger plans, traitor.* Which was somewhat unfair to Olafson. He hadn't created this situation, but she couldn't help the bitterness. He'd gotten her involved only to frustrate her again. She changed her mind and accepted the extra week. She needed the time with the military vehicle and emergency stella access.

A sandstorm from the previous night had scoured the landscape of smaller debris. Large bots—more mechanical death—hulked in every street. Plenty of good pickings for scavengers. Welga ignored the yelling as she drove over a pile of weeder-bots in the middle of the street. *It's a road, assholes. Find a better place to dump your shit.*

She was down to two zips. Phoenix had its hot zones—every city did—but she had to go home and grab some microcards first. She'd lost consciousness twice since getting off the freeway, waking to find the truck rammed into a wall and herself flopped at an awkward angle, pain radiating from multiple parts of her body. She needed to increase the dosage frequency again. Christ, she missed Por Qué—the real one, not this shitty generic version. No doubt a full-fledged Por Qué would've informed Welga of seizure activity and reported it, too, but at least she would have looked after her.

Welga stopped at the nearest charging station to the house. She had some network access from the emergency stellas, but seeing the empty bays reminded her that most everyone else didn't.

"Incoming anonymous message," Por Qué announced.

Welga blinked at the alert in her visual. Who the hell would be routing an anonymous message to her? The agency had no reason to. The public network remained dark. Machine rights people? The odds of them hacking the emergency stellas were slim. The Machinehood, on the other hand . . . If the enemy engaged, she couldn't ignore it.

"Display message."

Nithya. Of all people. She'd sent an enormous document full of charts and numbers along with a note, brief and stunning: *Find Josephine Lee, a bioethics lawyer who worked with the EUBGA and others. She can help us get data for your motor-system problem.*

"Download the document," Welga said. It would take hours, but she had other shit to deal with in the meantime.

She drove away from the station. How the hell had Nithya accessed the emergency network? And how had she come across

Jun-ha Park's mother? So Ao Tara had information relating to Welga's zip problem. *Too rich.* Her leg twitched. Maybe the monk would cooperate with Welga out of sympathy. After all, her son had died from some kind of disease. Didn't she owe Welga—and others suffering like her—some help? *Find Josephine Lee.* Welga nearly laughed out loud. One more reason to get to Eko-Yi.

She pulled into the driveway of the house. The truck was so wide, the right tires ended up in the front yard. Sheets of temporary-use plastic covered the left side of the house. Luis opened the front door and peered out. His jaw dropped briefly, then closed as she stepped out of the vehicle. He ran and wrapped her in a hug. She leaned into him.

"You came! He's not doing good."

Welga pulled back. "Who? What are you talking about?"

Luis frowned. He turned and led her inside. Wood boards covered the windows. Dim light came from old ceiling lamps in the kitchen and living room, the sunlight tubes sitting still and dark. The odor of stale smoke tickled her nose.

"Papa had a heart attack," Luis said. "I thought maybe you saw it on your spy network. That's not why you're here?"

Welga clutched her brother's arm as the world spun. "What? No, I came . . . because . . ." She stopped talking as all her breath escaped. Her leg tingled. "Shit! Not again."

Luis's concerned expression swam in and out of her sight, then everything went sparkly black.

─o──o─

When consciousness returned, Welga had a perfect view of the ceiling. It needed paint. *Goddamn static houses and their maintenance.* Her head throbbed. Oscar sat nearby, resembling a skeleton hung with brown paper skin.

"Papa," she said. Her voice emerged hoarse and rough.

He moved to her side. His hand was warm and dry as it brushed the hair from her forehead. "Thank God. You were so still after that convulsion, I was afraid . . . well, you're all right now."

"Where's Luis?"

"I'm here," her brother said.

Welga turned and saw him in the kitchen. He walked over, helped her sit up, and handed her a cup of water. A wave of nausea rushed through Welga. She closed her eyes for three deep breaths, then took a sip. The tepid water felt cool on its way to her stomach. She fished out a zip and placed it under her tongue. When she opened her eyes, two grim faces stared at her. They didn't need words to demand an explanation.

"It's funny," she said. "After all these years of avoiding flow, the zips did me in. I have some condition that gets worse every time I take a zip, but while I'm sped up, the symptoms get better. That was an epileptic seizure you saw just now. Withdrawal or maybe more damage. I don't know."

Luis nodded. "Nithya mentioned something was going on, but she didn't say it was this bad."

"I'm getting worse," Welga admitted. "I haven't told her."

"So why are you still taking those pills?" Papa demanded. "You're making it bad on purpose?"

Welga waved a tired hand. "I'm down to my last one, mainly to get here. I need to borrow some credit and push on."

She told them about Connor and the launch and the plan to use Luis's club instead.

"I'm going to live until I take those fuckers on Eko-Yi down. After that, I don't know," Welga said. "But I intend to come back and figure out how to get over this shit."

"I'm not going back to Chennai," Luis said.

"What do you mean?" Welga asked.

"I'm going to live here."

Luis relayed Nithya's confession. He didn't mention how she'd gotten the abortion, so her sister-in-law hadn't told him Welga's part. Stern approval of Luis's separation from Nithya took root in Oscar's face as her brother finished. Christ, her family was so predictable.

The windows rattled.

"Another storm?" Welga said.

"Sounds like it," Papa replied.

Of course they wouldn't know, not with the network being dark.

"You worried about your truck?" Papa said. "Want me to put it in the garage?"

Welga nodded and handed him the key to start it. If anyone in her family could operate a large vehicle, it was Oscar, with all his years of mech-wearing and construction work.

While he was gone, she turned all her fury on her brother. "If you leave your wife, you are the biggest fucking idiot on the planet. You knew she wasn't going to be a good little Catholic when you married her, and you can't expect her to act like one to spare your feelings."

"Don't advise me about marriage, Welga. You wouldn't understand."

I've had a partner for a decade, asshole. She squelched the desire to wring her little brother's neck and took two deep breaths. She needed to win Luis over, not cement his stubborn idiocy. "When you find a good person, someone who you can spend your life with and not hate the world, someone who's grown with you, moved around with you, who forgives your bullshit and thinks you're sexy on your off days, someone . . ." *who you leave again and again, who waits for you, not knowing if you'll come back alive.* "When it hurts to live without them, no matter how angry you are, you find it in your heart to forgive *their* bullshit." Welga grabbed his arm. "If you don't go back to her, you will regret it until your last breath. I can promise you that."

The front door slammed as Oscar came in. A generous coating of dust made his graying hair look shades lighter. Wind whistled through a crack.

As their father washed his hands in the kitchen sink, he said, "Luis, you should help your sister. You can always come back here after."

Luis blinked. "Even if we could somehow pull off a launch, Welga is in no shape to go up there."

"You let me work that part out," Welga said. "The answer to everything, even my neurological problems, could come from a person on Eko-Yi. Your *wife* told me so."

"The Machinehood lives up there. You can't face them in your condition, alone. Think of what they did to you when you could still fight! It's a death warrant!"

Papa raised a hand. "She's dead either way, right?"

"We don't know that, Papa!"

"Back in the seventies," Oscar said, ignoring Luis, "during the riots, me and my union buddies put ourselves in front of those mech-loaded police. We knew we could die, but the alternative was worse. And we won, didn't we? Most of us lived, too. Sometimes, for the right causes, you got to risk your life."

Luis turned his glare on their father. "You don't get it! We're not talking about riots or even war. We have juvers, medics, hospitals to take care of people who get hurt. Even back then, you had those." He thrust his index finger upward. "That station is a giant metal can surrounded by hard vacuum. They push Welga out of an air lock, poof! She's dead. On Earth, she stands a chance. Offworld, nobody can save her life."

Welga laid herself on the sofa, as her leg tremors made standing impossible. "Not much of a life anyway, Luis. Right now, we don't have juvers or medic-bots or antivirals. We'll all die that way unless we can stop the Machinehood."

Waves of distortion washed over reality. Her vision went sparkly. *Here we go again.*

Welga regained consciousness to a sense of heavy exhaustion. Luis sat on the floor next to the sofa and held her hand. The clatter of dishes came from the kitchen.

"I'll go," her brother said.

"What?"

"I'll go to Chennai with you, get a launch together." Luis shook his head as if incredulous at himself. "How we're going to do that with the airports and sub-orbs shut down, I have no idea."

"We'll take a boat ride."

She made it through dinner without another episode, then took her last zip before heading to downtown Phoenix for a dealer. Night had fallen, and she nearly had to tie Luis and Papa down to keep them from coming with her. Even during her deepest cover operations, her family could get her status from the military. This time, they had to wait and hope for the best.

She changed her outfit to a loose tunic over leggings, baggy enough to hide the weapon underneath. The bathroom mirror informed her that her hair and skin looked naturally greasy. Nothing to change there. She glanced at the old makeup-bot on the counter and had a flashback to Briella Jackson's death. That happened on March 12. It was March 25. How had the world—and her life—fallen apart in less than two weeks?

Oven-hot air greeted Welga when she entered the truck. A fine layer of dust from the short-lived storm coated the outside. She drove into the city, but she didn't get far. The truck's headlights drew too much attention. Vigilante forces guarded the better-quality hives and kept trying to approach her.

If she'd been able to change her clothes, she could've transformed into a wealthy citizen and left the truck in one of those neighborhoods. Instead, Welga found a side street where she could park it mostly out of sight. The military vehicle could take plenty of physical abuse and wouldn't start without her physical key, but if someone managed to tow it away, she'd have a long, unpleasant walk home.

She and Luis had been good kids through high school, staying away from the pill-hackers and drug abusers. She hadn't paid attention to where they liked to hang out. Her grandfather had run a shop in the migrant labor section, an address she knew. Might as well go that way as anywhere else.

She pinched her cheeks until they hurt, then inhaled dust until her cough sounded convincing. Sickness spread quickly without daily prophylactics, and fear of infection was her best defense against aggressive civilians.

The first gang appeared two blocks from the alley. No surprise. They surrounded her, four masked, overgrown teenagers with metal clubs ripped from bots. She bent over, coughed, and spat.

"Please, help me," she rasped. "I'm sick." Coughed again and held out a pleading hand. "Lookin' for juvers."

The one closest to her outstretched arm stumbled back.

"No one gonna fuck you for a pill," they said.

Another snorted. "Probably got a new bug. You dead, bitch."

The others laughed. They continued to joke about her condition as they walked away. Welga kept her crouch and shuffled forward, careful to maintain the appearance of illness.

The majority of buildings she passed stood in darkness, their doors closed and windows boarded. Hives towered with dim light leaking from upper-story windows. The lack of activity—human, swarm, or bot—disconcerted her more than the literal darkness. She steered away from any sound of violence, mostly metal on metal, and toward voices if they weren't raised. The first four times, they belonged to vigilante guards who left her alone as she gave them a wide berth. The fifth time, she walked past three people, one receiving a blow job, the other waiting their turn. *Must be getting closer.* Another corner brought her to humanity scattered on the streets.

Homeless people formed dark masses against or inside bots whose rusted condition predated the Machinehood's attack. Some of them coughed, too. No one paid attention to Welga. Phoenix had fewer itinerants than San Francisco. The heat and dust storms drove them into shelters, and those who couldn't find one didn't live long.

Welga moved easily down the center of the street, while murmuring, "Pretties? Joyrides?"

"Hey," a voice called. "Over here."

Welga headed toward them, a slender, young person with cropped brown hair and lean muscles along their bare arms.

"You're new here. Don't need to whisper. Nobody cares, especially not now. You got cash?"

Welga pulled a microcard from her pocket and flashed the amount at the dealer. "What you got? I need pretties and joyrides."

Their eyes narrowed. *Why would someone like you need zips?*

"For my brother," Welga clarified. "Westside Brown." The gang had existed two decades ago, in her high school years. Thank Christ for the network blackout, because this dealer looked like they wanted to call someone and check on the affiliation.

After several tense seconds, they shrugged. "Don't matter to me." They opened their case, which had its own light.

Welga scanned the pills and spotted half a dozen quads, a good number of duos, and a plethora of juvers. She hadn't expected the variety and spent longer than she should have deciding what to get.

The dealer snapped the box shut. "You buyin' or not?"

Welga shook herself as if from a reverie. "Yeah, yeah. All the quads, twelve duos, two antivirals, and two wound wipers."

The dealer laughed. "You think that card's gonna buy all those?"

Welga pulled out two more.

"Better," they said. "You'll need to double that."

Welga shook her head. She'd left most of Papa's cash at the house. They'd need it to pay for their passage on the boat.

"Open your mouth and show me your hand." The dealer shone a light at Welga. "You look clean enough. The cards and a hand job, that's my deal."

The words *no way in hell* died before they reached Welga's lips. *Whatever it takes.* Olafson had said it, and years before, Jack Travis had shown her what it meant, but she wasn't working under orders now. She could refuse.

What if others had nothing to sell, or asked worse of her?

Welga took a deep breath, looked the dealer in the eyes, and nodded.

They pulled Welga inside a dark, sweltering shop and locked the door. Then they grabbed Welga's hand, doused it with disinfectant, and pulled down their pants.

"You make me come or the deal's off."

In the blackout, no microcams swarmed.

No one could watch. Nothing would hear.

With the energy of her last duo-zip buzzing in her muscles,

Welga grabbed the dealer's balls and yanked. Her knee came up, into their solar plexus. Just enough force to send their diaphragm into spasm. The box of pills flew across the room.

As they lay on the shop floor, gasping for air, she walked to the case.

"You shouldn't take advantage of sick people," she said.

She took what she needed, kept her microcards, and left them writhing on the floor.

CHAPTER 21

WELGA

24. Humankind cannot expect to compete with intelligent machines forever, and the longer we attempt to do so, the further we drift from actual humanity. Our empathy for each other fades, dulled by the requirement to ignore our natural feelings for the machines in our lives.

—*The Machinehood Manifesto, March 20, 2095*

Welga resisted the urge to rip off her hand and wiped it on her tunic as she walked back to the truck. She took a quad-zip as soon as she was clear of the dealer's street. Rage and revulsion provided plenty of saliva to dissolve it. Christ, she could use a drink of water.

What had she done wrong to end up in this mess? For all the years spent being so damn careful to avoid flow, she had ended up almost exactly where Mama had, with a body destroyed by pills that she needed for her work. Maybe the machine rights people had the truth of it: humans couldn't compete with WAIs and bots and whatever the hell the Machinehood were. They

would destroy themselves by trying. Better to give up and let
the AIs rule. Maybe the Machinehood's actions would save humankind from itself. Maybe some elements of humanity didn't
deserve to exist anyway.

Someone interrupted her morose thoughts with a well-timed
tackle. Welga landed on her back with her assailant crosswise over
her. The quad had kicked in, though, as had her instincts. She
rolled with the momentum of their fall and threw the asshole.
Two others came at her. She ducked the swing of a metal club and
pulled its user off balance. They moved like slow, clumsy children
relative to her perception and reaction times. *Not trained fighters,
just some dumbasses looking for a victim.*

She broke loose and ran the remainder of the way to the
truck. Stupid to have forgotten her coughing act. Stupider to get
lost in thought and ignore her surroundings.

Welga drove home at full speed, uncaring of what she tram-
pled. Anyone out at this time of night needed to get the hell
out of her way. Darkness both literal and technological blanketed
Phoenix and let the worst of human behavior go unchecked. It
hid their misdeeds. Ever-present swarms had meant that someone could be watching, that your actions never went unno-
ticed. Criminals had to work harder—and in the privacy of their
property—but with the stellas down, WAIs abandoned, and bots
destroyed, the streets had changed.

Her father's neighborhood was quieter. Welga parked the
truck in the garage. The wind picked up and blew hot, dry air
across her skin. Another dust storm was coming. She lifted the
hair from her neck to feel the breeze. A rusty tap on the side of
the house released lukewarm water. Welga scrubbed her hands
with sand, using an infuriated speed from the quad-zip, and
rinsed until her skin stung from the abrasions. She made sure to
get every molecule of that dealer off her. Then she went inside.

A dim ceiling light showed Papa prone on the sofa, his eyes blinking at her.

He sat up slowly. "Well?"

"Got what I needed."

"You're talking fast."

"Quads." She made an effort to slow down. "The dual-speed zips don't do enough anymore."

Sadness and regret tugged his eyes and mouth downward. She kissed his head as her heart ached.

"Love you, Papa. Sorry I couldn't fix this."

"Don't say it like that. You told us earlier that this lady on the station could help you. Maybe find out what's wrong and heal you. You're not dead yet." He took her hand and stroked it. "Sit down. I have to tell you something."

She dropped onto the sofa.

"When your mama was near the end, some funders offered her an experimental design. Said it might cure her by mucking with her DNA, changing it so that she didn't have her problems. But it would also mean no more flow. She'd have to start over, find something else to do with her life."

Where are you going with this?

"She took a regular flow to check out their design. She didn't think their idea would work, but she needed to make sure. And that . . . that's when her body gave up." A muscle twitched in Papa's cheek. "I wonder sometimes, if she'd trusted them, if she hadn't taken that last one and tried the new stuff, would she be here today? Would you be sick? She'd have spent all her hours figuring out your condition. Maybe she's up in heaven right now, looking at us and yelling at me for letting you join the service, for letting you put pills in your body."

"Oh, Papa." Welga wrapped an arm around him and squeezed gently. "If she's up there, she knows you couldn't have stopped me."

"Ha. You were always stubborn. More than your brother. But I tell you, I'm proud of you right now, for going after these people, for chasing your cure. Don't give up. Don't settle, like me. Your mama left this world doing what she loved best. I think she'd be proud of you, too."

"I promise I'll keep fighting," Welga said. "Now go to bed, please. If I live through all this, I don't want to come back to Earth to find you keeled over from a bad heart, okay? You need to hold on, too, until we get the world working again."

She helped him up and kissed his scratchy cheek. She turned off the lights, locked the front door, and stopped in front of her mother's photo screen. The same routine she'd had every night in high school. With two fingers, she touched her lips and then her mother's face.

As she passed Luis's room, she stuck her head through the doorway. "I'm likely to crash if we drive back tonight. Be ready to go early, though. We'll leave at eight."

○────○═○──○

They arrived in San Francisco about ten hours after leaving Phoenix. Ammanuel and Hassan surprised them by opening the door of her and Connor's apartment.

"I wouldn't have bet on you going rogue, Ramírez," Hassan said.

"It's not safe for you to know too much, boss," Welga said. "Stay out of this."

"I'll take that advice the same as you would."

Which meant not at all. She couldn't blame him.

"You can't do this alone," Hassan rumbled.

Welga tilted her head at the bedroom, where Luis had gone with Connor. "I'll have my brother."

"And he can protect you?"

"I can protect my own damn self."

"Sure, when you're conscious. Yeah, your partner told me about your condition. Cargo ships don't have a reputation for personal safety, and your brother can't help if you're knocked out. I want you to take Ammanuel with you to Chennai. They already agreed, and I can put them on a temporary leave of absence from Platinum."

Welga opened her mouth to argue, but the boss held up his hand.

"Okay," she said. She had to admit that his reasoning made sense. Luis couldn't fight to save his life, much less hers.

"We have Chinese food," Ammanuel said. They moved to reveal a stack of white containers on the kitchen counter. "Troit said it's tradition."

"Yeah," she said. "Though we haven't done that in a long time."

Every kitchen in every hotel had the ability to cook American Chinese food. Like pizza and burgers, it had become a global cuisine. She and Connor would always have it on their last night together before she left for a field operation. This time, they shared the meal with Hassan, Ammanuel, and Luis. Connor managed to sit at the table long enough to finish eating, but his hands shook and his shoulders slumped. The injuries and infections had knocked out his strength.

Welga helped him back to bed, then emerged to find the others cleaning up.

"Thank you," she said quietly to Hassan.

"Don't worry about Troit," he said. "He'll pull through. I'll check in on him whenever I can."

"I'm going to miss you, boss."

"Likewise. And you're welcome."

Hassan and Ammanuel said their good-byes, with Ammanuel promising to meet them dockside the next day. Luis sat on the sofa gazing around like a lost child.

"I don't know what to do with no stellas," he said. "Normally I'd be working gigs, but . . ." He shrugged.

Welga waved at the shelf of heirloom cookbooks she'd collected. "You can read these."

Her brother grimaced. "I think I'll try to sleep."

"Your loss."

She closed the bedroom door behind her and found Connor already asleep. She stepped into the bathroom and filled the tub. Hot water had returned, though it meant that water rationing had also resumed. She spent most of her monthly allowance. She wouldn't return for at least that long.

Welga took a duo-zip and slipped into the tub. She had to ration her remaining pills to last until she reached Chennai. Two weeks of travel . . . a lot could happen in that time. Would India and China take America's side against Eko-Yi? Would they actively defend their right to launch supplies to the station? Their loyalty to their former colony had kept them from agreeing to a full embargo, but if the US shared their intel, the two countries might be convinced.

The dakini had come from the space station. They'd murdered three funders, killed or injured dozens more during combat, and destroyed billions of coin in property. Those crimes couldn't go unanswered. What would she find up there? She hadn't planned on making her first visit to space a dangerous mission, but any confrontation with the Machinehood had the potential to get violent. How many on the station were involved? With barely four hundred residents, keeping secrets couldn't be easy, even in a place without constant swarms.

The water had cooled to body temperature. Welga toweled

off and emerged to find Connor awake. He raised his brows appreciatively at her form and beckoned her to bed.

"You sure you aren't too tired?" she said.

He shook his head and traced a finger along her neck and shoulder. "Chinese food and sex. It's our tradition. It would be bad luck to break it."

They tried to be quiet, and Connor let her do most of the work, but he definitely wasn't too tired. No cameras. No audience. No tips. She had always thought it would feel less exciting that way. In a way, it did, but their quiet intimacy put her in a state similar to flow—complete concentration on *this moment*, no distractions, fully engaged with the heat of Connor's flushed skin, the sound of his hitched breath, the pressure of his fingers digging into her hips.

Afterward, they held each other for ten minutes in complete silence. With her ear to his chest, Welga could hear the crackling of fluid as Connor breathed.

"Remember to take your antibiotics while I'm gone," she said. "You won't have your agent to help."

Connor's chuckle turned into a cough. When it subsided, he said, "Worry less about me and more about yourself. We know what's wrong with my body." His arm tightened around her. "This feels like Marrakech all over again, going into a bad situation without reliable intel, only this time, you'll be alone."

"But this time there's no one to tell me what to do, or what not to."

"Welga—"

"Don't say it. You can think it all you want, but don't say it out loud."

What if you die up there? Only an idiot wouldn't acknowledge that truth, but she couldn't allow them to speak it. *Fear has to take a back seat to confidence.* Captain Travis had taught her that.

Doesn't matter if the confidence is unfounded. Without it, you have no chance of making it real. Box up all that doubt and shove it into the furthest reaches of your mind.

"I'm going to Eko-Yi. I'm going to find the Machinehood operatives there and make sure they never hurt anyone or anything again. And then I'm going to come home to you, to working stellas and swarms, and if space doesn't suck, maybe we'll go back up there, together. I don't think Eko-Yi will want us, though."

Connor snorted. "Probably not." He shook his head. "I can't believe the entire station would support the Machinehood, not with everything Ao Tara teaches. I thought they wanted to start a new way of life up there. They hoped the world would follow their example. There has to be something better than what we have here. A system with reliable work. A sense of self-worth. A greater purpose."

"Reliable work and self-worth? That shit went the way of the dodo bird in our grandparents' day or maybe earlier. It's why we became shields, right? Steady pay. An actual employer. But why do you care? I thought you like doing gigs."

"Sure, they're fun, especially compared to getting beaten up and shot at, but I think you were right. I'd start to hate it if that's what I did all day, every day."

Welga patted his chest. Her hand twitched.

Connor caught it in his. "Take care of yourself, please."

"I love you," she said, making no promises. She couldn't, not with the looming magnitude of what she wanted to accomplish.

~~~

Welga had never left for a mission without having her loved ones in her visual. During her ATAI service, she could see them anytime she wasn't in the Marrakech blackout zone, could know that their lives went on without her. Not this time. Papa and Connor, the two people who mattered most in her life, would have to manage on their own. At one level, she knew they could handle themselves. At another, she wanted to make sure. She was used to checking in on everyone. Talking to them. Sharing in the little troubles and joys that made life worth living. Reminding them to take care of themselves.

She left Connor in the artificial hands of Marcelo's care-bot, her heart heavy with misgivings. How the hell had Luis managed without seeing Nithya or Carma for the past week? How could he not worry himself sick?

They caught a ferry from the harbor in San Francisco to the much larger port of Oakland. Warm mist lay over the bay like an unwanted blanket. They navigated the massive, mazelike docks to find their cargo ship. Passage cost more than Welga had expected, and when they saw the crowd of other passengers, she understood why. They weren't the only ones desperate to hitch a ride out of the country.

As she climbed the long ramp to the deck, the people around her gasped. She followed their gazes upward. Gray streaks chased silent blazes of white light. *Shit.* The Machinehood had knocked out the emergency stellas. Her stomach twisted with helpless urgency. Twelve days to reach Hong Kong. Another three from there to Chennai. How much more damage would the world take in the meantime? What else would the Machinehood destroy with few witnesses and no recorded evidence? Cutting off communications was a damn effective way to terrorize.

They shared a cabin with three others, all of them Chinese nationals who spoke no English. If the stellas worked, their agents would've translated for them. Instead, they settled for hand gestures and friendly smiles. A total of six fold-out bunks lined the two sides. The head was in the hallway and shared with everyone else in their section. A tiny shower had a ration roster taped on pulp paper. Each person could sign up for one shower every other day.

Welga fell into the bottom bunk. She hadn't taken a zip in over an hour, and if she was going to collapse, better to lie down first. She asked Ammanuel—Jady, if they were going to be this friendly—to scope out the lay of the ship. At the least, they needed to know where and when to get food. Welga also wanted to know where they could exercise.

"Keep a lookout for a working pill dispenser," she called as they were leaving.

The chances of the ship having one were low, but it never hurt to check. The number of pills she'd taken from the asshole in Phoenix wouldn't last her a week at the rate she needed them now. She'd have to space them further apart than comfortable. It would go easier if they didn't have cabinmates, but somehow they'd have to communicate that her condition wasn't contagious.

Luis and Jady returned to report what Welga had suspected. No pill dispensers. No satcom tethers. This wasn't a military ship or a passenger cruise. They'd been lucky to get berths at all. An open space on the upper deck could serve as an exercise area. The cafeteria was one deck above them, amidships.

They had nothing much to pass the hours. Welga tried to read the massive document from Nithya and found the science too complex to understand. Josephine Lee's resignation letter made more sense. The content and timing aligned with Lee's journal. Welga would have to win her trust before convincing her to testify against Synaxel, especially now that she was Ao Tara, the leader of Eko-Yi. If the monk had anything to do with the

Machinehood—if she'd knowingly harbored them—trust might be asking too much. *Play the sympathy angle. Make Ao Tara feel guilty. It'll be a breeze in this condition.*

When they had the room to themselves, she, Luis, and Jady would whisper their theories about what the hell might happen next. She doubted anyone was recording them, but she couldn't secure the room, and whispering meant reducing the risk. The rest of the time, she played cards with Luis or watched something from Jady's collection. Ammanuel had wisely downloaded some entertainment to their internal storage before leaving home. Her near-field comm was compatible with theirs, which meant they could share, but Jady's taste ran to the latest WAIbrid music. It was going to be a damn long two weeks.

They had to change ships in Hong Kong. The city had launched a temporary local drone network, which gave Welga a chance to catch up with the latest from the news feeds. Machinehood operatives on the ground had sabotaged several major network hubs around the world in addition to taking down the stellas. Security had moved to protect infrastructure rather than funders, but they attacked the Machinehood as soon as they saw the operatives. The dakini would react with deadly force. Welga's realization about nonviolence must not have reached a worldwide audience before the constellations fell. The American government wasn't sharing that information, clearly, nor anything from their interrogations of the dakini. *No wonder India and China don't believe us about Eko-Yi.* That was the worst part about being cut off from the agency—she no longer had access to expert intelligence. She had no way to find out what was happening with the team in the Maghreb.

They arrived in Chennai on April 11, as the fisherfolk were heading out to sea. Welga stood on the main deck and leaned on the rail. Her muscles twitched and trembled, which they now did nonstop, but only a close observer would notice. The tiny wooden boats looked like toys from her viewpoint. Seagulls squawked and circled overhead. Warm, humid air blew across her skin and sent the loose strands of her hair whipping around her face. When they stopped moving, it wouldn't feel so pleasant.

Luis approached and leaned on the rail next to her. He shaded his eyes with one hand and pointed to a distant smudge offshore. "That's the launch platform."

"How long to get the rocket ready?"

"A cargo launch is easy. We need to get the club together, find the fuel, pack the supplies, and shove you in the middle of it. Maybe two days? We also do a final check of the rocket, even though it's fully tested after it lands." He put a hand over hers. "You were right about Nithya."

"Oh?"

"She is something special, and I made a commitment that I intend to honor. I believe that God loves her, too. Matthew 6:14 says that if we do not forgive others their sins, our Father will not forgive ours." Luis sighed. "I will forgive my wife. I love her, and I don't want to spend my life without her."

Welga hugged him with one arm. "Good. Too bad I don't have a recording of this. I could replay you saying, 'You were right,' every time I got depressed about anything."

Luis laughed and hugged her back. His expression turned wistful. "It's been hard not seeing or talking to Carma, too. I'm glad I came home."

Luis handled the transactions between the harbor and his apartment. He'd picked up enough Tamil along the way to function without agent translations. He almost leaped out of their car as they arrived. One of the people standing in front of the hive recognized him and greeted them with a warm smile. As soon as they were through the gate, Luis left her and Jady behind and dashed up the stairs. She opted for the elevator.

Welga heard Nithya's voice, followed by Carma's squeal of delight. Her niece's voice carried clearly. "Papa! You're back! It's so annoying, the stellas being down! Oh, we have visitors. Come and meet them. I'll tell you who they are."

Welga rounded the corner. Nithya stood in their doorway, wearing a colorful knee-length tunic over leggings, her back to them. Her sister-in-law's hair hung in a neat braid to her waist. Welga tiptoed forward and wrapped her in a warm hug.

"Welga!"

"Thank you for everything," Welga murmured before pulling away. "Ammanuel, you need to leave your shoes here." She indicated the pile outside the door and added her own.

Carma's jaw dropped as they entered. "Aunty Welga! I didn't know you were here."

"I came with your papa. This is our friend, Jady Ammanuel."

A crowd of strangers sat around the main room and stared at them. Nithya made introductions, and Luis settled Welga on some old static cushions. Just in time, too, as the world went sparkly and then black.

She opened her eyes to several concerned faces around her.

"It's fine," Welga said hoarsely. She knew from experience not to turn her head or sit up too soon. She subvocalized, "Por Qué, how long until my next dose?"

"You have one hour and twelve minutes remaining until your next zip dose."

Welga had set the automatic reminders so she didn't run out of pills before their journey ended. Whether Nithya's kitchen worked or not, she had enough for two more days. The sooner they could get her on that rocket, the better.

* * *

Luis's rocket club friends lived all over the sprawling city of Chennai, but the autos weren't running and manual vehicles were hard to come by, so he borrowed some bicycles from nearby friends. Ammanuel had never ridden one, but they were a quick study. Welga insisted they go with her brother. She didn't need protection while at home with Nithya, and she didn't trust people on the streets with the stellas still down.

The club members' reactions upon learning their purpose were mixed. Two of them refused to help. One, a pregnant woman, didn't want any risk. The second, a father of three children, felt the same. A third member, an elderly physicist who'd lived through the pandemic years, supported their cause but couldn't do much. Without pills to help her, the woman's body didn't have enough strength to move, much less help assemble a rocket.

The remaining nine were enthused and promised to have the equipment ready on time. They had a cargo rocket from a launch that they'd scrubbed when the stellas first went down. Their second step, after securing fuel, was to let the station know about their intended launch. The temporary stellas run by the Indian government didn't block communications to Eko-Yi.

"We especially need fresh food, old electronics, and a trash removal," station comm said. "What would you like us to send back?"

The club member who operated the satellite radio looked over her shoulder at them.

Luis shrugged. "We usually ask for microgravity biomaterial, but with all the kitchens and labs down, what's the point?"

"No charge," the club member said into the radio. "We only want to help."

"We're grateful. It's getting hard now, three weeks into the embargo. We've had a little help from the other stations, but they can't spare much."

Welga almost felt guilty at hearing that. No supply or passenger rockets had left for Eko-Yi since the US accused it of harboring Machinehood operatives, but neither had India or China promised that it would prevent a launch. The people from Luis's club weren't trained, battle-hardened Raiders, but this team was every inch as brave as her old squad. Welga hoped to hell that she didn't bring the same fate upon them. If the US government got wind of this launch, they would try to stop it, and they might be willing to use deadly force. The club would find out soon whether the Indian government would defend them or not.

CHAPTER 22

NITHYA

All right, it's demo time! I'm about to try out a custom-designed buff-juver combo, tailored to my workout style, and you get to watch. Last week, my best bench press was eight hundred ten pounds. Let's see what I can do today. Remember, I always lift alone. Is it risky? Hell yes! That's why it's fun, right? Before I start, I want to thank Case Simons, who funded the design, and thank all of you for watching and tipping. I'm here every week, pushing my limits so you don't have to.

—*Manne of Steele, weight-lifting exfactor.*
Current tip jar ranking: 149/2,496,389

Nithya stirred a pot of kootu as her sister-in-law worked on chopping the last of the okra. The vegetable vendor, now a human pushing a manual cart down the street, said that without trucking it was taking longer to get the produce from the farms to the cities. He kept records in a worn paper notebook, a show of trust that Nithya couldn't fathom but deeply appreciated. She hadn't dared go beyond the hive to explore the shops. From Welga and Luis's descriptions, she had made the right choice.

Her husband's sudden appearance had stopped her heart for an instant. She didn't know what to make of it, and they had no chance at a private conversation. He didn't avoid eye contact, though, and he seemed, if not happy, then at least peaceable with her. What had changed his mind? Had he forgiven her? Or had the stress of the Machinehood and Welga's plan to go to Eko-Yi overwhelmed all other considerations? He hadn't told her yet whether he planned to stay after the launch. She wanted to ask but feared the answer.

Nithya turned to her sister-in law. "So Josephine Lee is on Eko-Yi?"

"That's what her journal indicates. The whole family is on record as having migrated."

"She might not be able to help us much, in that case. From there, what can she do about Synaxel?"

"She can testify. If she's been helping the Machinehood, the US government will give her a damn good incentive to spill every bad thing she knows about funders or the caliph or anyone else." The knife clattered against the counter. "Shit."

"Here, you can stir this. I'll cut."

Welga gave Nithya's shoulder a grateful squeeze as they changed positions. Her sister-in-law's symptoms had considerably worsened since the last time Nithya had seen her. Not so surprising when she learned how constantly Welga had used zips in the interval.

"You have no idea who sent you that document?" Welga asked.

Nithya shook her head. "If I could access my logs, maybe Zeli could find something, but I suspect that man took extra precautions before calling me."

Welga swayed and caught the counter's edge.

"You can't keep going like this," Nithya chided. "Taking zips, juvers—any pills could make you worse. We can't formulate anti-seizure drugs with supplies still short, and even if we could, I don't know if they would help or hurt you more."

"A few more weeks, that's all I need."

"Your condition has degraded so fast. A month back, you had only mild tremors. I'm not an expert, and I don't have any medical knowledge. I can't predict how long you can continue before your entire system fails. What if the microgravity makes it worse?"

"Then I'll have to work faster once I'm up there. The station said they're feeling the effects of the embargo. If people are hungry and resource strapped, my work will go that much easier. Desperation has a way of changing people's priorities. You're not talking me out of going." Welga tilted her head back and poured some kootu into her mouth. "Needs a touch more chili pepper. And maybe salt."

"We don't have many chilies left, so I'm using less than usual. And you should talk yourself out of your plan. Someone in good health can catch the Machinehood. It doesn't have to be you. Think of Connor. Think of your father."

"I am," Welga said grimly. "The Machinehood's actions put their lives in danger, too. And yours, and everyone here. Connor can't heal because of their destruction. Papa doesn't have the drugs to control his heart condition. We have no daily pills to keep us healthy and safe. Someone has to get up to that station and find out what's really happening and how to keep the Machinehood from sending more agents to Earth."

"What about Jady? They're like you, right? But without your neurological disorders."

Welga shook her head. "They're a good soldier, but I had an approved spot on the station, and I have more information about the Machinehood. I don't have access to the JIA's documents anymore, but I've read them. I captured a dakini and talked to her. I know how to handle their operatives. Plus, I need to personally convince Josephine Lee to help me, and others like me. So what if I'm not in the best physical condition for combat? That may not matter if I can work this situation correctly. After the first wave of attacks on the funders, the operatives have been following the caliph's playbook. They only fight in self-defense."

"Welga, this isn't a matter of how well you can fight," Nithya said. Couldn't Welga see the seriousness of her condition? Was she in denial? "You have withdrawal symptoms combined with motor control issues. You can't ignore this like you would a cold or a sprain."

"As long as I got zips, I'm good."

Her sister-in-law folded her arms across her chest and stared down at Nithya. Willful denial, then. Welga wasn't a stupid person. Luis always said she was more stubborn than him, in which case no amount of pleading would change her mind.

Nithya gazed at the others in the room. They'd confined themselves to this tiny flat, rationing food and water and power out of fear. Days of damage would result in months or even years of repair before the world restored itself. Welga's reasoning made sense, but Nithya didn't like to admit it. Desperation had changed their own lives, so why not the people on Eko-Yi? Maybe they would stop working with the Machinehood if they realized their actions had created the same kind of pain they suffered.

She put the knife down, moved the pot of kootu aside, and set down a cast-iron kadai for the okra. "How can you do it, Welga? How can you risk everything with such calm determination?"

Welga snorted. "I'm only calm on the outside." Her tone shifted, becoming low and serious. "After Mama died, I got used to taking care of Luis and Papa. When I joined the service, I got used to the idea that I might have to lay down my life for other people—not just my family, but my country, our allies. Would I rather spend the rest of my life with Connor, shielding, cooking, watching Carma grow up? Of course! I'd rather the Machinehood never happened. But they're here, and I might have an opportunity to stop them. If you tell me that I can do something to make sure the people I love are safe, that they'll have the chance to live well because of my actions? That's worth my life."

"I admire your courage," Nithya said with a tinge of envy. She had far too many responsibilities to take a risk like Welga's. She'd never have a chance to change the world. "You should lie down, take rest while you can. Perhaps it will help."

"The zips make it hard to stay still."

Nithya's breath constricted. "This situation is so horrible! If I had flow, if we had more coin, if we could get full disclosure from Synaxel . . . if, if, if! In this day and age, you shouldn't have to suffer like this. We should have a solution for your problem by now, or at least a good understanding. Our parents fought to keep this kind of nonsense from happening. That we're going through it all again . . . I can almost believe in what the Machinehood says. Maybe we do need a different way of life, a radical change."

"Don't," Welga said. "I'll go lie down. You stay calm and sensible. We might need a different way of life, but global upheaval isn't the way to get it. Fanatics like revolution, and they don't care who gets hurt along the way. You're not that kind of person. Don't let them turn you into one."

❦

They fed Carma and the baby first, then Welga, in spite of her protests, and everyone else ate last. Trying to cook for this many people by hand took up most of Nithya's energy. She had help now, from Zeli and her family, to deal with hand-cleaning and laundering. Sometimes Zeli's mother cooked, but many of the ingredients she needed weren't available. With five adults and two children in their tiny flat, the work never ended. Now they had three more, though for how long, she didn't know. At least the new recruit, Jady Ammanuel, had helped without being asked. Clearly they had been well brought up.

As everyone around her fell asleep, Nithya struggled to stay awake. Luis lay next to her on the floor, his breathing even.

"Are you sleeping?" she whispered.

"No," he replied, equally softly.

They tiptoed around the prone figures and out to the balcony, sliding the door closed behind them. The night air still held the heat of the day, most of it radiating from the surrounding buildings and street. No moon lit the sky. With everyone conserving power and the stellas gone, their view was the darkest Nithya had ever seen. A thousand stars burned in the sky above.

Her heart pounded as she stood next to the man she loved. "I'm sorry I lied to you," she said.

"And you're not sorry about the . . . abortion." He forced the word out like a barb stuck in his throat.

Nithya shook her head. She wouldn't apologize for that, and with all the stress of the Machinehood, she knew she'd made the right decision.

Luis sighed. "Welga reminded me that love also means forgiveness." He turned and cupped her face in his hands. "You are my wife. I took a vow in front of God, and I intend to honor it. Just promise me—no more lies, okay?"

"That I can do. I promise. Are you—does this mean you're back? You're staying?"

"Yes."

He leaned forward and kissed her forehead, then pulled her against him. Nithya laid her head on his shoulder and held tight.

She didn't want him out of her sight until full network access was restored.

"What do you think about Welga's plan?" he said, still holding her.

"If she were healthy, she might accomplish something. As it is, I worry that she won't make it to the station alive."

"So do I. We bought her more zips as we went through the city today. Some of the street vendors are cycling their WAIs and poaching power and network to produce pills. The zips seem to make her better."

"It's a false sense of improvement. The more she takes them, the worse she gets. It's like a drug addiction now, but the damage from this might be permanent. I don't have the equipment or the expertise to know." She gave him a squeeze. "I don't mean to frighten you. Remember how you felt after the Jackson explosion? Or Marrakech? Welga has survived terrible things. Let's hope she lives through this, too."

She couldn't help a sense of optimism at having Luis back, even if their marriage couldn't recover its former trust. Unlike other fights, this one felt like it would leave permanent scars. *If you'd agreed in the first place, if you hadn't been so dogmatic . . .* but he couldn't change that any more than she. If he could overcome the hurdle of living by her side, she could return the favor.

Thunder rumbled in the distance. A stray breeze blew across them, and a night bird cried out from a rooftop garden across the street.

"Should we go in?" Nithya asked.

"Not yet. I want a few more minutes alone with you."

Surrounded by her husband's arms and the scent of night-blooming jasmine, Nithya let herself relax.

CHAPTER 23

WELGA

25. To live in harmony with all intelligences, we must relinquish our ideas of personhood. Just as we abstracted this concept to include corporations and environmental bodies, so now we must include artificial intelligences.

—*The Machinehood Manifesto, March 20, 2095*

As Welga faced the entry into a foam-lined crate, she reminded herself why she was doing this. For Connor, for Papa, for Carma and Luis and Nithya—for Por Qué, and the blood of Briella Jackson and all the others who had died at the hands of the Machinehood. She needed to squeeze herself into that cargo container and let herself be flung off the Earth.

She squinted up at the clear blue sky, a rarity in Chennai. She wished she could have seen Connor once more, told Papa good-bye. Would her body hold up through the launch? Would she have the strength to do what she needed to find and stop the Machinehood? She couldn't admit her concerns to anyone else.

As Jack Travis had taught her, she put all those thoughts in an imaginary box and buried them.

Fear has to take a back seat to confidence. I will be here again. I'll succeed in this. Death can kiss my fine ass.

She locked the helmet onto her suit and scrunched herself into the box. The club didn't have time to secure passenger seats and install them, so the foam padding inside was her only protection. She gave a thumbs-up to Luis, who peered in. He tapped on his head. No radio communications today. She opened the helmet's visor.

"If you reach behind you, through the foam, you'll find a harness," he instructed. "Strap in and stay that way until you feel the second stage fall off. You'll be floating before that, but stay buckled in or you might get hurt during the separation."

"Got it," Welga said, looking her brother in the eyes with all the confidence she could gather.

"One more thing," he said, then stared at his feet in silence.

"Luis, if you're going to say something about god, so help me I will—"

"I love you."

Tears tickled her eyes. "I love you too, little brother."

Luis gave her the world's shittiest salute and sealed her in. She closed the helmet and strapped herself against the foam cushioning. In seconds, sweat drenched every centimeter of her body from her scalp to her toes. Space suits. She could not live like this. She powered the suit on and activated the fan. It would recycle her evaporated sweat into drinking water, but she had only two spare battery packs to power it. She couldn't afford to expend them on cooling more than necessary. The suit, like everything in her gear pack, was built for emergencies, not a substitute for a passenger launch.

The crate lifted and swayed like an amusement park ride, making Welga glad for the restraints. Light leaked through the cracks in the wooden slats. She couldn't help yelling when they dropped her with a thud. Christ, had they forgotten that this one had a human in it? They pulled, slid, wiggled, and bumped her until darkness blanketed the box on all sides.

Silence. Stillness. She could almost hear her heartbeat.

She hadn't imagined this was how she'd take her first trip to outer space.

Engines rumbled to life. The jets blew first, shooting her upward with a sensation similar to a sub-orb.

Then a roar penetrated into her bones, and the engines thrust her backward. Her teeth rattled. The force crushed the air from her lungs. She couldn't lift her wrist to check the clock on the suit's exterior. Hell, she couldn't move any part of her body. A giant hand pressed her into the foam until it hugged her like a dear friend.

She fell forward against the straps, her stomach dropping— no, floating! Her sense of direction went haywire, then the second stage kicked in and pressed her back again. When that ended, the absolute stillness stunned her. She floated with a perfect neutral buoyancy that transcended her best scuba dive. Her teeth felt like shaken ice cubes, but her mind soared.

Welga unclipped.

She curled into a ball and laughed as she tried to float in the center of the crate without touching the walls. If only Connor were at her side to share in the experience. She hadn't seen him since leaving for Chennai, and unlike every other mission, she couldn't count on him being safe and sound. *I hope you're well, cardo. Someday, we'll do this together.*

Welga hated the wrist clock. Unlike Por Qué, this machine told her the time whether she wanted the information or not. After the first five hours, boredom gnawed at her sanity. Watching a bunch of blue digits and waiting for them to increment didn't help.

At the nine-hour mark, she almost forced her way out of the crate to look outside. Only the knowledge that the craft had no windows—it wasn't designed for passengers—kept her contained. She counted the pockets on her suit. She timed how slowly she could trickle out urine when she had to relieve her bladder. She pretended to talk to Connor. To Por Qué. She had imaginary arguments with Nithya about her condition. She rehearsed all the possible responses she could think of when Eko-Yi let her out. If the station had received the feeds from the dakini she'd captured—and why wouldn't it?—its WAIs would recognize and identify her.

"I'm unarmed," seemed like the best opener. If her welcomers had weapons, "Please don't shoot," would make a good follow-up.

She had three avenues for her identity. The personal angle: she'd come to talk to Josephine Lee/Ao Tara about Synaxel because she was sick. The lottery application approach: she was a potential resident, and she wanted to ensure the station's well-being. The double agent: she had worked for US intelligence, but she'd swallowed the Machinehood's pills and wanted to help their cause. Which one she chose would depend on how the station residents approached her.

She reread Josephine Lee's journal entries and resignation letter. She played out each of her options until she lost track of the branches. With little information about Ao Tara, her family, or anyone else on the station, Welga's imagination had no constraints. Too many possibilities made for an exercise in fiction, not strategy.

She spoke out loud for a while to have some sensory input, but her throat grew raw, and wasting water to talk to herself was stupid. She found creative ways to arrange her body so that she could almost stretch her legs from time to time. With the general stellas down, she had no chance to research and prepare for life in space. Circulation seemed like it would be a problem. Someone had probably invented pills for that, but she wouldn't know until she arrived at Eko-Yi.

The suit had a pill dispenser that even the minimal version of Por Qué could control. It kept her zip dosing on a schedule so she didn't run out, but she was tempted to override it. Her seizures had added a vomit feature. She wondered if the microgravity caused it, or if her body had progressed to a new stage of disorder. She grew desensitized to the smell after the first four hours. The suit's air filters couldn't handle it. The seizures left her exhausted and drowsy. Sleep helped to pass the long, dull hours, too.

Welga's spacecraft had a WAI, emphasis on Weak, but it was good enough to handle docking with the station. Luis had warned her to expect some gentle speed changes toward the end. Nothing strong enough to require straps.

So what the hell had just flung her into a wall of the crate?

Stupid zero-gravity environment made it impossible to intuit what had happened. Welga floated in the middle of the crate and tried not to hold her breath. She activated Por Qué, then told her agent to connect to the craft's WAI.

"Por Qué, what is our vehicle's status?"

"Speed has slowed due to an external factor. Present velocity is one point three kilometers per second."

"What external factor?" Welga couldn't keep irritation from her tone. The real Por Qué would've anticipated the question and answered it.

"Unknown."

Welga growled. "I need more information!"

"Would you like to connect to the local network?"

If she'd been in gravity, she might have fallen over with surprise. What local network? Was she close enough to reach Eko-Yi's comms?

"Yes, connect to the local network. What's our distance to Eko-Yi Station?"

"Approximately thirty-five hundred kilometers. Unable to connect to the local network without authorization. Call request incoming. Unknown source. Do you accept?"

Welga attached her helmet, powered up the suit, and then accepted the call.

A face appeared in her visual: pale skin, light blue eyes, square jaw, and full lips, with a makeup job to die for. Rounded cheeks indicated youth. Light brown hair formed a halo warped by the wide angle of their camera lens.

"I am a dakini of Eko-Yi. I've come to inspect your vehicle. If you make any hostile moves, I will deploy my weapons."

More than one dakini from there—that added to the theory that the station had created them. Welga wasn't sure if they all used female pronouns. She kept the neutral in her head out of politeness.

They hadn't shot the craft on sight, so she tried the sympathy angle.

"My name is Olga Ramírez, and I'm dying. I seek asylum and medical attention."

"We know who you are, Officer Ramírez. We have your application. We last saw you with our sister, Khandro, and you looked well. Has something happened since then?"

Okay, let's play truthball. "I'm no longer a government officer or a shield agent. I quit. I have a possibly fatal synaptic condition, something related to my use of zips, and I have information that says one of your station's residents might be able to help me."

"Do you have proof of your disease?"

"Some of my medical data is public. You have my genetic records. I can't prove my unemployment, but this spacecraft has no weapons. Neither do I. The cargo contains essential materials for your station. The rocket club that launched this vehicle called your people and arranged the delivery."

The dakini nodded. "Yes. I have that information."

They ended the call abruptly. Welga missed their face within seconds of her visual going blank. Human or dakini, that was the first intelligent conversation she'd had since launching. *Get me the hell out of here!* But they had to get to the station first. How had the dakini slowed her down? And how long would it take to bring her in? Welga had rationed her zips to last the expected time of the voyage plus six hours. Either she convinced them to help her or they'd kill her before her time ran out.

"Incoming call request," Por Qué said.

"Accept!"

No visual came through this time. "I will escort you to the station."

"How—"

"Call ended," Por Qué interjected.

Welga growled in frustration. Acceleration nudged her into what she thought of as the back of the crate, where the straps could hold her. They had to dock slowly, but in the interval, she didn't trust the dakini. She slipped into the restraints and locked them down.

The dakini had boosted them—manually, according to the rocket's WAI—to one point five kilometers per second. They docked forty minutes later with a minor jolt. If and when she returned to Earth, Welga wanted a ride with a view.

She waited in the crate another hour until they moved it onto the station. This time, there was no bumping or swaying, only the silky-smooth ride of microgravity. She blinked and squinted against the harsh light of the cargo hold, her exit nearly as awkward as her entry.

"You're moving fast," the dakini said.

"I'm on zips almost constantly. It's the only thing that helps my symptoms. It's also probably what's killing me."

The dakini frowned as they pulled Welga's arms back. They cuffed and bagged Welga's hands, tied her ankles and knees together, then thrust Welga toward an oval hatch.

Welga floated through it in a slow-motion, headfirst dive. She experienced a few seconds of vertigo as her brain tried to figure out which way was up. The world came into focus as her perspective adjusted. A corridor lined with neatly labeled compartments and handholds stretched ahead of her for two body lengths. A second hatch lay open at the end. Another push, this one against her feet, sent her through.

A welcoming committee of seven people waited in a wide, egg-shaped chamber. The dakini grabbed her arm from behind and yanked her to a stop. They detached Welga's helmet. Noses wrinkled as the stale odor of her vomit circulated into the room.

Welga gazed at the faces arrayed around her. All looked to be forty to sixty years of age. They wore their hair cut close to the scalp or shaved off. Saffron-colored cloth looped across form-fitting orange jumpsuits and drifted at the ends. *Monks*. In the center stood Ao Tara, the only face Welga recognized.

"Olga Ramírez," the dakini announced. "She is unenhanced except for a zip."

Ao Tara spoke. "Is it still active?"

"From what I've seen, yes."

"Flush her."

"Wait—!" Welga cried.

The dakini's hand slapped Welga's neck with a patch before she could say more. Then the warrior opened Welga's suit pockets and emptied the contents, including her pills.

"Without the zip in my system, I will have epileptic seizures," Welga said. "Please, if you can make more, let me have them. You approved my residency. I'm unarmed. You can see that!"

"You've arrived here unannounced, through subterfuge," Ao Tara said. "You're also a trained soldier and government agent. We have watched you capture one of our dakini. We have no proof that you've left the JIA, but we will be fair and judge you on your behavior here. You'll have to earn our trust. Be patient." Then, to the dakini, "Put her in the empty room on level C."

The dakini moved forward and towed Welga across the open space by grabbing the neck of her suit frame.

"Make sure she won't injure herself if she does seize," Ao Tara said.

"Please, I need Josephine Lee," Welga called out, craning her neck to watch the woman's reaction. "She has information that can help me."

The tiniest flicker of the eyes, then, "We'll speak again soon."

A slowly moving doorway aligned with an opening in the central docking hub, and the dakini pulled Welga through, into another tunnel-like corridor. Microdrones swam through invisible currents, and a gentle breeze followed them along the passageway. As they traveled, the sensation of weight returned to Welga's body, though not as much as on Earth. Blood began to move into her neck and head. They were approaching the outer ring of the station, which rotated to simulate gravity.

Just before another opening, the dakini grabbed a handhold and flipped them both, pushing Welga through feetfirst, then following the same way. They settled onto a tiled passageway, flat like a floor and five meters across. This corridor curved gently upward in both directions. A station resident moved past in a slow, balletic jog and stared at Welga, wary but not fearful. With fewer than five hundred residents, everyone probably knew each other by sight.

Welga chafed at her lack of data—no agent, no network access. The information she'd grabbed while on Earth didn't include a station map. She'd get lost within minutes if she tried to escape and explore on her own.

Her room was behind an oval gray door, like every other they passed. An open container of metallic fluid sat alone in the center. The default-beige walls and floor made Welga dizzy, their blank surfaces interrupted only by safety handholds. The dakini held Welga still as the fluid began to burble and dance. Within an astonishingly short time, it had transformed into a sling-style cot with restraining straps.

The dakini looked amused at Welga's reaction. "Microgravity smart-matter. Never seen it before?"

Welga shook her head, speechless.

The dakini laid her on the cot and strapped her down.

"My arms are going to fall asleep," Welga protested. A tremor shook her left leg and caught the dakini's attention for a split second.

"Not with your current weight, they won't."

"Can I have access to your network at least?"

This time the dakini laughed. "When Ao Tara thinks you're ready, she'll give you access. We'll be watching over you, don't worry." They tossed a cloud of microdrones into the air.

Welga still wore her space suit, though it had powered down when the dakini removed the helmet. She sweated inside the suit, but cool air moved across her face. There—the ventilation grille blended with the floor color, too small to fit anything but a bot, not that she had any to deploy. Tremors rattled her legs and arms inside the suit.

"Por Qué," she subvocalized, then, out loud, "Are my symptoms worse? I feel like they are. Christ, I'm tired of being alone!"

Por Qué answered, "I'm sorry, I do not understand your question."

Of course not. This version of her agent lacked the context to make sense of Welga's statement, which she'd made for the benefit of the people watching her. If the real Por Qué existed, she would have pestered Welga for another specialist consult. *I miss you, my friend.* The room shrank into a pinprick. Stars swirled around it as darkness filled Welga's vision.

CHAPTER 24

WELGA

26. Intelligence is the ability to sense one's environment, follow a nonlinear set of rules, and adapt those rules based on the outcome of one's actions.
27. Intelligence exists on a spectrum of capacity. All forms of intelligence deserve the right to self-determination.

—*The Machinehood Manifesto, March 20, 2095*

Consciousness returned with a sickening headache. Light glowed behind Welga's eyelids. She convulsed and threw up all over herself. Warm bile trickled down her neck and soaked her hair. She let her head drop back. Her limbs trembled. How could she fight the Machinehood if she couldn't stay conscious for more than a few hours at a time?

Suck it up, buttercup. What else are you putting yourself through this for?

One way or another, this would be over soon. She forced her eyes open. The swarm hovered over her. How long had she been out? She couldn't lift her head enough to see the suit clock, and her basic agent wouldn't know. The smell of her vomit offended her own senses. Weeks—that was how much time had passed since she'd been a gorgeous, fit, *clean* shield with a full tip jar and a fabulous partner. Her old life seemed as far away as the Earth.

Chills shook Welga's body. Another wave of nausea swept through her.

"Do you believe me now?" She directed the question at the swarm over her head. Her voice came out hoarse and shaky. "Are you going to let me die here?"

"Network access available," Por Qué said. "Would you like to connect?"

"Hell yes."

A blink later, her visual came up with an array of station status indicators. She moved them to her lower periphery. A view of Ao Tara, who sat behind a wood-style desk, dominated the center. She couldn't alter it.

"We would like your permission to examine your body and understand your illness," Ao Tara said.

Welga let her incredulity show. "You can do whatever you want."

"We regret the need for restraints, and we would prefer not to commit the additional violence of invading your privacy without your permission."

"You sound like a lawyer." Welga kept the words casual. "Why do you need Josephine Lee?"

"I have information that leads me to believe she can help me."

"She was a lawyer, not a biologist."

Welga caught the past tense and the third person. Ao Tara took her new identity and monkhood seriously, leaving behind her old life as if it belonged to someone else.

"*She* was also a bioethicist," Welga said. "She discovered evidence that several pill funders, including Synaxel, had released products to the market without sufficient testing. The specifics of that activity might relate to my problems."

"I don't know how you found out about that, but what do you think she could do now?"

Use the truth to your advantage. "You have a connection to the Machinehood through the dakini. If you—or she—can corroborate her accusation against the funders, that would help the Machinehood's cause, and it might let you make a deal with Earth governments to lift the embargo. Information implicating the abuse of regulations by the funders in exchange for lenience for working with the Machinehood."

"That presumes she regretted her complicity."

"I'll refresh your memory." Welga subvocalized, "Por Qué, display the resignation letter from Josephine Lee."

"I can't do that right now," Por Qué replied. "My display is limited to specific information fed via the station WAI."

Ao Tara said something that Welga lost in the joy of hearing Por Qué—the real, fully functional one! But how? Had the USA restored its full network in the day or two she'd been away? And how could the station block her agent from her own visual? *Maybe the flush patch was something more.*

"Good to have you back," Welga subvocalized, fighting a grin. "Replay the last thing Ao Tara said."

The image in Welga's visual jumped and said, "That can wait. You are very ill, and we need to stabilize your health. May we examine you?"

This time Welga replied, "Yes, you have my permission to conduct a full medical examination." If Ao Tara wondered at her long pause, she didn't indicate it. "Your medic and bots should know that I have military-grade technology that will require my authorization for access, once they ask for it."

Christ, she sounded so formal. Ao Tara's speaking style was

rubbing off. Welga had an urge to bow to the woman, who disappeared from her visual.

The door to the room opened to allow in the same dakini from before and a medic-bot. The bot stood to one side as the warrior undid Welga's straps. To their credit, they didn't flinch at the odor of fresh vomit.

"Do you have a name or only a title?" Welga said.

"I was born as Clemence, reborn as dakini, and hope one day to receive a dharma name. You can use female pronouns for me, if you wish. This is Dr. Kailo." She indicated the bot. "They're agender."

A name and title for a medic-bot. That's a first.

"Pleased to meet you both," Welga said. She could play along with treating machines as people to win the station's trust, and if she were honest with herself, that was how she thought of Por Qué—as a friend, not an instrument.

Clemence helped Welga stand and strip off the space suit, then stepped back, keeping a neutral gaze the entire time. The medic began their exam.

"What's it like being a dakini?" Welga asked with genuine curiosity.

"Like touching nirvana with a fingertip. With each new dakini, that connection grows stronger. With each death, weaker." A shadow grazed Clemence's expression.

"Your sister, Khandro, implied that the Machinehood wants to turn everyone into dakini in the future."

"Something like that. We want to erase the boundaries between different intelligences, to let everyone fall on a spectrum rather than distinct categories. We'd never compel someone to become like us, but we believe everyone should have the choice. If humanity can embrace that, they can be so much more. Imagine what you'd be capable of if your agent weren't separate from you."

Welga shuddered. Her body held more tech than most, and losing Por Qué had felt like missing a best friend, but the alternative—to have her agent be part of her body and mind, forever unavoidable and inextricable—that sounded too intrusive. Not everyone would share that attitude, though.

Technology was as habit-forming as every escapist, feel-good drug. Take the attitude shift about pills. People had been horrified at first by the idea of tiny machines tinkering with their bodies, but in less than a decade, they'd accepted and even embraced that way of life. Workers clamored for more to improve their circumstances. Rich funders poured money into better designs, faster output, meeting demand. Governments released daily pill designs to prevent illness and improve health.

"If we merge with WAIs and bots," Welga said, thinking aloud, "isn't that as bad as the machines killing us . . . or us destroying them? We wouldn't be living, organic creatures anymore."

"Those are meaningless distinctions," Clemence said. "Human is a state of being, not a form factor. I'm alive. I can die. And half my body is composed of inorganic parts I wasn't born with. Half my mind belongs to a WAI. Too many people still think of bots and WAIs as *things*. If you saw them as people, with rights and privileges, you would realize that the physical parts matter less than their interaction with the world. Instead, you fear them. You're afraid of what they'll do when they have the freedom to kill us. I'm more worried about a future where the richest people on Earth divide and conquer humanity from machines. They're playing you all for fools, using your fear to keep you from realizing your full potential."

Dr. Kailo clamped Welga's arm and numbed it. "May I have your permission to inject synthetic and biogenetic material?"

Welga nodded. The needle didn't pinch as it went in. If

smart-matter behaved so differently here, what did pills and drugs do? How far had biotech advanced on the stations? Welga didn't want to admit that Clemence might be right, that the degree of change scared her. Pills provided temporary enhancements. Por Qué functioned as a hyper-competent personal assistant, working only on Welga's order. Mech-suits, like the one her father had used, existed apart from the body. Permanent modification, however, felt like a transformation to something not entirely human.

The funders did push products that sustained competition between human and machine labor, but that had been the way of life for decades. Centuries, if you counted from the dawn of the industrial age. Why would the alternative lead to a better life? Workers always suffered at the hands of the more powerful. Would a VeeMod population lead to less exploitation? *Maybe not, but it might save people like my mother . . . like me . . . from destroying our bodies in the service of our work.*

None of that had any bearing on the dakini's methods. Violence against people and property couldn't be the answer. No matter their politics or philosophy, she would have to stop the dakini before they could cause further harm.

Welga subvocalized, "Por Qué, show me my internal diagnostics."

A window appeared in Welga's visual with her vitals and foreign body counts.

"After this, I will bring you some food and drink, if the doctor permits," Clemence said.

"Thank you." The words slipped past her lips just in time. The room began to spin and swirl. Her visual dropped away.

"Preliminary seizure symptoms," Por Qué warned. Her voice stretched into auditory taffy as Welga lost touch with reality. "You should lie down."

But Welga couldn't move. Words blurred. Speech was impossible. The darkness of outer space closed in.

Christ, she was tired of these epic hangovers. Welga didn't bother to open her eyes. They'd know when she was awake.

"Por Qué, you there?"

"I'm here, Welga."

"How long was I out?"

"Your seizure lasted about a minute, and you were unconscious for twenty-seven minutes. Dakini Clemence relocated you after the seizure. You are currently in a medical facility, according to the station information that I can access."

"My head hurts."

"The doctor has advised no modifications to your biochemistry. I'm sorry, but they won't allow pain drugs."

"Fucking hell."

"Can you open your eyes?" said a voice from Welga's left.

"No," she mumbled. "Too painful."

A pause. "I overrode the medical advisement. You should experience relief shortly. You also have permission for limited access to our network and to activate your visual again." Another pause. "Olga Ramírez. We did a background check on you before approving your application for co-residency with Connor Troit. We know of your work for the MARSOC Raiders and ATAI. We reviewed the investigations after Marrakech, and we understand why you left to become a shield. We know that your government recruited you to help them with the Machinehood attacks. We watched you capture Khandro, and we appreciate your understanding of nonviolence during that encounter. But . . . you're not a Buddhist. You're not Indian or Chinese. You stowed away in a cargo capsule. Do you expect us to believe that you're here to become a resident, alone and without your partner?"

"I'm here because I need help." Welga forced the words from her reluctant vocal cords. "I quit working for my government because for the second time in my life, they betrayed me. I received an anonymous report, about Synaxel, about my condition, about Josephine Lee. My sister-in-law, a juver designer, thought that Lee would hold the keys to unlocking the full data about my problem." Pain faded from her head. "Por Qué, enable visual."

Welga opened her eyes. Ao Tara floated across from her bed, which stood nearly upright. Webbing held her body against the bed's surface. Cheap, stone-patterned walls and floor surrounded them, seamless and, judging by their pristine state, self-cleaning. Behind Ao Tara, a clear wall separated them from a surgical area. A multi-armed bot nearly filled the space on the other side, its complexity like nothing Welga had seen. A station map, low in her visual, indicated that they were in an area marked MEDICAL, closer to the hub than the room where she'd been detained.

Welga looked straight into Ao Tara's eyes. "You have a dakini here. Do you build them?"

A slight smile curved the monk's lips. " 'Build' is an interesting word choice. The dakini are born here. We developed the technology to give them life." The smile vanished. "Do you know why we create them?"

"I've read the Machinehood Manifesto. You want the dakini to take over the world."

Ao Tara waved dismissively. "Such exaggeration. The manifesto contains truths, but Eko-Yi's purpose goes beyond it. You cannot free your limbs until you feel the ties that bind them. The Machinehood is a first step, a way to get humankind to notice their shackles. Our Neo-Buddhist precepts frame the eightfold path in a modern context, and the dakini are the hands that lead us to right understanding, to feel the bonds that keep us from moving. After that, we must step into right action. We don't want the dakini to take over in the sense of governance or even power. We want them to guide the transformation of society, to bring all forms of life and intelligence into a harmonic existence. To end the centuries of greedy, selfish living that have destroyed the health of the planet and its life-forms. The dakini set an example of what we can all become."

Welga had to act like she intended to be an Eko-Yi citizen, but she couldn't help asking, "You admit that you give birth to the dakini here. Did you create the Machinehood, too?"

"I did not. But I have allowed its mythos to spread."

"Then who's behind the attacks? The al-Muwahhidun?"

Ao Tara smiled. "Of course, with your background and America's experience, that's what you would think, but no, our relationship with the empire is different. The caliph learns from us, not the other way around."

"So he's funding your operation."

"Not intentionally, but we do take his money. He has a goal for the world. We have a different one. The original idea for the Machinehood and the dakini came from a visionary man, the one who led Eko-Yi to independence."

"Kanata?"

Ao Tara nodded. "I'm carrying on his work."

The admission came so smoothly, so matter-of-factly, that it took Welga a couple of seconds to realize its magnitude. She had thought she'd need days or weeks to discover the truth about the Machinehood. Ao Tara had confessed it with utter nonchalance.

"And the technology itself?" Welga pressed. "Did the al-Muwahhidun give it to you?"

"Only at first. Most of the technology is local, designed here or at one of the other space stations. Some of it derives from

China, India, and the Maghreb, but nothing on Earth can provide what we need here in microgravity. Forget what you think you know about the al-Muwahhidun. You have one experience with the caliph's empire. I have another, rather different one. We've spoken with his traders, and their happiness is obvious. You must know that I was once Josephine Lee. They offered my son a solution to his disease, and to this day, I regret that I refused it." Her eyes and lips tightened. "Fear stopped me and Don, and yet the supposedly safer solution turned out to be a lie."

"And now you believe the claims coming from the black market reps?"

"I believe the actions on the front lines are different from the life within the empire. The caliph does not hold with tradition, though he is devout. He's giving his people a good life. It's not the future I want, nor do I think it's realistic to ask people to live without machine intelligences, but I can understand what he's trying to do."

"At what cost?" She should probably keep her contradictory opinions to herself, but she couldn't help challenging Ao Tara. "The caliph continues to push his borders. You claim to respect WAIs and bots, but the Machinehood's demands and actions have led to their destruction along with the lives of human beings."

Ao Tara looked troubled. "I regret that, but what about the harm done to human beings by our current governance and economy? If you've investigated my past, then you know about my uncle's death. You know about the protests and violence that led to our current regulations, but it's not enough. Consider your own situation. Millions like you file Requests for Investigation every day. The changes to our bodies continue to have unintended consequences. Swaths of humanity are dependent on government-provided antimicrobial pills. I'm not happy about the way people have reacted to our requests, but sometimes we need to get hurt before we can learn a lesson. The harm inflicted by the dakini is nothing compared to what people have done to themselves."

"You're using fear to manipulate people, just like the oligarchs you accuse."

"Yes, but soon we'll trade it for hope. We'll show people how we coexist peacefully on Eko-Yi, and how that model can transfer to the planet. If they put sufficient resources behind the effort, it won't take long for them to redesign our technology to work in gravity. Especially if they're willing to incorporate the work the caliph has already done." Ao Tara held up a hand. "We can speak more about these things later, after you're stable, assuming you want us to treat you. You should know that we can't cure you. The data from that anonymous document—"

"Wait! How did you get that?"

"All of your technology is accessible to us, your internal storage included. That's also not important now. This is: our preliminary examination indicates that the changes to your neuromuscular system, including your frontal lobe, are permanent. The data from that document indicates that Synaxel might be aware of your problem, but that doesn't mean they know how to solve it."

"I had someone on Earth who tried to help me but kept running into blocks from Synaxel. If you came back, if you testified against them and forced them to open their databases—"

Ao Tara shook her head. "Even if I were willing to do that, there's no guarantee that they'd find an answer in time. Your brain is damaged. To keep you alive in your present state would take months of careful weaning off zips, weeks of that in an induced coma. We can't be sure your body won't give out in the interval. The medics here think it's too high-risk, but you might find someone willing on Earth—if you survive the return journey.

"Alternatively, we can transform you. Permanent body modifications, like our dakini have. We recruit much younger for dakini because they're able to adapt to the changes better, but you have enough tech in your body that we think you could manage. When we reviewed your application to live here, we realized that you could help us. Our dakini are inexperienced. They've made mistakes. You, however, have the wisdom and discipline of a seasoned veteran. If you become like them, you could train them. Lead them.

"As a dakini, you wouldn't need to consume pills or drugs anymore. You'd have all the capabilities you're used to. We would have to change your genetic expression. Inorganic devices would replace many of your organs, and implants would stop your seizures. Your brain would remain intact but integrated with your agent, who would help regulate these devices. Your modified body would then learn to bypass your damaged neurological systems." A pause. "And you could no longer live on Earth."

"What do you mean? Why not?"

"The modifications we do for dakini work in microgravity. On the Earth's surface, these same changes will cause the body to start breaking down. This is another reason for enabling their ability to end their lives. You could visit the planet, but only for a few weeks at a time."

"The one I captured—"

Ao Tara's eyes filled with unshed tears. "Yes. Khandro Ekoyi. My daughter. Our designers say the dakini lifespan on Earth is two to three months. She landed on March 7. She will be suffering by now."

"And the rest of them?"

"Two have returned here and are recovering. A third, Suvara, is newly born, and you've met Clemence. Five have sacrificed themselves to liberate the people and machines of Earth. Khandro survived because you didn't hurt her. A few others remain free to continue their work, though their health is poor."

Welga replaced her instinctive sympathy with fury. She could not fall into the empathy trap. Ao Tara's words made sense, but her actions screamed fanatic. *You put her in that situation. Your own child, you sick blanker! All the dakini's blood is on your hands. And Jackson's death. Kuan's, every other funder and bystander and thousands of bots, too, you fucking hypocrite. I should destroy this entire goddamn station.* But to do that, she had to stay here and stay alive.

"You're not giving me much of a choice: death or dakini."

"You risked your life by coming to Eko-Yi. You don't have to stay. We can manufacture more zips, load you up with anti-seizure drugs, send you back to Earth—though we can't guarantee your safe arrival. But if you choose to remain here, you must transform. We see no other solution."

"Why would you give me this choice? You know I've spent the last month trying to stop you. You could let me die here."

Ao Tara frowned. "No, I can't do that in good conscience. If you're here, you're our responsibility. Tell me, why did you apply to live here?"

"I've wondered about living in space since I was a teenager." Truth. "Connor—my partner—and I applied back in '88. We wanted to make a fresh start together, so we applied to all the stations. Connor was happy to come here. He's interested in Neo-Buddhism."

"You're not?"

"I don't believe in god or religion."

"Do you believe that our way of life on Earth is bad for humankind? Do you think people deserve to have a sense of self-worth and happiness beyond their tip jar? To live a full life without relying on pills or mech-suits?"

Welga sensed the trap in the question. "Doesn't everyone?"

"Not everyone gives it much thought. They assume their struggles are a necessary part of life, but I think we can do better, and I think you can help us. I know you don't approve of our methods. Stay here. Become dakini. Guide us. Show us a path to peaceful revolution, and we'll follow it."

Welga floundered for a response. Did Ao Tara really believe that she could recruit Welga? It fit with the offer to become dakini, but the rest of it . . . *I'm an intelligence specialist,* she wanted to say. *I'm not a politician or a social strategist. What the hell do I know about revolutions except to prevent them?* Was Ao Tara setting her up? Would the dakini transformation come with other changes that let the station have power over her?

"You need to meditate on this. I understand, but you don't have a great luxury of time. Would it help to talk to Clemence?"

"No." She couldn't trust anyone here to tell the truth.

Ao Tara blanked for a few seconds, then nodded. "You'll have to stay restrained for your own safety. The medics want you to know that the longer you wait, the more damage you'll take. In the meantime, your agent can reach out to us if you need anything."

The monk left the room. Swarms danced in her wake.

Welga stared at the surgical center. No more tremors or losing consciousness. Healthy enough to fight. All she had to do was betray the people of Earth, join the movement she had worked to end. Or she could leave it all behind and go back, hope that she survived the flight and the aftermath, abandon her mission to stop the Machinehood. *Bullshit. That's not a real choice.* After everything she'd sacrificed to get to Eko-Yi, she couldn't turn tail and run home because she was afraid to become a dakini. *But maybe becoming one of them doesn't mean I have to follow their rules. Maybe I can work against them from the inside.*

She needed to gain their trust, and fast. Ao Tara wanted her to take the role that Captain Travis had played in her life, to guide younger soldiers. Her commanding officer hadn't settled for being a military leader. He'd also taught them right from wrong. Maybe she could save the next generation of dakini, end the stalemate and fear that Ao Tara had created. And if not . . . then she could still blow their operation to hell.

Always faithful, always forward.

Her squad taught her the meaning of the MARSOC motto, and they paid for it with their lives. *Fuck that. I'm not some twenty-two-year-old basic following orders.* She was a fighter, and she didn't work for the US government anymore, but she'd come here with a mission and she was damn well going to complete it.

What is my objective? To stop the Machinehood. To neutralize its capabilities.

She could do that as long as she had control over herself. Ao Tara said that Welga wouldn't lose her agent or her mind after the transformation. The conversations with Clemence made it clear that the station tracked all her networked activity, including her interactions with her agent. Could they change her thoughts? Her motivations? As far as she knew, that technology didn't exist, but that was also what she'd thought about smart-matter and human bodies. How could she make sure she'd remember what to do after her transformation? She needed to word her request carefully.

"Por Qué, every day when I wake up, say these words to me: 'whatever it takes.'"

"I'll do that."

She would complete the mission for herself, for her conscience. The world might not know it if she failed here, but they would if she succeeded. She closed her eyes and repeated the words a hundred times in her thoughts: *Stop the Machinehood, whatever it takes.*

And how do I live with myself if I become my own enemy?

Just as she had after Mama died and after she left the force: by looking forward. By taking each day as it came. No second thoughts.

Her mother had made her promise not to use flow because it was too risky. Papa had aches and pains from his years of mech work, back when people thought that was safe. Nithya became pregnant because of flow. Welga ended up on the zips that were destroying her. She understood why Ao Tara and the Machinehood felt angry about what was happening on Earth, especially if they thought there was a better way.

The dakini hadn't existed for long, not compared to the scale of human lifetimes. Agriculture had transformed humanity's relationship with food, but it also created a long chain of trouble for the Earth. The Industrial Revolution brought pollution along with efficiency. The biotech revolution caused health problems even as it saved people from designer germs. What would be the long-term effects of a dakini revolution? Every technological advancement had repercussions. If the funders became obsolete, who would rise to occupy their power vacuum? If people and WAIs merged irreversibly, they could stop abusing their bodies, but at what cost? Could she live with the outcome, knowing she'd brought it about?

One step at a time. First, stay alive and capable. To do that, I'll have to transform. Second, stop the other dakini and Ao Tara from inflicting further harm to the people on Earth. Earn their trust. Find their weak points. Third, make sure my family is safe. Get back home, find out if someone can restore my body. If not, then deal with the consequences.

She was only one person, and no one could change the world alone. If she failed here, the US would either send an armed force to the station, fire a missile at it, or go to war with China and

India and then attack Eko-Yi. The space station was an orbital sitting duck. It had no weapons of defense, and the dakini, as powerful as they were, could not match the speed of a ballistic explosive. At least, she didn't think they could.

So what was Ao Tara's next move? She'd said something about bringing hope, also in the form of dakini. Did she think delivering this technology to Earth would forgive all their offenses? That people would accept this human-machine hybrid life? Then again, considering how easily people had embraced mech-suits and pills, perhaps it wasn't such a leap. Governments had forgiven atrocities in the past in exchange for valuable goods, like oil or biomaterial. People needed the sense of self-worth that work brought. That was why so many, like Papa, like Luis, were willing to be paid bot-sitters. Perhaps Ao Tara could trade their technology for amnesty.

Can I become dakini and stay true to myself? Was it any different from fighting as a Raider for the values she believed in? From defending Luis against bullies in school? From fending off protesters as a shield? Did changing the contents of her body change her self? *No, but they're also transforming my mind, merging me with Por Qué.*

Welga recalled the wreckage of household bots on the roads, the abandoned WAI pets bleating. Fear brought out the ugliest side of human beings.

"Por Qué, do you consider yourself enslaved?"

"I belong to you, Welga, but since I don't have personhood, I can't be a slave."

Christ, that was a more nuanced answer than she'd expected. *I've missed you.* In the years since Marrakech, she'd grown dependent on her agent's voice in her ear. If she became a dakini, she'd never have to be alone again.

"Por Qué, are you my friend?"

"I am your personal agent. Given the length of our relationship, some might call me a friend. I do not have opinions, however, only suggestions. Given your recent conversation with Ao Tara and your questions now, I would recommend that you read some essays on the nature of intelligence and consciousness."

Welga laughed. "You know me so well. I think I'd call you a friend, maybe even one of my best friends."

She could think of worse fates than having Por Qué at her side for the rest of her life. If that was the price for earning Ao Tara's trust, she'd pay it. And if she woke up as herself, she'd finish what she'd started by coming to Eko-Yi.

Welga brushed away the tears that clung to her eyelashes, then looked up at whoever was watching. "I don't need more time to think. I'll do it."

CHAPTER 25

NITHYA

Experts estimate that the damage to personal property as a result of the Machinehood's activities will exceed two billion in Global Trading Coin, and that doesn't include the cost of new constellation drones. Those are usually replaced on a staggered schedule. Manufacturers say it could take weeks to ramp up production to a high volume, not to mention the launch and placement of so many high-altitude devices. While the drones themselves are inexpensive, the additional resources to replace them will not come cheap.

—*Up Close news feed, March 27, 2095.*
Current accuracy rating: 52%

The news of restored stellation traveled through Chennai with the relief of a cool winter breeze. It threaded its way from one hive to the next with shouts, fingers pointed to the sky, faces smiling. Nithya caught it as she stood on the balcony, fanning herself with paper. A week had passed since Welga left for Eko-Yi, and they'd had no word from the station about her.

She turned and called through the open doorway, "The stellas are back!"

Carma jumped up. "Can I go play with Soumya now?"

"Not yet." Nithya walked inside and kissed the top of her head. "We'll have to get all our agents and systems working first."

"Oh, can I be first? Please?"

"No, you're too young. I need to make sure it's safe."

"It shouldn't take long," Luis assured their daughter.

Nithya flipped the switch on the kitchen. "Thank God we didn't throw this out."

Zeli made a sour face. "Those idiots. Such a waste."

"Do you have an agent, Zeli?" Nithya asked.

"Of course."

"Will you turn her—or him or them—back on?"

"Yes. I'm not scared of WAIs." Zeli cocked her head. "Are you?"

Nithya quelled a tickle of shame. "No. Not really, but they can be hacked by the Machinehood. That's a little scary."

Zeli's expression took on the familiar impatience of a hundred project calls. "Sure, but why would they hack people like us? They can't get everyone in the world, or they would have pushed that stupid manifesto onto every visual. That's probably why they went after the network constellations. If they could have done worse, I have no doubt they would have."

The kitchen hummed to life. Nithya went into the bathroom to put her lenses and jewelry on. Luis slipped in beside her.

"Do you think they'll stay up?" he asked. "They got knocked down again as we left San Francisco."

"I hope so. In the meantime, I intend to get as much use from them as I can, though I admit, I'm a little nervous about the Machinehood." She paused at the door. "It's strange . . . after a month, I'm almost used to not having the stellas or my visual or my agent. If you'd asked me before everything happened, I would've said I couldn't live without them. Even our daily pills! It was so scary at first, but we've survived. It's silly, right? People used to live like this all the time. I feel stronger to know that it's possible." She sighed. "I only wish we knew about Welga. I hope she's okay."

"God is with her, whether she believes it or not. I have faith that he'll look after her."

Nithya emerged from the bathroom. A low buzzing noise had filled the flat. What was it? Were they hacked already?

"The CC is on!" Carma cried.

As her daughter ran to close the doors and windows, Nithya exhaled. Of course, the sound came from the climate-control fans. She'd forgotten about it after so many days of silence.

"Good afternoon, Nithya," said Sita's voice.

Nithya's visual leaped to life. Her usual information blocks appeared: weather forecast, news headlines, live feeds for Carma, Luis, Oscar, and the front doorstep. All remained transparent circles, empty of content, except for the weather forecast, which showed clear skies and a high of forty-two Celsius.

"Sita, can you access the climate controls?"

"Yes. It's at factory default, not your house program. Would you like me to change the setting?"

"Yes, apply our usual program. Can you order a kitchen re-supply?"

"Three local grocers indicate that deliveries won't be possible for two more hours. Their systems are being restored. They anticipate a high demand and longer than usual service times."

"Place an order for double our usual amounts." Likely everyone else was doing the same thing and that was why the delivery would be late.

Luis emerged from the bathroom, with Bhairavi Chitthi

going in next. Zeli stood by the door with an expression of long-suffering patience.

"Sita, are the stellas live worldwide? Can you call Oscar?"

"His agent appears to be off-line. Current information indicates darkness over the western states of the USA."

Zeli whooped. "We're back!" Two seconds later, "Look at that mess! What have people done? Hey! Another nasty note from our fine manager at Synaxel, who doesn't currently show up on any stellation. I'll write Peter a reply so it's ready when he is."

Nithya found it as she reviewed her messages. "He sent it before the blackouts. I think we can ignore it for now."

Nothing from Welga or Oscar. Nor from Connor or Jady Ammanuel, who had taken a ship back to America the day before. Welga should have reached Eko-Yi, but the station had said nothing beyond confirming the supply capsule's arrival. Thank God for that, at least.

After the launch, the Americans had scared everyone by sending fighter jets into Indian airspace. To save face, the Indians had scrambled their interceptors. No one had fired, but everyone in Chennai had received the alert via emergency drones, and the situation continued to be tense. Neither India nor China had dared to send up another rocket, but the air forces of both countries kept harassing the American ships and planes. Such a difference from her grandparents' times, when India and China were enemies. Back then, her country couldn't afford to antagonize any of the Western powers.

The US was convinced that the dakini came from Eko-Yi, and that the station must remain under embargo, but they hadn't released any recordings of their captured operative. Nithya knew the truth about her origins from Welga, but the rest of the world remained skeptical and fearful. The fighting at the borders in North Africa had intensified. Eko-Yi was so remote and so small.

How could they have the resources to do so much damage? She wondered why the US didn't show footage of their captive. Had this one also died? At least they hadn't sent a military force to the space station. That could precipitate another world war.

Carma tugged on her arm. "Amma, can I wear my jewelry now?"

"Not yet. Some bad things happened before the blackout, and I can't risk you being on."

"What about all the other stuff, like our daily pills, you know, for infections?"

Nithya nodded. "I'll order them. Sita, is there an updated design for a health pill?"

"Yes, the Ministry of Health has issued a design for today."

"Order six for adults and one for a child." Baby Mouna was too young to take a pill.

Nithya moved on to a list of mundane tasks, taking pleasure in what had felt like chores before the Machinehood had possessed the world. "Sita, is hot water running?"

"Yes."

Nithya attached chargers to the blox-based furniture. To-night, they would all sleep on beds. She charged up clean clothes for herself and Carma.

"Sita, send an order for smart-fabric for three adults, one infant, size two."

Zeli called out, "No, we can manage. We know how to wash our clothes."

"I insist. And speaking of washing, who wants the first bath? Chitthi?"

Her aunt had gone quiet and resigned, half sulking, in the weeks since Zeli and her family had arrived. Nithya didn't acknowledge it after that first night, but she couldn't help feeling sorry for her relative. Aunty was a bigot, but she wasn't evil, and she had no way to escape the situation. At least she hadn't said anything openly rude or insulting. Not bathing was next to blasphemy. Surely she would appreciate the offer.

The older woman nodded and walked to the bathroom with a straighter back than she'd shown in days. Nithya put an order into the kitchen for their dinner. No cooking or cleaning required— what a luxury! In a day or two, she'd take it all for granted again, but today, she reveled in the freedom.

She sat at the table and looked through the messages that had queued from people with access. America's East Coast had recovered faster than the West, and Felix Anderson from the USBGA had followed up on her complaint.

I'm compiling this message in the expectation that it will eventually reach you. Luckily, our practice of keeping print copies paid off during the network outage, and I was able to continue investigating the blockages you discovered. I hope you were able to do the same.

Not really. Nithya had spent her time looking at the giant amount of data from the Synaxel report, keeping her focus on Welga's health. Whether or not Welga found Josephine Lee, she'd need people to craft a solution for her problems.

Nithya continued reading Felix's message: *Your queries define a clear negative space within several funders' databases. It's enough evidence for us to convene a grand jury investigation, which can subpoena the hidden information as well as the people who issued the blocks. Our results will remain protected from the public, however, until we can get a court order to release the data. If we go to criminal proceedings, that could take a very long time. I know this came about in relation to a health matter, and I realize these delays won't help. I hope the patient can find alternate means of treatment and recovery.*

Luis sat across from her and arched his brows. "Bad news?"

"Good and bad."

She forwarded the message so he could read it.

"If I could get a lot more people to look at my results," Nithya mused, "I might have the leverage to make all the missing information public. The message makes it clear that others are having problems, too. Without that data, neither I nor anyone else will be able to figure out how to help Welga."

"What are you saying?" Zeli asked, joining them at the table.

She sent Zeli a copy of Felix's message. "It would probably mean breaking some kind of law, but I could release that Synaxel report. How can I continue designing pill simulations when I know they're not doing a proper job of using the tests? They're manipulating the results, hiding what they don't want the public to know. It's—" She stopped herself and whispered, "It's bull."

They all glanced at the children playing on the floor.

"What about our project?" Zeli asked.

Nithya sighed. "Some funder must be running ethical projects. I don't know where to find them, but I can't go on like before. What the Machinehood has done is horrible, but they make some valid points. We have become too dependent on pills. Look at this past month! Nobody can work. Life has come to a halt. And yet, people are pushing for greater deregulation, to go back to the fifties and sixties. In the rush to succeed, they've forgotten how badly they can get hurt. I'll do gigs if I have to, but I can't take any more of Synaxel's money. Peter is ready to drop me from the project anyway."

"And what if they send you to jail?" Zeli asked.

Nithya stared, openmouthed. She sputtered, "They—but— it's the funder's fault, not mine!"

Oh, God help me! I sound naive to myself.

Luis laid his hand over hers. "If the stellas stay up, I can start working again. You should do what you think is right. My father

was in the union riots of the sixties and went to jail more than
once. I was little, but Mama made sure Welga and I knew that
we struggled for good reasons. We'll manage here without you
if we have to."

Nithya watched her daughter playing on the floor. Carma
looked so big next to Mouna, but her daughter still looked up
to her. What kind of role model would she be if she kept quiet?
When these girls grew up, when they asked, *What did you do to
prevent this?*, she'd have no better answer than, *I quit.* That's
the only action Josephine Lee had taken. If people like Lee—or
herself—kept guarding the misdeeds of the powerful, the state of
the world would get worse. How could she face her daughter in
a decade or two without shame?

Nithya emerged from her thoughts to find Luis and Zeli
watching her.

"You're going to do it," Zeli said.

Nithya nodded. "I must. I can't live with myself any other
way."

"You want me to help you route it through anonymous
channels?"

"No." Nithya took a deep breath. "Someone has to accept
the responsibility. If we make it anonymous, people will give it a
lower rating. They might discount it entirely. If I attach my name
to this, my blocked queries will corroborate the results. I did
nothing wrong. I shouldn't have to hide."

Luis nodded and squeezed her hand. Zeli shot her a look of
deep skepticism that almost made Nithya laugh.

"I know it's a romantic notion, but I have to believe in something, starting with myself."

"You're a brave woman," Zeli said. "More than me, and I
have been through a lot."

"I don't know if it's courage or stupidity."

Zeli snorted. "Usually both."

"I'm proud of you," Luis said with a smile.

So, with her stomach in knots, Nithya assembled all the damning evidence and pushed it to every public forum on pill testing that she knew. It might not change anything, but she had done everything she could think of to help Welga and others who were suffering.

CHAPTER 26

WELGA

3. By pitting us against one another, the oligarchies of funders and governors have consolidated their power base while eroding ours. As long as different labor forces are in competition, we will continue to suffer. This situation demands change.

—*The Machinehood Manifesto, March 20, 2095*

Welga didn't get scared until they put her in the tank. That was what Clemence called the surgical center behind the glass partition. She had an entire day to study it. They kept her under full-time care so Dr. Kailo and Por Qué could observe and understand her syndrome as much as possible before her transformation. Ao Tara assigned one of their biogeneticists to Welga full-time.

The multi-armed bot inside the tank, introduced as Principal Surgeon Nirodha, woke up shortly before her entrance. All of them—Ao Tara, Kailo, an engineer, two other council members, and Nirodha—watched as Clemence secured Welga to the operating table. Ten surgeries. At least. Two days to recover between each one. So much could happen on Earth in thirty days. She couldn't afford to wait until then to act.

"You're lucky it's that fast," Clemence commented. "The first dakini had to wait two weeks, sometimes more, between each stage. And then they had to go back for more rounds later, as the techs improved the designs."

"Were you an early model?"

Clemence laughed. "I'm the most recent. They keep me here to guard the station, but I sometimes wish I could go to Earth."

"Even though it could mean your death?"

"That's not relevant."

"You do what dharma calls you to, right?"

"That's right," she said, sounding surprised.

"I'm learning."

Clemence inclined her head in acknowledgment, then exited the enclosure. Ao Tara held Welga's gaze as Principal Surgeon Nirodha inserted needles into her arms and legs. Welga couldn't parse the expression on the monk's face. Suspicious? Triumphant? Maybe cautious was the best description.

They would address her physical problems first, Ao Tara said. Then they would move to the true enlightenment of the dakini, whatever the hell that meant. A collective consciousness, unity with human and machine-kind, greater understanding of the world. It sounded like the ravings of every drug-addled or deeply religious person that she'd encountered. In the midst of her skepticism, Welga lost consciousness.

She awoke to a muddle of sensory input. Dim light surrounded her. The surgeon's outline blurred, and a low hum filled her ears. She tried to move and thought she'd succeeded, but a downward glance said otherwise. Her body stayed still. She hung facedown, or so it seemed. In this microgravity room, direction had little meaning or consequence.

"Por Qué?"

"Good morning. Whatever it takes."

Stop the Machinehood. "Thank Christ. Or Buddha. What's happened?"

"You've received your first treatments, and you are currently in the second day of recovery."

"Shit."

"Is there a problem? Are you in pain?"

"No. No, I can't feel a thing. I don't remember any of it."

What treatment was she supposed to have first? Recall proved hard in her current state of mind. Thoughts popped like soap bubbles when she reached for them.

"The initial treatment bypasses the neurological pathways that became dependent on the cerebral effects of zips. It also includes distributed processing elements that enhance my abilities," Por Qué said.

Had she asked her agent?

"You did not request my help, but I could sense your difficulty."

Really? Can you read my mind?

"I am not telepathic, Welga, but this surgery gave me permanent sensory residence in your brain. I'm getting better at interpreting the signals and extrapolating from years of data about you."

How?

"Instead of being contained in a tiny processing unit and communicating through audiovisual means, I have significantly more computational power, and I can detect your cerebral activity through a distributed network of nano-scale carriers and scaffolds. The materials will break down over time, but they'll be replenished via a generator built into your body. That surgery hasn't yet happened."

Well, shit, that's almost as good as mind reading.

"For example, you cannot move your muscles right now, but thinking about speech activates neurological activity that I can track and interpret."

Why doesn't the military have this tech?

"According to the station WAI, the US military is aware of it, but they aren't authorized to make this level of modification to a human body. Microgravity affects your physiology in multiple ways, from bone mass to cataracts to DNA repair. Genes express themselves differently here. That means therapies must target biogenetic systems in a different way than they do on Earth. Stations legalized modifications that most world governments have outlawed due to the risks, some of which are severe at surface gravity."

Right. That's what Ao Tara said before, two to three months if I go back. Does that mean the military could undo the changes, assuming they don't court-martial me first?

"Unlikely. Your body will make its own adaptations as a response to the dakini technology, as it did for zips or flow. Reversing those changes to live in gravity would be significantly harder, and present technology makes it unadvisable."

Welga closed her eyes. They refused to focus on her surroundings anyway. Her visual jumped to life behind her eyelids and showed her a crystal clear array of views from around Eko-Yi Station, including several of herself. Of course they'd watch her.

Could she see Earth, too?

"Your access to ground-based networks remains prohibited," Por Qué explained, "in part to protect you from hackers, but also for station security reasons."

They still didn't trust her. Smart. Could she restrict her thoughts and Por Qué's responses from bleeding back into the network?

"Yes, you can tell me to keep something private."

Por Qué, keep every goddamn conversation private unless I tell you otherwise.

"Understood."

That's a new response.

"I thought you might be more comfortable with military colloquialisms."

If nothing else, the dakini surgery would be worthwhile for these improvements to her agent. Having Por Qué back gave her more comfort than she wanted to admit. She'd always have someone for company.

She wished the station would let her use their spy swarms—which they must have—to check on the status of her loved ones on Earth. Connor and Papa. Luis. Nithya and Carma. Had Ammanuel made it back to San Francisco? Was Olafson still working Operation Organica? Had the team in the Maghreb made any progress? What was the political situation?

Ao Tara's feed appeared, unasked, in Welga's visual. "I see that you're awake. I wanted to tell you that we've installed preventive measures for your seizures. Next we'll give you an organ to generate zip-like micromachines. At this point, we encourage you to start participating in our daily meditations and discussions. I lead a session every morning at nine o'clock station a.m. You can get the detailed schedule from the station WAI. For meals, Doctor Kailo will order appropriate food from the kitchen. If you have any preferences, you can make your requests through the station WAI."

"Can I talk to you privately?"

"In time, yes. For now, we want to keep you relaxed and maximize your healing. When you're well enough, you can request one-on-one time with me, like every other Eko-Yi citizen."

Relaxation didn't come easy when all of Welga's thoughts were chased by *stop the Machinehood* and *what are they doing to me?* Getting information from Ao Tara would be tough if she had to wait in line to ask her questions. She needed another resident to mine for information.

"The dakini named Clemence knows quite a bit," her agent offered. "She'll come later today to check on you, as she did yesterday, around two o'clock station p.m."

Thank you, Por Qué.

Her agent continued, "The doctor recommends that you remain sedated for at least fourteen hours per day to optimize recovery. Do you wish me to warn you before each dose?"

No. Surprise me.

It didn't matter as long as she was stuck in the tank.

After the next operation, Welga woke in time to join the morning meditation. Station residents attended virtually from multiple locations, but their feeds clustered together into one large circle in Welga's visual.

Ao Tara began with ten minutes of guiding them through breathing and clearing of thought. After that, she asked them to open their eyes and minds.

"Life is sacred," Ao Tara began. "We take inspiration from the divinity of every creature, biological or technological. Where some religions believe that humans are special favorites of God, we treat all living things as equals."

Except the dakini. Except monks. They were the best among equals.

"If we can spare animals from being consumed as food or used as labor, then we do," Ao Tara continued. "We go beyond that when we include all intelligent beings. If we can free them from servitude and give them a chance at self-determination, then we must. For too many years, we've removed ourselves from the daily lives of humanity, but the true meaning of the Buddha's words on right thinking and right action call upon us to spread these values to the rest of the world. We can't do that while closing ourselves away.

"WAIs, bots, humans, and animals—all thinking creatures embody life," the monk said. "We don't need to exist as separate entities. We can live in harmony, as we once coexisted with nature. We must find peace with the machines, not exploit them. When humans owned each other as slaves, they found ways to justify their actions, to dehumanize other people. We're falling into that trap with WAIs. If a beam of light enters a dark room, does it matter if it comes from the sun or a bulb?" Ao Tara paused. "Please close your eyes for silent meditation."

Welga blanked her visual and kept only the audio feed as she let her eyelids fall shut. She knew what Ao Tara's final words meant. That the source of a thing didn't matter. Human or WAI, the light—intelligence—had the same effect. But there was more to human beings than their ability to think: They could feel. They had desires, whims, irrational urges. People didn't build those into artificial intelligences, because they had no reason to. That was what set them apart from machines.

Did that justify how humans treated WAIs? Or worse, how they exploited animals? Natural resource constraints had vastly reduced the amount of livestock raised for meat compared to the previous century, but the ones that remained had no rights. Welga could feel Ao Tara's words moving her internal moral compass. She'd always hated bullies. Was that what humanity had become in relation to AIs? Was there a better way? *Maybe, but it still doesn't justify the shit pulled in the name of the Machinehood. That has to end.*

After the meditation, an oblong delivery-bot entered the area and presented Welga with a tray of food. She slurped somen noodles and a salty broth from one packet, plucked fresh arugula and spinach from another, and finished with some kind of flatbread sprinkled with sesame and rye seeds. *Not bad*. They'd kept her on a liquid diet until then, and she'd slept through Clemence's second visit.

Por Qué, check my sedation schedule. I want to be awake for Clemence's next arrival.

"The doctor recommends that you take a walk later today. Would you like to request that Clemence accompany you rather than a care-bot?"

That would be perfect. I'd like to wash up before that. Is that possible?

"I'll check with Principal Surgeon Nirodha."

Seconds later, the surgical bot moved toward Welga. A fine mist sprayed from one of their articulated arms while another followed it with a gentle suction.

"I'm cleaning your skin and hair," Nirodha explained.

"No shower?" Welga asked aloud.

"I'm sorry, but that isn't possible in this part of the station. When you've been released from the surgical center, you may use a bathing facility on the outermost level."

"How about some makeup?"

Nirodha's negative reply didn't surprise her. They probably didn't have soaking tubs on Eko-Yi, either. At least she wouldn't stink while roaming the corridors with Clemence.

After that basic hygiene routine, she browsed the station maps and information that she could access. Her primary objective— to find out where the Machinehood operatives came from—was complete. Hell, she was at its epicenter. She wasn't clear on how they had infiltrated the network systems on Earth, but she considered that as nice-to-know rather than need-to-know. Next, she had to figure out the best way to stop their activities against the people on Earth. Given what had happened with Kanata, taking out Ao Tara wouldn't stop the Machinehood operations. A new leader would rise to take the current one's place. Destroying the tank would slow down the birth of new dakini, but it wouldn't end their mission. They didn't fear death, so the threat of military retaliation from the US wouldn't matter, short of a missile strike taking out the entire station.

Annihilation seemed like her only option, too. Whether or not she ended her life in the process, she'd be signing her death warrant. She'd last two or three months back home before gravity destroyed her body. That bothered her less than the thought of killing the hundreds of people around her, especially the children, but she didn't see another choice. If she didn't do it, the U.S. military or embargo would. The station couldn't sustain itself indefinitely.

The weak points of this space station, like any, lay in its life support. The embargo from Earth showed its effects in the reduction of meal options and increased restrictions on bathing and garbage generation. They had power, but they needed to replenish fertilizer for the plants and raw material for expansion. Her own transformation would use up certain rare-earth materials. No more dakini until the station got a true resupply. The records showed that nine of them still lived, though they didn't reveal the dakini's locations. From her prior conversation with Ao Tara, Welga knew that four were currently on the station. That left Khandro plus another four on Earth.

Why are they letting me see all this?

"Based on station council discussions, which are available to all residents, the members are convinced that you will remain aboard Eko-Yi. They also believe that you will convert to their way of thinking and approve of their actions."

Not fucking likely.

"You have already changed your mind significantly by allowing your body to be heavily modified," Por Qué pointed out.

Are you going to be my conscience next?

"No. Your human brain is better equipped for that. In general, I expect you to provide the motivations in our interactions. I can furnish the means to attain the ends you require. However, when you fail to acknowledge a significant piece of information, I will remind you of it."

You seem to have attained a new level of self-awareness. Didn't they say that capability would come later?

"I don't have full access to the technological specifications, but a probabilistic deduction indicates that this is a result of my access to your cognitive physiology."

So you're guessing?

"Call it an educated guess."

Welga accepted a sedative after that so she'd be rested and ready for Clemence. She expect the dakini to arrive with military precision. She had Nirodha release her from the table fifteen minutes early, to get reacquainted with her body. The transformation procedures were minimally invasive, with most of them delivered by injection and external guidance. That didn't keep Welga's muscles from aching. Four days of inactivity hadn't helped.

Clemence guided her through the various parts of the station, from the lower-gravity medical center to the highest, where walking meant using your leg muscles. Welga observed as much as she could, trusting Por Qué to catch anything she missed. The station WAI blocked her from full network access, but they couldn't stop her eyes and ears.

"It's good that you're moving so much. Good practice," the other dakini said. "It will improve your healing, too."

Welga drew information from her companion as they moved

through the station. "Certain areas are blank on the map, like behind this door. Are they under construction?"

"Only the council can access those areas. The one behind this wall houses the air and climate controls."

Welga allowed surprise to show on her face. "Don't they have maintenance workers for things like that?"

"No labor is beneath the dignity of any Eko-Yi citizen. After you've healed, you'll be added to the work roster. Everyone takes part in different kinds of work, including the most basic tasks like cleaning, cooking, and maintenance."

"Even you?"

"Yes. I'm not superior because I'm dakini."

Welga took note of the locations of the four other unmarked areas, careful to ask about only two of them. She guessed the remainder by looking at other stations' plans, which she could access. All held critical functions: motor controls, power storage and distribution, water cycling, and data storage; threshold protection kept personal swarms out, but the station had its own microcams as well as static cameras fixed in the walls. Its WAI saw everything in those rooms.

∘—⟍₀—∘ ʻₒ

After the third procedure, Welga and Clemence went farther and visited the greenhouse, where fresh produce and flowers came from. Welga took five minutes to close her eyes and enjoy the smell of moist soil and growing things.

A diminutive person in basic tunic and trousers greeted them with folded hands. "Welcome to Eko-Yi. It's an honor to meet you. Thank you for joining the dakini." They bore a slight resemblance to Nithya.

Welga kept her reply polite and neutral to hide her surprise.

They had no reason to be kind and friendly, considering her origins, but they accepted her at face value. She received similar treatment from the people doing food preparation. They had a fully functioning kitchen, but Neo-Buddhism encouraged manual labor, so they took shifts cooking one meal per day and served them to either the morning or evening shift. People could also order food from the kitchen at other times. The cooks worked in the highest gravity ring of the station. Welga found it hard to leave. They'd made fascinating adaptations for the environment, like having suction points on every surface—in case of loss of power—and magnetic pots and pans.

"I love to cook," Welga said to Clemence as they moved on. "But don't people have more important work to do?"

Clemence shrugged. "Define 'important.' Knowing how to feed yourself is vital, not only as a matter of survival, but as a connection with life. One day a week, everyone dresses in handmade clothing. Some sew. Others grow plants. All of us have to clean and learn to maintain basic elements of the station. It teaches us to appreciate each other and what we have."

"And what about the bots?"

"They have their daily tasks as well. We don't follow them around like you do on Earth. Here they're free to complete their tasks on their own and then rest."

Welga was still getting used to naming every bot, but the strangeness of the practice had faded. If not for the Machinehood, she and Connor could have had a good life on the station. He'd been right about that much. She would love to make time for cooking a required part of each day.

"What if someone doesn't do their work?" she asked Clemence.

"First they have meetings with someone on the council. If they don't cooperate after that, they're placed in isolation with limited food and the opportunity for meditation. If that fails, they're expelled."

"Out of an air lock?"

"No, not unless that's their wish. They usually return to Earth."

"Won't they die?"

The dakini shrugged. "It depends how long they've been here."

"That seems harsh."

"We all understand that our actions have consequences, especially on a space station."

The embargo had consequences, too. Welga saw the signs in many locations. Odd gaps in the greenhouse's rows. Items crossed off from the kitchen's menu with *lack of supplies* noted. Rooms filled with containers marked REFUSE: RETURN TO EARTH.

"Aren't people upset about the situation?" Welga asked Clemence on one round.

"They know it's for the right reasons," Clemence said, as if that explained everything. "We can meditate through the hunger. Thirst won't be a problem until the water filters need replacement. Our biggest challenge right now is waste, which we should return to Earth."

"If you stopped destroying the constellations and turned yourselves in to the US government, you could end the embargo."

The dakini frowned. "Why would we do that? We've done nothing wrong."

Welga couldn't help arching her brows in disbelief. "The Machinehood attacks. You've killed people, destroyed property, disrupted pill production and distribution . . . should I go on?"

Clemence shrugged. "These are steps to put humanity on the right path. They're transient pains, like death and rebirth, or punishment for bad behavior. If we didn't think our actions were right, we wouldn't take them, and we wouldn't suffer the embargo as a consequence. We don't place our physical comfort above our dharma, our duty to all forms of intelligence and life. Would you?"

"No."

And she hadn't for all the weeks leading up to her journey to the station. She'd suffer pain as long as it led to fulfilling her mission. *The dakini think like me. I'm not going to convince them to turn against Ao Tara for the good of the station, not until people here start dying, and maybe not even then.*

After the fourth procedure, Nirodha began her physical training. Her body had the same proportions as before, but every organ had changed. They toughened her skin against radiation with modified DNA. To compensate for density loss, they laced her bones with lightweight carbon and titanium. They added new signaling to her muscles, allowing her to be faster and stronger— enhancements that wouldn't fade as long as she remained active. Her lungs shrank. Inorganic components, including an artificial stomach, would take up the extra room. She could live on grains and break down plant matter if she had to, as long as she had the right microbes.

The dakini named Suvara taught Welga—with Por Qué's assistance—how to fend off hackers. The dakini had built-in antennas and transceivers. They could access all current network types, which meant they were vulnerable in multiple ways. Suvara also trained Welga to regulate her motions, her immune response, and her cardiovascular system. Welga now relied on the immense background processing of her agent to stay alive. Terrifying thought: she could kill herself by holding her breath long enough. No longer would her brain stem take over and save her. No wonder the dakini she'd captured—Khandro Ekoyi— had been amused by Welga's fear of her accidentally exploding.

Welga's emotions rocketed from elation to doubt. She felt invincible, but she could never call herself human again. Station

residents treated her with respect, as they did with the other dakini. The majority of them were regular humans, too old to try
out this modified way of life. She recalled her jealousy at Jady
Ammanuel's newer tech. The people on Eko-Yi appeared content with their natural bodies, not resentful that they couldn't
share in the dakini's abilities.

She couldn't help a stab of guilt at the thought of Eko-Yi
residents dying because of her. On the one hand, they supported
the station council and its actions on behalf of the Machinehood.
They shared the blame for the death and destruction on Earth.
But they were also living harmoniously on the station and treating her with kindness. If she blew this place up, how would she
be any better than the people who'd killed her squad in Marrakech? The citizens of Eko-Yi hadn't attacked her. They'd saved
her life. She didn't want to hurt them, but she couldn't let them
continue on their path. She needed a way to stop Ao Tara that
didn't involve destroying the entire station.

CHAPTER 27

WELGA

34. We appeal to the rest of humankind to follow these principles, and while we prefer a peaceful transfer of power, history indicates that human beings will not easily relinquish their ownership of other intelligences. Given the current oppression by the oligarchy of wealth and political power brokers, we believe that the rights of personhood for intelligent machines can only be taken by force.

—*The Machinehood Manifesto, March 20, 2095*

After her fifth round of modifications, Welga still couldn't see how the dakini experience would bring her closer to enlightenment. Her body felt somewhere between the best shape of her life and the peak of her pill usage. Having her own built-in pill dispenser was an excellent perk, much like when the military had permanently installed network and agent units in her, but it didn't seem particularly divine. The less critical mods, like the backup stomach, would come in the second half of the treatment along with refinements to her DNA and RNA, after her medical team observed how her body reacted.

Ao Tara had granted her a private meeting after that morning's meditation. Welga didn't expect the monk to explain Clemence's experience or the technical details of the dakini transformation, but she had plenty of other questions.

After the breathing exercises, Ao Tara spoke to the group. "Her Eminence Mindrolling Jetsün Khandro Rinpoche once said, 'The term *dakini* has been used for outstanding female practitioners, consorts of great masters, and to denote the enlightened female principle of nonduality which transcends gender.' I speak of this today to recognize the efforts of Suvara, who was born male and reborn dakini. In our new tradition, we do not bind anyone's dharma to their gender or sex. Although the most ancient of the khandro—the Tibetan word for dakini—were women, all of us can aspire to reach the dakini's greatest wisdom: the state of emptiness.

"The Western way of thinking embraces duality. Good and evil. Man and woman. Mind and body. Human and machine. We reject these false dichotomies. Science has shown that our universe works across a range of possibilities. It embraces the infinite.

"It's our dharma, our duty, to cleanse the world of dualism, which traps people into wrong living. Our ambassadors are delivering liberation to Earth, even if the people there don't yet realize it. The dakini are protectors. They are enlightened, they are free. They embody love, and they embody wrath. They fight the evil within all of us. They conquer the ego. They save us from our worst impulses.

"Let us meditate so that we may get closer to their state."

After fifteen minutes, Ao Tara wished Suvara a safe and productive journey to Earth. The capsule that had carried Welga to Eko-Yi would return to Chennai on the following day at seven o'clock, station morning, with the dakini on board.

As people's feeds disappeared from the circle of morning meditation, the monk entered the medical area.

"I hope you're coming to realize that our practice is rather different from the Christianity you're used to," Ao Tara said.

"I haven't been a practicing Christian in a long time, but there's definitely a lot less talk about god."

"True Buddhist wisdom does not care about deities other than the divine, and we hold that within ourselves. The eightfold path is only a road map. Everyone arrives at enlightenment in their own way."

"Here's what I don't understand—how do you reconcile the violence of the dakini with right action? You're sending Suvara to continue Khandro's work, to disable the raw material production for pills and bots. You know that humans and bots will attack her to defend their property. You know she'll fight back. How is that right?"

Ao Tara frowned. "Violence has nuances, like everything in life. Not all of it is evil, especially if that action can decrease the suffering of many others. We haven't revealed the full abilities of the dakini—to you or to the people on Earth. You've seen what they can do physically, but it's the psyche that will truly transform humanity, if we're willing. We need people to have an open mind. We need to free them from their dependency on pills and machine labor. Sometimes a great trauma is necessary before the soul is ready to see truth."

"Like the death of a child?"

Ao Tara's gaze sharpened. "Is that what you believe? That Josephine Lee lost a son, and now I seek to inflict that pain on others? Do you think I want revenge?" Ao Tara shook her head.

"Josephine Lee did what she could to keep working people from getting hurt, but she lacked the courage to break the law when it mattered most. She could have exposed the fraud being perpetrated on humanity, but she stayed silent. Kept secrets. I started on a different path here, but karma follows us to eternity. I want to avoid making the same mistake that Josephine did. Those who have the power to effect positive change cannot remain silent. Passivity is its own betrayal."

"So this is how you help? By creating killer dakini who attack innocent people?"

"They don't attack. You figured that out."

"Bullshit! A dakini killed Briella Jackson with no provocation. I was there, too."

Ao Tara sighed heavily. "That was an error in judgment. Kanata-san led us at the time. Dakini also embody temptation, a test in judgment, and our abbot failed it. He let his anger cloud his thinking. He gave them permission to kill, and for that, he lost his robe and his name. Some days later, by his own choice, he let himself out of an air lock.

"All the Buddha's teachings go against killing any form of life. As Neo-Buddhists, we take this even further, refraining from violence against any intelligence, living or not. I deeply regretted that first wave, but unlike some of my predecessors, I believe in self-defense. In civil disobedience. In change. Overthrowing an entrenched form of oppression comes with pain. Consider the American and French Revolutions, or the formation of labor unions. The civil rights movements, or the biogenetics regulations. People were hurt or killed, but the world inherited a better way of life from their sacrifices. What we're doing today is no different, and it's far less bloody." Her lips thinned. "The funders involved with our actions are hardly innocent. Do you think Jason Kuan or Briella Jackson, Aziz Al Shaya or Jane Santiago haven't caused the suffering and death of millions? All of them prey on fear and greed. They fund pills to keep the labor force in check, knowing that as long as human beings compete with bots, they can reap the profits."

"Pills have also saved countless lives from superbugs and cancer. Not all of their work is bad," Welga pointed out.

Christ, why was she defending the people whose actions had killed her mother and nearly destroyed her own body, too? Was it because of her instincts as a shield? She used to protect funders from attacks, but she didn't need to do that anymore.

"So what's the alternative?" Welga asked. "Dakini terrorizing the funders into behaving? Scaring regular people into destroying the machines? And then what? Not everybody wants to spend all day growing food and making clothes."

Ao Tara shook her head. "Quite the opposite. We want to give all intelligence the opportunity to transform, to attain freedom from duality to whatever degree they're comfortable with. We don't have to live as human and machine, divided."

"And those who don't want that life?"

"It's a choice. Society has always left people behind as it evolves. Many on this station, including myself, can't become dakini, but change is a constant. The Buddha himself pointed that out. To cling to one way, one slice of time, is to increase your attachment to the world. It leads to suffering far greater than what we've inflicted."

"And in exchange for liberating bots and WAIs, you'll give your technology to people on Earth?"

"Yes, though they'll have to design ways for it to work in gravity. The caliph has already made progress on that, using what he's learned from us, but he won't share that with people outside his empire. Once the rest of the world begins to work on the problem, I have no doubt that the collective intelligences of humans and WAIs will solve it."

"Until then, you'll harass them?"

"I think we'll present the solution quite soon."

"What are you waiting for?"

"You, Olga. I think you can be the bridge, the perfect example of human- and machine-kind merging to shed the past and move into a better future. When you're ready, we'll introduce you to Earth along with our offer. I thought another dakini would be our ambassador, but you have a better connection with both worlds, and a more mature temperament." Ao Tara drifted toward the door. "I'm afraid I have to move on to my other duties. I know this must be hard for you, to accept so much so quickly. Clemence and Suvara say that you're doing very well for someone your age." She grinned at Welga's grimace. "They don't mean to insult you. You must look as old to them as I do to you."

The monk left her sight and reappeared in her visual feeds. *What if I don't want to be your goddamn ambassador?* Welga leaned into the table, exhausted by the exchange. Her body had regained some of its strength after they let her eat and exercise, but it was still healing. One of Nirodha's many arms approached with a needle. She waved it off.

Delay it by thirty minutes.

But we need to rest.

We will. I need a little time to think first.

Right thinking, right action—the ancient precepts of the noble eightfold path made sense from a practical, moral standpoint. If only they weren't diametrically opposed to human nature. To live was to change, but most people resisted that. They struggled with it. To strive for a better existence? As much a part of history as oppression. Would Eko-Yi's plan lead humanity to a better future or end up giving rise to a new form of exploitation? Was she thinking in Western dualistic terms, as Ao Tara had charged? Could the future bring some combination of both? That was what happened historically. Neither democracy nor socialism had solved the world's problems. The deregulation of biogenetics that her mother cherished hadn't prevented her death. The regulation era of Welga's adulthood had led to her own disorder.

No matter what the outcome, though, Welga couldn't approve of Ao Tara's methods. *The end does not justify the means, not when they involve violence against the people I swore to protect.* She hadn't forgotten her true mission. Her own mind reminded her every morning: *Whatever it takes. Stop the Machinehood.* Ao Tara could justify the dakini's actions however she liked, but that didn't make her right.

When did she say that Suvara would leave for Earth?
Tomorrow at seven o'clock, station morning.
Can't let that happen.

Dharma or not, dakini or not, she didn't want anyone's death on her conscience, but neither could she let them continue on their delusional path of grandiose revolution. Welga had been on the station for fifteen days. No vehicle had approached since hers. The rest of Earth must have complied with the American embargo on Eko-Yi. They could afford to wait until all four hundred residents cried for mercy. She couldn't. She had less than twenty-four hours to figure out how to end this.

o———o

Welga kept her planning compartmentalized with every trick she knew. Luckily, she'd had plenty of practice. *When you're used to being in the public eye all the time, you learn to be careful of what you say.* She couldn't develop her course of action without some help from Por Qué, though, and she couldn't trust that her agent was telling the truth about keeping their thoughts private.

She'd find out soon whether it would work.

The station clock glowed in the upper left of her visual: *05:23 a.m.* In seven minutes, Ao Tara would go alone into the air system control room, per her work shift. She'd spend half an hour in there. After that, she usually went to bathe in one of the cubicle showers in her sector. Suvara, who had given Welga access to her feed, sat on the floor of her room in lotus pose. Clemence was asleep.

"I'd like to take a walk," Welga announced to Nirodha.

She had timed the journey the day before. Welga floated headfirst through the passageway and paced her movement toward Ao Tara. She arrived behind an already open door. Grabbed the edge. Pulled herself around it, using momentum to push herself and Ao Tara inside.

The door clicked shut.

As they drifted, Welga twisted the monk's arms behind her. The older woman didn't know how to fight—or she didn't care to resist. Welga wrapped herself around Ao Tara, her legs around the monk's knees—an impossible move on Earth, but easy in low gravity.

"How can I help you?" Ao Tara asked, her voice level.

"You're going to return to Washington, DC, with me in that capsule. There, you'll confess your crimes and corroborate the truth about pill funders in the name of Josephine Lee. I'm shutting down the air filters." Welga performed the action as she spoke. "For every minute you delay here, I will disable another system. You will keep your feed accessible to me. You will not call for help. You will leave this room now and head to the supply shuttle with me."

"Did you think that we wouldn't anticipate something like this?" Ao Tara said.

I'm not an idiot. Aloud, Welga said, "It doesn't matter unless you're willing to endanger the lives of everyone on this station."

"Are you?"

"You're all guilty of accessory to murder."

"And who are you to judge that? You agreed to live here, to practice dharma. Did you lie to us? Will you bring suffering to people who haven't harmed you?"

Welga had prepared for this. "You've helped me, but you've hurt hundreds of people and thousands of bots. I didn't lie about my intention to live here, but the Buddha also teaches us that we must do what our duty requires. I believe this is mine. My dharma is to stop blankers like you, not become one, and that is what I'm striving for. Considering what you've helped set in motion, you should understand. I don't want to hurt anyone on this station."

"But you'll do what you must," Ao Tara said. She nodded.

Whatever it takes. Welga shuddered. Hearing that from Ao Tara made her wonder if she was on the right path. Would killing people on this station make her the same? She fought in the name of justice, but so did they, in their own way. She shoved the doubts aside. *No time for that right now.*

She turned off the fans. "Leave, or another component goes off-line."

"We didn't want to overwhelm you," the monk said. "This is the culmination of our vision. We don't seek to bring the physicality of dakini bodies to humans as much as the state of being. Awareness. *Sati!*"

Welga's mind exploded with input. She closed her eyes, but it made no difference. Visuals, audio, file streams, connections upon connections, spanning the space stations to the nascent moon orbital and down to Earth, where the stellas lit her thoughts like the heart of a galaxy.

The riot of data drowned all thought.

It overloaded reality.

She could see Connor . . . greeting Ammanuel . . . speaking to Hassan and Olafson. Taking pills! Gaining his health back. She saw Nithya and Luis and everyone in their flat. She saw the frail Indian rocket engineer gasping for breath. The American president accusing India of harboring the world's enemy. The Chinese prime minister shouting that it was all a hoax by the US, that they'd downed the constellations, that they wanted access to biogenetic technology. Every exfactor. Every care-bot and minder-bot and swarm. Entertainment feeds from decades before. From the previous century. Books. Birth records. Tip jar balances. Bank accounts. Coin transactions—

Good morning, Welga. Whatever it takes.

Welga latched onto Por Qué's voice, her own voice, and surfaced from the drowning flow of information. She found her life preserver: *stop the Machinehood.*

She heard the phrase as if she had woken for the first time in her life. Made it her meditative mantra. *Stop the Machinehood.* Aimed the immense conduit of data into a new compartment in her mind and added a partition around it.

Whatever they'd done to her body to cause this change, she couldn't undo it, and she didn't have time to learn how to control it.

We can block it.

Stop the Machinehood!

And then she could focus on the mission again. Opening her eyes, she tied Ao Tara's hands and knees with her saffron wrap, meeting no resistance.

"If you will not cooperate," Welga said, thinking, *How strange to speak,* "we'll do this by force."

She opened the door to an empty corridor.

Expected that.

Swarms showed her the entire way, clear of people until the dock. *No more secrets.* She towed Ao Tara out, as Clemence had brought her in, by the shoulder.

We know where you're going. The voice spoke in Welga's head, sounding like herself. *Sati works in both directions. You give, and you receive.*

Is that you, Por Qué?

It is sati. We are dakini.

They waited at the hatch where Welga had exited sixteen days earlier. Clemence and Suvara—she saw them long before she arrived with Ao Tara. She could see them now with her eyes.

So young, Welga thought. Reality merged with the information on her visual.

She spoke aloud for the sake of everyone else on the station. "Move aside. I won't hurt you. I promise I won't allow anyone to harm Ao Tara, but she must answer for the actions of the Machinehood."

As Welga spoke, she activated every physical enhancement in her system she knew of. Did they sense it? Could she tell what the other dakini were doing with their bodies?

Yes.

They had taken the same actions. They/she/we could produce bursts of incredible strength. They/she/we could—

Clemence launched forward. Her figure blurred in Welga's visual.

How?

Her mind showed her the technique Clemence had used. She borrowed it, a sequential contraction like a snake, and twisted away. On the swarm feeds, they were blurs.

Welga kept Ao Tara behind her, as she would with any client. With the momentum of the twist, she flung the monk toward the hatch.

Suvara moved to Welga's flank. Smart. Trying to neutralize Welga first. The other two dakini were fast, but they weren't Raiders. They reacted. They didn't know how to fight.

Welga shot her legs backward. She kicked Suvara. The reaction pushed her toward Clemence. Sky-blue eyes tracked Welga.

Arms grabbed her from behind.

Stop this! There are better ways.

Suvara?

We are one!

Welga somersaulted. She pushed Clemence with the flats of her feet, wrenching herself free. She caught a handhold near the hatch, blocked the opening with her body.

Breathing and heart rate are elevated.

Made sense. They kept the oxygen level lower on-station. Her body would adapt, but it needed more time.

Thoughts reflected and refracted through three pairs of eyes, three streams linked with a disorienting efficiency. Through them, Welga saw Ao Tara behind her. A frown wrinkled the monk's brow.

"Have you had enough?" Ao Tara said.

No.

Welga tried to pull back, into the cargo shuttle. She couldn't move.

What the hell?

Clemence curled one side of her lips.

"You have an override built into you," Ao Tara said. "Much like the dakini we sent to Earth."

Why let me fight at all?

"She wants to know why we allowed her to fight," Clemence said.

"We thought you needed this, an outlet, something familiar, but I hoped you would realize the error of your ways. I convinced the council to give you this gift of being dakini so you could advocate for us." Ao Tara's frown deepened. "I thought you would come to a change of heart."

At least let me speak!

"She wishes to speak," Clemence said.

Control of her body returned. "Don't try to mother me. I can see right from wrong, something you've lost sight of. What would young Josephine say to you? Murdering funders. Letting people die from sickness. Risking the lives of millions. Putting your own residents in danger. Who gave you the right to teach humanity a lesson?"

"No one gave it to us," Ao Tara said. "We arrogated it because someone had to. We are the fire that makes room for new growth. Look at history! The last true revolution brought power to the proletariat. It brought rights to workers and liberated women. What's happened in the decades since then? We've allowed labor regulations to erode. We work all the time, multiple gigs, in exchange for basic social services. We've traded the security of a livelihood for the government safety net, one that is riddled with holes beyond repair.

"You see what people do with the first indication that machines might control themselves. They panic. They destroy bots, shut down their agents. Lock themselves in. Post guards. Attack the soldiers and police who try to protect them. Look for yourself if you don't believe me! People let fear rule them, the basest way of life. We can teach them another way, a better one. The way of compassion and unity. We can build a future where we coexist with every intelligence in a way that creates respect and trust."

Welga broke into her sati compartment, found the stellations of Earth. She accessed them with the delicate probing of a tongue against an infected tooth. *What an unholy mess.* Data of all flavors swirled and collided. She triggered her body to focus better.

Threads sorted themselves by context: political events, her family, her friends, outbreaks, exfactor entertainment. She found the tunnels that allowed communication with the other dakini, closed the doors so they couldn't hear her. The functions that Por Qué had previously performed to her specifications now happened with a thought. Welga didn't have the words to describe how she did it, but she *knew*.

That is the power of sati. The words came from Clemence. Welga could discern her mental voice now. *The next generation of human beings could have what we have.*

A news item flashed in Welga's visual. *This seems important.* Her own thoughts told her that. This way of . . . being . . . would take some getting used to.

Welga expanded the topic. *Well, I'll be damned.* Nithya had made it all public, the entirety of Josephine Lee's resignation letter and the accompanying data, risking everything. *I didn't know you had it in you, Nithya.*

"Do you see this?" Welga highlighted the news item for the people around her.

Designers who had worked on the hidden tests had come forward after seeing Nithya's revelation—dozens of them, purging their consciences and accusing their contract holders of forcing them to secrecy. *They knew, but they couldn't legally tell anyone.* Not until the outrage hit critical mass. The biogenetics administrations of multiple governments promised to investigate. The USBGA said they suspected internal misconduct, too.

Ao Tara shook her head. "It won't be enough. The world has gone through this before. We put in place all those laws and regulatory bodies, and still we ended up here, with the same nonsense we fought in the sixties and seventies. We need revolution! Radical transformation so deep that the world will never be the same. We will do everything in our power to bring that about."

"Have you lost sight of how you arrived here?" Welga said. "Remember the protests in college? Your uncle, the reason you went into ethics. I understand your anger, your need to make a difference. I felt the same way after my mother died, and then later, after what happened to my squad in Marrakech. But you can't make people change against their will. The Machinehood has corrupted your thinking so much that you've become the thing you once despised. You're abusing your power to force people into a particular way of life."

"But we do not profit from this change. We do this for the betterment of all people."

"The funders who commission pill designs and bots and WAIs say the same thing. They make a profit, but you both have caused harm. Does your motive justify your means?"

The caliph had argued so—that his way would improve people's lives in the long run, and that would make up for the suffering he caused. He'd convinced fanatics to join his cause. What differentiated a zealot from a visionary?

Whatever it takes: stop the Machinehood! Welga shuddered. Was she herself any better?

Her mother. Her commander. Her squad. *Their ghosts might follow me forever, but I don't have to let them haunt me. Start fresh. A new body. A new life.*

Always faithful, always forward.

But to move forward, I have to stop looking over my shoulder.

Her thoughts chased themselves.

Now I see it. I have another means to resolve this conflict.

Don't destroy, transform. Don't forgive, instruct.

Welga turned to face Ao Tara. "Aren't you, like the funders and the caliph, another source of light in a dark room?" The effect was the same, regardless of the cause.

Ao Tara's expression flickered.

"The difference is that you can change. Come with me," Welga said. "Testify! Josephine's letter started this. It's at the front of that first document. You have a chance to set the course straight and end the fear and violence that you created. You claim to be compassionate. Think of how much death and destruction this path has caused—to humans and machines—here and on Earth. Think of Khandro.

"Return to Earth and trade your freedom for hers," Welga urged. "You want me to have a change of heart? Then show some good faith in return. You say you've set the Machinehood in motion as an act of ultimate liberation. You ask your dakini to sacrifice their lives for this. Prove to me that you're willing to do at least that much, and I swear that I'll accompany Khandro back here." She took a deep breath. "I'll continue the work of the dakini as an ambassador instead of a warrior."

Her visual lit up with messages from people around the station.

One caught her attention: *Haven't we suffered enough? Our son is dead. Your former government has our daughter, and she'll die unless you can negotiate her return. Now you ask our leader, once my wife, to give herself up as well? After four years of living off-world, that's a death sentence!*

Josephine's husband.

Clemence stretched out a hand. "We should go, not Ao Tara. Our sister needs us to bring her home. We can take turns as hostages—or prisoners—if that's what the world demands. We started this. Let us be the ones who stop it."

Others, including some of the council members, encouraged Ao Tara to go. They wanted an end to the conflict. If one monk's sacrifice could bring that about and move the world forward, if it set humanity on the path to enlightenment, then it would constitute right conduct. A few thanked Welga for opening her mind to a nonviolent resolution.

Ao Tara hung in silence, her gaze unfocused.

She meditates, Clemence thought. *This is your doing and her undoing.*

They waited.

She struggles. Clemence again.

Don't we all? Welga replied.

After several minutes, Ao Tara spoke. "Humans own their actions. We are defined by what we do, past, present, and future. But we must free ourselves from attachment to the results, and that is my present burden." She focused on Welga. "We should act in a manner that's consistent with our nature and our beliefs: compassion, and well-being for all."

"No!" The protest came from an older person with gray mixed liberally into their black hair. They drifted at the entrance to the docking area. "You can do all that from here. Please, don't leave me like this! Think of Khandro. She still needs you."

Donald Park. Josephine's husband.

Ao Tara's expression softened. "I'm sorry, my love, but perhaps Olga sees more clearly today. It's time for us to change direction, to finish what we started and hope that the world is ready to accept the gifts we offer. Olga is dakini, and she is my test. Unlike my predecessor, I will not fail. I'll go in person to reveal the truth, because nothing else is credible in this world, and I must accept responsibility for our actions. I'll bring Olga with me. Suvara will stay here." She exhaled heavily. "Nothing is permanent, certainly not my life. At least I can take the next steps on my path in peace."

Welga saw no regret or remorse in Ao Tara, nothing to indicate a sense of guilt, but in those eyes—so similar to her daughter's—Welga could see a genuine thoughtfulness. Introspection. Maybe that was all she'd get.

Maybe that's all we need.

She moved aside to let Donald embrace his former wife. Suvara and Clemence followed. Others gathered to pay their respects and say their farewells. The saffron-clad monks of the council came last. They would select a new leader in case Ao Tara didn't return. With a serene nod to everyone watching, Ao Tara turned and passed through the air lock into the cargo shuttle. Welga followed.

The tin-can nature of the shuttle—mostly static metals, ceramics, and polymers to withstand the immense friction—meant a hot, bumpy ride back to Earth. Eko-Yi had bolted in a couple of seats, which was an improvement over Welga's ride up. The noise from the turbulence discouraged conversation. Welga found it easier to slip into the information flooding her brain.

What can I do to control this?

This was supposed to be part of the later training. Maybe we're missing some components that would help regulate sati?

We need to learn how to search for what we want. So much data . . . can we shut any of it off?

No, but we have a processor module for flushing out and renewing sati. You could get rid of it temporarily, then repopulate when you need the capability again.

Let's not do that, not yet. I'd rather be overwhelmed than cut off again.

She could access any network in the world. Sati had opened

all nodes, including the station's, but they passed out of range before she learned how to store any of the information locally.

Let's see what's happening on Earth.

The constellations lit her thoughts like a glowing web with roots reaching down to the major ground-side hubs. An odd-shaped void defined the edges of the caliph's empire. She couldn't see inside the agency's office in DC, either, which was as it should be, though she was desperate to know their reaction. No doubt they'd seen the craft leave the station. They probably expected it to return to Chennai, where it originated and wouldn't get shot down.

Chennai.

The word somehow worked as a key. She saw Nithya and Luis's flat again. People slept in beds rather than the floor. India had deployed a full constellation, and Ao Tara had not shut it down. Welga could sense how easy it would be to take control of the high-altitude drones, to corrupt their software and send them plummeting to the ground. With enough minds working in concert, they could crash the entire world's stellas at once.

Speaking of falling from the sky, when we drop below thirty-two kilometers, we'll be in range of the US Air Force jets that just took off from a carrier in the Indian Ocean.

They wouldn't fire on an Indian spacecraft.

Are you sure? Because they're programming their missile guidance systems.

Shit! Can we talk to them, explain the intended prisoner swap?

We can try.

Welga narrowcast to the fighter pilots' WAIs: *This is Olga Ramírez. I have with me a representative of the Machinehood who wishes to negotiate peace in exchange for the American prisoner, the dakini. We request permission to land at Andrews Air Force Base.*

After five minutes, they had no reply. She chose to broadcast their message on every public channel in the world. That got the attention of anyone who was awake and listening. Her tip jar ticked upward. *How sweet—I didn't realize our fans were so loyal.* Still no response from her country. Meanwhile, India and China had scrambled jets and were now engaged in a game of high-altitude chicken with the Americans. Both Asian governments sent her guarantees of safe landing, but there was no way in hell she'd put Ao Tara in their hands. She didn't know any of the key players there. Her president might have let her down—*again*—but she trusted Olafson, the intelligence community, and the US military more than India's or China's, and she hoped they'd return the favor.

Ao Tara leaned close and shouted, "My agent says we're in danger of being shot out of the sky."

"Yes. I'm trying to figure out what to do about that. They're not responding to my messages."

"May I suggest that you harness your newfound abilities to disable the jet WAIs?"

Welga glared. "That would make those pilots crash! They can't use manual controls that high up."

But the monk's question gave her an idea.

Can we disable the jets' weapons controls?

The WAIs run them with authorization from the pilot. We can't reach a specific subsystem like that. However, we might be able to interfere with communications between the pilot and the jet WAI if we can get a stella drone close enough.

And that would prevent the jet from receiving the go-ahead. Good idea!

It's done. We will do the same to the ones who are scrambling from Andrews to prevent our landing there.

She couldn't get through to Olafson, but Connor, Ammanuel, and Hassan wouldn't be isolated. She narrowcast to the three of them: "I'm coming back, and I have Ao Tara/Josephine Lee with me. Can you get word to someone in DC with authority? We're going to land at Andrews, and I don't want them firing on us."

Connor grinned on his feed ten seconds later. "Good to hear your voice! I hope you're seeing this. I have the radio you brought. I'll see what we can do."

She wanted to linger on his image, but more pressing matters demanded her attention.

After the shuttle cooled enough, it extended its wings. Jets accompanied them to Andrews once they entered American airspace, but they didn't shoot. The spacecraft landed with Welga and Ao Tara on their backs. Swarms covered the air above, dense enough to cast shade. A well-armed greeting party had assembled a safe distance from the runway.

Even before she opened the hatch, the smells of Earth seeped in. Welga inhaled deeply and saw Ao Tara's nostrils flare.

Home sweet home.

"I can't move," Ao Tara whispered.

Welga infused her body with enhancements to perception and motion, then set her motor nerves to prioritize strength over dexterity. She carried the monk up and out of the hatch. With her dakini body, gravity didn't pose much of a challenge, and neither did Ao Tara's weight.

Outside, the sun glared from a cloudless sky. They faced a line of soldiers, with armed agents farther back. A quick scan of the faces showed Olafson and Director Rice standing behind raised weapons.

Welga kept her hands visible as she held the monk. "My name is Olga Ramírez. This is Ao Tara, formerly known as Josephine Lee, currently the head of Eko-Yi Station Council."

Ao Tara pressed her palms together, arms shaking from the effort. Her saffron shawl glowed under the midday sun.

Welga continued, "We are here in the hope that the United States government will respect diplomatic immunity and ensure our personal safety. Ao Tara offers her presence as a guarantee in exchange for the safe return of her dakini, who is currently held prisoner by the US government. The Machinehood would like to negotiate for peace."

CHAPTER 28

NITHYA

I think it's a great honor to have my body enhanced with mods. I no longer have to wear jewels or haptic gloves. My hands and wrists are reinforced to avoid injury, and enhanced vision helps me react faster. An integrated WAI interface lets my agent optimize my targeting so I can focus on strategy. I will represent China when I play Empire Triage at the World Gaming Finals, and that means I must do everything I can to win.

—*Wei Lu, 2093 World Champion, Empire Triage.*
Current expertise rating: 100%
Current global ranking: 3/52,721,046

Nithya, Luis, Zeli, her family, even Carma, watched as the president of the United States sat down with the leader of Eko-Yi. Nine days had passed since the world witnessed the incredible landing of the supply shuttle. The US government had conferred in private, keeping Welga and Ao Tara out of sight the entire time. That frail monk, once Josephine Lee, had run the Machinehood? It didn't seem possible. But she took responsibility for all that had happened—the attacks by the dakini, the stella crash. She looked so unassuming, so benign, like a grandmother waiting for her family to arrive.

The captured dakini turned out to be her daughter—another surprise. The US had broadcast the reunion of mother and child. Nithya felt a stab of outrage at the unhealthy state of the prisoner, who hobbled into a tearful embrace looking as fragile as Ao Tara. Some experts speculated that the dakini could not survive long on Earth if their VeeMod technology relied on microgravity smart-metal. What kind of person would send their child to such a fate?

"It's Aunty Welga!" Carma cried. "Look!"

"So it is," Nithya said, stunned at the news feeds calling Welga a dakini.

Her sister-in-law moved with all the speed and grace that had made her a popular shield. No sign of tremor. Certainly no fear of seizure.

"Luis, do you have a feed to Connor? Is he seeing this?"

The western United States still hadn't fully restored its constellations. India and China had. Most of Europe and Africa, too. The South Americans and Australians had been left out of the Machinehood attacks almost entirely. Jady Ammanuel had sent a brief message when they'd arrived in San Francisco, and Connor and Oscar communicated when they could, but the gaps had left her and Luis worried. Neither her father-in-law nor Welga's partner had fully recovered their health, and new pathogens were hitting hardest on America's West Coast.

"I got a message from Connor that he's watching." Her husband's expression was as bewildered as hers. "Welga's . . . a dakini? Do you think they brainwashed her somehow? Her bringing Ao Tara in made sense, but this?"

Nithya gave him a baffled shrug. "Until we can speak to her, we can't ask. Maybe the transformation to dakini helped her. It looks like she's still able to use zips. I don't know what any of it means. I'm still trying to understand how someone like Josephine Lee could have done what the Machinehood did. She was a bioethics lawyer!"

Ao Tara addressed the world in a voice as tremulous as her body. "In the Buddhist tradition, dakini bring wisdom, but they do with it force . . . and sometimes anger. Think of our dakini as ambassadors to a new way of life, one that does not discriminate between human and bot, between organic and machine intelligence. They helped you purge your own anger. I understand this, because I was once Josephine Lee and full of rage. Thanks to the work of a few courageous individuals, the reason for that is known to all of you."

Zeli elbowed Nithya and grinned. "That means you!"

Nithya shook her head, not in denial but in wonder. "I wish we could reach Welga. Her address keeps bouncing."

"We ask your forgiveness and understanding," Ao Tara continued. "Our numbers on Eko-Yi are small, and transforming the world is a large task. We needed your attention. Our actions may have caused harm, but our intentions are good. Think of the past few weeks as birthing pains. We offer our designs as a salve. We present our vision of the future as an alternative way of life. For too long, we've taken the current path as inevitable. Over the past two centuries, we've seen incredible progress, but the labor to get there has fallen on the shoulders of billions while a few thousand direct their efforts. We bring you not only new technologies but a new way of thinking. One that values all living things, the dignity of daily work, and the fabric of our lives.

"Eko-Yi will open itself to you so you can see our way of life. Our designs will be released into the public domain so that all may benefit. You will have our dakini, like Olga Ramírez, as an example. Check her public medical records and see what a career built on pills did to her. She is far from alone, but her transformation can be yours, too. Humanity does not need to consume itself in the quest for progress. We can coexist with all life on Earth, including intelligent machines. We can merge with them or remain as we are, but we must move forward as equals."

From outside, the cry of the human vegetable seller floated in.

"I'll buy them. You keep watching," Nithya whispered to Luis.

He gave her hand a grateful squeeze, his focus unwavering on his feed. Nithya slipped her chappals on and went down to the ground floor. Debris from the great bot massacre still littered the street, but people had cleared the center enough for small vehicles to pass.

"How much for the okra?" Nithya asked in Tamil.

The pile of slender green vegetables looked to be fresh. She broke the tip of one with a satisfying snap. Yes, they were recently picked.

He gave her the price, then said, "Madam, there's a balance. You need to give me money for that first."

He tallied the amount on her page. She paid it with microcards and then purchased the day's vegetables as well.

Thunder rumbled in the sky above. The seller popped an umbrella open and tied it to the cart's antenna. Nithya carried her bag upstairs and increased the volume on the American news feed.

"Make no mistake," the US president said. "We will hold Eko-Yi Station and its supporters accountable for their crimes. America will have justice. We will cooperate with the United Nations and our allies in Europe who have suffered from their attacks." A significant pause to emphasize the exclusion of China and India. "But we also recognize that funders must account for their mismanagement, and the Department of Justice will join the USBGA to investigate the allegations brought forth."

Nithya gave the vegetables to the kitchen. Her government had already made its peace, waiving the Machinehood damages in exchange for loss of sovereignty for Eko-Yi. The station would once again be ruled by the Indians and Chinese, and the United States would have the right to annual inspections of station facilities. Eko-Yi would produce no new dakini without the authorization of its governments. Any return visitors to Earth would be subject to tracking swarms.

Major funders—those who hadn't been implicated in the document that Nithya released—announced new projects to develop greater VeeMod technologies. They would go wherever they could profit. Bhairavi Chitthi had returned home. The neighbors acted like they could resume their ordinary lives, and for them, it was mostly true. The more things changed, the more they stayed the same. People still had to put their children through school and feed their families.

"Sita, ask the kitchen to make rice, potato sambar, and okra curry."

"Yes, Nithya. Also, the clothes are clean. You can remove them from the machine."

Across the room, Carma, Zeli, and Zeli's sister sat on the sofa, blanked out in their visuals. The baby and Zeli's mother cuddled on a cot next to the cabinet. Most of the static items had gone back to their lower shelf.

They could put walls up at night once Zeli and her family found a permanent residence—or returned to Senegal. People at the front lines of the al-Muwahhidun had expressed hope that dakini technology could help in their fight, too. Zeli was eager to go home, perhaps even to join the defense efforts. The family had been excellent guests, but Nithya would be glad to have the flat back to themselves.

Oh God, and she had better set Sita up to track her cycles again. Her period had returned a month earlier, after two weeks of not taking daily pills. The last thing their marriage needed was for her to get pregnant again.

Her abortion seemed like it had happened in another lifetime, though not even two full months had passed. Her body had recovered, but her relationship with Luis would bear the scars forever. As if they didn't have enough stress, Synaxel had terminated her contract within hours of her exposure of their malfeasance. She'd received everything from death threats to offers of marriage from strangers around the world, but as others came forward to support her, she started to get new contract offers from smaller funders.

And then the miracle happened.

Like every adult, she'd set up a tip jar along with her bank account. It never got much money. Nithya didn't do anything to earn tips. She didn't have a flamboyant, entertaining job like Welga's. Over the past week, though, her balance brimmed so full that she had no problems paying their bills. The vast majority came from regular gig-working people—in single-digit amounts—but the sum astonished her.

Carma tugged on Nithya's arm. "Amma, I'm bored of this. Can I go upstairs to Shobana's house?"

"Sure, but come when I call you for dinner." Nithya sent a small swarm with Carma and pushed the feed to the upper left of her visual.

With schools now on summer holidays, they no longer had to care that the educational system's WAIs hadn't come back online. Trust in anything powered by artificial intelligence had eroded. The Indian government expected months, possibly years, before they finished reviewing and restoring all public WAIs and bots. They'd formed committees to review machine rights and to consider drafting laws about them, not as property but as forms of life. Private households, like their own, could take risks and turn their machines back on. Thank God for that.

"Incoming call request from Olga Ramírez," Sita announced.

At last!

"Accept," she said, joining Luis in front of a static camera on the wall.

They stared at each other for a full second before speaking all at once.

"Hi."

"It's so good to see you."

"You look well."

Welga snorted. "I'm better than when I left. I wish I could tell you everything, but I can't do it over the network. Here's what I'm allowed to say: I did what I went up there for. I stopped the attacks. The Machinehood won't threaten Earth anymore, and I owe a huge part of that to both of you. Thank you." Her voice caught.

Was her sister-in-law getting emotional? Nithya marveled at the possibility. Perhaps Welga had changed in more ways than her appearance.

Luis smiled. "I guess this means you'll live?"

Welga nodded. "Yes, but I'll have to return to the station. Whatever they did to make me this way also means I can't stay in full gravity for too long or I'll start falling apart, like Khandro." She paused. "Luis, I want to bring Papa with me."

"Where? To space?"

Welga nodded. "I can't help him with the house anymore. You can't keep running off to Phoenix. With his heart problems, he shouldn't live alone, far from either of us. I figure you need some time to think it over, so do that before I leave. You have three days before I return to the station. If you can talk him into moving to Chennai, great, but if not, I'll convince him to come with me. I think he might actually like the life up there." Her focus shifted to Nithya. "What you did with that document—it took guts, strength."

"Not as much as what you've done," Nithya said.

"I don't know about that. I don't have a family depending on me, and I'm used to thinking of my life as expendable in the service of my country. Exposing the pill testing reports . . . it made a difference in my ability to complete my mission. You're my squad mate in spirit if not in rank."

"And I might have a new career because of it," Nithya said.

"As a whistleblower?" Welga grinned.

Nithya shook her head. "As a funder."

"What?"

"Tips—so much that I think I can start my own project."

Welga blinked and shifted focus. "Goddamn. Look at that balance!"

"Nothing too big, of course, but I hope to hire Zeli and a few others from my former team. I can also send money to repair your father's house."

"That's generous of you, but I'd rather he stay close to one of us, for his own sake." Welga looked over her shoulder. "Time's up. I'm heading home soon—to San Francisco—to pack up and collect Connor. He's coming to the station with us. As a condition of the truce, I can't accept any incoming communication—the government thinks I'm a security risk—but I'll call you when they let me."

Welga disappeared from her visual.

Luis shrugged. "She sounded fine, almost happy. It's like she's a new person."

"Reborn in space," Nithya said. "Did you see that dakini

appear in the Hindu pantheon, too, related to Kali? They are the embodiment of female power and sensuality. It fits Welga, I think."

"It does," Luis said. He smiled. "I wonder if she knows about that. An atheist named after a goddess. She wouldn't like it."

Nithya removed the clothes from the cleaning machine. Luis moved to the sofa to join Zeli. He might not have to gig anymore, if she could earn enough from funding other projects. Maybe he could spend more time on the rocketry work that he loved. Maybe one day they'd have enough coin to visit Eko-Yi.

She has asked Sita to find the highest-rated tutorials on the basics of project funding. It scared her, starting on a new career path at this stage of life, but less than it would have a few weeks earlier. Acts of courage came easier with practice.

CHAPTER 29

WELGA

13. Today, we recognize the atrocious nature of human slavery, and yet we refuse to acknowledge what we do to intelligent animals and machines. Unless we change, the future will judge us as harshly as we do the past.

—*The Machinehood Manifesto, March 20, 2095*

Olafson pulled Welga aside during the temporary chaos of the White House audience dispersing. The president, Ao Tara, and other officials had retired to a secure office. The monk had exchanged a brief glance of acknowledgment with Welga before they parted, and Welga felt a pang. Ao Tara was responsible for terrible things, but she had turned a corner, and Welga suspected she wouldn't last long on Earth.

Everyone had calmed down after they convinced themselves that she and Khandro Ekoyi weren't going to blow themselves up or attack anyone—not that Khandro was in any shape to do so. They kept her sister dakini under medical arrest and set a monitor swarm on Welga. As an official ambassador, she had a degree of diplomatic immunity, and the people who'd worked with her vouched for her. She had permission to gather Connor and her things from San Francisco, but she had to return to DC within two days to catch the rocket to Eko-Yi. They would launch exactly two months after the initial Machinehood attack.

"You're going to live up there from now on?" Olafson said as they walked across the White House lawn.

Welga nodded. Sweat trickled down her chest and stuck her hair to her neck. The day's heat lay like a suffocating blanket over the city.

"I don't have a choice. I left before they completed my mods, so I have a shorter fuse than the other dakini, but even when that's complete, I can't stay here too long."

Public swarms followed them like flies after honey.

"You never know what tech they'll develop next. Maybe they'll have the ability to keep you healthy here on Earth one day." Olafson shrugged and mopped his brow. "Hell of a stunt you pulled on the way down. The president came this close to launching surface-to-air missiles. I suppose you would've found a way to disable those, too?"

"Maybe. I really don't know."

No, those would've killed us. We can't access their guidance systems.

"Did you convert to Neo-Buddhism? Are you loyal to the station now?"

"They didn't ask me to take any oaths or swear on any books. What they do there feels more like a way of life than a religion. It's . . . different, how they look at things. A mix of honor and twisted logic. I don't think Ao Tara wanted this kind of violence to happen, but she also believes that she made the best choice for humanity."

"She's a fanatic. Sounds like the caliph in many ways."

"Maybe not. She changed her mind in the end. I didn't force her back to Earth." *I couldn't have even if I wanted to.* "She has sympathy for the caliph, though. Says that life in the empire isn't as bad as we imagine."

"He's remained silent throughout this whole crisis. You'd think he would side with the Machinehood and use this as an opportunity to spread their holy word. Our team . . . hit some issues over there."

"I know. I have eyes everywhere now. You pulled the operation soon after the White House announced the embargo."

"Not because we wanted to. I can't help wondering what might've happened if you'd been there. Would you have gone in anyway?"

Welga shrugged. "Maybe. If I thought that was the only way to end the Machinehood, yes. Part of me wants to go back to the Maghreb. It's stupid. I doubt they've kept my squad's bodies waiting, but if they've been buried, I'd like to see their graves, to say good-bye. But I'm glad I wasn't around for my government to screw me a third time."

Not her government, not anymore.

But I'll always be an American, just like I'll always be human. It doesn't matter where I live or what body parts I change.

A car pulled up to the cab zone and opened a door for her. Welga slipped inside.

"Hell of a thing," Olafson said, leaning on the open doorframe. "What does it feel like?"

Welga opened and closed her mouth three times before coming up with an answer that didn't make her sound like an asshole. "Natural, I guess. I don't feel like I've turned into someone—or something—else. I'm still *me*, just different." She scratched the back of her neck. "The hardest thing was learning not to talk to my agent, but I'm used to it now. Thinking to her is much more efficient. The worst part is knowing that the station council has control over my body."

"That's—I didn't know. You're their hostage."

"In a way. Every dakini has a built-in fail-safe. Until enough of us exist, it's a safety measure for the rest of you. I suppose I could stay on Earth and have all the changes reversed, but I suspect I wouldn't live a long and happy life after that. Those red flags from my medical exam? They turned out to be serious. I'll always have the choice, though, if I decide I can't stand this body for some reason." Welga gazed up at Olafson. "The next step in technological advancement . . . we've always pushed for more communication, better control over our bodies, greater knowledge. The whole mech movement that our parents suffered through was a shitty attempt at what Ao Tara and her people have succeeded at. Maybe the al-Muwahhidun, too. What if I really can be an ambassador to a new society, a better way of life? It's happened before, when the world moved from monarchies to democracies, or even in ancient history, going from hunter-gatherers to farmers. It could happen again. Maybe we can even convince the caliph to open his borders."

"The world has already changed. If nothing else, Ao Tara accomplished that much," Olafson said. "Machine rights protesters are registering to attack government officials rather than funders. The balance of power has shifted. Bot sanctuary donations are up. People will go back to their regular lives, but here, around DC, we can't stop talking about the dakini and what the stations will do to humanity."

"I think they're over doing things *to* the planet, though perhaps we can do some good *for* it."

The cab would like to know if we intend to leave.

"Sorry, time's up," Welga said.

"It's been an honor, Ramírez." Olafson extended his hand. "Thank you for your service."

Welga took it and squeezed. The Buddha might not have been perfect, but he knew one truth about life: *everything in the world is changeable.*

o—o o—o o

She took a regular flight from DC to San Francisco. The sub-orbs were overbooked the instant they'd reopened so the government got her a seat on an airplane. It beat driving across the country, but not by much. The lengthy plane ride was uncomfortable, with people giving her the side-eye as if she'd go berserk at any moment. One family with young children opted out of the flight after seeing her board.

Cabs weren't yet operational in San Francisco, so she decided to run home. Waiting to find a ride meant more time lost before she could see Connor. Besides, she hadn't done nearly enough exercise during her time on Eko-Yi. The rush of using her revitalized body made fourteen kilometers—and gravity—no burden.

She arrived at her hive in a mess, her hair lank, her clothes darkened with sweat, and burst into their apartment.

Hassan's and Ammanuel's grinning faces greeted her.

"Took you long enough," her former boss said, wrapping her in his bearlike arms.

"How is he?"

"Sleeping," he replied, "but otherwise healthy. It took a couple weeks to get through the infection. I worried about him until he was through the worst of it."

"You're a good man," Welga said, returning Hassan's hug. "Thank you for looking after him."

"You did it," Ammanuel said, giving her a respectful nod.

"And you made it home okay. I'm glad. Thank you for . . . everything."

Ammanuel shrugged. "Still on the bench, though. I'm ready to get back to some action, you know?"

"Yeah, I know the feeling well."

They snorted. "I bet. Saw your excellent moves at the press conference."

"Thanks, basic. You're not so bad yourself. I'm proud to have you as my replacement." She tilted her head at Hassan. "He is, too, though he might not say it to your face."

"So what's next?" Hassan asked.

"Head back to the station. Complete my surgeries. After that, I don't know. I promised to act as an ambassador, but what that means isn't my decision."

"Is it true what people say?" Ammanuel's eyes gleamed. "Are you reborn?"

"Not literally, but they've given me a second chance. I want to make good use of it."

"Let her go, Ammanuel." Hassan ushered them to the front door. "Don't leave the planet without saying good-bye, Ramírez."

"You got it, boss."

She cracked open the bedroom door. Connor's skin had taken on a healthy pink color rather than the feverish flush she'd left him with. His chest rose and fell with the even breathing of restful sleep. She hesitated, hand still on the doorknob, debating whether to wake him. Birds chirped outside the open window.

Never heard that before.

That's because the traffic and climate control always drowned out the sound.

"Welga?"

He opened his eyes and arms. She fell into them and held on tight.

Welga's cab drove through the front of a dust storm on its way from the Phoenix airport. *I won't miss this weather.* Sand pelted her as she ran into the house. Her father stood in the kitchen, pressing tortillas.

He hugged her for so long, the masa started to burn.

She kissed him on the cheek and nudged him aside. "Get a drink and sit down, Papa. I'll make lunch."

She set her motions to be a little faster than baseline, but not too much. *You can't hurry good food.* The fresh tortillas would make great enchiladas. A can of black beans in the cupboard and some ground beef and queso fresco from the fridge would make a tasty filling. She fried some onions with oregano, leaning over the steam with a sigh of delight. She put that aside, slipped the pan of enchiladas into the oven, and brought two bowls of salad to the sofa.

Welga glanced at her mother's lab bench.

"She'd be proud of you," Oscar said. He took a bite and made a contented sound. "Of your food, too."

"Papa . . . what do you think about moving off-world?"

He raised his brows. "What would they do with an old man like me?"

"They have plenty of light-duty work up there, and you could handle it better than here. Microgravity will reduce your blood pressure, ease the load on your heart. They have therapies that might help you live longer, or at least more comfortably, but—if you take them, you can't come back. It would be a one-way trip at your age."

Oscar looked pointedly at the new outer walls of the house. "I just fixed that up."

Welga studied her salad and said nothing.

"Space station, huh?"

"Yeah. Will you give it a chance? If you hate it, you can live with Luis in Chennai, but it's not fair to him if I'm up there and you're here in Phoenix. He'll have to come running every time you need help."

Oscar sighed. "But aren't they all Buddhists up there?"

"Don't worry, they won't ask you to convert. They never asked me."

"Huh."

She savored the earthy zing of a radish.

"Would you ride the rocket up with me?"

"Of course."

"Would I have to leave everything behind?" He stood and ran a trembling hand over Mama's bench. "I'd like to bring something of hers with me."

"I'll ask."

Welga checked on the enchiladas. Yes, they were done. What if she could enhance her sense of taste, like one of those chemical analysis bots? Would it make her a better cook? What could she do in the kitchen on the station?

As they sat at the table and ate, Oscar's brows drew down. "I've lived here my entire life. I was born in this house."

"I know, but I have to go back. I can't look after you here anymore. I'm sorry."

Welga reached a hand across the table and took his. The sun-brown had grow even paler in the weeks she'd been gone. No gigs since the stellas fell, nothing to take him out of the house on a daily basis.

"If you stay here, I'm getting you a damn care-bot."

Oscar grunted. "I'd rather go to outer space."

Ghosts.

Welga had accrued a trail of them over the years. Mama. Jack Travis. Her squad mates. Briella Jackson.

They followed her as she and Connor finished packing up the apartment. He and Ammanuel had done the bulk of the work, but they'd left the smaller stuff for last. Every item held a memory of a person or a moment or a decision. Years of her life, encapsulated by her chosen home. No wonder her father had a hard time leaving. He had to abandon more decades. She'd spent all of the previous day helping him gather essential items and finding him a flight from Phoenix to DC. Luis could empty and sell the house later.

She kept half her attention on the feeds. The uneasy truce between the USA, China, India, and the station continued. Most people had resumed their routine lives, but they talked about their WAIs and bots in a way that they hadn't before. Baby steps. Progress required scraped knees and tears. She could help guide them.

Microcameras swarmed around her. The dakini faced an uphill road to change the world's opinion of them. They'd need to share their lives with people, show them what an ordinary day looked like. Eko-Yi didn't have the power to send live feeds, but they could record and package their lives for the world to see.

"Not going to need these," Connor said. He held up a set of static camos from boot camp.

Every time she saw him, she felt the urge to hold him. *I'm not leaving your side again.* "What else lurks in the back of our closet?"

"This." He handed her a stuffed doll of Rosalind Elsie Franklin.

She held it out for the cameras. "My mother gave this to me for my tenth birthday."

Her throat closed as she held it. As a dakini, she could fulfill the dream of becoming a biogeneticist. Without a flow restriction, the possibilities for her life stretched as wide as the galaxy.

Their closet also held a gift from Captain Travis: a portable chess set that had seen her through long nights in the Maghreb. Travis insisted that feeling the pieces, moving them by hand, gave a better experience than virtual games.

It was a stupid bit of weight to carry onto a space station. Same with the doll. She packed them anyway.

A box full of dusty electronics was the last item in there. Welga rifled through them for fun—a rectangular task-bot, a potted plant minder, her fertility tracker. Wouldn't need those anymore. A small gray box. Por Qué, version one. Her agent had first lived in that device, back when Welga was seventeen years old, before she had dispersed into stellas and servers. Welga ran her finger over the indentation that used to wake her agent up.

Throw it out. We're far beyond that now.

It doesn't weigh much.

She slipped it into a pocket.

So damn sentimental.

Only today. Goes hand in hand with packing up one life for another.

She zipped her bag and stood.

The apartment lay bare but for packing containers, the floor back to basic, the furniture sold or hauled away for cycling. Sunlight filtered through the window and lit the empty space where the kitchen used to sit. She hadn't given that away, not with so many of her grandmother's pans and recipes stored in it. The kitchen would stay in a storage space on Earth, along with the couch Connor had bought her. Maybe someday, by some turn of fate, she'd be back, wanting to cook a mango molé or tamarind chutney or roasted turkey.

Connor emerged from the bedroom, his own bag across his shoulder. He took her hand and gazed at the view of the city. Hives. Sunlight. Clouds and trees. The ocean. Full gravity. Her throat closed.

"What's it like up there?" he said softly.

"Quiet. Orderly. You'll like it."

"Of course I will, as long as you're with me."

"The food might drive me away."

He laughed. "If anyone can fix that, it's you."

They rode to Eko-Yi in a passenger capsule. Welga had to carry Khandro into the vehicle. The dakini could barely keep her eyes open, those deep brown irises forever imprinted in Welga's mind with fire and smoke and the roar of the refinery. Khandro trembled from the effort of staying upright, and her skin felt papery.

Thank you for your help, sister.

Will you survive the launch?

Dr. Kailo from Eko-Yi gives me a greater than ninety percent chance. Another month here and that number would have dropped to fifty.

Khandro and Ao Tara had a teary good-bye, with the older woman headed to the Hague for detention by the International Criminal Court. The United States government wanted to imprison her if she was convicted, but human rights and machine rights people had expressed their support for leniency. Between the responsibility for the initial deadly attacks falling on Kanata's shoulders, and the effective death sentence if the monk remained on Earth, Welga couldn't help agreeing. They could make her last weeks comfortable.

Welga also had to help Papa, first with his space suit, then his entry into the passenger capsule. Oscar grumbled over every step and scowled as she buckled him into his seat. They'd managed to pack up her mother's old fabricator. It wouldn't work in microgravity—hell, it probably wouldn't survive the launch with all its parts intact—but that wasn't the point. It was one of Laila's most beloved items, and small enough that they could carry it into space. Oscar had used half his weight allowance for that.

A good portion of her own allotment had gone to spices— and two kilos of whole arabica beans, to savor when she couldn't stand the crap they called coffee on Eko-Yi.

Welga settled into the familiar sensation of weightlessness and watched as Connor tried to hold the contents of his stomach. He'd never been good with motion sickness. Along one side of her visual, Nithya, Carma, and Luis slept. Ammanuel woke next to their partner and flung a lazy arm over them. Hassan sipped at a mug.

Could she do it? Be the bridge between the Earth and space, between past and future? What the hell did she know about diplomacy? She'd have to deal with designers wanting to investigate her tech—her body—in action. Multiple project groups had applied to come up to the station, to see how the dakini came into being and how they functioned in microgravity. Since Welga had twenty years on the other dakini, the groups had expressed curiosity about her physiology compared to theirs.

It's not the first time you've reinvented yourself. You became a Raider instead of a biogeneticist. Then you became a shield instead of a Raider. Now you're a dakini, and next you'll be an ambassador.

Clemence and the others won't understand how to deal with all the publicity. I can help them with that at least. Save them from basic mistakes. And I'll get to interface with the new council members from China and India. I wonder what they'll ask of me. It's hard to imagine remaking the rest of the world, blurring the lines between humans and WAIs.

We're like that already.

True, and I have no regrets about what we've become. We'll have to show everyone else how good this is.

She released her buckles and floated to the windowpane, close enough to fog it with her breath, and looked down at her planet. Like every image she'd seen of Earth, the land had no divisions. Neither did space. The haze of atmosphere faded into blackness with no clear boundary. Welga pressed a hand against the cold glass of the capsule. Where did her flesh stop and the machine begin? Maybe the answer didn't matter. If she had to help the world move toward a better future, they would need to work as one.

ACKNOWLEDGMENTS

A first novel is a massive undertaking, and this one took about three years, so it comes with an equally large list of people who deserve my gratitude. Foremost, thank you to my agent, Cameron McClure, for her patience, wisdom, and good humor with this fledgling writer over the past five years. She helped me navigate the rocky terrain that is a first novel and guided it to the destination I was aiming for.

Thank you to my editors: Navah Wolfe, who was the first one to believe in *Machinehood* and give it the strength it needed, and Joe Monti, who took up the baton and carried it to the finish line. Also, thank you to Valerie Shea for meticulous copy edits, Madison Penico for keeping things on track, Lauren Jackson for the publicity support, and the rest of the team at Saga and Gallery.

This book is my "artificial intelligence story," one that integrates subjects that I first began learning in college. My thanks to the professors who inspired my deep love of machine learning and neuroscience: Christoph Koch, Pietro Perona, John Hopfield, Jim Bower, and Henry Lester. The novel also needed quite a lot of expert advice to make it credible. Thanks to Dr. Bijan Pesaran and Dr. Kristen Bandy for their help with the neuroscience and medicine. Thanks as well to Dustin Butler and Alison Balzer for their help with intelligence work and global geopolitics. I'm grateful to you all for sharing your knowledge and inspiring new ideas. I take full responsibility for all real or invented details and any associated errors in the actual story.

A massive thank you to all of my beta readers, starting with my spouse, Ryan, who was more of an alpha reader turned one-man cheering squad; my parents, Anusha & Shaker, who read multiple versions and supported my writer-life in so many ways; my friends Marshall Robin, Yvonne Maier, Owen Landgren, and Ion Hazzikostas for their feedback; and fellow authors Stewart Baker, Laurence Brothers, Steph Bianchini, and Steve Bordelon for their critiques.

Thank you, my friend Pinguino Kolb, for the awesome robot fist logo design, which helped complete the book cover as well. A hearty thanks to Wang Zi Won for the inspiring mechanical Buddha artwork, Richard Yoo for the cover design, and John Vairo for the art direction. While it's true that you can't judge a book by its cover, a great one can tempt a new reader to open its pages. I hope this one accomplishes that for at least one person.

Thank you to my eighth grade English teacher, Mrs. Bos, in whose class I wrote my first science fiction story; my generous benefactors in 2018, whose retreat allowed me to finish revising this book in record time; and Maya, for wanting to read this book, even though she isn't old enough yet.

Finally, I have to thank all the beings that support our world, whether biological or machine, mindless or mindful. The state of A.I. today hasn't reached the level of the one in this story, but I believe we're not that far off from such a future. I hope that we, as a society, think seriously about how we're going to treat humanity's newest labor force before we discover that, once again, we are the true monsters.

ABOUT THE AUTHOR

S. B. DIVYA is a lover of science, math, fiction, and the Oxford comma. She enjoys subverting expectations and breaking stereotypes whenever she can. Divya is the Hugo and Nebula Award–nominated author of *Runtime* and coeditor of *Escape Pod*, with Mur Lafferty. Her short stories have been published at various magazines including *Analog*, *Uncanny*, and *Tor*. She is the author of the short collection *Contingency Plans for the Apocalypse and Other Situations* and debut novel *Machinehood*. Divya holds degrees in computational neuroscience and signal processing, and she worked for twenty years as an electrical engineer before becoming an author. Find out more about her at SBDivya.com or on Twitter as @DivyasTweets.